New York T... ... s
had over *thirt...* ... f
fans with *her...* ...
ceived numerous honours t... ...
being a nominee for the Rom... ...
and receiving a Career Achi... ... *...om Romantic*
Times, and has been published in multiple languages and in
many formats, including audio book, ebook and large print.

Visit Christine Feehan online:

www.christinefeehan.com
www.facebook.com/christinefeehanauthor
@AuthorCFeehan

Praise for Christine Feehan:

'After Bram Stoker, Anne Rice and Joss Whedon,
Feehan is the person most credited with
popularizing the neck gripper'
Time magazine

'The queen of paranormal romance'
USA Today

'Feehan has a knack for bringing vampiric
Carpathians to vivid, virile life in her
Dark Carpathian novels'
Publishers Weekly

'The amazingly prolific author's ability to
create captivating and adrenaline-raising
worlds is unsurpassed'
Romantic Times

By Christine Feehan

SHADOW
REAPER

CHRISTINE
FEEHAN

piatkus

PIATKUS

First published in the US in 2017 by Jove
An imprint of Penguin Random House LLC
First published in Great Britain in 2017 by Piatkus

1 3 5 7 9 10 8 6 4 2

A CIP catalogue record for this book
is available from the British Library.

ISBN: 978-0-349-41647-2

Printed and bound in Great Britain by
Clays Ltd, St Ives plc

Papers used by Piatkus are from well-managed forests
and other responsible sources.

MIX
Paper from
responsible sources
FSC® C104740

Piatkus
An imprint of
Little, Brown Book Group
Carmelite House
50 Victoria Embankment
London EC4Y 0DZ

An Hachette UK Company
www.hachette.co.uk

www.littlebrown.co.uk

For Cindy Hwang, who always has my back.
Thank you for your patience and understanding.
Thank you for your willingness to allow me to go
to places most editors wouldn't. Mostly, thank you
for the incredible friendship over so many years.
With much love.

FOR MY READERS

Be sure to go to christinefeehan.com/members/ to sign up for my PRIVATE book announcement list and download the FREE ebook of *Dark Desserts*. Join my community and get firsthand news, enter the book discussions, ask your questions and chat with me. Please feel free to email me at Christine@christine feehan.com. I would love to hear from you.

ACKNOWLEDGMENTS

As always, there are people to thank for helping me with this book. First and foremost, Lee Harrington (passionandsoul.com). I studied Shibari in many books, but you took the time to Skype with me and answer all my questions. You went out of your way to help me, and I thank you for that. You gave me an understanding of the culture, the history and the various ways Shibari is used. When I needed additional help, your books were invaluable and you answered even more questions. Any mistakes made are mine alone. Thank you so much for your patience. I appreciate Midori for allowing me to attend one of her classes. Thank you, Marc Kennedy (TinyK.net), for stepping in when we desperately needed a rope master to tie for the trailer. I know you drove through a snowstorm to help us out. Thank you so much! Thanks to Domini Stottsberry for being with me every step of the way to get this book out when disaster after disaster occurred. And thanks to Brian Feehan for working out the fight scenes with me, brainstorming fight sequences and encouraging me when everything that could go wrong did. Denise Tucker, during the worst times, when my hard drive melted and I thought the book lost, you were the calm in the middle of a terrible storm and you found a way to get it back and kept me from a major meltdown while it was all happening. Thank you!

CHAPTER ONE

Ricco Ferraro wanted to punch something. Hard. No, he *needed* to punch something—or someone, preferably his brother. It would be satisfying to feel the crunch of his knuckles splitting open flesh. Cracking bone. Yeah. He could get behind that if his brother didn't shut the hell up. They were in a hospital with doctors and nurses surrounding them on every floor. If he really went to town and made it real, Stefano wouldn't suffer for too long.

"Ricco," Stefano hissed again, using his low, annoying, big-brother tone that made Ricco feel crazier than he already was feeling. "Are you even listening to me? This has got to stop. The next time you might not make it."

Stefano had been lecturing him for the last ten minutes; Ricco figured no one could listen that long, let alone him. He didn't have the patience. He knew damn well how close he'd come to dying. They'd replaced every drop of blood he had in his body not once, but twice. He'd been in the fucking hospital for weeks.

His car had hit the wall at over two hundred miles an hour, but he knew he hadn't driven into it. Something broke and the suspension went, driving pieces of metal through his body like shrapnel. He'd lived it. He still felt it. Every muscle and bone in his body hurt like hell.

"I'll listen when you make sense, Stefano," Ricco snapped and finished buttoning up his shirt. It wasn't easy. The pain was excruciating when he made the slightest movement, but he was getting out of this damn hospital whether the doctor signed the release papers or not. He'd had enough of all of them—especially his older brother.

He turned to face them—his four brothers and one sister with their expressions so concerned. Grim. But there was Francesca, Stefano's wife. He focused on her and the compassion in her eyes. She had nudged Stefano several times to get him to stop. It had worked twice, but only for a moment or two.

"I'm going to say this one more time and never again. You don't have to believe me." He spoke to Francesca, because surprisingly, it was Francesca who believed him. They all should have—they could hear lies. That gave him pause. *He* could hear lies. If no one believed him, it was because he had to be lying to them—and to himself.

He turned his back on them. Just that little motion hurt. His body protested the slightest thing he did. "At least wait until you get the report on the car before you jump to conclusions. I didn't have control. The car's system just shut down." That much he was certain of. He drove at speeds of over two hundred miles per hour and had no trouble; his hand-eye coordination and his reflexes never failed him. The car had failed. He knew that with absolute certainty, so why couldn't he convince his brothers and sister that he hadn't tried to end his life? Why couldn't he convince himself?

It took everything he had to stand there, trying not to sway when his body broke out in a sweat and he could count his heartbeats through the pain swamping his muscles. What had he done to try to save himself? Nothing. He'd done nothing. He'd let fate decide, closing his eyes and giving himself up to the judgment of the universe. He'd woken up in the hospital with needles in his arm and bags of blood going into him.

His room was filled with flowers. There were boxes of cards, all from people in Ferraro territory, the blocks of city considered off-limits to any criminal. Their people, all good and decent. He hadn't looked at the cards, but he wanted to keep them. He didn't deserve those cards any more than he deserved the concern on his brothers' and sister's faces, or the compassion Francesca showed. Still, he was alive and he had to continue.

"Something went wrong with the car, Stefano," he repeated, turning back to look his brother in the eye.

"We're checking the car," Vittorio assured him. He was always the peacemaker in the family, and Ricco appreciated him. "We towed it immediately to our personal garage and it's been under guard. Only our trusted people are working on it."

Ricco flicked his brother a quick glance that was meant to serve as a thank-you. He didn't say it aloud, not with Stefano breathing down his neck.

"You almost died," Stefano said, and this time the anger was gone from his voice and there was strain. Apprehension. Caring.

That was Ricco's undoing. It was impossible to see or hear the stoic Stefano torn up. He was the acknowledged head of the family for a reason. Ricco didn't deserve the way they cared so much. There were too many secrets, too many omissions. He'd put them all in jeopardy and they had no idea. Worse, he couldn't tell them. He just had to watch over them night and day, a duty he took very seriously.

He shook his head, sighing. "I know, Stefano. I'm sorry. I lost control of the car." That was true. He had. He remembered very little of the aftermath, but in that moment when he realized the car wasn't an extension of him anymore, that it was a beast roaring for supremacy, separate from him, he had felt relief that it was over. If he had died, it all would have been over and the danger to his family gone.

"Are you convincing me? Or yourself?" Stefano asked quietly. "We're taking you out of here, but you have to pull yourself together. Enough with the craziness, Ricco, or I'll have no choice but to pull you off rotation even when you're physically fit and have the doctor's okay to work."

Gasps went up from his brothers and Emmanuelle, his sister. Francesca uttered a soft "no" and shook her head. Ricco's heart nearly seized. He was a rider. A shadow rider. It was who he was. What he was. A rider had no choice but to do what he'd been trained for from the age of two—even before that. It was in his bones, in his blood, he couldn't live without it. He dispensed justice to those the law couldn't touch.

Stefano stepped directly in front of him, close, so they were eye to eye. "Understand me, Ricco. I won't lose you. I'll do *anything* to save you. Anything. Give anything, including my life. I'll use every weapon in my arsenal to protect you from yourself and any enemy that comes your way. You do something about this, whatever it takes, and that includes counseling. But there aren't going to be any more accidents. You get me, brother? There will be no more accidents."

Ricco nodded his head. What else could he do? When Stefano laid down the law he meant every word he said. It wasn't often Stefano spoke like this to them, but no one would ever defy him, including Ricco. He loved his brother. His family. He'd sacrificed most of his life for them gladly, but Stefano was more than a brother. He was mom, dad, big brother, protector, all of it rolled into one.

It had been Stefano who had always been there for him. His own mother and father hadn't even come to the hospital to visit him after the accident, but Stefano had barely left even to eat. He looked haggard and worn. Every time the pain had awakened Ricco from his semiconscious state, Stefano and his brothers and Emmanuelle had been right there with him. That solidarity only reinforced Ricco's decision to keep them safe. They were everything to him.

"I get you," he assured softly.

"It's done then. When the doctor okays it, you resume training, but you don't train any more than the regular hours. You sleep even if you have to take something to get you to sleep. You stop drinking so fucking much, and you talk to me if you are having trouble doing those things."

Ricco's heart was pounding overtime now. He couldn't promise Stefano that he would stop with his extra training hours. He had to make certain he was in top form at all times, that he didn't—couldn't—ever make a mistake. That was part of him as well. But how did he explain that to his brother when he couldn't explain why? He just nodded, remaining silent so no one could hear his lie.

He drank sometimes to put himself to sleep, but he could stop with no problem, he just wouldn't be able to sleep. He wasn't about to say anything more to Stefano. It was impossible to lie to him and he didn't want his brother to worry any more than he already did.

Staring into the mirror as he finished buttoning his dove-gray shirt, he looked at the vicious bruises and the swelling, the side of his head that had nearly been caved in. Beneath the shirt his muscles rippled with every movement, a testimony to his strength—and he was unbelievably strong. It had been his superb physical condition that had saved him from certain death—at least that was what the surgeon said, his strength and a miracle. His frame was deceptive in that his roped muscles weren't so obvious, the way his cousins' were, but they were there beneath the skin of his wide shoulders and powerful arms.

He reached for his suit jacket. The Ferraro family of riders always wore pin-striped suits. Always. It was their signature. Even Emmanuelle wore the suit, fitted and making her look like a million bucks, but then she could wear anything and look beautiful. He sent his sister a reassuring smile because she looked as if she might cry. He knew he looked rough. He felt worse than rough, but his sister didn't have to know that.

"I'm fine, Emme," he reassured softly. He wasn't, but then he hadn't been for a long, long time.

"Of course you are," she said briskly, but she looked

strained. "Walking away from a crash like that is easy for a Ferraro."

He hadn't exactly walked away from it, but he was standing now. He forced himself not to wince as he donned his jacket. Once the material settled over his arms and shoulders, he looked the way his brothers looked, a fit male, intimidating, imposing even.

There was a rustle at the door. His brothers Giovanni and Taviano moved aside to allow the doctor and nurse to enter. The doctor glared at all of them. The nurse kept her eyes on the floor. He noted her hands were shaking. She didn't want to confront the Ferraros, but had no choice when the surgeon insisted on saying his piece.

"You shouldn't be up, Mr. Ferraro," Dr. Townsend said.

"I'm fine," Ricco assured. "And very grateful to you." That had to be said whether it was a lie or not—and he honestly didn't know if it was.

"I refuse to release you. You could have blood clots, an aneurism, any number of complications," the doctor continued.

"I won't." Ricco gave them the look every Ferraro had perfected before their tenth birthday. His eyes were cold and flat and hard. Both the doctor and nurse immediately moved back. That, at least, was satisfying. He took another step toward them and they parted to allow him through. He might look like hell, and feel worse, but he was still formidable.

"I want the boxes of cards, but you can distribute the flowers to other hospital patients," Ricco continued, ignoring Stefano's frown. He knew what that meant. Stefano would want to talk to his doctor. A shadow rider could hear lies and compel truth—even from someone in the medical field. He kept walking, knowing his brother would never let him walk out to face the reporters alone.

"You're leaving against medical advice," the doctor reiterated.

Ricco didn't slow down. Immediately, his brothers and Emmanuelle fell into step around him. Surrounding him.

Shoulder to shoulder. Solidarity. The moment he was outside his hospital room, his cousins Emilio and Enzo Gallo moved in front of them. Tomas and Cosimo Abatangelo, also first cousins, dropped in behind. The cousins always acted as bodyguards for the Ferraros, and Ricco knew he needed them. He might say he was ready to leave the hospital, but he wasn't. His body needed rest desperately as well as time to heal. He just couldn't do it there.

The press had been all over the accident, trying to sneak into the hospital and get photographs of him covered in bandages. One nurse had been suspended while they investigated the fact that she'd taken numerous pictures of Ricco unconscious and sold them to the tabloids. There had been several other attempts by orderlies and a janitor. Anyone getting a picture of playboy billionaire Ricco Ferraro after he'd crashed his race car in a fiery display stood to make hundreds of thousands of dollars.

"Did Eloisa come to visit you?" Stefano asked, walking in perfect step with him.

Ricco glanced at him, one eyebrow raised. "I crashed, Stefano. Not perfect. Why would you think our mother would ever come to visit me when I showed the world I was less than perfect?" Stefano had raised them, not Eloisa.

Stefano glanced at Francesca. "I thought she was attempting to turn over a new leaf. Guess I was wrong."

Ricco didn't answer. He knew Francesca had been trying to make peace with Eloisa, but his mother didn't have one maternal instinct in her body. He couldn't care less. They'd had Stefano growing up, and he'd watched out for them—just as he was doing now. His oldest brother might be annoying, but Stefano loved his siblings. A. Lot. And he looked after them. It was something they all counted on.

Ricco hated that he'd caused his brothers and sister so much concern. He knew he had to change, turn his life around. It was time. He just didn't know how.

"Ready?" Stefano asked as they approached the double doors leading to the parking lot. No one broke stride, all moving with the same confident step. The town car had already been brought to the entrance. It was only a few feet away, but the paparazzi, several rows deep, had flashes already going off.

"Yeah," Ricco said. He wasn't. He could barely walk upright. Every single step jarred his body and reminded him he was human.

He was afraid he would fall before he reached the privacy of the car, but he kept walking. He had to get out of the hospital before he lost his mind. He'd had his own private wing complete with bodyguards, but that hadn't stopped the madness of the press or his fear that they'd catch him at his most vulnerable.

Stefano and the rest of his siblings had stayed the three weeks he was kept unconscious, at least that was what Francesca had whispered to him. They only left if a job was imperative. Once he was awake, it was mainly Stefano with him while the others took care of work. He felt their love, and in that moment, facing the paparazzi with his siblings surrounding him, he knew it had been worth every sacrifice he'd made to protect them. He'd do it all over again in a heartbeat.

Ricco kept his head up as they moved as a single unit to the town car with its tinted windows. Emilio and Enzo cleared a path through the reporters. None of the Ferraros even looked at them. Ordinarily they were friendly with the paparazzi. They needed the reporters and photographers to provide alibis for them. Today, the family just wanted to get Ricco home.

To his dismay, Stefano slid into the car with him. Ricco sighed and shook his head as Tomas shut the door on the frantic cameras and shouted questions.

"Stefano." God, he was tired. He lifted a hand to wipe at the beads of sweat dotting his forehead. "You don't have to escort me home."

"I wanted a private word with you."

Evidently the fact that his first cousin was driving the vehicle and Emilio was in the front seat didn't matter.

Ricco laid his head against the cool leather. "I'm listening."

"I've been patient since you returned from Japan."

Ricco stiffened despite all his training. It was the last thing he expected Stefano to bring up. He'd been barely fourteen when he'd been sent to Japan, and had just had his sixteenth birthday when he returned. It seemed a lifetime ago. He'd tried to bury those memories, but nightmares refused to go away. They haunted him no matter how much liquor he consumed.

"You have to talk to someone about what went on there. It's colored your life. You're the best rider we have, Ricco, but you're too reckless. You don't care about your own life, and that's something I won't allow you to risk. You've gotten worse, not better."

He couldn't deny that. "I've never once failed a mission. Not one single time, Stefano." Ricco could barely breathe. His brother couldn't possibly be saying what he thought he was.

"No, but you don't give a damn about whether you live or die."

It was the fucking truth, and if he opened his mouth, Stefano would hear it. Ricco forced air through his lungs and stared out the window at the buildings as they drove through the streets of Chicago. Outwardly, he looked calm. Confident. There was one truth he could give his brother. He turned back to face him. "There is no surviving without being a shadow rider. You take that away from me and I've got nothing to hang on to."

Swift anger crossed Stefano's face. "That's fucking bullshit, Ricco. You have us. Your family. How do you think I will do without you? Or Emme? The rest of them? You're important to us. Do you even give a damn about us?"

He loved his brothers and sister fiercely. Protectively. He'd alienated himself from them—for them. Fury burst through him, that rage that sometimes threatened to consume him. "What does that mean? You think I would do this if I had a choice—" He broke off. That was a mistake, and shadow riders didn't make mistakes. He couldn't afford to have Stefano launch an investigation. It was the painkillers, loosening his tongue when he knew better.

Stefano fell silent. That was a really bad sign. He was highly intelligent and little got by him. Ricco tried desperately to think of something that might distract his brother, but nothing came to mind. He hurt too much. Every muscle. Every bone.

Most people didn't realize how physically demanding it was to race a car for the length of time a race took, let alone wrecking at such a high speed. Even with all the safety measures built into the car, the jolting and spinning on one's body was incredible. Add an actual crash into the wall and his body felt as if he'd been beaten by an assembly line of strong men with baseball bats—or run over by several very large trucks.

"I get what you're saying to me, Stefano, and I'll do something about it. I must be a rider. You won't have to replace me in the rotation. As soon as I'm healed, I'll be back to work." He poured truth into his voice, knowing his brother could hear it.

That wasn't going to be enough and he knew it. He made a show of sighing, so it would be more believable when he caved. "I need to change my life." There was nothing truer than that. "I can't wait for a woman to walk down our streets throwing shadows out like Francesca did. I need to find someone now. I've been giving it some thought, but I had decided it wouldn't be fair to find someone, allow them to fall in love with me and then have to give them up to marry a rider just so I can produce children."

All riders were expected to marry another capable of producing riders, even if that meant an arranged marriage. Emme had it the worst because she was a woman, and if she didn't find her man by the time she was thirty, her marriage would be arranged. The men had a few more years, but there was no just falling in love and getting married to anyone. That was one of the prices they paid being shadow riders.

Stefano's dark gaze never left his and Ricco forced himself to continue. "I've thought a lot about this. I'm an artist. I've continued studying Shibari and I love the artistic elements, but the only place to actually display or practice my art is in one of the clubs." Ricco felt grounded when he practiced rope art using the human body as a canvas.

Stefano blinked, his only reaction.

Ricco nodded. "I know I can't be protected in the kinds of clubs I'd have to frequent. Sooner or later the paparazzi would find out and it would be in every magazine from here to hell and back. But if I find a good rope model, one I can work with in the privacy of my home, I can photograph my art. I've always wanted to do that. I have my own darkroom and can develop the photographs myself. You know I'm a good photographer. Eventually I can put the photos on canvas or in book form. I just need to find the right model. I'm hoping if I do, I'll feel a strong connection with her."

Stefano rubbed the bridge of his nose as the car slowed and then turned through the heavy throng of paparazzi standing on the sidewalk nearly blocking the drive leading up to Ricco's home. Both men ignored them as the driver inched his way through the crowd to the high iron gates. "It's a risk, Ricco. Not the art. The woman."

Ricco nodded. "I'm aware of that. I want to find someone I can fall in love with. Someone who could love me and maybe understand if I have to be with another woman."

"That's highly unlikely."

"I know. I know that. I just can't live like this anymore." Staying up all night, drinking himself into a stupor or partying until the sun came up with multiple women at the same time. Never feeling anything. He watched as the gates swung open to allow them inside. He didn't realize he was holding his breath until they closed behind the car, locking out the paparazzi.

"Someone threatened us, didn't they?"

Stefano asked it quietly—so quietly Ricco almost missed it and almost asked what he meant. Stefano said it like he already knew, that he was just confirming. Of course he would figure it out. He'd been the head of the family for years, since he was a teenager. He'd taken care of them all when he was even younger than that. He would know. He'd probably considered that possibility all along.

"I can't talk about it." That was confirmation and it wasn't.

Stefano swore, a long tirade of Italian. He kept his voice low, vicious, and Ricco heard the promise of retaliation there.

He shook his head. "Just let it go."

"Let it go?" Stefano looked at him as if he had grown two heads. "They threaten my brother, a fellow rider, and you want me to let it go. We have a council—"

"Don't. I mean it, Stefano. Let it go. There are reasons."

"There are never reasons for one family of riders to threaten another family."

"It was a long time ago. I'm asking you to let it go." He didn't allow desperation to show on his face, no matter that he was feeling it. Stefano would go to war in a heartbeat over him, but there was no way to know how many families in Japan would unite against them. Ricco wasn't willing to risk his brothers, sister, or cousins.

He'd remained silent for years. They'd been long, hard years of always looking over his shoulder and training harder than ever. Often, when he couldn't sleep, he'd go to one of his brothers' homes and watch over them, paranoid something might happen to them. After several years had gone by, he was certain they were safe, and he didn't want Stefano to stir up trouble.

"I think finding a partner for your art is a positive move, Ricco." Stefano switched subjects again. "Looking for a woman to be your partner when you know you'll have to walk away later is something else altogether."

Ricco already knew that, but he was losing too much of himself. Going too wild in a desperate attempt to feel something. Anything. He was already too far gone and didn't know if there was anyone who could bring him back. He'd deliberately separated himself from his family, spending less time in public with them and more time racing or partying in the hopes that others would think he didn't care about them. He must have done a good job for Stefano to ask him if the family mattered to him.

Ricco dropped his hand to the door, needing to escape. Stefano shifted in his seat as if he might follow him. "I need to lie down," he said, knowing his brother would hear the ring of truth. He did need a bed and fast or he was going to topple right over.

Stefano subsided. "Angelina Laconi is going to come check on you, and don't give me any trouble over it. She's a nurse."

"She makes eyes at me." Now she'd have excuses to touch him. Life sucked. He wasn't going to get out of having a nurse drop by, he could tell by Stefano's expression.

"Live with it. Emmanuelle made certain your fridge was stocked and Francesca made several meals for you. They're in the freezer. One's in the fridge."

"Please thank them for me." Ricco shoved open the door and forced his legs to work. It wasn't easy, but he had discipline in abundance, a trait every rider needed. He was very, very aware of Stefano's eyes on him as he made his way up to the door.

"Francesca." Ricco bent his head to brush a kiss along his sister-in-law's cheek. The weeks of healing and physical therapy had helped. Pain didn't crash through him every time he took a step, and he'd begun training again, although Stefano watched him closely. His older brother was still unaware of the training hall Ricco had installed in his home a few years earlier. Most gatherings were in Stefano's penthouse in the Ferraro Hotel.

"Ricco." Francesca flashed her amused smile, the one that mocked him a little for his greeting.

He rarely said hello or good-bye. He said her name, and she retaliated by saying his. He loved that about her. He loved everything about her, mainly that she loved his brother more than anything or anyone.

He'd never learned the art of relaxing. He could play his part out in public, but at home, with his brothers and sister, he had always been the one to pace around, help Taviano, his youngest brother, in the kitchen, or find his way to the training room and work out while the others conversed. Since the accident, he'd made a few attempts at being better.

"Smells good."

"I hope it tastes good. I've been working with a few new recipes for the artichoke sauce you said you liked and I think I've got it for you now. I'm serving homemade pasta with artichoke sauce, zucchini flan, guinea fowl and stuffed flowers fried. Oh, and for dessert, tiramisu."

"Nice. I've never had anything you've ever cooked that I didn't like." It was the truth. He wasn't into flattery, but Francesca was truly the nicest woman he'd ever met. She loved and accepted them all right along with her demanding husband. "Where's the boss?"

She laughed. "He only *thinks* he's the boss. I still have my job at the deli, don't I? You know how much he hates me working."

"Here's a little news flash for you, honey," Ricco said. "We all hate you working. We've got enemies."

"I don't."

They'd taken care of her enemy. Permanently. "They can get to us through you," he pointed out. It was an old argument and one he was certain Stefano had tried many times. Francesca might be the sweetest woman he knew, but she was no pushover.

The fact that Francesca still had her job surprised him. He couldn't imagine his oldest brother allowing his woman to put herself in danger, and Stefano had no trouble bossing all his siblings around.

Ricco shrugged out of his jacket and let her take it to

hang up along with his tie. "Just us tonight?" He was already unbuttoning the top three buttons of his shirt.

"Yes." She made a face at him. "Family business."

He found himself relaxing. He was good at family business. Francesca would have told him if Eloisa was present. As a rule, his mother didn't show up for family events at Stefano's—which meant she was almost never present.

Taviano had come to him three weeks earlier with his findings. A casing had cracked on the shock absorber. Stefano had yet to talk to him about it, so he was fairly certain that was what this night was all about. He didn't really care what it was that brought the family together, only that they were together.

"Stefano told me you're advertising for a rope model," Francesca continued. "How's that coming?"

"There's a lot of fucked-up women in the world," he replied.

She laughed. "You're just finding that out?"

"Since meeting you, I had high hopes." That was partly true, but mostly he was teasing her. Something new for him with an outsider, although he'd never considered her that. Francesca fit right in with his brothers and Emmanuelle. She was family, and every one of them would lay down their lives for her.

She gave him another smile. She really was a beautiful woman. Stefano was lucky to find her. Not only was she sweet, intelligent and beautiful, but she also could have been a rider, had she been found and trained from the time she was a child. She was rare. Very rare. She had accepted their way of life, shrouded in secrecy and living outside the accepted laws of the land.

Ricco sighed. He'd secretly hoped that by advertising for a rope model, the woman of his dreams would appear. She would be tall, with red hair, because he liked that look, slim like a model and very willing to accept him as the focus of her life. More, she would be an untrained rider, one who could give him children so his family would be happy. So far he'd gotten every body type, hair color and a variety of curves, a lot of women willing to do kink and more who wanted money. A lot of money. He hadn't connected with any of them—not even physically.

He hadn't conducted the interviews, but he'd been there, in the shadows, watching where the parade of women couldn't see him. He was determined to find one woman that aroused him at least emotionally, if not physically, but nothing happened. It was depressing.

He'd always liked women—especially when he came out of the shadow tubes after a job. He never connected with them on any level but physical. He never wanted to spend any time with them outside of having sex. He was adventurous sexually and surrounded himself with women who were the same way, but he played and he left. He always made that clear. He wasn't a man who stayed. Lately, even that was fading. He played with the Lacey twins occasionally, but he wasn't into it anymore.

He envied Stefano his ability to have a relationship. He wasn't certain he could do it. Now that he'd been in on the interviews with the various women applying to be a rope model, he was fairly positive he would never be that man. He wanted it, but he just felt indifference or annoyance. None of the women knew who the rope master was, but they'd tried to find out. He'd been careful to have Emilio conduct the interviews in a neutral location—the conference room of the Ferraro Hotel where many interviews for a variety of jobs were often conducted.

"It's going to happen for you, Ricco," Francesca said, walking with him through the enormous open room toward the kitchen where the family usually gathered. "I know you don't think it will, but I feel it. She's close."

He glanced at her sharply. Francesca wasn't given to fantasy. He shook his head in denial. He'd given up that dream a long time ago. "Done too many things in my life to ever have a decent woman throw in with me."

"I'm a decent woman and I love you," Francesca said.

"Yeah, but you're my sister."

"I love you, too." Emmanuelle joined them, slipping her arm around his waist as well. "But then, I'm your sister, too, and it's well known by the lot of you that I have no sense."

Ricco couldn't help but laugh. Emmanuelle could always make him smile, no matter how bad his nights had been. She was a ray of sunshine to all of them.

She turned her face up to his, her eyes moving over his features, seeing things he didn't want her to see. At once the smile disappeared. "You aren't sleeping."

He shrugged, trying to look casual. "Never been good at sleeping, honey. Tell me what's happening in our neighborhood. I've been out of the loop for a while."

"Francesca knows far more than any of us. Working at Masci's she hears everything, don't you?"

Francesca went to the stove, where Taviano was turning the guinea fowl in the frying pan. Using olive oil, he'd sautéed garlic and scallions and then placed the fowl skin side down before adding sage. He glanced up and winked at Ricco. "Francesca was just going to let this burn."

"She never burns anything," Giovanni objected. He mixed the homemade pasta noodles with the artichoke sauce. "Stefano scored big-time with this one. He just needs a few bambinos running around, her pregnant and barefoot, and the man will be happy."

"He's already happy," Francesca said smugly.

"Well, I'd be happy," Giovanni clarified. "I'd make a great uncle."

Francesca blew him a kiss and sat on the barstool between her brothers-in-law. "Lucia and Amo are having the time of their lives with their new daughter, Nicoletta. Extremely happy."

"Is she going to a regular school yet?" Stefano asked, coming up behind his wife and circling her around the waist with his arms.

Ricco had noticed Stefano couldn't get near Francesca without touching her. He envied his brother that and wanted it for himself. He just wanted to feel for someone. Connect with someone.

"She's smart," Vittorio said. He stabbed his fork into the pasta and took a bite, then held up his thumb, indicating it was good. "But she doesn't want to go to a regular school. Amo asked me to talk to her. I did, but I don't think she was impressed. She didn't say much, just looked at me. I don't envy them. The girl is gorgeous. Every young man from here to hell and back is going to be knocking at their door."

"Why do you all want her in a regular school?" Taviano asked. "More trouble if you ask me. All those horny bastards leering at her. Do we really want that kind of problem? One of us would have to go scare the crap out of them and then she'd be embarrassed or pissed and we'd get the blame. Keep her home. Locked up. It's for her own good."

"It's her last year of high school," Francesca said. "She deserves to have fun."

Ricco wasn't positive Francesca was right about sending her to the local high school. Nicoletta had come from New York, from a terrible situation. She'd been brutally abused, physically, sexually and emotionally. Stefano and Taviano had rescued her, but the damage had been done and it had been severe. Ricco knew the girl, like him, didn't sleep. He knew because he often pulled guard duty at night.

Nicoletta was one of the rare potential riders, her shadow throwing out feeler tubes to connect with the other shadows around her. The riders all took turns watching over her. He took the night shift because it suited him, and she went out her bedroom window and sat on the rooftop listening to music. He kept watch, but he didn't interfere. She looked so young and alone, and he knew he'd just scare her if he suddenly appeared beside her.

"She likes being with Lucia and Amo," Stefano said. "I've talked to her often, and she wants to stay with them."

"Who wouldn't want to be with them?" Taviano asked. "They'll spoil her rotten. She's good for them as well."

"It was a cracked casing, Ricco," Stefano said abruptly.

"On the shock absorber. Not you, a cracked casing. The wrong metal alloy was used and passed off to us as the real deal. I've already informed the other racing teams."

Ricco didn't look at his brother. That was the most Stefano was going to give him, when both knew that everything else that had been said between them still stood. He just nodded and sank down into the chair at the table beside Emmanuelle. It wasn't exactly news, anyway. Taviano had come to him immediately a good three weeks earlier and told him. Taviano preferred to race Indy cars, and he was the one, along with Vittorio and Emmanuelle, who designed their engines.

"How you coming on your hunt for a partner?" Vittorio asked, sliding into a chair at the long table.

Ricco shrugged. "I guess I've got to choose someone soon. I'm doing one more round of interviews in a few days and then I'll have to pick someone."

"Or not," Francesca said. "Seriously, hon, don't hook up with just anyone. It won't work."

He knew that, but he was determined to try.

CHAPTER TWO

Ricco sighed and raked his fingers through his hair, spilling thick dark strands over his forehead. "I guess that's it, Emilio. I didn't spot anyone I was wild about, but I'll go over the applicants again and see if anything hits me." That was pretty much a lie, and any one of his brothers or his sister would know he wasn't about to go through those applications again.

"The one whipping off her shirt was good," Emilio pointed out with a grin. "I'm keeping her phone number and address."

"She'll expect you to tie her up," Ricco warned.

"I can do that." Emilio rolled his shoulders to get the kinks out. "I hate sitting around. Even with all the models coming in, seriously, Ricco, this isn't my thing. Next time, have Enzo help out."

Ricco knew there wouldn't be a next time. He knew none of the applicants were going to work out. He was going to go home and toss every single one of the submissions in the fireplace. That last ray of hope he'd held out had died a violent death when the very last model had sat there chewing gum with her mouth open and with the top three buttons open on a shirt three sizes too small, all while her hand kept straying to Emilio to stroke his arm suggestively.

Every one of the models had thought Emilio to be the rope master. They'd advertised a good wage, stating the photographs would be used in a book but would be exclusive to the rope master. Out of three hundred applicants, only about fifteen were clearly models with experience in rope art.

A timid knock on the door had them both turning as a woman clutching a book in her arms pushed halfway in. "Am I too late?" There was a note of apprehension in her musical voice.

Ricco went absolutely still. The pitch was low and sweet. That tone pushed into his chest, right into his center, as if it were a key unlocking something tight and hard in him. He moved his hand over his heart as an unknown emotion seized it hard, wrenching, twisting, forcing that lock to open so that his own music could be heard pounding in his ear, beating like a lost drum seeking the right rhythm.

He inhaled sharply as something he didn't understand spread through him like the rays of the sun, driving out the pressure that was always with him, always weighing on him. He couldn't have moved if he wanted to. The sensation was unlike anything he'd ever known, but it was so strong it was overwhelming. He had to hear her again. Had to be close to her. It wasn't a want so much as a need.

He remained locked in place, his gaze drifting over her body, taking in every detail. She was unexpected. Not the tall, slim woman he'd always imagined he wanted. She wasn't short and delicate, either, but somewhere in between. She wasn't a redhead, and he'd always thought that his favorite. She had curves and pale skin; her eyes were large, hazel, and shaped like a cat's. She had blond hair and was graceful, a bit fragile-looking, reminding him of an exotic flower. She looked mixed race to him, part Asian—Japanese perhaps—in spite of her coloring. He never would have looked in that direction after so much trauma, yet every cell in his body responded to her.

"Sorry, sweetheart," Emilio said. "Interviews are closed."

The woman stood there, right in the center of the doorway, clutching the book to her chest. She was taller than both Emmanuelle and Francesca, but lacked the height of the supermodels he often dated. It was impossible to tell how long her hair was. The shiny blond mass was swept up with long hairpins in some intricate style he couldn't begin to figure out, but it left her neck bare and vulnerable. Her skin was flawless. Soft looking. Beautiful. Already his palms itched for his rope. Red, he thought, to complement her skin and that glossy blond hair.

At Emilio's answer, the woman took two more steps inside the room, right under the blaze of lights they'd purposely set up. His heart, now a pounding drum, nearly stopped. The lights threw her shadow into sharp relief behind her on the wall. The shadow was dark and thin but threw out strong tubes, feelers reaching toward other shadows. When there were none, the feelers reached farther for connections, elongating, seeking, prompting another step from her.

His breath caught in his throat as the tube slid along the floor, moving through shadows until it connected with the shadows where he stood. It hit like a freight train. Jarred him. Shook him. Filled his cock with hot, urgent need. Lust was sharp and terrible, almost uncontrollable. He felt that same wild pounding in his heart hammering right through his cock. He knew she felt it, too. Her head came up as if scenting danger and her eyes moved around the room warily.

"Come in," Ricco managed, but he didn't know how he could speak in a normal tone. No part of his body seemed his own, not even his voice. He was grateful for his strict training. He kept all interest from his tough features when his entire being reacted to her.

Her gaze jumped from Emilio to him. He was in the shadows and she probably hadn't spotted him immediately. She hesitated, and he couldn't blame her. He was intimidating and knew it. The Ferraros were born intimidating. Time seemed to stand still as he waited for her to obey his order. It had been an order. Ricco was used to obedience from everyone around him—obedience and deference. When he spoke, he expected and got an instant reaction.

Emilio glanced at him sharply, heaved a resigned sigh and sank down into the high-backed chair at the conference table. He beckoned to the woman. "I guess you're not too late, sweetheart." He indicated the chair across the table from him. "Did you bring a portfolio? Anything with your picture?" He held his hand out for the book.

Mariko Majo could barely breathe through the need rushing through her veins like molten lava. She didn't understand what was happening. One moment she was perfectly fine, a little worried she was not going to get the extremely important interview, and the next, she was overwhelmed with need—with a hunger she'd never known. For the first time in her life she had the urge to turn around and flee. She knew danger when she saw it, and Ricco Ferraro was pure danger.

The two men were both waiting. She lifted her chin and forced her body into movement. She hadn't expected Ricco Ferraro to be in the interview room. She knew the hotel belonged to the Ferraros but not one woman had come out of the conference room talking about him. She knew it was him because, of course, she'd seen photographs of him; who hadn't? He was in all the magazines, online and paper both. He had quite a reputation as a ladies' man and she could see why he would deserve it. He was gorgeous. Stunning. Scary.

She took several steps into the room, but then the door swung closed behind her and her heart jumped and then began to pound. Fear had a distinctive taste. She glanced back at the door. She wasn't a coward, she never had been, but the Ferraros were reputed to be in organized crime, a dangerous family to have anything to do with. She felt a little desperate trapped in the room with the two very intimidating men. It was whispered that they could hear lies. She had secrets. Too many. The last thing she needed was for one of the Ferraros to ask her questions.

No one spoke, not to encourage or discourage. This was her decision and both men made that very clear. She tightened her arms around the book she held as if that could give her the necessary courage. Mariko was not a woman afraid of much, yet in the presence of Ricco Ferraro, she found herself trembling. That wasn't a good start. Straightening her shoulders, she walked across the floor toward the conference table. It was large and intimidating, just like the men.

"I didn't bring a portfolio. I've never been a model, but my mother was. She died long before I ever had the chance to know her." Her voice was low and very soft, a soothing, pleasing sound, cultivated by the elders as she grew. Now, she didn't know how to raise her voice. She wished she could. She was raised to sound seductive, pleasing to a man's ear and body. She didn't want to attract undue attention, not when she was alone in a room with the two men, one an obvious Ferraro, the other clearly related.

Emilio sighed again and glanced up at Ricco. "I can do this and catch up with you later." The idea had been not to ever allow the models to know who the rope master was. If they knew it was a Ferraro, they would have had even more women looking to fill the position, hoping they'd have a chance of seducing him.

The hotel was often used by businessmen for a variety of meetings. No one would think twice about interviews being held there. It would not be unheard of for a Ferraro to be spotted in the hotel or talking to one of the men using the room. Most of the models had been disappointed that they hadn't seen one of the famous family members.

Mariko held her breath. She wanted Ricco out of the room, yet she didn't. She was confused with the way her body had suddenly come to life, every nerve ending aware of him. His eyes were dark and hooded, giving nothing away. He looked invincible. Disinterested. She was a mass of nerves and he was totally in control. She wanted to run, but she needed to do this—to convince them she was perfect for the job.

She'd watched the other models leaving one by one. They were mostly American, although not all. Some were from Brazil and Mexico. A couple had been from Spain and Argentina. There had been an Icelander. She was gorgeous.

Most were beautiful, with lots of height—something she didn't have. The moment she thought that, the voices rose to taunt her. She was mixed—Japanese and American. Nothing. A nothing. A nobody. The *kanji* in her last name meant "female devil." She didn't even know what her real last name was because she'd dishonored the family simply by being born.

She wasn't beautiful, or like any of the women she'd seen Ricco with in the magazines. There were two in particular he favored. Twins. The Lacey sisters—both actresses. She'd read all about them numerous times, the fact that the tabloids had caught them all naked in a hot tub together had been splashed across every tatty little rag and gossip magazine. She forced that image out of her mind. She had one shot at this and she had to make it right. Already she'd made a bad impression by being late, waiting too long to make up her mind.

Taking a deep breath, she continued forward, keeping her steps soft and light. She knew how to keep the nerves out of her face and voice, but she'd never felt under such scrutiny. Ricco had one scar across his face, a long line that ran from his left eye almost to the corner of his mouth. He was handsome, but in a rough, all-male way: the shadow along his stubborn jaw, his high cheekbones, straight nose and amazing eyes. Those dark eyes took in far too much but remained flat and ice-cold. He was reputed to be the most violent of the five brothers, and looking at him, she believed it.

"I'll stay," Ricco said. "I might have more questions."

Her heart jerked hard. She kept walking, feeling as if she might be headed to her doom. She didn't look around her, but she'd noted the exits the moment she'd entered the room. She had given the huge room a quick glance, taking in everything. She wasn't one to walk into a fancy hotel and be dazzled like most of the women leaving had been. She'd deliberately waited and watched from the lobby as the hopeful models had exited. None seemed particularly certain they'd gotten the job. She hadn't been all that sure of trying out for the position and she wanted to make certain the opportunity was a legitimate one.

"Sit." Ricco waved his hand toward the chair across from

the other man. "I'm Ricco Ferraro. This is my cousin, Emilio Gallo."

Ricco was definitely in charge. He was making that very clear. Emilio glanced up at him again, one eyebrow raised. So, Ricco hadn't conducted the other interviews. That wasn't good. Why had she ever thought she could do this?

She pushed the application across the table to Emilio but she knew Ricco was looking at it as well. "I'm Mariko. Mariko Majo." She bowed her head, her gaze sliding away from his in shame. That was unusual for her, she usually stared defiantly, daring anyone to notice her name. To comment. Still, she watched Ricco carefully from under her long feathery lashes. She'd perfected that particular art many, many years earlier.

His gaze drifted over her face so that she had to fight to keep color from rising. Very slowly his hand, large and strong with long fingers, turned the application toward him. All the while his eyes remained on her face, and then his gaze dropped to the writing. His features went utterly still.

He knew. He could read those characters and he knew what her last name meant. The name she'd been given, not born with. She didn't know her true last name; that had been taken away from her and her brother. Humiliation almost had her snatching the paper out from under his hand, but pride won out and she lifted her chin and her gaze to his face, steeling herself for his snide comment. Let him judge her. She was used to it. She lived with disapproval every day of her life.

"May I call you Mariko? I prefer not to be formal."

She inclined her head, surprised that he would forgo any reference to her surname. Female devil. She'd kept the devil character out of defiance. If she was being strictly truthful, sometimes she was the devil. She noticed he hadn't given her permission to call him by his first name, but then he would be her employer if she got the position.

"You have no experience, yet you want to be a rope model. Why?"

She'd known she would have to answer that and she could

tell the strict truth. She pushed the book across the table to him. "I never knew my mother. This is all I have of her. She was a rope model in Japan."

He continued to look at her, not at the book, although his palm dropped to the cover. "Tell me about your mother."

Her breath caught in her throat. She knew very few facts, most of which weren't good, but she was determined to be honest. "She traveled to Japan with the express purpose of finding a rope master. She was very interested in the art." Make that the erotic elements, if those raising her told the truth. It had been a terrible scandal, her father dishonoring his family by wanting to marry her. That had been the story she'd been told, but when she'd done the research, looking for him . . .

"Her name?"

She fought to keep the color from rising. Of course she should have started with that. Why was she allowing him to shake her usual composure?

"Maria. Maria Hammond. She met my father there and they wanted to marry." To the horror of his entire family. According to what she'd been told, her father had reputedly nearly destroyed his family with his choice. Her mother had been everything his family had predicted and more. In the end he hadn't married her and she'd lived on the streets, making her living as a whore. She'd abandoned Mariko and her brother to the streets and had taken off.

"The name of the rope master?"

She hesitated. She was no longer certain he was her father. There was a long silence. "I prefer not to say."

Ricco kept his eyes on her for a moment and then he spun the book around and opened it. He studied the photographs. "This appears to be Eiichi Hayashi's work."

Mariko had traced her mother through the names in the book, but the rope master was dead. He'd died of old age, and his children had told her that he'd had numerous models over the years and had never married any of them. Mariko suspected the story she'd been told wasn't altogether the truth, but she'd met dead ends everywhere she'd turned. Eiichi was too old to be her father.

She inclined her head, waiting for his denouncement, but again he surprised her by remaining silent, waiting for her to continue.

"Is that what you're hoping to do?" Emilio asked. "Marry your own rope master?" There was the slightest touch of sarcasm in his voice.

She flinched. She'd heard that note of derision so many times growing up, children taunting her about her American mother. Her "family," the ones so gracious and honorable to take in two orphans, was harsh with her for her own good so she wouldn't become the whore her mother had been.

"Emilio." Ricco's voice was very low, but it was a whip, lashing at the other man.

She never wanted him to use that tone with her. It was terrifying, and she wasn't a woman to be terrified by much of anything. Her family had been strict, at times bordering on brutal, and she should have been used to such a soft but harsh reprimand. Clearly, Ricco was a force to be reckoned with.

"I've got this. Thank you for your help."

It was a dismissal and Emilio instantly stood. She didn't want him to leave her alone in the room with Ricco Ferraro. It was dangerous. The tension in the room was tangible and growing more so every moment. Mariko kept her head slightly down, just as she'd been taught since she was a child, a respectful position when the men were talking, but her eyes were moving, noting everything about them, body positions, the way they moved, Emilio like a fighter, Ricco like a panther.

This was the most difficult thing she'd ever done. Sit quietly, absolutely still, feeling more vulnerable than she ever had in her life with the exception of once, but that was a very long time ago when she was a child. She was an adult and fully capable of choosing her own fate. She had come to this place determined to get this job—and she was still

determined. She just hadn't expected to feel so defenseless
or susceptible to Ricco Ferraro.

There was silence after Emilio closed the door, leaving
her alone with the panther. She counted her heartbeats but
refused to raise her eyes. Her body was already humming,
alive, a strange rhythm she'd never felt before, one that not
only alarmed her but puzzled her. Physical attraction to date,
at best, had been mild. This was anything but mild. It was
shocking in its intensity, her body reaching for his. She could
barely breathe with him so close. She'd never been so aware
of another human being.

"Look at me."

She didn't dare lift her eyes to his. She had to gather her
courage first before she went into battle. This one she had
to win or she might be dishonored for all time.

"If you can't even look at me, Mariko, how do you expect
this to work?"

His tone was mild, but there was a hint of a reprimand
in it and she winced. She didn't like that voice, but it wasn't
because she wasn't used to the tone, it was more she didn't
want to disappoint him—or herself. Swallowing hard, she
lifted her gaze to his.

At once she fell into those dark, dark eyes. She'd never
seen anyone with eyes so compelling. Her heart drummed
even louder. Fight or flight? She was frozen and couldn't do
either. She touched her tongue to her lip, a leftover childhood
habit she'd been beaten for. The moment she did it, she was
ashamed of herself. She forced air through her lungs and
held his gaze.

"That's better. You said your mother was a rope model
so you know what it entails." He made it a statement.

She nodded just slightly.

"You're going to have to actually speak to me."

She was an idiot to think she could do this, but she was
already in the situation. She hadn't expected to feel anything. Certainly not attraction. To hell with her childhood
and all the voices whispering in her head. She moistened

her lips, watching him watch her. That slight action of her tongue on her lips, the nervous giveaway. "Yes." The single word came out low and husky.

His lashes didn't so much as flicker. He had long lashes. Beautiful lashes. His mouth was pretty amazing as well. It was just that he was far more daunting than she'd expected.

"Have you seen a performance?"

She nodded. He kept looking at her. Waiting in silence. The color slid under her skin. "Yes."

He remained silent.

"After I was given the book, I studied the art and went to several demonstrations. I guess I wanted to feel closer to her." She'd wanted to understand her mother.

"What did you think?"

What had she thought? She'd been taught that her mother was a slut. A whore. That she'd destroyed an entire family, dishonoring them. She'd been told time and again that her mother had made her living whoring, that she had abandoned her two children to the streets. It hadn't been an image she wanted to think about. Until now. Until she learned everything she knew might not be real. The ground had shifted out from under her and now she was here, trying to figure out what she could do next.

"I thought the art was beautiful. I didn't understand why or how she could do it." The photographs were stunning. But to be tied up at someone's mercy. That was disturbing. Mariko wasn't certain she could actually do it.

"For this to work, you have to trust me. Implicitly. You have to know that I would always take care of you in any circumstance."

She blinked. The breath caught in her lungs and felt trapped there. She trusted no one. Especially not a man like Ricco Ferraro. She'd done her homework before applying for the position. No one else seemed to know Ricco was the rigger, but she'd suspected all along. There weren't that many real rope masters in the United States.

He waited, and she couldn't think of a single thing to say.

No one took care of her. Not ever. She took care of her brother, but no one took care of her. She wasn't even certain what that meant to him.

He moved then and her heart clenched so hard in her chest she feared she might have a heart attack. All he did was step forward, but she couldn't breathe.

"You know that we have to get to know each other fast. The contract is for six months."

"I thought three." The words came out strangled. She sounded like a scared little mouse and that annoyed her. She wasn't a mouse.

"Six." It was firm. "Six, and you live in my house. With me. You would have your own suite of rooms within the house."

She shook her head and went to stand. She couldn't breathe. She had to get out of there. The moment she moved, he did as well, stepping back to allow her to get up. She didn't expect that. Why? She wasn't his prisoner. She was applying for a position she wanted. No, needed.

"Are you staying?"

His voice was pitched low. Mesmerizing. She loved music and she responded to musical notes. This was different, but no less perfect. He had the kind of voice that made a woman go soft and damp. That made her want to do anything he said. Even her. She'd thought she was immune to anything like that until this moment.

"Do you want me to stay?" She held her breath. She needed his answer more than she needed air.

"Yes."

She didn't understand how she could be so affected by his voice. By that simple answer. She took another breath. "I honestly don't know if I can do this." She didn't know. That was the truth. She was walking on eggshells, giving him as much truth as possible without revealing the dark secrets shadowing her every step.

"Of course you don't. You don't know me at all. You have to get to know me before you'll have faith that I'd never hurt or harm you in any way."

He took her hand, closing his very gently but firmly around hers, and led her out away from the table. Grasping her shoulders, he turned her until she was facing the door. "Stand here for me. I don't want you to move."

Mariko found she was trembling. His touch was terrifying. Not because he hadn't been gentle, but because she felt the absolute command in him, telegraphed through those warm, strong fingers. It was impossible not to think what it would be like to have those fingers stroking caresses over her skin. She tried to shut down those thoughts, but they refused to leave her. She didn't want to look at him just in case he could read her most intimate desire.

Ricco moved then, like a stalking panther, circling her slowly, silently. When he moved behind her, out of her sight, she nearly panicked. It was all she could do to keep from running to the door. He had positioned her right in front of it, almost like he was daring her to make a run for it.

She *felt* him. His breath on the nape of her neck. The skim of his finger from the nape of her neck down her spine. His touch was so light it was barely there. Did she imagine it? If so, the caress was so real it sent flickering flames licking at her skin. She didn't want to move. She wanted to show him she was strong. She was powerful. She could be what he needed. She *was* what he needed.

"Put your hands out in front of you. Palms together as if you are praying."

His voice was even and low. A mere whisper, but if she thought he was commanding before, now she heard the real thing. No one could possibly disobey that soft, powerful tone. A whisper of trepidation slid down her spine. At the same time, she felt her sex clench, go damp.

She was slow to bring up her hands but he didn't look impatient. He simply waited. Never once had she been restrained. "I thought we would get to know each other."

None of the other models coming out of the room had said they'd been tied by Ricco Ferraro. She was certain they could never have resisted bragging about it. That was what

Shibari was, wasn't it? She hadn't thought about the fact that she'd be placing herself in such a vulnerable position. That she'd be helpless, and entirely at his mercy.

Ricco moved in front of her in that silent way of his. He was too strong. Too powerful. Too scary. It wasn't just his looks—and he was a striking male. It was the predatory vibe he gave off. The look in his unblinking stare, so focused on her. Now he had a rope in his hand. This one was red and it slid through his fingers as if a part of him. At once she was mesmerized by that single movement. She couldn't look at anything else. The rope appeared an extension of him, coiling, uncoiling, slithering, just as suddenly coming alive with sheer power.

"We are getting to know each other, Mariko. You should know yourself as well. This is an exchange of power. We're in it together. You must be able to talk to me. Let me know what is uncomfortable, what you like. What you don't like. What frightens you. What makes you feel as if you're flying."

Did people actually feel that way in the ropes? She couldn't imagine it. Still, she had committed to this, but if she allowed him to tie her hands, she would be in such a bad position. She glanced around the room. The shadows had lengthened just a little bit, telling her time was slipping away. He was patient. He didn't speak again, didn't try to persuade her, leaving it entirely up to her to make the decision.

Taking a breath, she extended her arms to him, her palms together. Her heart was wild now, and she felt a little faint.

He didn't slip the rope over her wrists like she thought he would. He leaned into her, his mouth against her ear. "Breathe for me, Mariko. Just breathe."

The rope slid along her cheek, a whisper of silk. It moved down her throat to caress her bare skin where her top exposed her shoulders and neckline—and it was a caress. It felt sensual. She found herself shivering. His breath had been warm, his lips brushing her earlobe. Ricco Ferraro was far more dangerous to her than she'd ever imagined, in ways she hadn't even considered and wasn't in the least prepared for.

There was no way to deny that voice. She forced air into her lungs, afraid if she didn't, she might faint, or worse, disappoint him and herself.

"That's my girl."

Her heart jumped at his praise—that soft note of encouragement, of approval, even admiration. He knew she'd never done this before and he was willing to see her through it. She had to hand it to him. He wasn't a man trampling on his model to get her to do as he wished.

"Look at me. Look at my eyes when I tie you. I want to see your expression, to know if you're okay. If you're not, I'll know and I'll remove the rope immediately."

It took courage to lift her gaze to his. Not because it would send him permission to tie her wrists, but because looking into his eyes was a very dangerous endeavor. A woman could get lost there, and Ricco Ferraro wasn't a man to trust with one's heart. She knew that much from her research of him.

She stared into his dark, dark eyes—so dark they appeared black. Gorgeous. Compelling. Intense. She almost forgot what he was doing, but then the silk moved against her bare skin, sliding sensually, an extension of his fingers. Not just his fingers, she realized; an extension of *him*. That was why the rope felt so powerful and sensual touching her skin.

She expected to feel claustrophobic and afraid, but she didn't. Not as long as she was looking into his eyes. She could read people, hear them for what was beneath their words, not just the pretty things they said. Looking into Ricco's eyes, she knew she was safe with him. She felt safe. More, she felt free. It was strange, that feeling of freedom, as if by tying her, he had released her spirit—beaten down, so encased in the beliefs of others, what was right, what was wrong, what she was—so that she could just be. Simply be.

"Look at your wrists. They're so delicate, so feminine. Your skin is extraordinary. To me, you're like a beautiful flower. Your fingers are strong, yet you look so fragile. Tell me what you see when you look at the ropes against your skin."

She could barely force herself to look away from his eyes. His hands were over hers, his thumb sliding along the back of hers, a small, light brushing, back and forth, that she felt deep inside her most intimate spot. It was as if he'd made a connection between him, her hands and her sex.

Slowly, reluctantly, she dropped her gaze from his eyes to her hands. The red rope stood out against her bare skin, but instead of looking bizarre or ugly, the knots were intricate and beautiful. They formed two wrist bands, wide and lacy, lying against her wrists like delicate cuffs. His hands enveloped hers, holding her with exquisite gentleness, almost as if he really thought her that fragile flower and he guarded her with care. That made her feel a fraud, but she couldn't bring herself to pull away from him.

"Are you uncomfortable?"

Was she? In so many ways, but not the way he meant. She'd never felt more sensual. More attracted to a man. More intimidated or exhilarated. This was a dance between them, and it could end up fatal to her—or to him—but it was beautiful and she didn't want it to end.

"No." That wasn't strictly the truth and her gaze jumped to his. She not only felt the censure but saw it. His disappointment. That hurt. An unexpected arrow. She shook her head. "No, but yes. The ropes aren't uncomfortable. I thought I would have claustrophobia, but I don't."

"Do you suffer from claustrophobia?"

That was a mistake to admit. He might not want her, and suddenly she wanted the position because she was certain she needed it to learn things about herself she had never known and would never again have the opportunity to find out. She nodded reluctantly. "Sometimes."

"Do you know why?"

It was impossible to ignore that soft, captivating voice. It played along her nerve endings, setting them on fire, making her so aware of him. Of her. Of the rise and fall of her breasts, of the fact that he was taller, broader and stronger. That his personality was unexpected. She thought he might be mean. A bully. Using his power and wealth to push others around. He didn't need to do that. He had that voice, so low and sensual—a temptation to sin. Put the voice, his eyes and his body together, and any woman might be lost. She certainly was.

When she didn't answer immediately, he tugged very gently on the rope so that she was forced to take a step into him. At once she was surrounded by his masculine scent. He smelled clean. Fresh. Outdoorsy. A powerful waterfall in a forest. Up close, he was daunting, and much more sensual. Every breath she took drew him deeper into her lungs until she didn't know where she left off and he started.

The red silk connected them. The ends had never left his hands. He controlled movement without seeming to do so. That shook her. He wasn't obvious about it, but he had complete control. "I require an answer, Mariko."

She closed her eyes to block him out but at once she heard the cries of pain. The screams of a woman. A man's voice as he died. Images rose, the crack in the closet door. Her arms around her baby brother. Her hand over his mouth to try to keep him from crying and giving their hiding place away. The streaks of blood running like dark shadows across the floor.

For a moment she couldn't breathe. It was all too real. All too close. She kept the door closed on her persistent nightmares, but now she was bringing it all to the surface and she couldn't go back. No matter what, there would be no going back to her other life.

"I have dreams of being locked in a closet when I was a child. I have nightmares about it nearly every night." He would hear the truth of that if all the rumors about his family were true. It was said one couldn't lie to a Ferraro, so she had no choice but to share her memories when he asked.

He removed the ropes and massaged her wrists, looking for marks on her skin. There were none, which didn't make her as happy as she would have thought. Belonging to him would be incredible, but he wasn't a one-woman man, and she would never accept less.

Ricco stepped away from her, coiling the rope easily in his hands without looking at it, proving it was an extension of him. "I will require you at all hours of the night. I don't sleep very well and I want to be able to practice my art anytime the mood strikes. I'm compensating you well for your time. You'll have your own rooms. During the time you're with me, you will have no other relationships. I made it clear in the ad that if you were married or seeing someone, not to apply."

"I'm not," she said.

"You have only to sign the papers. Read them carefully. My lawyer drew them up and he's very, very thorough. I think we'll suit each other, but I want you to be happy with the arrangement."

He was waiting and she had to answer. Take that last irrevocable step. She would have her own room, her own place where no one could get to her. She would be able to think without panicking. She'd do whatever was necessary, but it had to be the right thing, no mistakes. What she was doing was very, very dangerous, but she had no choice.

She took a deep breath and nodded. "I think this arrangement will suit me just fine."

"How soon can you move in?"

"Immediately. I don't have much. Just my personal clothes and a few items."

"I'll give you the address and a key."

It was done. She had gotten the position when all odds seemed stacked against her. She didn't smile because the consequences were too severe, but she was elated. She had stepped on the path she needed to be on.

CHAPTER THREE

Ricco paced across the floor with the restless energy that always marked him from his brothers. He could be utterly still when needed, but most of the time he was in motion. He trained hard and he worked and played harder, but that energy inside him never quite left him alone. He was aware of Francesca casting him little anxious glances. His beautiful sister-in-law, the true mother of the lot of them now. She'd taken them all on when she took on Stefano.

She'd made the monstrous penthouse at the top of the Ferraro Hotel a home. How she'd transformed it, he had no idea, but it felt welcoming where before it had been cold. She was everything, in Ricco's opinion, his brother needed. Soft when she needed to be, and tough as nails when Stefano got out of hand—which was often.

He sent his brother a quick look. Stefano, as always, was still. He simply waited for the explanation of why Ricco had called an emergency meeting. He sat on the leather couch, a drink in his hand, regarding Ricco thoughtfully. It was impossible to think one could put anything over on Stefano, nor did Ricco want to try. This was too important. On the other hand, Stefano hadn't been blowing smoke when he'd informed Ricco he would do anything to save him.

"What's up, bro?" Giovanni asked, throwing himself into one of the wide, very comfortable armchairs. He was the last to arrive. "I had to cancel a date tonight. This had better be good." He grinned at Ricco, but his eyes were worried.

Ricco looked around the room at his family. They were all worried. The only one who didn't really show it was Stefano, and he was the most worried of all of them. He hadn't taken his eyes from his brother, not from the moment Ricco had entered the penthouse.

He took a breath and turned to face them. Emmanuelle and Francesca would be his allies no matter what. Possibly Taviano. Stefano would be a fight. The others, he wasn't certain. This was the most important battle of his life and he had to win. If he lost . . . he was lost. That was what he had to convince Stefano of. If Stefano sided with him, they all would, and they'd help him. God knew, after all the wild things he'd done privately and publicly, he would need the help.

He stalked across the room to the bar and poured himself a Scotch on the rocks. Tossing it back without tasting it, he turned and faced his family. "I found her." He announced it quietly. He didn't raise his voice because he never had need to, but there was a part of him that was filled with exhilaration, so much so he could barely contain it.

Stefano put his drink down and leaned forward, his eyes never leaving Ricco's face. Never blinking. Emmanuelle and Francesca exchanged a long look and then both broke out into smiles. Giovanni, Vittorio and Taviano all stared at him without comprehension.

"Found who, bro?" Giovanni asked.

"Her. The one. She just walked in at the last minute. Emilio and I were giving up. I wanted to throw all the applications into the fire and then she walked in. She's a shadow rider. Her shadow reached out and connected with the shadows in the room and then hit mine. It was a little like being drunk only way, way better." He wasn't about to tell them the connection had been so strong that she'd given him a permanent hard-on, but he was certain Stefano knew all about that. He'd found Francesca.

"Just because she's capable of being a rider doesn't mean she's *your* woman," Vittorio cautioned. "There's more to it than that."

Ricco nodded and pressed his hand to his chest. "She walked in and asked if she was too late, and I felt that note press into my chest and unlock something chained up in me. I don't even know how to describe it, but from the moment I saw her, and heard her, I knew. I feel different. For a long time now I haven't felt anything for a woman, not even desire."

There was embarrassment and shame in confessing that to his brothers. They thought he was the stud of the century. Vittorio gave a small snort of derision and Giovanni coughed, nearly spraying his drink everywhere.

"No, it's the truth. Nothing and no one excited me anymore. All the games, they didn't work." He didn't dare look at Stefano. He was too silent. Too observant.

"How about the Lacey twins?" Taviano asked.

He shook his head. "Nothing. Then she walked in and I haven't been able to get a moment's peace. It's not going to be easy living with her in my house and trying to seduce her slowly."

Vittorio laughed. "That shouldn't be a problem for you, Ricco. I'll take bets you get it done in less than a week."

They all laughed. Happy for him. All but Stefano. He kept watching him. Waiting. Ricco had to convince him that this was the real thing and that he needed it more than he needed safety. More than anything else. He wouldn't survive without it—without her.

He put the glass down on the sideboard and looked directly at his older brother. "You were right, Stefano. I might not have caused that accident, but once the casing cracked I didn't do a thing to try to prevent myself from going into that wall. I'm tired. So damn tired. I didn't feel there was anything or any way out for me. The work kept me going, but I don't sleep and that was beginning to affect the job."

Vittorio and Giovanni glanced at each other, but Stefano kept watching him, unblinking, knowing there was more. He always knew.

"I need this woman. It isn't just about wanting her, and

I know that's wrong. I know it should be about want, not need, but I'm not going to make it without her." Stefano had to know it was that bad. Admitting it didn't make him feel very good about himself, but then he hadn't for a long, long time.

"You worried she isn't going to like your relationship with the Lacey twins?" Giovanni asked. He wasn't being sarcastic: it was a legitimate question and they both knew it.

"No, she's not going to like that or any of the other stupid things I've done, but hopefully we can get past that with the help of all of you. Francesca and Emmanuelle, I'm really counting on the two of you to make friends with her."

"Of course," Emmanuelle said.

Francesca echoed her, nodding, but now both women looked worried. He couldn't blame them. He was never nervous. Never. He was still looking at Stefano, and by now, all of them were aware of it and they were looking at the head of the family as well. Stefano hadn't said a word. Just waited. Because he knew. He always knew.

"What's wrong?" Francesca voiced what they were all wondering.

"There's a host of small problems, ones that are of my own making, and it's up to me to convince her I'm worth taking a shot with, even though I've got the worst reputation in the world." He shoved a hand through his hair. "The biggest problem is that she's a shadow rider and I'm fairly certain she's here to kill me."

Emmanuelle gasped. Francesca reached for Stefano's hand. He remained immobile, still as a statue, his gaze never leaving Ricco's. He held up his hand for silence when the others began to all talk at once.

"You're positive she's an actual rider?" he asked, his voice strictly neutral.

"There's no way to be positive," Ricco said. "She was too good at what she did. Acting nervous. I knew she was totally aware of me, that the connection between us hit her just as hard. I know when a woman wants me, and the physical attraction was definitely mutual. What woman wouldn't flirt just a little? She didn't. She has tremendous courage. She actually allowed me to tie her wrists. I could tell it was terrifying to her, but she went through with it. The pins in her hair were definitely not women's normal hairpins. Still, there's no way to be certain. The only thing I can tell you is that I just *knew*."

"We know every family. If she's a rider, we'll know of her," Stefano said. "I can reach out . . ."

He shook his head. "Wait. I need you to wait."

"Why wouldn't she just kill you without ever showing herself?" Vittorio asked.

He shook his head. "I have no idea."

"Are you guilty of something we don't know about?" Stefano asked. "Something that would put you in the path of a rider?"

A shadow rider carried out justice when the law couldn't. Always, always, they had to be certain, which meant a thorough investigation of the facts.

"She would have to be one of the Archambault family. There is a female rider. They're the only riders allowed to go after another shadow rider family," Stefano said.

"She's not French." Ricco took a breath. "I have to tell you. It's time, but Stefano, we have to be very careful, otherwise we're going to end up in a war and everyone will lose."

He didn't want to tell them the truth of what happened in Japan, yet he did. It would be such a relief to get the entire mess off his chest. To know that his family would look over their shoulders instead of him guarding them night and day would be a relief. Telling the truth would be liberating in a lot of ways.

"Start talking, Ricco." That was Stefano, all business.

"The riders are different in Japan. When we train other riders, we welcome them as family and treat them as we treat one another. There, riders from other countries are looked down on—especially the ones from the United States. We're considered lazy and undisciplined."

He didn't know if he was making excuses or just needing to find a place to begin. The entire sordid affair had been bottled up for far too long. Wrapped in guilt and fear for his family, he had stayed silent until he almost didn't know how to tell them what had occurred.

"No matter what we did or how hard we worked, those of us who weren't from the families there were never acknowledged, not even during the tournaments. It pissed me off. I have a temper and I got into a lot of fights proving myself, beating the crap out of some of the boys from the host families. Of course, that just proved to them that I was undisciplined and not fit to be a rider."

It was still painful, those memories. He'd trained harder than anyone else, and it hadn't mattered. "If I defeated the sons of the host families, if I beat their times riding the shadows, or in any way bested them, it was never acknowledged, but the boys were punished and the hatred and bitterness grew for all the other riders training, in particular me and one other rider—a female. You can imagine what it was like to be a female rider there where the women were supposed to wait on their men and be subservient to them. She was never considered as good, and the boys were mean to her."

"What country was she from?" Vittorio asked.

Just his voice was soothing. Vittorio, the peacemaker. Vittorio, the brother who always seemed to bring calm and sense in the middle of any storm.

"That's the thing, she was from Japan. Right there. She was the daughter of a council member. I didn't stay with her family, none of the foreign riders did. Her mother had died and her father was a former rider, he didn't go out on any jobs anymore. Her grandmother was very mean and ugly with her and the other kids. She put our parents to shame."

"Name," Stefano said abruptly.

Of course he would get down to the facts immediately. Nothing was going to get by him. Nothing ever did.

"Her name was Akiko Tanaka."

Stefano nodded. "She came from a fierce line, but they're all gone now. She was killed in a car accident along with the last of that lineage, her father and grandmother. I think three other riders, sons of some of the best families there, died as well. One survived, but was in a wheelchair for the rest of his life. It was a horrible tragedy."

Ricco shook his head. "None of them died in a car accident. I killed the three riders and put the remaining one in the wheelchair." He dropped the bomb right into the middle of the room. No one moved. No one spoke. They all just stared at him, shocked. There was absolute truth in his voice, and he knew they all heard it.

He didn't take his eyes from Stefano. He loved his brother. He was mother, father and big brother all rolled into one. He was the family's measure of what it was to be a shadow rider, a Ferraro, someone to be respected. Killing other riders, especially young, untrained riders when they needed them so desperately, was the worst sin a rider could commit, so much so that it was forbidden and would bring a death sentence down on the perpetrator. Only an Archambault rider could bring justice to another shadow rider.

"Ricco," Emmanuelle whispered, her voice filled with a mixture of horror and compassion.

He didn't look at her. He kept his eyes on Stefano, waiting for judgment, waiting for condemnation. He should have known better.

"You wouldn't have done so without a good reason, Ricco," he said. "What happened to Akiko and her family?"

Ricco shook his head. There was no way to put himself in a good light. He couldn't spin it or leave out details. "There was a tournament that afternoon and Akiko defeated Nao Yamamoto. He was seventeen and considered the fastest of the shadow riders coming up in Japan. His family was extremely proud of him. According to everyone, he brought them great honor. But he was a terrible human being. He bullied everyone, including the boys who followed him. He had his own little gang. His buddies were seventeen and sixteen. If anyone ever slighted any of them, or in any way made them look bad, they would ride the shadows, go visit them and beat the holy hell out of them. They bragged to the rest of us that they visited girls they liked and did whatever they wanted."

"Oh my God," Emmanuelle said. "I hope you reported them."

"Several of us did the day before the attack took place, but the elders said it was merely boys bragging. That it wasn't the truth. We knew differently because *we* heard the truth when they were bragging. Nao and his pack beat the shit out of two of the other riders who reported them, and I was waiting for them when they came for me. All in all, I didn't do too bad against the four of them, and if I'm being strictly honest, Nao was hurting when he went into that tournament."

"Wait a minute," Stefano said. "I want you to be very clear on this. You reported what you'd overheard about these boys using their abilities to harm girls and beat up other riders and the council dismissed it as untrue?"

Ricco nodded. "Women aren't treated nearly the same there as they are here. We know we need them for the riders to survive, but there, they are less than a man. Outsiders are treated the same. The council was comprised of the fathers of these boys. Had it come out that such a thing was going on, their entire families would have been dishonored. They're very traditional and old-school."

"Honor among riders is traditional," Taviano said, "or at least I always thought it was."

"If all the families were dishonored, and their sons were banned from riding, stripped of their abilities, the families would be left with nothing. I can't explain just how dire the consequences for them would be there. No one would acknowledge them or have anything to do with them. Cousins, anyone outside the riders would demand their last name be changed—" He broke off as it occurred to him that Mariko's last name couldn't have been the name she was born with.

Giovanni had to be thinking along the same lines as he was. "Did any of these boys have siblings? A sister? Could your woman be related to one of them?"

Ricco tried to remember. As far as he knew, none of them had sisters. Or brothers for that matter. He shook his head. "That's why the way they treated Akiko really got to me. It didn't make sense when they needed female riders and there was one right there, not related, and they treated her like dirt. I didn't understand them at all, other than the fact that Nao was on a power trip. He kept bragging that even the Yakuza would fear him."

"So this Nao went into the tournament already injured from the previous night when he and his little gang jumped you." Stefano redirected him, wanting to keep him on track.

He nodded. "Akiko defeated him by such a margin there was no way the judges could pretend it was a tie or that she had in any way fouled. The trophy was given to her, and Nao was shamed. His father was furious with him and humiliated him right there in front of all of us. Even his own friends laughed at him. I knew he would try to retaliate."

He ducked his head for a long moment. He had to confess to Stefano. There was no way around it. He looked directly at his brother. "I had been so disgusted with the way they treated me that I'd stopped working so hard. I knew no matter what I did, it wouldn't be recognized. It was only later I realized recognition didn't matter. Training did. But I had become what they said. I didn't have discipline."

He knew that was shocking to his brothers and sister. He trained night and day. No one could ever turn him around in the shadows. He could find any place—anytime, anywhere. He was fast and he was vicious when he needed to be. He shook his head and held up his hand when his brothers would have protested.

"I was a hothead, worse than I am now. I thought I was proving a point, but instead, I got a lot of people killed."

"How?" Stefano asked, his voice nonjudgmental. Waiting for the evidence of his brother's crime.

"I went to a class on *hojojutsu*-tying prisoners that evening. Two riders overheard Nao and his friends conspiring to go after Akiko, and they told me before I went to class, asking my advice on what to do. I advised them to go to the council again. I thought it was taken care of—until I got home and found the boys gone. I knew they were going after her. I'd never been to Akiko's home. None of us had. I didn't have the exact address. I had to find it. I thought I'd get there and warn her father, but I got turned around. I ended up on the wrong side of town and had to backtrack. If I'd been studying like I should have, I would have gotten there first and I could have stopped them. Akiko would still be alive."

There was silence, and he stalked over to the bar and poured himself another drink. He needed it, and he couldn't quite make himself look at his brother. He didn't want to see the disappointment he knew would be in his eyes. They'd been raised by Stefano to always give their best. Stefano would never have shirked learning. Not for one moment. It didn't matter how much Ricco trained, all the extra hours, the skills he had now, none of it made up for his getting lost in Tokyo that day.

The riders were sent to Tokyo because it was Japan's largest city, or more properly, prefecture. It was very confusing to the young riders, easy enough to get turned around, but they were expected to learn directions and be able to move freely from one end to the other quickly.

"That's bullshit, Ricco," Taviano burst out. "Complete and utter bullshit. No one could possibly blame you for that girl's death. What the hell? You were *fourteen*."

Ricco downed the Scotch, feeling it burn all the way down his throat and into his belly before he turned and faced the others, trying not to see the images burned so deeply into his mind he'd never been able to get them out. "It wasn't just Akiko. They killed her father and grandmother as well as two servants. Akiko fought them, and the noise brought her father and grandmother running along with two of the people who had worked for their family for years. The four boys killed them. I got there late and found the bodies of her grandmother and servants. There was blood everywhere."

"Ricco," Francesca murmured, "how awful."

"I still can't close my eyes without seeing that sight. When I entered the house I almost stepped on her grandmother's body. They'd nearly sliced her into pieces just outside the door of the small room where she held court. One of the female servants was just to the right of her. She'd been slashed with a sword down her back and was still dying. The other was nearly decapitated. The attacks had come from behind. Two of the boys had lain in wait for the father and servants while Nao and the other one dealt with Akiko and her grandmother. When I got there, the first two were still hacking at the bodies of the servants. I took the swords away, and I killed them. It wasn't easy—I have the scars on my chest and down my thigh."

He touched the three slashes he kept covered by his clothing at all times, remembering the feel of the blade cutting through his flesh.

"Oh my God, Ricco," Emmanuelle whispered. "You were only fourteen, younger than they were. You took on two riders with swords and managed to stay alive?"

"I had no choice," he said. "Not if I was going to try to save Akiko."

"You're telling me four riders from four of the families in Japan used their abilities to murder innocents?" Stefano asked. His voice was low, but it was a whip. "Which families? Tell me now. I need to hear you confirm that these boys were the sons of the riders on the council."

He had known Stefano would be furious. Breaking the code of a shadow rider was the worst thing one could do. The code of honor was put in place to protect every rider, their families and every innocent human being they came across.

"Three families," Ricco corrected. "You know Nao Yamamoto. His father, Isamu Yamamoto, was head of the council overseeing all riders in Japan at that time. The other two members had sons."

"Ricco." It was a warning. "Stop stalling." Stefano pressed his fingers to the corners of his eyes, putting pressure there.

He wasn't stalling so much as trying not to go back to that moment when he stood before the council members, knowing he'd killed their sons and they could do anything to him and no one would know.

"Eiji and Hachiro Saito followed Nao anywhere he went. They were bullies, believing, because their father, Dai Saito, sat on the council in Japan, no one could touch them. They both had swords that night. They were the ones who killed the two servants."

Stefano swept a hand over his face as if trying to sweep away the things his brother told him. "This should have been taken to the International Council. Those men *lied* about the deaths. Who was the last boy?" Of course he knew. His mother had attended the funerals of the boys, paying their respects to the riders who had lost their children. Mikio Ito was the other council member.

"Kenta Ito, Mikio Ito's son," Ricco confirmed.

"This is a disgrace. A fucking disgrace," Stefano bit out. "The top three families of riders. Council members. Lying to other riders, pulling that shit off because as council members they had the ability to tell a story with emotion that could muddy hearing. Their sons were murderers. Damn it, Ricco, we should have been told."

Ricco's gaze swept the room. His brothers were stunned. Shock showed on Emmanuelle's face. Such a thing was unheard of. Lying to the world of riders. It was a small, closed group, and they counted on honesty. On truth. On honor above all else.

Ricco shook his head slowly. "I couldn't tell you."

Stefano opened his mouth and then snapped it closed. Giovanni got up and took the cut crystal glasses and poured more Scotch, handing them back before seating himself again. He took his time, making certain everyone had a chance to recover from the sheer shock.

"Tell us all of it," Vittorio encouraged. "This is turning my stomach, but we have to know."

"It was Kenta Ito who killed Akiko's father. He painted his face with her father's blood and was dancing around Akiko and Nao. They wanted her to see that her family was dead. Nao had raped Akiko and he cut her to pieces. She was still alive, and Nao told her he was going to kill her little brother and sister. He told her he would violate her sister in front of her before he killed her. Her sister was three years old. Her brother was fifteen months."

Francesca gasped and put a hand to her throat. Stefano immediately drew her close, beneath the protection of his shoulder.

"Power corrupts." Taviano repeated what Stefano had drilled into them from the time they were toddlers. "Clearly those boys believed themselves above everyone else rather than servants of the people."

"I came into the room and overheard what he was saying. Kenta turned to face me. He had a sword, just like the others, and he was big and very strong." He had known fear back then, facing that blade and the anger and hatred of Kenta and Nao. "They believed me to be less than what they were. Akiko was less. Her family. Her father could no longer ride the shadows and was considered an outcast and dishonored. I had to fight them no matter how afraid I was of them. Akiko was still alive and I could see the desperation on her face. She didn't have anyone else to save her siblings."

Ricco couldn't stand any longer. The restless energy was there inside him, demanding he move, but his body, still recovering, couldn't oblige him. He took the chair facing Stefano. This was a confession, pure and simple, and it was

Stefano who would judge him. Giovanni, Vittorio and Ta-viano would stand solidly with him. Emmanuelle had the softest heart and would never think him guilty of anything. She would most likely view him as a hero.

He knew he held responsibility. He hadn't studied the way he should have and he'd gotten turned around in the shadows of Tokyo. He hadn't gone with the boys that night to try to convince the elders that the others were up to no good because he didn't believe they would listen. He knew the council members would make his life even more mis-erable than it already was. Then there was the matter of the actual killings. The boys, no matter what they had done, were riders. There was a code—an unbreakable code.

"Kenta and I fought and while we did, Nao went to the closet and yanked open the door. I could see the little girl crouched on the floor holding her little brother, her hand over his mouth. He dragged the boy out and threw him on the floor, stomping on him over and over. Bones broke. I heard them. The sound was sickening. The little girl, only three years old, rushed him. She leapt into the air and kicked Nao with both feet right in the balls, driving him away from her brother. When she landed, she hit Akiko's blood and slipped, falling almost at Nao's feet. Kenta had sliced me a couple of times. I had to get possession of the sword and take him out. I stepped close and he swung just like I knew he would. I pulled my head back, but the tip sliced my face open."

Ricco touched the wicked scar. He hadn't even felt the pain of that cut. He'd been desperate. Kenta was good with the sword. "I kept moving into him. Akiko must have been doing homework when they attacked and her desk had turned over. I found a pen on the floor and I shoved it into his eye, hard. He dropped the sword. I picked it up and slammed it down over his head, splitting his skull in two." The aftermath had been horrific, with blood and brains ev-erywhere.

He hadn't had time to think about those first lives he'd

taken when he'd killed the boys he'd trained with. It was only later, when he tried to sleep, that he remembered their eyes, wide open, the horror in them, the light fading away. His stomach lurched. He'd brought many men to justice since that time, but nothing had affected him the way the deaths of those boys had.

"I didn't have much time. Nao had caught the little girl by the hair, pulling her through the blood to his lap. He was going to cut her throat. I lifted the sword again and jammed the blade into his back, down low, with every bit of strength I had left, which wasn't much. The sword was sharp and it went in."

He took a deep breath and pressed his fingers to his throbbing temples. "I've never seen anything so horrific before or since. Nao kept screaming and screaming. The baby was absolutely silent. We both collapsed right there on the floor. I crawled to Akiko. There was blood bubbling around her mouth and she couldn't talk. I didn't move until she died. The little girl had crawled to her brother and she was holding him like a rag doll and rocking him back and forth."

He couldn't look at his siblings. All he could see was the blood soaking into the floor of the Tanaka home. So many dead around him. He hadn't saved Akiko. He had felt numb. He hadn't known he was shaking until the sword slipped from his nerveless fingers. It hit the floor and was instantly coated from blade to hilt in red.

"I don't know how long I sat there before I realized the boy was still alive and needed medical attention, as did Nao. I called Isamu Yamamoto and told him what happened and we needed help fast. They came, and I don't remember too much after that. I was taken to a room back in the host home with orders not to speak to anyone. I didn't want to. I wanted to come home, but they refused to allow me to call you, Stefano."

"I'll just bet they didn't let you call me or Eloisa." Stefano's voice was a lash of pure anger. A promise of retaliation.

Ricco winced. "There was an investigation and I was questioned repeatedly by the council members."

"The council members? Not investigators?" Stefano clarified.

"Council members," he reiterated. "I honestly expected them to kill me. It was clear they weren't going to allow outsiders to know what happened. The dishonor would be too much for the three families. They called me in and told me if I dared to tell my family or any other council the truth of what happened, the three families would unite to wipe out every member of my family in retaliation because if I brought them that kind of dishonor, they wouldn't have anything to live for. They said that they would tell the rider world that I had killed their sons. They also said they would make it known that I had murdered those boys in cold blood when they caught me raping Akiko. That I had been the one to kill her family."

"Those fucking liars. Any of us would have heard the lies they told. If we'd brought them up before the international governing body they couldn't have made those charges stick." Stefano's eyes blazed with anger. "They would have been stripped of their abilities. Only a member of the family of the international governing family can do that, but Yamamoto knew that would have happened immediately if this came to light. He fed crap to a fourteen-year-old boy and then forced him to stay there for appearances."

Ricco nodded. "They wanted me to know just how powerful they were. It was a difficult time, but I was determined that nothing would happen to any of you. When I came back, I trained even harder than I had in Japan, every day, to make certain I would never make another mistake. I guarded you at night as best I could just in case they decided to come after all of you."

"You should have told me, Ricco," Stefano said. "I would have put a stop to this nightmare for you."

Nothing could stop the nightmare. He'd have those deaths on his hands until the day he died. The images were branded into his brain. "We don't want to start a war with the families in Japan," he cautioned. "My host family were good people. They, at least, treated me right. From there I went to Mikio Ito's home for six months. The rest of my time was spent with the Yamamotos."

Stefano went into another round of inventive curses.

Ricco kept talking. He wanted it all out and over with. "Nao was in a wheelchair and very, very bitter. His mother and father were bitter. It was an extremely difficult situation, with constant beatings and threats, but I had resolved to learn as much as I could and all those beatings were done in the training halls by Isamu Yamamoto, and while he bested me time and again, it only served to make me train harder and grow stronger."

Stefano was the one to begin pacing across the floor. "It doesn't make sense that they would send someone after you at this late date. The Saitos retired years ago. I believe Dai and his wife Osamu live in their home in Tokyo. He gave up riding the shadows after his sons were killed. Mikio Ito stopped riding after his son was killed as well. His wife is still alive, and I believe they retired to a small cottage in the country. She never was a trained rider. It was an arranged marriage. And Isamu Yamamoto lost his wife to suicide. She walked out in front of a train. They said he began to drink heavily. A few months ago, he committed suicide by disembowelment."

"I heard about that," Ricco said, slightly ashamed that he'd wished they were all dead and the threat to his family was over.

"Nao Yamamoto has run their company here in the States for the last ten years or more," Vittorio volunteered. "They've been losing money. According to their publicist they've been under attack by an industrial spy. Nao spent money like water, and I think he ran the company here into the ground."

"The shadow riding lines of these families are gone," Stefano continued. "It was rumored Saito and his wife had two other children, but neither was suited for shadow riding so they were never talked about publicly."

Ricco frowned. He was already putting pieces of the puzzle together, although it still didn't make sense. "She said she was claustrophobic, that when she was a child she'd been locked in a closet. Mariko. She could have been that little girl."

"Nothing was ever said about any of the Tanaka line remaining," Stefano objected.

"I study the history of all the rider families," Vittorio said. "There was a rumor that there were other children, babies, but they died in the accident as well."

Stefano shook his head. "The Tanakas only had Akiko. They had a very famous line and it was regarded the world over that no one was left."

"That's not true," Ricco said. "There was a little sister and brother. I was there. They came to the tournaments to cheer Akiko on. They came with their father. And the girl was in training. You should have seen her take down Nao with that double kick. I'm telling you, she was a Tanaka. So was the baby boy."

"It wouldn't make sense that this child would want to assassinate you when you saved her and her brother," Taviano said.

"What did she say her last name was?" Vittorio asked.

"Majo, and the *kanji* characters mean 'female devil.' The name was given to her. She said, and I heard truth in her voice, that her mother was an American. She'd been told that her mother was a whore on the streets. Later she abandoned her children and disappeared. Mariko believes that to be true."

"Tanaka married an American woman. She left him, and their shadows were torn apart. She didn't remember her children or marriage or anything about riding shadows, and he was lost to all of us as a rider," Stefano said. "But there was no mention of any child other than Akiko that I can remember; however, if Vittorio heard about more, then it is probably so. The lineage was remarkable. Admired and respected despite what the family thought about his marriage. Surely a son and daughter would have been welcomed by every rider family."

Ricco shook his head. "Akiko was looked down on by every family, all riders and her own grandmother because she was mixed race. The grandmother, in particular, treated her horribly, and all the families followed suit. Although Akiko was mixed race, she looked more like her father. If Mariko is a Tanaka, she obviously looks more like her American mother. Still, when I asked about what happened to the two remaining children, Yamamoto told me a family took them in."

"It still wouldn't make sense for the girl to come after you. It's pretty hard to forget the boy who saved your life," Giovanni objected.

"She was three, Gee," Francesca pointed out. "What do shadow riders do?" she asked softly. "They carry out justice. It's ingrained in them. It can't be personal, right? You call in other riders to cover anything personal. If Mariko is a rider, then someone called her in. Someone investigated, and someone called her in. The fact that she didn't carry out her assignment in the prescribed way means she isn't convinced that you're guilty and she's conducting her own investigation. What other reason is there for her waiting to try to kill you? She didn't have to come out into the open. She could have slid into the shadows like you all do and it would be over. You wouldn't have seen it coming."

Except Ricco was always vigilant. He made certain of that. Made certain there were unseen alarms that would be tripped by anyone moving around his house at night or during the day whether they slid out of a shadow or not. For several years he'd been convinced someone, a shadow rider, had slipped into his home on numerous occasions. He'd invented a screen to hook under the doors of his family to prevent riders from sliding into their bedrooms unseen. The weird feeling that an intruder had visited had ceased when he began using the screens.

"Francesca is right," Emmanuelle said. "Why take a position unless she needs to know more?"

"Say that's all true," Taviano said. "Who sent her? Someone had to have contracted with her people in Japan, Ricco was investigated and she was sent. Whoever sent her must believe he's guilty of killing the Tanaka family just as Yamamoto threatened. Maybe the findings were turned over to the new council when Yamamoto died?"

"This has to go before the international governing family," Stefano decided. "Or we're going to find ourselves in a war."

"If you go to them, we may find ourselves in a war anyway. The moment the new council in Japan comes under the governing family's investigations, they'll feel dishonored. They'll believe Saito and Ito. Both will lie. They'll have to. The culture is very different from ours," Ricco objected. "I know I'm asking a lot, because every one of you is at risk, but I know this woman is mine. I know I was born for her. I need a chance. I'm asking all of you to give me that chance."

Stefano sighed and looked around the room at his siblings and wife. "Ricco, more than risking us, because I doubt anyone is that stupid to come after our family, you're asking all of us to allow this woman, a trained assassin, to remain in your home with you."

Ricco nodded. "I know what I'm asking. I need this chance."

"I'm willing to take the risk," Taviano said. "Ricco's been through enough and I'll stand with him."

Stefano looked at Vittorio. "You?"

"I'll stand with Ricco, but I want added protection for him."

"The last thing I need is my brothers or sister standing in the shadows while I'm trying to seduce a woman," Ricco said, faint humor coming to the surface. That was his family, in the worst of circumstances, siding with him and making him want to laugh.

"I'm in," Giovanni said. "I could use some pointers, Ricco. You've always been good with the women."

"As if you need any help," Emmanuelle said and threw a wadded-up napkin at her brother, striking with deadly accuracy. "I don't like it, but I'll help. I'm befriending her, Ricco, and if she so much as blinks wrong toward you, I'll break her neck."

He was a bit startled by the intensity of his sister's attitude. She meant it. Even smiling at him, she meant it. He inclined his head.

"If I get a vote, I'll help, too," Francesca said. "I can be her friend and tell her why I adore you."

"Of course you get a vote," Ricco said. "You're family." He looked to Stefano. They all did, waiting for the verdict.

"I'll contact our cousins in New York and Los Angeles. If a war is starting they need to be aware as well. I'll contact the international governing family and ask them to keep the investigation quiet, but not for long, Ricco. If someone is after you, we'll need to know who it is. And we're starting our own investigation as well. I don't much care whose toes in Japan I step on."

"Thank you." He should have known his family would back him.

"You were fourteen years old, a kid, Ricco. They were adults. Their children fucked up and they would have had honor if they'd faced that with courage. Instead, they tormented you and threatened you. God knows what they did to this girl and what they've told her. We're going to find out what happened to Tanaka's other two children. There has to be a trail, elders who knew about them. God help them if they turned over those innocent children to the Saitos and left them in their care. Those three families would have kept the details of their sons' deaths secret. They told everyone they'd died in a car accident with the Tanakas. There's a trail, and we'll uncover it."

Ricco nodded his head. "I'd like to know what happened. I'm fairly certain Mariko is a Tanaka. She has to be that same three-year-old."

"One more thing. You will be guarded at all times. I don't want you trying to give us the slip. Obviously, we can't be with you twenty-four-seven, so you watch your back at all times."

"Consider it done."

"You weren't guilty of anything, Ricco," Stefano added. "Not one fucking thing. They twisted what happened in your mind. You did the honorable thing, fighting for that family. Finding your way through Tokyo when you'd just arrived a few weeks earlier would have been difficult for any of us, let alone a teen. I'm proud of you. You honored our family with what you did to save those children and then coming home and watching out for all of us. You carried that burden alone for too many years. You should have trusted me, but the decision was made by a boy who feared three powerful families threatening to kill his own. I understand, and I can look you in the eye and say I'm proud of you."

That meant more to him than anything else could have. He looked around the room at his family, the men and women who stood with him. He wanted Mariko there with them. His woman. He just had to find a way to seduce her without being killed.

CHAPTER FOUR

Mariko slept fitfully, expecting Ricco to make his move any moment. Every creak, every shift of the outside branches had her jumping up, her dagger in her hand. She would lie back down, sliding the reassuring weapon under her pillow, the hilt in her palm, eyes wide open, waiting for him to take advantage of a woman silly enough to put herself in such a position for money.

It was a great deal of money. She contemplated that as the first rays of the sun streamed into her room. It was a beautiful room, very spacious and appointed with every luxury. The fireplace was old stone, the floors gleaming hardwood. A bank of windows faced the east, allowing the sun to stream in if the drapes were open. Sheer lace panels covered the windows and the darker, thick drapes were open or closed via a remote by her bed.

She could get lost in that bed. It was big enough for several of her. The mattress was comfortable, but she couldn't relax. She'd bought herself time and a place to hide, but now she had to figure out what to do. It came back to the money. She'd read the contract carefully, looking for hidden clauses that might put an unsuspecting woman in jeopardy, but she didn't find any. He hadn't asked her to remove her clothes—and she'd been expecting that request. Most of the photographs in the book she'd brought along were of her mother as a nude model in the various poses.

So why so much money? He hadn't mentioned sex and

there was no mention of it in the contract. There were locks on her door. She'd gone exploring—he'd told her to familiarize herself with the layout of his home, just to stay out of his master bedroom. She hadn't planned on obeying that directive, especially when he'd left her alone while he went out.

She was a shadow rider—and a good one. She had little pride, but she knew she excelled at her work and few were faster than she was moving through shadows. She could deliver justice quickly and painlessly and did so often. She couldn't penetrate the shadows to slip under Ricco Ferraro's bedroom door. She used light in order to throw shadows, but each time she stepped into them, feeling her body wrench apart, she hit some kind of barrier and couldn't continue into his room.

She'd picked the lock and broke in the old-fashioned way. She needed to know what it was he was hiding. Nothing, it appeared. She expected to find a dungeon with all kinds of bondage toys. He liked Japanese art and had amazing pictures of various forms of rope art on all the walls. The bondage was beautifully portrayed and tastefully photographed. She didn't find a single cane, whip or flogger.

There was a room where the lighting was perfect with an entire wall of ropes, all of various colors, made from hemp, silk or cotton. She found herself touching them almost reverently, running her finger along the rope as if it were his arm. A part of him. It had felt like an extension of him when he'd looped the silk around her wrist. She found her heart accelerating and turned abruptly and left his side of the house to go to her room.

All down the wide halls were numerous pictures of Japanese art. Gorgeous prints. She looked closer and gasped. Not prints. The real thing. One extremely large room held a collection of ancient Japanese weapons. Each era had its own space on the wall, and the weapons, as old as they were, were cared for and displayed behind glass. There were hundreds of them. Old books, all in Japanese, were displayed as well, carefully preserved, and she knew they were first editions.

The house itself was two stories, beautiful and quite large. Outside he had amazing gardens, all protected from the outside world by high, thick walls. There was a waterfall that fell into a cool, shaded pool where trees wept lacy leaves and ferns grew along a narrow stream. Koi swam lazily, protected by water lilies in the large pond. Everything in and out of Ricco Ferraro's home spoke of peace and serenity when he was anything but. He was a puzzle and one she had to figure out fast.

He was extremely wealthy and very good-looking. He exuded sex appeal. He was the most sensual person she'd ever met in her life. He didn't need to offer that kind of money to find a partner who would indulge in kink with him. Most women would be more than willing. So why advertise for a rope model and pay such an exorbitant amount if he wasn't planning to use the woman for sex?

She dressed carefully, needing to feel as if she had some armor. Ricco had stripped her bare with just the sound of his voice, and she needed to feel on equal footing. She'd wanted a simple solution, for Ricco Ferraro to be a monster—a man preying on women, perhaps—but that didn't make sense. She sighed and picked up her brush, stroking through the shoulder-length blond waves. If she were honest, his being guilty wouldn't have been a solution, either. She hoped it would, but she knew better.

A knock on her door made her jump. She wasn't a woman to be startled, nor did anyone sneak up on her, but she hadn't heard a single footfall.

"We're leaving in ten minutes."

She took a breath. His voice was very compelling. "I'll be ready." That was part of the contract. They were to spend most of their time together in order to get to know each other. That suited her fine, although . . . She twisted her hair up into a loose bun that wrapped around the back of her head and gave her more height as well. She secured the mass with long hairpins that could be used to defend herself if necessary.

She dressed Western, in slim, dark jeans and a cream-colored thin sweater. She wore elegant boots. They were made of soft leather and gave her several advantages. She slid a knife down into the specially made sheath. They also had a bit of a heel, which gave her a little more height.

He was waiting just outside her room, leaning against the wall, looking amazing in his suit. His gaze jumped immediately to her face and she felt the impact as if it were physical. He didn't need to touch her in order for her to feel his fingers on her. He straightened, his eyes moving over her.

"You didn't sleep well. What do you need to make you more comfortable?"

His voice poured over her like heat. Instantly she was aware of him, the wide set of his shoulders, his height, the muscles moving beneath the soft gray shirt. Everything. Just like that her body came to life.

"I was quite comfortable, thank you." She took a breath and forced her body to relax. "It's a new place, and I'm a little nervous committing to this project when I don't really know what to expect."

Being honest was always the best policy. She found that she wanted to give him honesty. Something. Anything. She'd come to him in full-blown panic, a state so unusual for her that she hardly recognized herself. Now she had a place to stop and think about things. To force panic from her mind and begin to hunt for solutions.

He held out his hand to her. Her heart quickened. God, he was gorgeous and intimidating when nothing and no one intimidated her. He didn't snap his fingers or insist, he simply held out his hand and waited, leaving the decision to her. She wasn't used to human contact. She hadn't exactly had a lot of it. It wasn't as if she'd had a mother who put her arms around her and held her. She couldn't remember a time when someone had held her.

She put her hand in his, and he smiled. It was as if, for

her, the sun had come out. His smile took her breath and made her inexplicably happy because, she sensed, he rarely smiled and it was like a gift. His fingers closed around hers and he pulled her close to him, almost beneath his shoulder. She had the strange illusion of feeling safe.

"We'll take the car to a small café I know for breakfast, and you can ask me any questions. It's important to build trust between us and the only way to do that is to get to know each other."

She nodded. "I've read quite a bit on the subject of Shibari, but no two poses seem alike, and I wasn't certain what to expect."

"It isn't about posing, Mariko," he said.

He reached to open the door for her. As she stepped through, his hand went to the small of her back. It felt intimate, his palm burning a brand right through the thin weave of her sweater. He smelled masculine. That same, strange outdoorsy, after-a-rain scent that she loved.

"When I come to you to ask you to be my model, whatever mood I'm in, the way you look, how your hair sweeps across your neck, those kinds of things determine how I'm going to tie you, which color of rope, the material of the rope. What you need."

She glanced up at him from under her lashes. His expression was very serious. "I don't understand. What I need? Why would it be about what I need?"

A dark town car waited for them. A man, looking very similar to Emilio from the day before, opened the door for them. Ricco smiled at him. "Enzo, this is Mariko. Mariko, my cousin Enzo. Emilio and Enzo are my keepers for the moment. I was in a car accident and my family is afraid I might faint and crack my head on the sidewalk, isn't that right, Enzo?"

She liked the easy camaraderie in his voice when he spoke to his cousin. She wasn't used to that easy. There was no laughter in her home growing up. Only duty. She also had read about the "car accident." He'd gone into a concrete wall at well over two hundred miles an hour. The video had been on the Internet and she'd replayed it over and over, watching the car fly apart and flames leap into the air as metal flew in all directions. She had no idea how he'd managed to live through such a thing. Even the surgeon, when he'd been interviewed, had called Ricco's survival a miracle.

"That's right, Ricco. We're supposed to chase after you with a pillow and get it under your head before you hit the ground." The man laughed and closed the door.

It was only then that she saw Emilio emerge from the drive, up close to the gates, to hurry and slip into the front passenger seat. Emilio turned and smiled at her. It wasn't quite as sincere as she would have expected, and that sent up a tiny red flag.

"Mariko," he greeted.

"Emilio," she answered, using a shy, demure voice. She allowed her long lashes to sweep along her high cheekbones, a gesture that usually put men at ease automatically. It didn't seem to work on Emilio. She saw his gaze flick toward the rearview mirror, clearly watching them.

Maybe she was wrong and his concern wasn't about her at all. "What should I call you?" she asked Ricco. In Japan she would have addressed him only formally. She didn't want to have to call him master or sir, but she would if it was necessary.

"I prefer not to stand on formality, but if it helps you to feel more at ease with me by keeping everything strictly businesslike, Mr. Ferraro is fine. Otherwise, Ricco."

She thought about that. Would a man determined to establish dominance over her want her to be informal with him? Probably not. "Ricco, then." Her accent made his name sound much more intimate than she'd intended. "I know you were in a terrible accident. Are you okay now?" Her eyes met Emilio's in the mirror. "Should I be looking for signs of physical distress?"

She hated the anxiety running through her system, making her breath catch in her lungs. For him. She recognized that she was worried about his health, and that was just plain laughable considering what she was there to do. She looked up at him, contemplating.

She'd come there trying to keep perspective, trying to be fair, when the cost to her would be so high. So dear. Already she knew her answer. She was looking for dirt. Very few people didn't have something they wanted to hide. Ricco Ferraro was hiding most of what and who he was from those around him, but that didn't make him a criminal. She needed him to be a criminal.

"It's been weeks, and I've gone through physical therapy. I still have to go a couple of days a week, but I'm much better. The headaches come and go. I haven't had blurred vision in a few days, and I haven't been dizzy in a couple of weeks." There was honesty in his matter-of-fact voice, but something warned her he didn't like talking about his recovery in front of his cousins.

She waited until the car had pulled smoothly up to a curb and Emilio had opened the door for them. She slid out and waited on the sidewalk, looking around her. This was the famed Ferraro territory. It started right on the edge of little Italy and went on for several blocks. She had studied it before she'd ever come, and she'd spent time riding the shadows from one end to another, familiarizing herself with the layout.

Ricco's hand on the small of her back startled her. He didn't make a sound when he moved and that was definitely a problem for her. How she didn't sense that he was close, she didn't know, not when every cell in her body seemed specifically tuned to him. He gestured toward the small glass door with gold hand-painted letters that simply read Biagi's. Many of the shops had only one name on the door, as if that were enough.

The aroma was a mix of coffee, sausage and fresh bread, making her stomach react. She hadn't eaten since she'd arrived in the United States. The entry was narrow, and it looked like there would be a long wait. Ricco didn't try to push his way to the front of the line, but the moment they stepped inside, all conversation ceased. Enzo and Emilio had squeezed in behind them, blocking the door, and she felt claustrophobic. She detested small places and now they were packed in like sardines in a can.

One by one heads turned until it seemed that every single person was staring at her. Ricco seemed to sense her dismay and he shifted, putting his body between hers and the rest of the room.

"Mr. Ferraro," the hostess said brightly. "Your table is ready. Emilio, we have yours ready as well."

"Thanks, Imeldia." Ricco sent the woman a smile and moved through the crowd, murmuring to several people.

Mariko noted Emilio and Enzo kept pace tightly behind him, as if they feared someone might try to hurt him—or that he might fall. She let her gaze sweep the restaurant as they followed the hostess back behind her small greeting table to another room that opened into a large floor space. The floor was tiled with wide red squares and the tables were very simple. Nearly every table was taken. Just as had happened in the entryway, every person looked up and conversation ceased.

"Does this always happen?" she asked as Ricco pulled out her chair. She was happy to see that the table was more secluded than the rest, one step up in a little alcove.

The hostess handed her a menu, hesitated, and when Ricco continued to look only at Mariko, walked away. Mariko realized that although Ricco had nodded to many of the customers, clearly knowing them, his attention had been centered on her. He made her feel as if she were the only woman he saw—maybe the only person.

"Does what always happen?" He seated himself across from her. "Everything is good here. Imeldia's parents are phenomenal chefs."

She picked up the menu because she needed to do something with her hands. She wasn't the nervous type, but she couldn't relax. She was just too aware of him and everything about him. She found herself looking for the shadows in the room. Immediately she realized this table was held for the Ferraros and it was where others couldn't overhear what was said. The shadows blurred their images so they had a semblance of privacy.

"Everyone staring at you."

He looked around. "I guess I don't pay attention anymore. We're in Ferraro territory, and most of those in here, I consider ours. If it bothers you, we can go somewhere else. I wanted you to get to know me, and these people are part of who I am."

She looked around as well. Most of those in the restaurant had gone back to eating, but Ricco Ferraro was clearly considered a celebrity. She wouldn't have been surprised if he had to sign autographs before he left. Enzo and Emilio were at a table close by and she realized they could—and probably would—stop anyone from bothering him as he ate.

"It doesn't bother me. I'm just not used to it. And they aren't just staring at you, they're staring at me, too."

"That's because I don't bring women home."

The admission was said in such a low tone she almost didn't catch it, but she heard the ring of truth. Her gaze jumped to his. "Never?"

"Never. This is part of my home. Our territory. My family owns quite a bit of the real estate here. I've known a lot of the business owners since I was a child."

She couldn't imagine him as a child. He was too intense. Even now, in a casual setting, he drew every eye. He exuded complete confidence, dominating the entire room without doing anything but sitting there. She knew she couldn't take her eyes off him.

"You didn't ask me to take my clothes off," Mariko blurted, her voice very low. He hadn't, and she didn't understand why.

He didn't pretend not to understand. "You don't know me. You would have been uncomfortable."

He used that word often. *Uncomfortable.* As if her comfort meant more to him than anything else. "You're not at all what I expected," she admitted.

"What did you expect?"

"I don't know exactly. Not you. Someone much more . . ." She almost said *dominant*, but he was. He had a hard authority about him, and when he wanted something from anyone, she was certain he got it. *Dominant* was a very good way to describe him, yet at the same time, he seemed incredibly gentle and thoughtful.

He waited. When she didn't speak he glanced up at the waitress, who'd brought him coffee and orange juice. Mariko knew immediately that he frequented Biagi's often for breakfast. The waitress stared at him, her mouth open.

"Coffee? Tea? Orange Juice?" he asked Mariko. Ricco, not the waitress. The waitress was far too busy trying to get his attention by flipping her hair. Again, he seemed to only notice Mariko.

"Tea and orange juice would be lovely, thank you," she said. If he could ignore the ridiculous eyes the waitress kept making at him, so could she. It was much more difficult to ignore the fact that so many of the other customers paid more attention to Ricco than to those sitting with them. She had no idea why the waitress annoyed her with her blatant flirting, as if she wasn't even there, but for the first time in her life, she knew she didn't want another woman to catch his interest.

"Would you have taken off your clothes had I asked?" Ricco inquired once they were alone again.

His voice was soft and dark with a sensual magic that sent heat rushing through her bloodstream. She felt that voice as if it had penetrated every inch of her body until he was stamped inside her like a brand. He wouldn't have asked, she was certain of that. Had he wanted her to remove her clothes, he would have made it an order. The command would have come couched in a phrase that allowed her to make the decision, but she would know that if she didn't do what he required, he would have been very disappointed in her. She didn't know how he could do that with just his voice, but she found herself wanting to please him when she didn't much care about pleasing anyone.

"I don't honestly know," she admitted, because he would wait forever for her answer. She was beginning to recognize that he was always patient. She noted he didn't take anything in his coffee, just drank it black. "Will you ask me to be tied without clothes?"

"I would like that, but if we never get there, we don't. It's that simple. It isn't in the contract that you have to take your clothes off."

"Did you ask any of the other models applying to take their clothes off?"

He shook his head. "It wasn't necessary. The female body is beautiful to me. There is beauty in any body type and it inspires me. Sometimes I can be moody and edgy and my art reflects that. The rope designs always look beautiful to me against bare skin, but again, it isn't necessary. I might ask you, but Mariko, it is always your choice. Your decision. When I told you Shibari is a power exchange, that is exactly what it is. You have to get something out of it as well. Yesterday, when I tied your wrists, you liked it. You didn't expect to, but you did."

He had noticed. She didn't think he would miss much and his entire focus had been on her. Of course he had noticed her heightened breathing, the rise and fall of her breasts, her wild heart singing. "It didn't feel the way I thought it would," she confessed.

The waitress was back with her tea and a goblet filled with fresh-squeezed orange juice. She was so busy looking at Ricco that she nearly dropped the teacup into Mariko's lap. Ricco caught it before it hit her. Her hands were directly under his when the teacup fell into his palm.

He glanced up at the waitress even as he held the empty teacup. "Perhaps you would send Imeldia to me immediately."

The girl bobbed her head. "I'm sorry, Mr. Ferraro, I'm really sorry."

"You owe Ms. Majo the apology, not me," he said softly, but his voice was a lash and the waitress winced, her color rising.

She looked at Mariko. "I'm so sorry."

Mariko inclined her head. "No harm was done. I'm fine." She smiled up at Ricco, who settled back in his chair and gently put the teacup on the table. "Thank you." He had fast reflexes. He was across the table yet he'd risen and caught the teacup before she had—and she was fast. She'd always been fast. That was something she would have to remember.

The waitress hurried away, her head down, tears in her eyes.

"She's young," Ricco said. "Still in high school. This is her first job and she's a little starstruck. Some people really enjoy the races and drivers can be considered celebrities."

He was being modest. The Ferraro family owned a prestigious international bank, the Ferraro hotels, and several casinos. As a family, they were considered in the billionaire category. She'd done her homework. Not one single thing she'd discovered about Ricco had confirmed that he was a criminal. He played hard—too hard. He partied hard. He liked women—a lot of women. He was fearless. Dominant. In control when the world he played in seemed utter chaos. Even without all her problems, she could never keep up with a man like Ricco, or hope to satisfy him.

She liked that he recognized that the waitress was very young and he wasn't angry with her for acting so silly. She waited in silence while Imeldia hurried to their table.

"You need to talk to our waitress, see if she can handle waiting on our table, Melda," he said, his voice indicating he was friends with the hostess. "I think she's having a difficult time of it."

"She said she nearly dropped the teacup in your friend's lap," Imeldia acknowledged. "Rita is friends with my youngest sister, Alessa, and insists she needs the work. Her parents were killed a few years ago, and she and her younger brother, Maso, have lived with us ever since. Rita wants to pay her own way and take care of Maso, although my parents insist the two of them aren't costing them any more than my sister and me. I think they both want to be part of the family business more than anything else and not be a burden to my parents—which they are not."

Mariko's heart clenched. For a moment she couldn't breathe or think. Chaos reigned in her mind. The waitress was a young girl trying to earn her keep as well as her brother's. She glanced toward Rita with new respect. She'd been that young girl and she knew how difficult it was to be the one always having to accept charity. In Rita's case, it sounded as if the people she was with genuinely cared about her. She resolved to find out.

"No harm done. Reassure her and see if she feels she can continue. Maybe tell her a little less hair flipping and more paying attention to my woman would get her a better tip." Ricco's voice was gentle.

Imeldia's eyes went wide with shock and she glanced at Mariko, her mouth forming a perfect *O*. Ricco didn't seem to notice what he'd called Mariko, or how possessive he sounded. He certainly was giving Imeldia the wrong impression, and word would spread like wildfire that Ricco Ferraro had claimed a woman if he wasn't more careful. She knew from reading the tabloids that it wasn't his style, he was the one-night-stand type, other than maybe the exception of the Lacey twins, actresses making a name for themselves, getting lots of publicity whenever they were with Ricco.

"She's a little starstruck, Ricco."

"Even with that she managed to remember everything without writing it down. I watched her wait on some of the other tables. She'll be an asset here."

"I think so as well." Imeldia turned away with a small smile, weaving her way through the tables, stopping every few minutes to talk to someone.

"That was nice of you," Mariko acknowledged. "Many people in your position would have been really ugly to the waitress, maybe even gotten her fired."

Something crossed his face, disappointment perhaps, she couldn't quite catch it, and then his features were entirely expressionless. "Is that what you think of me? That I would use my status as a Ferraro to get a young girl fired?"

His face might not give anything away, but his voice held just enough of that disappointment she'd seen slip across his features seconds earlier. The lash made her wince. His gaze held hers, forcing her to face him with her accusation. She had thought that just from reading the tabloids. Investigating a Ferraro was difficult. No one knew anything at all personal about the family. Everything was speculation or clearly made up for headlines. Maybe the rumor about the Lacey twins wasn't real, either.

"I'm sorry if I've offended you. I merely thought it was sweet of you that you didn't do what others in your position might." She chose each word carefully. She found she hadn't liked upsetting him and she didn't want him to think she thought badly of him. That wouldn't fit with the image of a woman taking such an intimate job with him—at least she told herself that was the reason she was so cautious.

He sat back in his chair, his gaze on her face. Compelling. Intense. She'd never been under such open scrutiny. "How is it you aren't with a man? You're beautiful. You're intelligent. You've got an amazing voice. I could listen to you talk forever."

He flashed a small smile at her and it lit up his dark eyes for just a moment. The lines etched deep in his face softened and that ghost of a smile made her stomach do somersaults and a flutter started deep.

"Not that you talk much."

"You're very intimidating." She had resolved to stick as closely to the truth as possible. "I didn't expect that."

His eyebrow shot up. "I'm intimidating?"

"You know you are." She was certain of that.

He burst out laughing, and even that was low and sensual. The man couldn't do anything without sounding or looking sexy. He had a way of focusing so completely on her that he made her feel as if they were alone and she was the only woman in his world. That low tone he used created an intimacy between them. She hadn't expected to like him at all. More, she hadn't, not even for one moment, considered that she might be attracted to him—and she was. The moment their shadows connected, the attraction had been intense, and it continued to grow with every moment spent in his company.

Rita was back, this time looking determined. Color had stolen up her neck into her cheeks, but she gamely smiled at Mariko. "Have you had time to look over the menu?"

"I'll have the vegetarian omelet," Mariko said. "It looks delicious. No toast or hash browns."

"And you, Mr. Ferraro?" Rita asked, her chin up.

"The scramble for me, and please include the hash browns and toast." He smiled at the girl and she nearly dropped the pad she hadn't been writing on. "How is your brother doing?"

"He's fine. He makes very good grades. He's been bussing here a couple of days a week." Rita nearly stumbled over the words, but she got them out.

Ricco nodded his head. "That's good. Boys can get a little wild as I'm sure you know. You or your brother need anything, you let me know." He handed her a card. "In case of trouble. Keep that with you."

She moistened her lips and nodded several times, pocketing the little card that held just a single number on it. "Thanks. I really appreciate it." She hurried away, a huge smile on her face.

"You just made a conquest for life," Mariko pointed out.

"She's not alone in the world. The Biagis are really good people, and they love Rita and her brother."

"You knew about her before the hostess ever said a word, didn't you?" she asked curiously.

He nodded. "My family owns quite a few of the buildings in this area and we lease them to the businesses. We like to know who the prospective tenants are before we do business with them. The Biagis have been here nearly as long as my family. Their parents owned the café before them. Bernado and Leah Biagi took it over about ten years ago. They were best friends with Rita's parents. She was eleven when her parents were killed in a botched robbery at their home. She took it very hard."

Mariko studied his face. He hadn't sounded any different than he had one moment earlier, yet there was something about the way he gave her the information that made her believe that botched robbery had been taken personally.

"Did they catch the robbers?"

"Murderers," he corrected. "They were murderers. And yes, they were caught and sentenced, but they escaped before they got to prison. They had brothers and parents every bit as brutal as they were."

"Were? I take it they were caught."

He shook his head. "They were found dead in an old abandoned warehouse along with two brothers and their father. The police speculated a rival gang had killed them. Their necks were broken."

She could guess how. The Ferraros had clearly considered Rita and Maso's parents under their protection. Shadow riders moved through shadows without detection, dispensing justice when the law couldn't. She didn't doubt for one moment that a rider or riders had extracted justice for the children.

She looked up at his impassive face. Expressionless. Tough. No one could ever doubt that Ricco Ferraro would handle his enemies with swift and certain death once he went on the hunt. A little shiver went down her spine.

"Hey."

Her gaze jumped to his. At once she felt the impact of those black velvet eyes. She couldn't look away from him.

"I shouldn't have brought up something so unpleasant. We're getting to know each other, and now you look a little afraid. That's the last thing I want."

Afraid? She looked afraid? That was impossible. She was

very good at keeping all emotion from showing, wasn't she? Was she so shaken up that she wasn't able to keep him from seeing inside of her?

"Tell me about you," he encouraged.

She had to stick as close to the truth as possible. Every shadow rider could hear lies and, in most cases, compel the truth. "I guess hearing about Rita threw me for a moment. You already know about my mother. My brother is eighteen months younger than I am. We were taken in by a family, but I could never understand why."

Osamu had said her husband had noticed the shadows coming from her body even then, when she was three and on the street. That had been the reason given for the family having taken her in. They had known she could be trained as a rider.

"The family despised what my mother was and the fact that I look American. My brother looks Japanese. He was very . . . broken. His bones were smashed when he was very little. Sometimes they were good to him; other times, not so much."

For a moment she could hear the sound of Osamu Saito's voice telling the two children what a burden they were. Mariko had scrubbed their home from top to bottom daily, cooked and served the woman, but was beaten for being sloppy. She was reminded daily that her mother was a whore and she would likely become one as well—that the beatings were for her own good. All the while, she had trained as a rider. The more she excelled, the worse Osamu had treated her.

She had thought she had Ricco's complete focus, but the moment she told him about the way she'd been treated, his eyes were on her and there was nothing and no one else in the room. Not even when Rita put their food in front of them. She felt hot under his gaze. She felt a glaring spotlight. He was so focused it was as if she had a laser on her. There was no telling what went on behind his tough mask, but she didn't like feeling as if she were always one step behind.

She needed to be in control at all times, yet she felt off-balance with Ricco.

She'd learned discipline in a hard school, and this was too important. The life of her brother was far too important to allow something like physical attraction to get in the way. But then, the problem was that the attraction to Ricco was far more than physical and she'd never experienced it before, so she didn't know exactly how to handle it.

"Tell me about your brother."

She hadn't expected that, either. Ricco kept her off-balance, but she didn't know how he did it. "Ryuu." she could barely say his name without choking up. She couldn't look at him, not into those eyes that saw right into her soul. "His name is Ryuu, and it means 'dragon spirit.' He's amazing. Truly amazing. A genius." Pride was in her voice. Love. She couldn't help it.

She loved her brother fiercely. Protectively. "When he was a baby, his bones were smashed and not all of them healed properly. He has trouble walking sometimes, but he's never once complained. He's so smart." She heard the pride in her voice, but she couldn't help herself. She was proud of him.

"Where is he now?"

Her stomach rolled and she pressed her hand beneath the table to it. "I don't know. I haven't heard from him in a while."

CHAPTER FIVE

Ricco kept up small talk throughout their breakfast, and as they rose to walk out, he put his hand on the small of Mariko's back again. She moved slightly, an indication that she was uncomfortable with the familiarity, but she had to get used to his touch. There was no doubt in his mind that Mariko Majo was in fact Mariko Tanaka from the legendary Tanaka family.

He knew his cousins Renato and Romano Greco were already conducting their investigation into Mariko, but this information was vital. He pulled his phone from his pocket and texted Romano one-handed. He kept the other firmly on Mariko. She could pull away if she wanted, but she would have to make that decision on her own.

Anyone could come to the Ferraro family and get an audience with the greeters. His mother, Eloisa, and father, Phillip, had acted as greeters since the death of his grandparents. They were former riders and could hear and compel the truth. Once in a while someone slipped through that shouldn't, but it was rare. Whatever the problem that needed to be heard, at first the visitor merely talked about his life, mundane things that allowed the greeters to get a feel for his voice, respiration and heartbeat. Once that was done, the greeters would ask the visitor to state his reason for contact. They would listen with no response and then stand up, dismissing the visitor without comment. That way, if they were under investigation by law enforcement, nothing could be recorded or said that might confirm anything illegal was going on.

The greeters would turn their findings over to the investigators if they felt the visitor had a legitimate claim against someone. There were two teams of investigators. One would study the crime and the person or persons accused, while the second set of investigators would examine those making the request and look into everything about them. They didn't want any mistakes made in their business, so there were checks and balances every step of the way protecting the family as well as those making requests.

If Mariko was a Tanaka, and her brother was in trouble, then Ricco was in far more danger than he'd first considered. Could someone blackmail a shadow rider? Shadow riders were human and they could make all kinds of mistakes, so yes, they could be blackmailed. They were born with serious flaws, just as everyone else was. He added that to the text informing his cousins. Find her brother immediately. Get everyone on it.

Ricco glanced down at Mariko as he guided her out of Biagi's café and down the sidewalk so he could show her the neighborhood. He loved their community and the people in it. He wanted her to feel that same sense of camaraderie he always felt. If Mariko was a Tanaka, she might not have been better off with her own family. He'd met her father, a shell of a man, but then, he was no longer capable of riding shadows and carrying out their work.

Ricco had a small taste of what it was like to be sidelined. He found himself restless and moody, edgy even. Not that he wasn't like that most of the time, but he was even more so without being able to do what he was born to do. He couldn't imagine what it would be like to be a rider unable to ride permanently.

Tanaka had married a woman who had eventually destroyed him. She'd left, and in doing so, she'd torn the shadows apart, rendering Mariko's father incapable of riding the shadows and carrying out justice for his people. The price her mother had paid was forgetting she had ever been married and had children. She remembered nothing about the Tanaka family or what they did. It was a heavy price for making a mistake in choosing one's life partner—or being forced to take one for the sole purpose of having children like his own parents had done.

"Ricco." Lucia Fausti waved at him from the doorway of her shop, Lucia's Treasures.

Ricco immediately picked up the pace. Lucia was the perfect person for Mariko to meet. There was no one he knew sweeter than Lucia other than, possibly, his sister-in-law, Francesca. Lucia stepped onto the sidewalk, holding hands with Nicoletta, the teen she'd taken in when the Ferraros had asked her. Lucia and Amo hadn't even hesitated. They'd lost their daughter to cancer when the child was three. Their son was murdered after coming home from serving in two wars and countless hot spots around the world, coming out of a theater with a date. Instead of being made bitter, the couple were closer than ever and truly wonderful human beings.

"Lucia, Nicoletta. This is Mariko." He deliberately put his arm around Mariko's shoulders, wanting everyone watching them to know she was under his protection.

"Ricco, so good to see you," Lucia greeted.

He kissed both of her cheeks. She was always warm and soft. A good woman. He smiled at Nicoletta. "And you, *tesoro*, how are you doing?" He leaned down to brush both cheeks with his lips. Lightly. Making certain not to touch her anywhere else.

Nicoletta took a breath, but she didn't step back until he straightened, and when she did, she stepped to the very edge of the sidewalk. "I'm good."

Two words, but at least she spoke. Up until that moment, Ricco had never heard the teenager say a single word. She still didn't quite meet his eyes, but her head was up instead of down. Her hair was glossy and thick, a beautiful, shiny color, so black it was nearly blue where rays of the sun hit it. He wanted the world to know this girl was also under Ferraro protection. They would shield her fiercely from any trouble.

"It's so lovely to meet you, my dear," Lucia said, reaching with both hands for Mariko's. Her eyes were alive with true happiness. She smiled from Ricco to Mariko. "Nicoletta *is* a treasure to my husband, Amo, and me. She just took a job at the flower shop helping out Signora Vitale. Her grandson, Bruno, needs help. The shop is thriving but he can't make the arrangements and the deliveries, and they lost their helper."

Ricco sighed and glanced at the girl, who looked a little defiant. The Ferraros wanted her in school. The teen was extremely intelligent and needed to know that. She hadn't been to a school since her parents had died and she'd been given to her step-uncles.

Deliberately, Ricco turned his back just a little on Lucia, knowing that if he gave her visual cues, her maternal instincts would have her answering for Nicoletta, and that wasn't the best for the girl. The teen needed discipline and training. She needed to recover enough to face the world. Enough that she would have confidence in herself to do whatever was necessary to protect herself and those she loved.

"Nicoletta, I believe you gave your word to my family that you would go to school. Where in your plan, helping Lucia here and working at the flower shop, does that give you time to work with tutors to catch up with your education?"

Mariko, probably sensing the girl's discomfort, shifted slightly out from under the hand on her back, that one physical connection between them. He caught her hand, enveloping her smaller fingers and holding her still, although he kept his attention on the younger girl.

"Nicoletta?" he insisted when she remained silent, looking to Lucia to answer for her. He kept his voice low, but the note of authority couldn't be denied.

"I want to work," Nicoletta said, looking more scared

than nervous. "I don't want to be a burden on Lucia and Amo."

"You could never be that," Lucia said immediately. "We love having you. We want you to think of our home as yours always."

Ricco heard the ring of truth in her voice and for a moment wondered if they'd made a terrible mistake. Amo and Lucia had suffered so much loss already. If they grew to love Nicoletta and she didn't return their feelings and left immediately, he didn't know how the couple would be able to cope with another loss.

"I know, Lucia," Nicoletta answered immediately. "I already think of you and Amo as my home, you've been so kind to me."

Listening to her voice, there was no mistaking that she meant every word, and deep inside, Ricco breathed a sigh of relief. Lucia and Amo were magic. The epitome of a loving couple going through life together. They were the perfect couple for a lost teen like Nicoletta.

"I still need an answer, *tesoro*. That you want to pull your weight with your family is admirable, but it doesn't tell me how you plan to keep up with your education." He was firm. Insistent. Nicoletta needed care, and gentle handling, but she also had to get an education. She needed her high school diploma and she had to catch up. She'd always feel inferior to others if she didn't, and she had enough trauma to contend with.

Nicoletta toed the crack in the sidewalk, staring down at it as though it might give her answers. "I'm doing four hours with a tutor in the morning before work," she said in a low voice. "After work, another two hours. Amo said he'd help me as well."

"Were the tutors vetted before they were hired?"

"Your family is doing that now," she mumbled.

He heard the resentment in her voice. He couldn't blame her. She couldn't turn around without stumbling over a member of his family. They guarded her carefully, knowing she truly was *tesoro*—treasure.

"It's to keep you safe," he said gently. When she didn't respond he used a soft, commanding tone. "Nicoletta. Look at me."

She raised her gaze to his reluctantly.

"It's for your safety. Yours, Amo's and Lucia's. You understand that, don't you?"

She nodded, color sweeping up her flawless complexion. She had Italian skin. A beautiful girl, one he knew would give his family trouble.

"What is it then?"

She opened her mouth twice, glanced at Mariko and Lucia, who were talking in low tones, clearly trying not to look as if they were eavesdropping.

"Nicoletta, you have to be able to talk to us. We're the ones that keep all of you safe. We need to know what's going on."

She shrugged. "Do you think the Demons are still looking for me?"

He refused to lie to her. "I know they are. We're watching them. They have no idea how you disappeared or how your step-uncles were killed. Unfortunately, you caught the eye of Benito Valdez, their president, and he's determined to find out what happened to you. They've reached out to all the various clubs saying they'll owe a favor for information leading to your whereabouts."

She swallowed hard. "He's the worst of them."

"I know. You're safe here. No member of the gangs or clubs come into our territory. They're in New York. You're here in Chicago. They have no idea."

"I don't want to take a chance with Amo or Lucia. They're . . . wonderful." She blinked rapidly and looked away from him.

"We would never take a chance with them. We consider them family."

She moistened her lips. "I don't know how your brothers saved me. I don't remember very much."

She never talked about the night her step-uncles died, not to anyone, not even her counselor. They knew, because Emmanuelle had been assigned to stay in the shadows just to make certain Nicoletta didn't make the mistake of revealing to anyone how she had been rescued. The girl was young, an unknown, and traumatized at that. They'd taken a huge risk rescuing and giving her to nonfamily members, but she needed constant care and love. Lucia and Amo were the two people the Ferraro family could trust to do right by the girl.

Nicoletta may have been born capable of riding shadows, but if she wasn't properly trained, her body would be torn apart by the energy field they entered. Riders were trained from the time they were infants. A few had learned later in life, but they were never fast at it. Ricco's father didn't take jobs unless Eloisa went with him; mostly he used the shadows to visit his mistresses. Still, Nicoletta could produce children capable of riding the shadows, and very few could do that. Nicoletta was truly the treasure Ricco called her.

There was no sound. Nothing at all to warn him. Instinct had him looking up to see a truck barreling straight at them. Someone screamed as he pushed Mariko into Lucia and caught Nicoletta around the waist. He took several steps to try to get them out of the path of the truck but it moved with them, engine roaring, coming so fast he was certain they wouldn't make it. Still running, he tossed Nicoletta away from him, uncertain if she was the target or if he was, but he had to get her clear.

Something hit the windshield with deadly accuracy, hitting the driver's side, head high. Ricco was so close he could see the glass spider-webbing. Without Nicoletta to hinder him, he leapt onto the hood to keep from being run over and to keep the driver's focus on him. It was impossible to tell if the man was trying to kill the teen or him, but it wasn't a random accident.

The driver spun the wheel, intending to send him flying.

The truck barely missed Nicoletta. Emilio dragged her away from the tires as the truck lurched back onto the street. Ricco hung on grimly as the truck pitched violently from side to side, jumped the curb again, swiped two trees planted on the sidewalk and bounced into the street again.

He was about to leap off when he glimpsed a gun through the cracks in the windshield. The driver seemed to be trying to shove it out the side window, but again, Ricco couldn't tell if he was aiming for Nicoletta or for him. He slammed his fist repeatedly into the windshield in order to keep the driver's attention centered on him and away from the teenager.

Cars had pulled over seeing the truck so out of control, but one, directly in its path, was hit, spinning it around. The impact jolted Ricco's body. The force felt as if someone had hit him in the head with a sledgehammer.

"Gun, gun," Enzo shouted as he ran along the sidewalk, trying to get a clear shot at the driver. "Everybody down. Get down."

Instinctively, Ricco rolled across the hood and landed hard in the street. Emilio was on him in moments, covering his body with his own, both bodyguards returning fire. Blood spattered the windows and the seat as the driver was hit. The truck lurched to a slow roll. Emilio leapt off Ricco and ran to the truck just as Enzo tore open the door to steer it to the curb.

Ricco was slower sitting up than he'd like. He'd hit hard, and his body was still healing. His head hurt the worst, every movement sending what felt like shards of glass piercing his skull. It took every single bit of discipline he had to set his teeth and just sit there in the street without keeling over. Sweat beaded on his forehead and trickled down his chest.

It took him a few moments to orient himself and understand what had happened. He'd managed to shove Mariko into Lucia and both had gone flying, but they were safe. He could only send up a short prayer that Lucia hadn't broken a hip or done worse when she hit the ground. He knew he'd gotten Nicoletta clear, but the driver had fired off several shots before one of his cousins had stopped him. He had no idea if anyone had been hit.

A cool hand swept back his hair. Mariko crouched beside him, her body between his and the sidewalk where half the village was watching. If anything told him she was a shadow rider, that instinctive need to protect a fellow rider said it all. His gaze moved over her face, examining her for injuries.

"Lucia?"

"She's good. I rolled under her and she didn't even hit the sidewalk. Nicoletta's fine as well. He fired several shots into the crowd but no one was hit, thanks to Enzo shouting for everyone to get down. Can you get up?" As she gave him all the pertinent information, her hand wiped away the beads of sweat.

She'd rolled to keep Lucia from hitting the pavement. Fast, fast reflexes. He'd shoved her hard to get her clear, deliberately making the choice to send both flying to get them out of harm's way. Even with a shove like that, hitting Lucia and going down, she had the presence of mind to roll before they struck the sidewalk. Definitely a shadow rider. Had he still been considering that he was wrong about her, the way she was guarding him from interested eyes and her astonishing reflexes said it all.

He had to get up. There was no choice. "Were they after Nicoletta? Or me?" he asked. "Could you tell?"

"I'm sorry, no. But it was deliberate."

He gave her a small smile. His head hurt just making the little movement to look fully at her. Damn, but she was beautiful. He could look at her forever. He planned to do just that, and sitting on his ass in the middle of the street wasn't helping his cause. He took a breath, steeled himself and forced his body into a standing position. Waves of nausea crashed through him instantly, but he made it to his feet.

Mariko slipped her arm around his waist. "Where should

we go?" She was asking him how to get him out from under the eyes of the public.

The sound of sirens was loud. The police would want to question him. He couldn't just leave, no matter how much he wanted to. Ricco straightened his body, ignoring the painful protests. "The deli. Masci's. They'll have chairs and I need to sit. Francesca will be there."

Mariko blinked up at him. *Francesca will be there.* She was helping him, but he thought Francesca could do a better job. She was *quite* capable of looking after his injuries without another woman interfering. She forced her mind away from jealousy. That horrible tiny flare of resentment couldn't be called anything else.

Ricco Ferraro didn't deserve death. Whatever crime he had supposedly committed to be on someone's hit list, there had to be extenuating circumstances. Mariko had been delivering justice to criminals since she was fourteen years old. She knew criminals and she knew good.

The moment Ricco had realized there was a truck barreling down on them, he'd shoved her into Lucia, moving both out of its path. He'd had to turn and catch Nicoletta up, running with her to get her clear. He could have saved himself and left the others to their fate, but he'd risked his life to get them all clear—especially the teenager. He had placed himself in jeopardy.

The driver had been determined to kill them. Or one of them. Mariko honestly didn't know which one. It stood to reason that the intended victim had been Ricco, but only because she'd been ordered to kill him. Even after he'd thrown the girl from him, the truck had continued on its course to crush her. Mariko had managed to throw a rock at the windshield to obscure the driver's vision and hopefully slow him down. He'd pointed a gun out of the driver's side window, but it was impossible to tell if he was firing at anyone in particular.

Ricco moved with his fluid, flowing walk, although she could tell he was really hurting. She was fairly certain no one else could. Emilio and Enzo moved in on either side of them. She kept her arm firmly around his waist, helping to support him without looking as if she were.

He went straight to Lucia and the teenager, who were pressed against the side of the building. He took Lucia's hand and bent to brush a kiss across her cheek. "Are you both all right?"

Nicoletta, her arms around Lucia, nodded. "I texted Amo. He's on his way. I'm going to take Lucia to the deli and get her something to drink. I've already locked the store."

She appeared suddenly very grown-up, not at all the young, uncertain teen Mariko had been introduced to. She was transformed, somehow, by the crisis, but she looked scared and resigned. She looked like a girl hunted—and haunted—yet standing up now that whatever the trouble was had found her.

"Nicoletta."

Ricco's voice was so gentle it turned Mariko's heart over.

"We don't know what this is about yet. We're going to wait and see before jumping to conclusions. We're heading to the deli as well, so we'll walk with you. Emilio and Enzo are with us, and my family will be here any moment."

So would the police. The sirens were louder than ever, and clearly that made Nicoletta nervous as well. Still, the girl's hands on Lucia were steady and she nodded, turning the older woman toward the deli. Ricco and Mariko walked behind them, and as they did, Mariko for the first time could see the shadows on the teenager. She threw tubes out, tubes that sought connections with other shadows. Her breath caught in her throat. The girl was more of a mystery than ever. Clearly she was a shadow rider.

Ricco walked upright, making every effort not to lean on her, but she kept her arm firmly around his waist, fitting under his shoulder when she never would have walked so intimately with a man. Strangely, she didn't mind. In fact, she liked thinking of him as hers to take care of and she dreaded getting to the deli where Francesca would take over.

She wondered why he'd had to advertise for a rope model if he had Francesca.

Instinctively, she knew Ricco wouldn't want her to ask him if he was all right. They both knew he wasn't and he wouldn't want to acknowledge the truth of that, or let anyone else know. She was well aware he was still recovering.

Looking up at him, at his handsome, rugged features, one couldn't tell that every single step was agony, but she could. She was connected to him through their shadows and she felt his pain. He was stoic, as every shadow rider had been taught to be, but she didn't like that he was so exposed. Out in the open. Every eye seemed to be on him.

She knew the impression they were giving to the watchers. She appeared to be his current girlfriend, something that didn't sit well with her. She didn't like the idea of being one of so many. His women never lasted long, most no more than a night, and the idea of the paparazzi getting ahold of her picture with him was distasteful. Still, she couldn't let go of him or move away.

"Thank you."

He said the words so softly she almost didn't hear. She glanced up at him again and found his eyes fixed on her face. He knew what she was feeling. As she was growing up no one could read her, not even her beloved brother. She kept a serene mask in place despite every humiliation, every beating. She scrubbed floors and trained harder than every male rider, uncaring how sore she was and never allowing anyone to see how much she hurt. She had more practice than any other rider that she knew of in hiding how she felt, yet Ricco read her.

"You're welcome." What else was there to say?

A beautiful woman with Italian flawless skin, lots of generous curves, and a wealth of black hair stood holding open the door of the deli. Instinctively, Mariko knew this was Francesca. Francesca put her arms around Lucia and drew the older woman and teen inside the store, but her eyes were on Ricco, assessing the damage to him. Mariko knew it looked bad. His clothes were torn and bloody from the fall off the hood of the truck to the street.

"No gunshot wounds, *cara*," Ricco assured her. "It looks worse than it is."

That was such a lie. Surely she wouldn't believe him, but Mariko could see the relief in her eyes as she turned away to help Nicoletta with Lucia. Ricco didn't let go of Mariko. If anything, he held on to her tighter. His touch all at once seemed possessive, although what had changed, she didn't know.

"Mr. Ferraro." A shorter man, clearly the owner of the deli, hurried toward them. "Is everything okay? What can I do? What do you need?"

"It's Ricco, Pietro," he corrected and pulled out a chair for Mariko.

She was afraid to let go of him, but he stood stoically, his face a little pale. There were beads of sweat on his forehead, but she knew anyone seeing him would put it down to the wild ride on the hood of the rampaging truck.

Pietro bobbed his head and watched anxiously as Ricco sat down at the table with Lucia and Nicoletta.

"We'd appreciate as much privacy as possible, Pietro," he said. "The police will be in asking questions soon. I imagine my family will show up as well. Emilio and Enzo must talk to the cops. I've texted our lawyer and he'll be here soon. We'll pay you for the loss of business, of course."

Pietro waved his hand to dismiss such a notion, but Mariko knew the Ferraro family would insist. Pietro clearly knew it, too. He rushed over to the door and locked it, turning the sign to closed, and then hurried back behind the counter. Francesca returned from the back with a washcloth and towel. Ricco took both and just held them.

"Lucia, should I call the doctor to look you over?" he asked.

"No, no, I'm just shaken. I thought I would lose Nicoletta, and I can't lose another child." She clung to the teenager. "Already Amo and I think of her as our family." She leaned into Nicoletta heavily.

The girl wrapped her arm around the older woman. "You aren't going to lose me. Did you see Ricco? He moved like lightning." The teen managed a small laugh, and Lucia responded with a smile, blowing him a kiss.

"Mariko, you hit the ground hard. Do you need a doctor?" Lucia asked.

"Thank you," Nicoletta added, looking at Mariko for the first time. "Lucia told me you saved her from the truck as well as a very bad fall."

"It was actually Ricco saving both of us from the truck," Mariko corrected. "He shoved me into Lucia hard enough that we both were cleared from the path. He did that before he grabbed you and ran."

A man emerged from the hallway behind Pietro. She knew immediately he had to be a Ferraro. He came striding out from behind the counter, his gaze moving first over Ricco, taking in the blood, torn clothes and beads of sweat, then moving on to Nicoletta, Lucia and finally to her. He was every bit as intimidating as Ricco. He looked younger, but no less lethal.

"Ricco?" One word. He injected more into that single name than she could imagine anyone doing.

"I'm fine, Giovanni. This is Mariko. She took care of Lucia for me."

She took the wet cloth from his hand, very annoyed at his darling Francesca for not bothering to try to clean up the wounds. It would be a wonder if he didn't get an infection. She glared at him when he tried to pull away. To her shock, he allowed her to dab at the blood and sweat on his face.

"Mariko," Giovanni said.

She was beginning to think just saying a name was a language in itself; she just didn't know the family well enough to know what the inflections meant. She nodded, noting Giovanni bent to brush Francesca's cheek first and then Lucia's and Nicoletta's. Nicoletta went stiff, but she didn't pull away.

Giovanni toed a chair around and straddled it, sitting across from his brother. "Was it deliberate?"

Nicoletta made a small sound of distress and instantly Francesca and Lucia put an arm around her. Mariko wished she knew where the girl fit in and what had happened to her, why someone might be after her.

"Yes." Ricco's voice was clipped. "But we don't know who. It looked as if they were trying for either Nicoletta or me, but it could have been Mariko as well."

"Or Lucia," Nicoletta said, her voice tight.

Mariko was aware of another brother. He emerged from behind them, where the deeper shadows were.

"Bullshit," the newcomer said. "No one would ever want to harm Lucia, would they *amore*? Well, not unless you stole some woman's man. Or ran off with one of your ten thousand admirers."

"Taviano," Lucia said softly. "You know if Amo throws me out, I will run to the Ferraro family. No other men can compare."

Taviano bent down to brush a kiss across her cheek, touched Nicoletta on the top of her head and hugged Francesca. "What trouble are you in now, Ricco?"

Mariko noticed that Nicoletta avoided Taviano's gaze, as she did Ricco's and Giovanni's. Taviano smiled at Mariko. "I'm Taviano," he announced. "One of Ricco's many brothers."

"Mariko," she said, concentrating on getting the blood off of Ricco's head. He'd hit the side of it fairly hard. The road had shredded his suit down one arm and part of his thigh. Blood seeped through the material. He sucked in his breath when she laid the cloth on his arm over the torn flesh. "Ricco, I don't think you need stitches, it's mainly surface, although there are a couple of spots that are deep."

"It's fine," he said abruptly and pulled away from her.

She knew immediately he was embarrassed in front of his brothers and the other women. He didn't want them to know he was hurt, although how he could hit the street like that and not get hurt, especially after the car crash, she couldn't see.

"Don't be a dick, Ricco," Giovanni said.

"I'm not being a dick," he objected. He took the cloth from her and tossed it on the table. "I'm being brave. Can't you tell the difference?"

He said it straight-faced and it was all Mariko could do to keep from laughing.

"Amo is at the door, Pietro," Francesca said, already hurrying to allow Lucia's husband inside. "Vinci is with him."

"Our lawyer," Ricco told Mariko. He caught her hand, curling his fingers around hers and bringing it to his chest as he leaned into her. "I'm sorry for being a dick. Sometimes I just am, but I'll watch it."

Giovanni snorted his derision. "Sometimes? Don't believe a fucking thing he says, Mariko. It's *all* the time."

She could hear the affection in their voices. They included her in their circle, and it made her feel ashamed. She should have pulled her hand from Ricco's but she told herself she didn't want to embarrass him. If she was strictly honest with herself, that had nothing to do with it, but she just couldn't go there yet.

As Vinci and Amo entered through the front door, two more men came from the back of the store. Mariko knew immediately that these were also Ricco's brothers and one of them was definitely Stefano Ferraro, head of the Ferraro family. The family was legendary around the world, known to other riders, respected and admired. He strode in, his gaze taking in everything, the minutest detail, but mostly he was centered on his brother, noting every detail, every road burn, his color and breathing.

She had the strangest need, almost a compulsion, to shield Ricco from his brother's scrutiny. From all of them. She sensed he detested appearing weak in front of anyone, but especially his family. He didn't relax; if anything, he became much more tense. She moved closer to him, not understanding her need to shield him, but determined to do so all the same.

From the back, a woman hurried into the room. She was dressed in the same pin-striped suit her brothers were wearing, and there was no mistaking she was Emmanuelle Ferraro. She was absolutely gorgeous with her blue eyes and her thick dark hair. "Ricco!" She rushed right up to him and flung her arms around him, practically dragging him out of the chair. There were genuine tears in her eyes.

"I'm all right, Emmanuelle. A little truck can't hurt me," he assured.

"No, but the fall on top of your car going into a wall might," she objected. She hugged him again.

Mariko wanted to tell her that just touching him had to hurt him, but she kept silent, wondering when the last time she hugged her brother had been. Had she ever showed him the love she felt? Told him? She'd let Osamu Saito stamp out every joy in her, every bit of personality. As she'd grown, she moved through life in silence, hoping not to be noticed, afraid of drawing attention to herself.

She was big. Clumsy. Ugly. She'd brought shame on her family with her American looks and her undisciplined passion, which clearly meant she followed in the footsteps of her whore of a mother.

She was surrounded by Ferraros. They were shadow riders. Americans. Their reputation was impeccable. They weren't considered undisciplined; they were almost revered. They freely showed affection to one another, and concern. It was clear they loved one another. She couldn't imagine that they would go very long without expressing that love. She loved her brother—*loved* him with everything in her— yet she couldn't remember telling him, not since they were very little and she'd whisper it to him, afraid of being overheard.

Suddenly she could barely breathe. She was always calm, yet now, in the face of the knowledge that she might never find her brother, never be able to tell him that she cared, she couldn't breathe. Couldn't find a way to catch her breath. She wasn't being fair to Ricco, contemplating killing him when she knew she never would. He was too good of a man. But she'd come with the vague idea that she might, and now she was using him to hide while she figured out her next move. That wasn't fair, either.

She'd tried to live a life of honor, but practically overnight she'd become the very person Osamu Saito had pounded into her night and day—that person she'd always told herself she wasn't and could never be. Her throat closed and it seemed impossible to draw in air. Around her, the talk continued, the brothers reassuring themselves that Ricco, Lucia and Nicoletta were all right. They thanked Emilio and Enzo as well as her.

She felt a fraud. A terrible fraud. If they all knew that she had come to kill Ricco Ferraro, that she was willing to harm a fellow shadow rider, none of them would want to sit in the same room with her. She had to go. Right then. She knew the police were coming to question everyone; she heard the lawyer assuring them that the cameras in the street would have picked up the action. Still, she couldn't stay. She had to leave.

She made one small move, a simple shifting of her feet. Ricco leaned back in his chair and wrapped his arm around her, drawing her close to him. At the same time, his head turned until his mouth was close to her ear.

"Stay with me, Mariko. I want you to stay."

CHAPTER SIX

Stay with me, Mariko. I want you to stay. That's all Ricco had said. In that voice. The one that whispered over her skin and seeped into her pores to drown her in him. In his will. He left it to her—her choice. But then, she was coming to understand, with Ricco Ferraro, she had very little will of her own. Once he told her he wanted her to stay, she'd been lost in the wonder of that. No one had ever wanted her. No one. Sometimes, not even the brother she loved with everything in her. Osamu had done her best to drive a wedge between them as they'd grown up until it had reached the point that Mariko wasn't certain Ryuu wanted her around.

She paced around the beautiful room Ricco had given to her to use. She'd never had so much space. She thought it would overwhelm her, but she found she liked it. She especially loved that the French doors opened into a gorgeous garden. The police had questioned all of them for what seemed hours. Coming home to the solace of this room had been calming after everything that had happened.

She could tell Ricco was exhausted, but no one else seemed to notice—no one except for his oldest brother. The police questioned everyone over and over until the Ferraro lawyer had objected. They presented a united front always, and they kept Lucia, Amo and especially Nicoletta in their center, surrounding them with strength. Vinci made it clear to the police that they weren't to question anyone without him being present.

She found it strange that Ricco's parents hadn't shown up when everyone else had, but then in all the conversations, she'd never once heard his parents mentioned by anyone. She knew they were alive, she'd researched the family thoroughly—although she'd missed Francesca's connection. Her relationship with Stefano was new.

She was going to have to tell Ricco the truth. There was no other option. It was only right. She didn't want to see the condemnation in his eyes, but she had to warn him. They all thought it was a possibility that the truck had been aiming at Nicoletta, but she knew better. She knew there was a hit out on Ricco and she wasn't the only assassin sent. She would lose everything. She would lose him. His family. This place. Her hideout. Most of all, she would lose a very important ally.

She had to find Ryuu before it was too late. She'd been given three weeks to kill Ricco or Ryuu was a dead man. She didn't know who had him, why they wanted Ricco Ferraro dead, but she knew even if she killed him, whoever had taken her brother would have no reason to keep him alive. Right now, she could demand proof of life whenever they called her, but once the shadow rider was dead, they would kill Ryuu. She had a place to stay in Ricco's home, a base to work from. If she came clean, there was a possibility he would help her. More likely, he would throw her out.

She opened the French doors and stared out. It was a cool night, the breeze moving the leaves and branches around, casting shadows across the ground. Something moved at the far end of the garden and she took several steps outside to get a better look. At once her shadow connected with the others and raced toward the ones at the farthest end.

She recognized Ricco before she saw him. The connection between them had grown that strong—so strong when their shadows touched, it sent a jolt of heat rushing through her. His head came up and he spotted her immediately . . .

or had he known the moment she opened her door and stepped into the courtyard? That was more likely. She didn't feel surprise on his side at all.

"What are you doing up, Ricco? I thought you'd gone to lie down for a while." At least her voice was pleasant. That was one attribute in her favor.

She had never been exactly desirable in Japan. She towered over the women there—and some of the men—but she'd always had a melodic voice. Osamu Saito had despised that about her as well, saying she tried to use her voice to seduce men. She'd become afraid to speak, just in case she'd incur Osamu's wrath. The beatings were difficult. She found she had a temper, and she wanted to rip the broom handle from Osamu's hands and give her a taste of her own medicine. She hadn't, of course, because she might have been banned from shadow riding and it was all she had, but more, she'd made a deal with Osamu to keep her from beating Ryuu.

"I rested for a while. I'm glad you're up. I'm in the mood to work." Ricco's voice came out of the shadows, low and intense. Sexy.

Her heart jerked hard in her chest. Fingers of fear crept down her spine. She'd applied to be his model, at his beck and call any time day or night for the next few months. She'd done that. Given her word. Signed a contract. Always her word had been gold. She would never go back on that with him if she could manage it. Fear wasn't the problem—she could deal with nerves. It was the excitement welling up in her that frightened her most. The unfamiliar emotion was too strong. Too needy. Too everything she was unprepared to deal with.

"What do you want me to do?"

"Get yourself ready. Hydrate, use the bathroom, dress in one of the one-piece things hanging in your closet, no underwear please. I'll take a few photographs because even if I don't use them for the book, I want to document your journey for you and this first session is an important one. In later sessions, we'll have a makeup artist here, but this one is just for us. Me, to get rid of the building edginess that always means I need to do rope art or I'm going to do something crazy, and you, so you realize I would never hurt you and you're always safe with me."

"Something crazy?" She had to ask.

"I can be an adrenaline junkie. Fast cars. Climbing. Jumping out of planes."

Fast women—but she wasn't going there. She couldn't. She had to stick to her plan as closely as possible. This might be her first and last session. One-piece things? When had they been put in her closet? She'd locked her doors.

Without a word she turned and went back inside. She needed to get her breathing under control. Her heartbeat was wild, a drum that wouldn't stop pounding. It wasn't fear of being tied and vulnerable as it should have been. There was some trepidation, but Ricco wasn't a man to force a woman to do anything. He wouldn't need to. A woman would want to do anything he asked of her.

She moved through her room to the closet, opening the double doors. She had brought very few clothes, but now there were several dresses, wraps, jeans and sweaters, and three of the one-piece, skintight suits all in her size. There was also lingerie that looked as if it would fit her as well. She'd had to provide her stats on the application. That had included her height, weight and clothes size.

She turned and glanced at the dresser. It was tall and ornate, beautifully appointed. Slowly, she crossed over to it and pulled out a drawer. It should have been empty, but it wasn't.

Mariko lifted the underwear from the lined drawer. The dresser was made of cedar and smelled delicious. The panties were sheer lace, covering her front—barely—but leaving her buttocks bare. She took a deep breath and picked up the matching bra. As a woman, she should have the courage to wear such things. She should be proud of her body, no matter what the type, and walk with confidence, but she felt ashamed. It had taken every ounce of discipline she had to force herself to walk with her head up and her shoulders straight always—but she had done it.

Courage and discipline. Courage was being afraid and doing the task anyway. She wanted this for herself. She'd told herself she was doing it to get close to Ricco Ferraro, but she'd researched him very carefully and as far as she could see, even before she met him, he was a good man. Wild. An adrenaline junkie just as he'd admitted. Not a good bet for a husband—ever—but a good man.

She walked to the mirror and stared at herself. Her father, according to Osamu, had been Japanese, her mother American. Her brother looked Japanese. She didn't look anything like them. Like any of them. She was used to being ridiculed, ignored, beaten and made fun of. She didn't understand why looking different had warranted all that.

She touched her pale skin with shaking fingers. Her blond mane was a legacy from her mother. She had large hazel eyes, with long sweeping lashes, and a pouty mouth with full red lips. Her nose was straight and she had good bone structure— that was what had made her mother so photogenic.

Where her mother had been five foot ten, she'd only managed to hit five foot six. It was annoying to be in the middle. Not short, not thin, not tall and not model material. She felt clunky next to the small women moving silently through the house growing up in Japan. She always seemed too big for everything.

She knew she was going to die and that knowledge made her question everything about her life, the family she never had. Even her love for her brother. As they'd grown up, Osamu had by turns loved and hated him. He'd grown confused. Osamu had told them Ryuu's twisted body was Mariko's fault. She'd blamed Mariko for his inability to ride the shadows. Ryuu had sometimes sided with his sister, but as he grew up, more and more, he tried to get Osamu to love him, often going against Mariko to prove to Osamu he was loyal to her.

Was he worth dying for? The answer was yes. Ryuu was her only family, and she loved him with everything in her. It didn't matter if that love wasn't reciprocated every moment of the day; it was in her heart—and his. He was her only family and the only person in the world she had. She couldn't live with herself if she didn't try to save him. On the other hand, she couldn't murder a good man to trade for her brother's life.

So that led her to this moment. She needed to know she'd done at least one of the things important to her. She wanted to feel beautiful. Just once. One time. From the moment Osamu had shown her the books with her mother as a rope model portraying all kinds of rope art from simple to bondage and suspension, she had studied that art. She knew the history. She'd gone to demonstrations. She had found herself moved by the various rope masters and how they treated their models—as if their partner were the only person in their world. Osamu's taunts had backfired. Just once, even if it wasn't real, she wanted to feel as if a man saw only her. No one else. For those moments, she was his world. His canvas. He saw beauty in her.

She began to remove her clothes in front of the mirror. She didn't have the slender, beautiful body the other women in her household had had. She was all curves. Full, firm breasts; wide, curving hips; she even had a butt. How many times had Osamu made fun of her butt, saying they could serve tea on her bottom. For one moment, in defiance, she considered going to Ricco in a bra and those indecent panties, but she couldn't make herself do it. It was bad enough to go with no underwear, even covered by the one-piece thing he wanted her to wear. There were three of them—red, black and white.

Mariko forced herself to pull on the black catsuit. It was tight, the nearly sheer, stretch lace material molding to every curve and emphasizing her narrower rib cage and waist. She could barely look at herself in it. It showed every single flaw she had, and that was her entire body. She nearly ripped it off and sank to the floor in a flood of tears, but that wasn't allowed in her world. She took a deep breath and forced herself to continue.

She was very aware of time passing. Ricco had said they didn't have much time. What did that mean? He didn't call out to her or try to hurry her in any way. She used the bathroom and spent time on her makeup. She'd learned from another shadow rider, a young sixteen-year-old girl from England. The girl had taught her in secret, because if Osamu had found her with makeup, there would have been hell to pay.

Again, she stared at herself in the mirror, afraid to move. Her inclination was to run. To just disappear into the night. Never see Ricco or his family again. Never think about this moment of utter terror. She was attracted to him and she didn't want him to see her as weak or ugly. She didn't want him to know she'd come there with the thought to kill him. She had so many secrets to hide.

It would be so easy to leave, but she couldn't pass up this one moment in her life. Face herself. She wanted truth. She'd been seeking the truth of her past, the truth about herself. Squaring her shoulders, head up, she turned away from the mirror. She was one of the best riders in Japan. She knew she was and had confidence that she could kill a man.

Could she find the confidence to look into her own soul? To be a woman and *feel* like a woman just once? She'd chosen this path because her mother had thought the art form beautiful. In studying the history and learning about each rope discipline, she had come to find beauty in it. She wanted to be a part of that before she died. She would become part of both her father's and mother's history and culture. She loved that idea. She just had to find the courage to do it.

Ricco was waiting in the studio. Lights were muted, which surprised her, and there was music playing, something soft and easy. The room, like all the rooms in his home, was spacious. Mirrors went from floor to ceiling on one wall.

Cameras were in cases and there was an open closet full of props. Her heart pounded when she saw the rigging overhead that told her he might at some point want to suspend her from the ceiling.

He had his back to her, his hands moving over the coils of rope on the wall. There were all types of materials in various colors and he seemed to absorb the textures of each as his hand moved over the bundles. She was mesmerized by the way he touched them, almost a caress she could feel on her own skin. There were far more ropes here than in his room.

She shivered and rubbed at her arms, wishing she could hide her breasts and the way her nipples pushed against the material of the skintight suit. It wasn't the cold, although the studio was cool. Her body had reacted to the way he smoothed his palm over the ropes. She held her breath as he turned, watching his eyes, needing to see that first expression, afraid it would be disgust and she would be humiliated all over again. She steeled herself. She was used to humiliation. She could handle it. *But not from him.*

Her eyes met his as the thought raced through her mind. For one moment his mask slipped and she saw his eyes go dark with desire. Every line in his face was etched with a sensuality that kept her breath trapped deep in her lungs. No one had ever looked at her like that in her life. Then the mask was back in place and he was stalking her. Like a great, fluid jungle cat.

She watched him come toward her, his muscles rippling beneath his tight tee. The material stretched over his chest so she could see the defined muscles beneath as he approached her. He looked utterly confident. The scrapes on his arms and face didn't detract from his good looks at all. If anything, he looked even tougher.

"You look perfect, Mariko," he greeted. "Absolutely beautiful."

No reprimand for being late. For taking her time. For almost running away. She was ashamed that she'd considered that idea—just opening the French doors and disappearing into the night. He circled her, his body heat reaching her. Enveloping her. His scent surrounding her.

"You're nervous."

That voice. She loved how low and intimate his tone could be. How commanding. She was strong. She needed stronger. "Yes." He'd made it a statement, just as he had said she was beautiful, as if she knew it and he was just acknowledging it. As if it were the truth. She heard the ring of honesty in his voice, but then he'd hit his head numerous times.

"It's okay to be nervous, Mariko. You're entering a journey that is both sensual and artistic."

He moved behind her and touched her shoulder. She jumped and immediately felt ashamed. "I'm sorry."

"Don't be sorry. Talk to me. Communication is very important between us at all times." He bent his head as he lifted the hair from the back of her neck. "For instance, I find your neck incredibly sexy. You look both vulnerable and sensual with your hair up. With it down, you look wild and beautiful. Just as sensual, but in a completely different way."

She closed her eyes as his breath touched the nape of her neck. So warm. So male. He made her aware of every cell in her body because each went on alert when he was close. She was a rider and trained in every aspect of warfare, of engaging an enemy, defeating them. She knew anatomy, knew every pressure point. She knew the exact angle one had to use to break a neck.

She had absolutely no knowledge of what he was doing to her or how he could arouse her with just his voice and a gesture so small as the brush of his fingers on her body. He had barely touched her shoulder, lifted her hair, spoke in that low, compelling voice, and her body was aroused. Her breathing came in soft, ragged pants. He couldn't fail to notice, he was far too tuned to the human body—especially a woman's.

"I want to do a breathing exercise with you, but I will be touching your body. You have to get used to my hands on you and I need to know how you breathe so I never restrict you when we're working together. Any time you're uncomfortable, you need to say so. I have to trust that you'll communicate what you're feeling at all times. If I lay a rope incorrectly and it hurts you, I have to know."

He was still behind her, his mouth against the nape of her neck, lips brushing tiny caresses with every word he said. That voice, so low and velvet soft, smoothed over her skin like his lips, until she couldn't separate the two sensations. Already her breasts ached with need and she grew damp between her legs.

"Mariko." His voice was gentle. "I need to know you're all right with me touching you intimately."

Just the way he said *intimately* was intimate. She wanted to groan and her mouth had gone suddenly dry. She not only wanted him to touch her, she needed him to do so. She swallowed hard and nodded. Slightly. A bare affirmation with her head because that was all she could manage. He didn't move. He didn't drop her hair back into place. He stayed behind her, his body very close to hers but without touching other than his hand and his breath. He simply waited.

"Yes. It's all right." She needed his touch more than she needed to breathe. How she managed to give him what he needed to continue, she didn't know. For the first time in her life she felt weak with wanting. With need. Yet at the same time, she did feel sort of attractive. She was aware of herself as a woman, as feminine, when she'd always felt masculine. He'd given her that, and she'd be forever grateful.

His fingers curled around the bicep of her right arm. His touch was firm. Possessive. Held her captured there. "I'm going to put my hand on your upper chest. I want you to just breathe normally. Feel my breath moving in and out with yours. Just let yourself feel those sensations, Mariko."

He placed his left palm gently on her just above the curve

of her breasts. She'd never been so aware of her breasts in her life. How they could ache with need. Burn for him. For touch. *His* touch. She became aware of his body, standing directly behind hers, his hand guiding her back into his chest, her buttocks pressed against him. He was hard. All muscle. Heat enveloped her. Her body seemed awash in sensation.

His cock pressed tightly against her, right into the small of her back, a sword there, a male weapon, an instrument of pleasure, she didn't know which, but she wanted to find out. She knew he wanted her, was very aroused, but then, he seemed to be very sexual and she was certain one couldn't separate this practice from sex and art entirely. It was a sensual bonding between two people. Intimate beyond belief. Very, very erotic. Had all his models felt this way? Had he wanted all of them?

"Relax, *farfallina mia*, breathe for me."

Little butterfly. She liked that. She forced air through her lungs and then let herself become aware of his chest rising and falling. It felt like a dance between them. She followed naturally. Easily. He kept his hand on her arm, strong and confident so that she felt safe with him.

"That's my woman. I'm going to put my hand on your breasts," he warned.

My woman. Did he call every rope model that? She told herself not to react, to keep breathing, to not wrap herself in his words. His palm slid from above her breasts, over the curve to cover her nipples with his palm. He just pressed heat there, feeling the rise and fall of her breath. He stood quietly, letting her get used to the feel of his hand on her. He was still behind her, taking more of her weight than she should have been giving him, but her legs were trembling.

Ricco's face nudged aside her heavy fall of hair so his lips could whisper against the nape of her neck. "You're doing great. Keep breathing as normally as possible. Feel me breathing with you."

She did as he asked, mostly because the flare of pleasure

she got from his praise shocked her. No one ever praised her. She excelled as a rider. Excelled in every area of training, yet not one instructor had ever praised her. Her fellow riders avoided her for the most part. They were never rude. None of the instructors or riders were rude, but they made it clear she was alone. She thought she would always be alone, until this moment. Even among the riders, she was the daughter of a whore, abandoned to the streets. She'd always be mixed race and not quite good enough.

She breathed in and out for him. For herself. To be someone strong and courageous. To be different because she needed to be different just once before she died. She needed to feel the freedom of arousal, and he gave her that. She wasn't certain how, but he did, but that connection between them was extremely strong and compelling.

"That's exactly what I need from you, Mariko," he said softly, his lips caressing her skin and sending little darts of fire streaking through her body. "I'm moving my hand to your belly."

He did, sliding his arm intimately around her to hold her to him with just his will. His hand didn't press into her hard, or try to force her closer. He simply stood there, breathing with her. She felt her body relaxing into his. He moved then, sliding his arm from around her, releasing her right bicep as he stepped toward the wall holding the coils of rope, and she felt bereft.

"I was in a foul mood when you came out to the garden, and you've already managed to transform that into an inspiration." He stood in front of the ropes but looked at her. "A pentacle harness I think to start. You'll get a feel for the ropes and know whether we can continue."

"I don't understand. Why wouldn't we continue?" What was he looking for in her? Panic rose. He couldn't already be thinking of replacing her. What had she done wrong? She needed to be here. She needed a base. She needed—him.

"Mariko, this is an exchange. You have to get something out of it as well."

He was paying his rope model a great deal of money, that was what she was getting out of it, but she kept her mouth shut, because so far, it was much, much more. She'd never felt so close to another human being. He hadn't even tied her yet and she wanted the feel of the rope. His rope.

"I think green to go with your eyes today." He pulled the bundle from the wall and ran it through his hands like an old friend.

"My eyes are hazel." Not green. Not brown. Hazel. Osamu had pointed out to her many, many times even her eyes weren't special. They were ugly with their combination of green, brown and gold.

He smiled. "Right now, they're very green. They change color. True hazel, like yours, is actually quite rare and very beautiful."

She blinked, astonished that she could hear truth in his tone, mesmerized by the way the rope moved through his palm. Sensual. As if part of him. She watched him breathe in and out as he ran the rope through his hand again and again. She could watch him all day and never get enough. It was shocking how much she wanted him.

Ricco took a moment to just look at her, to breathe her in as he folded the rope in two, resting the center point in his palm. She was unexpectedly gorgeous. A treasure beyond any price. She was nervous, but excited, giving him the greatest offering he could ask for—her trust. She was a shadow rider. A woman meting out justice, always in control. She was giving that control over to him.

Mariko didn't realize the incredible gift she was giving him. He'd watched her. Her reflexes were extremely fast. She was in not just good physical condition but superb condition. A rider needed control always. If she had come there to kill him, as he suspected, allowing him to tie her up was the last thing she should do, yet she was giving him her complete trust. Making herself vulnerable to him. Only to him.

She was a woman any man would be lucky to have, but

he knew she belonged to him. He hoped he could get her to feel the same way. He would be asking a lot, to have her accept him as he was—with all the dark places inside of him. Her courage humbled him. The immense trust it took to allow herself to be tied by him, even in the name of art, was astonishing for a woman like her.

It was a true power exchange between them and he loved that. Even craved it. He needed a woman strong enough to accept that he would always need his ropes. They anchored him. Centered him. The moment he touched them, those dark shifting shadows inside him subsided.

He had been careful not to spook her. Right now, with their shadows connected, he could feel her slipping through his fingers. She had fight-or-flight syndrome in full force and he had to make every single moment with her count. He'd risked touching her to get a feel for her breathing. He needed to know in order to minimize the risk to her for potential trouble when he laid the ropes on her skin. He was very careful in his tying, always making certain his model was comfortable and safe, and now, having found Mariko, it was doubly important to him.

He wanted to be further along with her, in a place where he could see her naked body, where she'd give him that as well. Already he could see patterns on her, so many he wanted to try with her, his greatest model, the only one he'd ever have now. He wanted to spend every moment with her.

He used a stalking motion coming to her. Something he couldn't help. This was his world, and she was his woman, his prey. He was going to seduce her into being just that for all time. He would do so with his ropes. His art. With the sheer force of his will. He would court her gently outside this room and teach her about her own body and that desire could be satisfied in many ways.

He had learned to kill and then he had killed. Many times. Fourteen was far too young for his artistic mind to accept the violence and he'd been fortunate that he'd met his teacher, a rope master of more than forty years. The art had saved his sanity and his life. He needed it like others needed air.

Deliberately moving into the light, so that his shadow connected with hers, he watched her body shiver with awareness as heat and need rushed over him and into her. She was drowning in desire. His? Hers? Their combined desire? He watched her skin flush and knew she felt the way he did. She was very sensitive to him. Open to him. With each line of rope, each pattern he created, he would wrap himself around her, adorning her body with—him.

Mariko couldn't take her eyes from Ricco as he approached her, the green rope moving subtly, but powerfully, with his body. She didn't want to panic, but she'd never been so aroused by or aware of a man as she was Ricco. His hands guided her, gently but firmly, in front of a full-length mirror. She didn't want to look at herself. He was so gorgeous and she was just . . . Mariko.

He touched the rope to her face, sliding it along her cheek like a caress so she knew he was once again going to use silk on her. For some reason the silken ropes felt intimate, an extension of him. When he touched her with them, even just to slide the coils over her skin, it felt like sex and sin all wrapped up with his scent and his sheer will.

Very gently he pulled both arms behind her, and she felt the ties. Her heart hammered in her chest at the swiftness of his movement, the casualness, as if he'd done it a million times and there was no effort on his part. Just that quick he deprived her of two of her weapons.

She gave that gift to him, her submission to his will. To his art. But she knew now that it was so much more. Maybe he wasn't aware of the enormity of her ceding power to him—she didn't know him well enough to know what he thought with other models—but she was certain she had little time left on earth and she wanted her surrender to be to him. To a man she not only found attractive, but worthy.

Keeping his hand around her wrists, he nuzzled her hair

aside from her neck so that he could press his lips against her ear. "You're doing great, Mariko."

He had to feel her tremble, but his hand smoothed back her hair and his voice held nothing but admiration, respect and praise.

"Are you afraid?"

He waited and she knew he'd wait forever for her answer. He wouldn't continue. She knew he was giving her the opportunity to stop. She moistened her lips and nodded. "A little, but only of the unknown." That was the truth, and yet it wasn't. She was afraid of how he made her feel. Not just vulnerable, but so in need. She was damp with desire. Floating. She'd never felt that before. Almost euphoria.

"That's my woman." He whispered the words against the pulse pounding in her neck. His lips touched her ear and then her temple.

She dared then to raise her eyes to look into the mirror directly in front of her. He stood behind her, his head against hers, dark hair falling like sin across his forehead. His gaze met hers in the glass and she knew she would always remember that moment. His expressionless mask had slipped and she saw him, his fierce demons and turbulent needs mixed with dark, ferocious passion. He would never be like other men. He would always be dominant, scary to enemies and yet gentle with those he loved.

He reached around her and wrapped the double line around her torso beneath her pectoral muscles, all the while looking into her eyes in the mirror. His movements seemed effortless, casual, yet she was drowning in his focus, in his complete attention. She was used to disappearing no matter how large the crowd, but it was impossible to do that with Ricco. She was hot under the spotlight of his complete concentration.

She felt dizzy with need. Already her breathing had changed again, from slow and steady to ragged pants of desire. It was impossible to hide it from him. Her needs and desires were completely exposed for him to see, naked on her face, bare and visible on her body. It should have humiliated her. She should have felt embarrassment at the loss of control, but instead she felt a curious freedom.

He reached around her again and did something with the ropes, pulling them snug under her breasts. Her breath caught in her throat as he wrapped her breasts and continued creating the harness.

His mouth moved against the nape of her neck. "Breathe for me, *farfallina mia.*"

She tried. His hands were smooth and sure as the ropes slid over her body, wrapping her up in him. The rope was clearly an extension of him. She felt him in every wrap, every tension. The rope seemed, like her, to be completely under his spell, flying out of his hands to surrender to his will, a sensuous snake dancing to his tune.

She could see a pattern taking shape. A star. He worked fast, efficiently, smoothly, but his concentration wasn't on the artwork so much as on her and the artwork together. Making her one with both Ricco and the rope, binding all three of them together.

Her mind slipped away as she gave herself over to his care. The ropes licked at her flesh, kissed her just as his lips moved occasionally on her nape as he worked. She lived for those moments. The rope seemed such an extension of him, giving her small sweet licks, gentle strokes, a scorching-hot bite and then back to the kisses. A tendril of fire curled through her body, spreading like a slow burn. Her clit pulsed in tune to her drumming heart. A shudder of pleasure slid up her spine.

She was wrapped in a rope embrace now, firm on her skin. Wrapped in him. There was no separating the two of them, rope and master. With every breath she took, she breathed in his power. Every sure movement of his fingers on the rope, on her, was a revelation. She had never thought there was beauty in such a thing as being helpless. She had seen art in ropes on a human body but she'd never *felt* that beauty until this moment. She had never, not once, considered that for her, there would be something sensual about the feel of being surrounded and embraced by rope—but there was that, too.

Her body came alive, humming, vibrating, even purring. All the while her mind floated, drifted on sensual pleasure she hadn't known existed—or that she was capable of feeling. A bright, hot flare exploded in the vicinity of her chest and spread like flames through her body, radiating outward from the ropes as he cinched her breasts tighter. The bite was scalding hot, so sensual her sex pulsed and clenched by turns. Close. So close. Her breathing changed again. Ragged. Panting. Her face was flushed. She could see herself in the mirror and she looked—sexy. There was no other word for it.

"Beautiful." He breathed the word. "You are so beautiful, Mariko. I would like to photograph you now, if you're comfortable."

For the first time, she believed him. She saw it. She saw herself through his eyes, the way he had the first time she'd walked into the conference room. She saw what the camera would see. What the world would see if he shared this moment, but instinctively, she knew he wouldn't. It was too intimate and just between them. Just for them.

She saw green against black, a harness that shaped her breasts and formed a beautiful star. Like the flower arrangements and paintings in Japan, his art had balance and perfect symmetry. The tension was even. There wasn't a single twist in the rope. There was no pressure on her body and she knew instinctively she wouldn't have a single bruise. There would be no abrasions.

She nodded her head, although she wasn't certain she wanted the camera to capture her wanton need, the lust she saw in the mirror. The invitation to him. It was only for him.

"Mariko, I need your consent."

It was the voice she had grown used to. Waited for. Found safety and pleasure in. It was always velvet over steel. Soft. Low. Commanding. His voice sent shivers down her spine and kept her nipples as hard as rocks. His hands went to her shoulders, steadying her, and she realized she was swaying. Her knees felt weak but she knew she wouldn't fall because he was right there.

"Do you need a few minutes?"

He was holding her. She wanted to keep him there, but this was what she had agreed to. He'd more than kept his side of the bargain. She had no idea she could feel so protected. So beautiful. So cherished. He made her feel all those things. She could give him his art—and it was beautiful. She knew whatever she had to learn for future artwork would be far more strenuous, but now that she had a taste of it, she wanted to know it all.

"I'm good now. Just for a moment I was somewhere else."

He smiled. "That's good. That's what I'd hoped. You're supposed to feel that, Mariko. If you didn't, this wouldn't work for us."

She felt his caution when he slowly removed his hands and allowed her to stand on her own. She smiled to let him know she was okay. "If you want photographs, then go ahead."

"Are you comfortable enough to last in the ties? You're in superb physical condition, something important for the longer and more strenuous ties."

He was already getting his camera, adjusting the light so that she felt its white-hot glare. Even that made her feel sensual. Every movement of her body in the ropes sent those little subtle licks and bites over her skin. Unexpected pleasure.

Over the next twenty minutes he moved around her, getting pictures from every angle in the same meticulous and decisive way he'd tied her. He checked each shot before he put the camera down and was back, standing in front of her, his fingers on the ropes. She felt each tug and vibration traveling through her body, once again, the ropes an extension of him. Her skin, beneath the thin, tight suit, was so aroused as he slid each rope off that every nerve ending flared brightly with a shocking flame of sheer desire.

He took his time. His hands slipping the bindings, fingers whispering along with the rope over her nipples, under her breasts, between them. Caresses that sent heat sliding from breasts to her feminine sheath so that her sex clenched and stayed damp in need. He murmured to her softly in Italian as the ropes slid away, leaving her feeling more exposed than if she'd been naked, praising her, telling her how pleased he was with their session, how beautiful she was. How courageous.

She found herself exhausted, as if she'd run a long race, and she didn't understand why. She worked out every single day. She trained hard. Still, she wanted to just collapse on the floor, but Ricco lifted her into his arms, and cradled her against his chest as if she were precious to him. He made her feel cherished beyond anything else.

He carried her to the single chair in the room, sank into it with her on his lap and reached for a bottle of water. "Drink this, Mariko. All of it." He kept his arms around her, holding her when she thought she might fly apart.

That had been the problem. She'd been soaring too high, unfamiliar territory for her, and now that she was back on the ground, a little disoriented and exhausted, she wasn't certain what to do.

"It was only a harness," she whispered against his throat.

He kneaded her wrists, first one and then the other. "It was your first experience. I'm sure it was unexpected." He inspected her wrists, hands and arms before beginning a slow massage on her shoulders and the nape of her neck. "I am so proud of you. I couldn't have asked for more for your first time." He nuzzled the top of her head with his chin. Strands of her hair caught in the shadow along his jaw and even that felt sensual to her. "Tell me how you're feeling."

"Scared. Excited. Exhausted." She hesitated. It seemed silly to not admit what he already knew. "Turned on. Very." She confessed it in a small voice.

"I was surprisingly turned on myself. As a rule I am quite controlled."

He gave her that back and it made her feel better. She let herself relax totally into him, enjoying the feeling his strength gave her. She'd been alone so long, she hadn't expected to want his touch, to need it, but she was fast realizing she craved it.

"Are you willing to take the next step with me?"

She turned her head to look at him. That beautiful, scarred face. "Next step?"

"Are you comfortable enough with me to wear more revealing clothes, or none at all, depending on what I'm looking for?"

Her heart thudded, the rhythm a little erratic. She started to turn her head away, afraid he would see that was exactly what she wanted, but she was afraid. Shadow riders didn't show fear.

He caught her chin before she could hide from him. At once she read satisfaction there. "Say it for me."

She moistened her lips and nodded. "Yes." A commitment then. To him. To them. Maybe before she died, she'd leave behind a book of beautiful Japanese art for Ricco. Someone would know she'd lived, and maybe he would think of her occasionally.

CHAPTER SEVEN

Ricco stood outside the door of Mariko's room. That rage in him he never quite managed to keep suppressed had risen to the surface as he'd carried her from his studio to her room. He'd placed her carefully on her bed, told her to drink lots of water and get some sleep. He'd thanked her and had to leave abruptly because she looked so beautiful and delicious lying on her bed he'd wanted to kiss her senseless. Kiss her until she gave herself entirely to him.

Every step back to her room, she protested she was too heavy for him to carry. At first, he'd been insulted. He might not be the tallest of his brothers, but he was in the best shape. No one trained harder or worked out more. He ran. He lifted. He did both heavy and speed-bag work. He took down his brothers and any other rider asking to train with them. Just because he'd been in an accident didn't mean he was unable to carry a woman weighing less than a hundred and twenty pounds around. It was a blow to his pride—at first.

He realized when he got a good look at her face, when he'd forced her to quit hiding against his chest, that her protests weren't about his lack of strength. They weren't about him at all. They were all about her. She believed she was far too heavy, and who had done that to her? Who had made her believe she was anything but beautiful? He knew women much heavier who, to him, were gorgeous. It wasn't about a woman's weight, it was about who she was, if that brightness shone through her eyes and skin and hair. Ricco found beauty in art. Women were a form of art. All shapes and sizes. All body types.

The thing that enraged him was that Mariko, by any standards, would be considered a beautiful woman. She had beautiful symmetry. She had gorgeous bone structure. Her hair was thick and wild, silky soft. Hair a man wanted to see on his pillow. Hair he'd like to grip in his fist when he was kissing her or she had her fantasy mouth wrapped around his cock.

She had a completely false image of herself. He had seen the stunned look in her eyes when she'd looked at herself in the mirror—as if for the first time she saw beauty. It probably was her first time. At least he'd been the one to give her that, but she should have had it from the time she was an infant.

He put his palm on the door, level with where her head would have been. He just stood there. Silent. He had never believed a woman could accept what was inside of him. He'd worked hard to get rid of his demons, but it had been impossible. In the end, he'd accepted who he was because he had no choice. He had demons. He lived with them. He would be asking Mariko to live with them as well.

There were two ways he could ease the rage when it overwhelmed him, when the devil rode him hard. He could beat the shit out of a heavy bag until his hands bled right through the wraps, or he could use his ropes. He needed a woman willing to accept those things in him. The good thing, he reminded himself, was that he knew what he was asking, and that made it easy for him to accept a woman the way she was.

He might be accepting, but he'd never connected with a woman on any real level. Not until Mariko. He wished things were different. He wished he were different. He wished he hadn't done so many of the stupid things he'd done publicly. He couldn't take those things back or sweep them under the carpet.

"Okay, baby," he whispered softly. "Give me time before you decide to kill me or run. I can feel that in you, the need to run away from me, but you're really trying to run away from yourself." All of them were. He was. Mariko. Nicoletta. He knew all about running away from one's demons. He had them, and he often didn't want to face them. He used everything he could to escape them. Nicoletta had them. Mariko had them. Maybe most people did, just not quite as ugly as the ones he carried.

He sighed and glanced at his watch. Vittorio was keeping watch outside of the Fausti home. It was past time for Ricco's shift. All of them were working in shifts tonight to keep Nicoletta from running away—also, on the off chance she'd been the target, to keep her safe. He knew they thought he'd drive to her house—he wasn't supposed to go into the shadows until he was completely healed—but he was late. A bad feeling had been growing in his gut and it was growing worse.

Working fast, he stripped and pulled on his pin-striped suit. The material was made just for the riders and blended into every shadow easily. The moment he was dressed, he turned and headed for the door, moving fast, suddenly worried about both Nicoletta and Vittorio. His gut had never steered him wrong. As he pulled open his door, that feeling got so much worse. There was no waiting. He was faster in the shadows than any other rider. They'd tried clocking him on one of the longer runs, but no one, not even Stefano, could believe the time.

He chose his shadow and stepped into it. The wrenching on his body was familiar, but it had never felt like this. Not even in the early days when he was just a child and practicing. Now it was second nature, but his body felt like he was being torn apart. He never would have made it if he hadn't believed his brother was in trouble. The pain was excruciating, worse than when he'd woken up from the accident. He'd had pain meds then; now his body was molecules, being pulled through the tube at reckless speed.

He could barely function, making the jump from shadow to shadow to take him to Amo and Lucia's home. It was in the middle of Ferraro territory, just down from the businesses in a quiet little cul-de-sac. All the homes were kept up, the yards filled with flowers and trees. He stayed in the mouth of the tube, gritting his teeth and enduring the way his body flew apart, the wrenching so terrible there wasn't a single molecule that he didn't feel as pure agony.

Ordinarily a rider took a moment at the end of the tube to let his body reorient, but the pain was so overwhelming he kept moving, bursting out of the shadow. He knew instantly, even as he was emerging, that he'd fucked up. He felt the attacker before he caught a glimpse of him. Turning as he emerged, he tried to block the swing of the bat. It hit him on the back of his right shoulder, but he kept turning despite the pain radiating through his body.

His roundhouse kick took his assailant high, in the face, driving him to the ground. Ricco was on him instantly, reaching to drag him up before he realized there were several men surrounding his brother. Nicoletta burst from the house as he rejected the idea of keeping his attacker alive. He snapped the neck of the downed man. He couldn't afford to have someone coming at his back.

He heard Vittorio grunt and saw the flash of a knife. Nicoletta jumped into the air and caught the knife wielder by the arm and yanked him back and away from his brother. She landed on her butt, and immediately one of the men surrounding Vittorio turned, a gun in his hand.

"Move," Ricco ordered the teen as he rushed the gunman, keeping his body between the gun and Nicoletta. At the last moment, before the man fired, he hit the ground, sliding along the shadows there with impressive speed. He didn't even register the wrenching on his body. His adrenaline had kicked in and he was fully focused on disposing of the gunman.

He took the man down with a scissor technique, rolling and toppling him hard without warning. At the same time, he remained wholly committed to securing the weapon first. The man hadn't aimed at Vittorio or him. He had gone after Nicoletta. He yanked the gun from the man's hand, continuing the roll, putting him on top. Turning, Ricco fired at the knife wielder as the man stalked Nicoletta. The attacker seemed to fall in slow motion. Ricco couldn't believe he missed, he'd fired at the heart and he was a marksman, but he squeezed the trigger again, not wanting to take any chances with Nicoletta's life.

A flash of movement told him he had to keep moving, but it was already too late, the kick taking him on the side of the head, right where he'd been injured a few months earlier. His stomach rolled and bile filled his mouth, his vision blurring, but he managed to fire directly into the man's gut as his assailant tried to plunge a knife into the back of his skull.

The man staggered back just as Nicoletta screamed a warning. Lucia and Amo both ran outside toward the group of men surrounding Vittorio, who was on the ground. After the initial grunt of pain, his brother hadn't made a single sound. Three of the attackers turned toward Lucia and Amo. The three held knives and, strangely, rope.

Ricco rolled away from the man he was on, twisting his head to break the neck as he did so. He had to get to his feet. The kick in the head made him sick and dizzy. He realized he couldn't make it up fast enough so he slid through the shadows on his ass toward Vittorio. Ricco could see four others working his brother over, kicking, punching and stabbing down at him with knives.

As he came out of the tube at Vittorio's feet, he swept his leg out to take down the four standing over Vittorio. He smelled blood, and to his horror, his brother had an intricately tied rope around his throat and multiple stab wounds on his body. The rage, always present since that day he'd walked into a slaughter, erupted. That dark presence always threatening to swallow him whole—did.

Physically he was a wreck, but his will was made of iron. He covered Vittorio's body as he took the knife from one man in a blue coat, who stabbed down at his brother's leg, and shoved the blade through the man's throat. Ricco took a hard kick to the gut, but moved into it, rather than away, catching the man's boot, rolling and breaking the man's leg. The crack was loud and the man shrieked. The demon that was Ricco stabbed him twice in the heart, both times twisting the blade as he dragged it out.

Nicoletta screamed again and threw herself in front of Lucia and Amo, arms stretched out wide to protect her foster parents from the bullets she was certain would come. Lucia's eyes widened and she gripped Amo hard as Mariko emerged from the shadows, flowing like water, a beautiful, deadly storm, sweeping past the three men aiming weapons at Nicoletta and her family. As she moved past them, she stuck one through the heart with a long hairpin. The second one she sliced across his throat, under his arms and over his thigh. The last one she caught around the neck and wrenched hard. The three men were down in seconds.

Lucia and Amo covered their mouths. Nicoletta spun around and jumped on the back of a man climbing to his feet. He had rolled out of Ricco's reach and was searching the ground for the gun he'd dropped.

"Call Stefano!" Nicoletta yelled to Lucia. "Call him now, and an ambulance. Hurry, Lucia."

The attacker slammed himself backward into one of the trees on the Fausti property in an effort to dislodge the teen. She sank her teeth into his neck and bit him, all the while pulling his hair with both hands. Her legs stayed wrapped around his waist, ankles locked at his belt buckle.

Amo ran forward and hit the man with his fist twice, breaking his nose and knocking out teeth as the attacker began to pound his fist into Nicoletta's leg. Lucia whirled around and ran for the house, rushing to get her cell phone.

The man spat blood at Amo and head-butted him. Amo fell like stone to the ground and lay still. Nicoletta screamed her fury again, and then Mariko was there, gliding by them gracefully, her dagger slicing through arteries before she turned to go to Ricco's aid. The way she moved was like the wind, one moment gentle and calm, the next a whirling storm of a tornado.

Ricco managed to get to his feet, sparing one more glance at Vittorio. His brother was covered in blood, his face ashen, his eyes wide with shock, but he held on, trying to warn Ricco of the danger behind him. He stayed absolutely still, the rope tightening around his neck with every tiny pull. Ricco knew already that there was another assailant behind him, but the man in front of him had a gun, and that was the most pressing. No one was going to shoot Vittorio or Nicoletta, not if he could help it. Now he had the added complication of Lucia and Amo.

He was on the gunman, using the wrenching shadow to slide past and behind the man. He chopped at the wrist with the edge of his hand and then grasped the head with both hands and broke the neck. Any moment he had expected a bullet to hit him, but when he turned, Mariko had taken the last man down to the ground with a superb kick that nearly took his head off. He dropped like a stone and she was on him, dispatching him in the way riders dispensed justice.

Ricco dropped to his knees beside his brother. He recognized every knot used, and they were intricate. *Hojojutsu*, the ancient form of tying prisoners. It was an art form, beautiful but deadly. He caught up one of their knives and cut through the ropes just as Stefano burst from a shadow tube followed by Emmanuelle, Taviano and Giovanni.

Mariko crouched down beside Vittorio to examine the numerous wounds. "Most of these cuts on his legs are very shallow, designed to hurt as much as possible without killing him. A couple of the cuts are very deep. They did more damage to him with the rope and the kicks and beatings. He needs to get to the hospital immediately."

Vittorio stirred as if he might protest, but Stefano dropped down beside him, running his hands over his brother even as his formidable gaze was on Mariko. "You're a shadow rider."

She nodded. "But my explanation belongs to Ricco. He's also injured and needs medical attention."

In the distance they could hear sirens.

Ricco glared at her. "I'm fine. Concentrate on saving my brother. Emme, get over here. You're better at this than any of the rest of us. I can't move. I'm plugging up the deepest hole. Get him to breathe properly."

"Let me see," Mariko said gently.

Terrified of letting go of his brother, Ricco shook his head. "Get him breathing right." Vittorio's lungs didn't appear to be working properly.

"They broke his ribs," Mariko said patiently. "His lung has collapsed."

Ricco closed his eyes and shook his head. He'd been late again. For the second time, and someone else had paid the price.

"Ricco, I need a report," Stefano said. "The police will be here any moment. Let the others take care of Vittorio. He isn't going to die. He's too tough for that. And he's given me his word. Haven't you, Vittorio." Stefano pinned his younger brother with a father's demanding gaze. "You. Will. *Not*. Die."

Vittorio's eyes clung to Stefano's. He nodded slightly, but didn't attempt to speak, every ragged breath a struggle. Stefano took Ricco's arm and tugged him back away from their fallen brother. "I need to know what happened."

Ricco allowed Mariko to slide her hands into the deepest stab wound to apply pressure until the medics got there. He tried to rise, but his legs were pure rubber. There wasn't a place on his body that didn't hurt, but most importantly, his head was pounding and his vision had gone back to blurred.

Giovanni slipped his arm around him and helped him up. The brothers closed ranks around Vittorio and the women.

Taviano aided Amo in his struggle to stand. Nicoletta hurried to help. Taviano cut her off with a smooth step, nodding to Lucia. "Take him inside and have him lie down. I'll send one of the paramedics in to him." He caught Nicoletta's arm. "We need you out here."

She nodded, her features a mask of worry as she anxiously watched Lucia help Amo into the house. When she turned back, Taviano's gentleness was gone. He gripped her arm and tugged her into the circle of his family, his fingers taking possession of her chin to turn her face, examining the bruising. "You're limping." It was an accusation.

Suddenly she had the attention of all the Ferraros. Anyone would find that uncomfortable, but a teenage girl especially. They knew her past. They knew she'd been raped repeatedly by her step-uncles and that the head of the bloodiest gang in New York had claimed her for his own. They were the only ones who knew, and Nicoletta had a difficult time in their presence.

"One of them pounded the hell out of her leg," Ricco said. "If it wasn't for Mariko, she'd be dead, along with Amo and Lucia. She ran in front of a gun, arms spread wide to keep the Faustis from being shot. She also jumped on the back of one of them to keep Vittorio and me alive." There was admiration in his voice.

Taviano touched her face in several places. "What the hell were you thinking?"

She jerked her head away. "I was thinking I didn't want any of them to die."

"Taviano, we'll discuss all this with her later," Stefano said. "I want a report, Ricco. You look like hell. Do you need to sit down?"

He did. He'd been surreptitiously looking around for a bench to sprawl out on, but now, with his brother's question, he felt he couldn't. "I was running late." He might as well confess right now. "I didn't want Vittorio to have to wait for me so I took the shadows." He didn't look at Stefano as he said so, but he heard his older brother swear under his breath. "I won't lie, it hurt like a bitch, so I was a little disoriented coming out of the tube. I didn't feel anyone there until I was stepping out. I took a bat across my shoulder and it was on."

"They were waiting for you? At the entrance to the tube? In front of a shadow?"

Stefano turned his cool, penetrating stare onto Nicoletta. "Did you see them attack Vittorio?"

She nodded. "I was climbing out my window and he stepped out of the shadows. I hadn't seen him. Suddenly all these men surrounded him, kicking, punching, beating him with a bat. I started to come all the way out, but he yelled at me to get inside. I obeyed until Ricco got there. It was only a few moments, but I thought they'd kill Vittorio and it would be my fault." Tears welled up but she turned her head away from them, embarrassed to be caught crying.

Giovanni stepped closer to her. Protective. "You did good, kid. Great."

The ambulance arrived, and the next couple of hours were a blur. Vittorio was raced to the hospital. Ricco lied and said Mariko and he had been together all along with Vittorio, watching the house because they all feared Nicoletta hadn't quite settled. Vinci was once again there and refused to allow Nicoletta to be questioned more than absolutely necessary. She went to the hospital with Amo and Lucia. Stefano sent two bodyguards with them. The doctors— and Stefano—insisted Ricco have a CT scan because of the blow to his head. He reluctantly agreed, mainly because Stefano wouldn't budge. Fortunately, aside from a whopping headache and blurred vision, he didn't have any significant damage that they could see other than the concussion he already knew he had. Ricco insisted Mariko could watch him at home.

Emilio and Enzo drove Ricco and Mariko back to the house with orders to stay no matter what Ricco said. No one, not even the little rebel Emmanuelle, defied Stefano when he was in such a mood. Ricco didn't feel defiant in the least. If Stefano wanted to send an army to defend him, he wouldn't argue. He wasn't up to defending himself let alone anyone else. His head hurt like a son of a bitch and every muscle in his body was screaming at him.

"Did Stefano say he had guards on Vittorio?" Mariko asked anxiously.

"Stefano will guard Vittorio. Taviano will be with him, and Emmanuelle and Giovanni will guard Nicoletta, Lucia and Amo," Ricco assured as he closed the front door to his home and leaned against it. "They weren't riders attacking us, but they knew to stand just outside the shadows." He made it a statement.

No one outside their family knew about the riders other than other riders and their families. There were very few of them in the world. Mariko stood in front of him, turned away from him, her head bowed, that sweet, vulnerable nape of her neck inviting his touch. He'd have done it, too, the craving was that strong, but he hurt too much to extend his arm.

"Were they targeting Nicoletta or me, Mariko?" He waited patiently for her answer, even though the room was spinning and it felt as if spikes were being driven through his head one slow beat at a time.

Several seconds went by before she slowly raised her head and looked at him over her shoulder. "You, Ricco. I have something to show you." She pulled a paper folded into a small square from inside the pocket of the pin-striped suit she wore, indicating to everyone in their world that she was a rider.

His eyes on her face, he took the paper from her, unfolded it while still looking at her and then dropped his gaze to read the contents. The message was typed in a bold font: **Kill Ricco Ferraro, a rider in the States, or your brother Ryuu dies. You have three weeks to complete this task.**

"You haven't killed me." He made that a statement as well. There was the faintest humor in his voice, because, after all, it was pretty evident she hadn't. He was standing there. He'd known all along she was a rider and probably there to kill him, but not for the reasons he first thought. Still, he was just a little hurt and more than worried that she'd slip through his fingers.

"I am a shadow rider. I can't kill unless it is in the defense of my life, the lives of those unable to defend themselves or when I bring justice to those escaping the law. Killing you would go against everything I hold sacred. The very code my life is built on. You're too good a man. I can't trade one life for another."

He almost sagged with relief, and the part where she thought him a good man felt great, but then he realized he was sagging because he almost went down. Alarm spread across her delicate features. She stepped forward and circled his waist with her arm, fitting under his shoulder. He didn't pretend he was all right, because frankly, he was going to fall on his face if he didn't let her help him.

"You should have stayed in the hospital, Ricco," she murmured, placing one foot carefully in front of the other, leading him toward the master bedroom. "I can call Emilio and ask him to bring the car around."

"Not going to happen," he said. "It's just a fucking headache. The scan said I was fine. I still get the headaches and once in a while blurred vision. One of those bastards kicked me in the head." So much for impressing her. She'd had to come to his rescue. "Did I thank you for saving me tonight? For saving Nicoletta?"

"I don't need thanks." She sat him on the edge of his bed and bent to untie his shoelaces. "Who *is* Nicoletta? Where does she fit in?" She tugged his shoes off. "Get out of the jacket and shirt."

"Don't think you're going to get out of the contract you signed with me just because you're a shadow rider," he said decisively, pouring his bossy tone into his voice. He shrugged out of the jacket, flung his tie onto a chair and began to unbutton the shirt. "After we find your brother, I'll expect your full attention." He tossed the shirt aside and lay back, trying not to wince as his shoulder and back encountered the mattress.

"We? You're willing to help me find Ryuu?"

"You're mine, Mariko. The moment you said yes and signed that contract, you became mine. No one threatens you or your family." He closed his eyes. "We'll find him. My family specializes in that sort of thing."

"Roll over. I have to see your back. You're already black and blue around your ribs. Are you certain they aren't fractured?"

With a groan, he complied, turning onto his belly, making himself completely vulnerable to her. If she wanted to kill him, now was the perfect opportunity. Right at that moment, he wouldn't have cared.

"I took a couple of hits," he admitted. "But nothing's broken. My head's the worst." He didn't know why he admitted that to her. He never would have told Stefano or his other brothers. Maybe Emme, but she would probably have ratted him out to the others.

Mariko's hands were on his shoulders, light, barely there, a whisper of movement across his back, almost as though she brushed away the pain. There was no white heat, nothing to indicate she had any healing powers, but something eased in him—whether it was pain or just happiness that she didn't take advantage and kill him, he didn't know.

"You haven't said anything about my coming here to kill you."

"I suspected you were a rider and you were here for that purpose. I informed my family just in case you or other riders were after them as well. But I gave you several opportunities and you didn't take them." He turned his head to look at her over his shoulder. "You let me tie you up. You're a shadow rider. Control is everything. I can't imagine how difficult that was for you." He didn't try to keep the admiration from his voice. To him, that moment had been such a humbling gift. He would treasure her surrender for his entire life.

"I wouldn't allow any other to do such a thing, but for some reason I don't understand, I trust you. I don't expect to live through this, so I wanted, before my death, to experience my culture. Your art. And it was beautiful." The admission was made in a low tone.

He rolled over, suppressing a groan as his head felt like it had exploded. "Why do you think you aren't going to live through this?"

Her hands went to his bare chest, fingers following the long path of the blade that had left three distinct scars. "He has to kill me. Whoever has my brother would have no choice. I'm a rider. He knows I'm one, or why choose me?

My home is in Japan. You're here. Still, he chose me. He would always be looking over his shoulder if he didn't kill me."

"And you have no idea who kidnapped your brother?"

She shook her head. "My brother is a genius." There was pride in her voice. "A software company in the United States offered him a job and to pay his way here and even help him find a place to live. He left very excited. I drove him to the airport myself. I received this message the next day."

"Was it mailed to you?" He couldn't sit up. His head was pounding beyond belief. Every movement sent more bile churning in his gut.

He wanted this woman more than he ever thought possible. Not just with his body, and there was that—an urgent, constant demand, no matter the circumstances—but with everything in him. He loved the way she moved. He could watch her all day. He found himself listening for her soft, musical voice. He'd just met her, yet he thought more about her, day and night, than he'd ever thought about the many women he'd been with throughout his lifetime.

Ricco realized he was in danger of falling hard for a woman capable of killing him. He especially loved that about her. She was soft inside, soft outside, but he knew she had a backbone of pure steel. She moved like the wind, or water flowing over rocks, a gentle breeze moving so quietly and softly most people might not even notice her, not until it was far too late.

"You're beautiful." He made it a statement because it was true.

She frowned, and he found that adorable. "Thank you. I want you to remember that you're suffering from a very severe head injury."

He couldn't help himself, he laughed. It hurt like hell, but amusement welled up out of nowhere, shocking him because it was genuine. He laughed with his family, but he never felt it.

"Why are you laughing at me?"

"Because you're adorable. I'm very glad I've tied you to me for the next six months. That gives me time to convince you to stay with me."

She sighed. "Ricco, you really have to go to the hospital. I can tell that you have a concussion."

"How is that?" It was true. He couldn't deny it. He knew he had a concussion. The doctor had said so. His head wouldn't stop pounding and if he didn't move his head, he could focus, otherwise his vision was impaired.

"Your way of thinking is really messed up right now and not at all like your normal way of thinking. You don't want a woman in your life for more than a night or two. It's a way of life for you, changing women the way other men change their shirts."

He winced because everything she said was the truth. Until now. Until she'd come into his life and turned it upside down. Until he knew the woman coming to kill him had to belong to him. He was born for her. To love her. To cherish her. To spend his life shielding her from men like the one who had taken her brother.

"Stefano told me my idiot way of living would come back to bite me." He hissed the last few words through clenched teeth. His head hurt like a son of a bitch. "You asked about Nicoletta." Changing the subject was the only safe path.

"You and Vittorio were willing to die to save her. That was twice that you fought for her. Who is she?"

"She's a woman capable of producing riders. That's rare, as you well know."

She shrugged. "None of the riders I grew up with would have done that for me."

"That isn't true. They might not have shown any interest, but I can guarantee, they'll be very upset that I have you here with me." He waited for her to protest, but when she remained silent, he continued, this time musing aloud. "If it was another rider who took your brother, they would have come after me themselves. Why involve you? Or take the risk of kidnapping your brother? I saw you out there tonight.

You're as good as a rider gets. Of course, coming from the Tanaka lineage, you would be."

Her head snapped up, her eyes moving over his face, probing for the truth. For the distinctive sound of a lie. "A Tanaka? Why would you think such a thing? That lineage is revered in my country. Everyone knows the tragedy."

"Do they? Tell me."

"Daiki Tanaka married a woman from another country and had one child, a girl, Akiko. She was on her way to being as great a rider as her father when she died in a car accident with her father and grandmother. Four other riders were killed as well. The accident nearly wiped out all the shadow riders in Tokyo. Everyone knows the story."

Every word she said made that horrible hole inside him bigger. It was filled with the helpless rage of a fourteen-year-old boy.

"You don't have it quite right, Mariko," he said softly. He forced himself into a sitting position and indicated she sit close. He was surprised when she obeyed him. His head protested the movement, but he ignored the crashing pain. This was far too important. She could very well leave him when she heard what he had to say, but he was through hiding the truth.

"I was there, Mariko, so I know the truth of what happened. All of it. I was training under Daiki Tanaka, Isamu Yamamoto, Dai Saito and Mikio Ito, the four top riders who also made up the council in Tokyo. At that time, Nao Yamamoto, son of Isamu, headed up a small-time gang. Nao was the leader and a bully. He despised the riders coming in from other countries, but more, he despised any female rider and considered them inferior to him and the other males." He fell silent, allowing the memory of that terrible night to sweep over him.

Mariko didn't say a word but remained quiet, not asking a single question or hurrying him. Her gaze didn't once leave his face.

"Akiko defeated Nao in a tournament. He was weakened

because I had beaten the holy hell out of him earlier that day. He and three of his closest friends—Eiji and Hachiro Saito, sons of Dai Saito, and Kenta Ito—had jumped me earlier because I'd gone with two others to the council and warned them of Nao's behavior. Then my times beat theirs in the trials. I kicked their asses. Nao's father was furious with him, first that I had beat the crap out of him, but mostly because Akiko, a lowly female, bested him in the tournament in front of everyone. The judges had no choice but to call the win for her."

Mariko didn't take her eyes from his face. She almost didn't blink she was holding herself so still.

Ricco pressed his fingers to his eyes and shook his head. "I was fourteen. That's not much of an excuse. It isn't an excuse. I knew Nao would hit back at Akiko. I heard him boasting about using the shadows to hurt his enemies. It was forbidden, of course, but two of the riders had gone with me to the council to tell them of our suspicions earlier and they dismissed what we told them."

Her thigh slid along his as she drew her legs up and put her chin on top of her knees, her face turned toward him, eyes never leaving his face.

"I had a *hojojutsu* class that evening . . . " He trailed off again. Little did he know it would be his ropes that eventually saved him. His artistry. He sighed. This wasn't about him. Mariko needed to know she had a past. She was part of a legendary family, a family respected and held in the highest regard by all riders around the world.

"I got lost," he said, telling her his greatest shame. "In the tunnels. When I returned to my room, I realized all four of them were gone and I just knew they were going to attack Akiko. I went after them and I got turned around."

The throbbing in his head took a backseat to the knot twisting in his gut. "When I arrived at the Tanaka home, the boys had already done their worst. Chiharu, Akiko's grandmother, was dead, her body on the floor just outside of her room. Nao lay in wait for her and murdered her as she rushed to the aid of her grandchildren."

CHAPTER EIGHT

The scent of blood hit him hard. It smelled like a slaughterhouse. He knew before he even emerged from the shadow tube that he was far too late. He nearly fell over the body of Akiko's grandmother. Chiharu. She'd been a strict, unsmiling woman, but she'd also been the first legendary female shadow rider. Chiharu was the reason the other girls were given the chance to prove themselves.

She lay crumbled on the floor, looking small. Blood covered her like a bright red blanket. A sword had nearly severed her body in half. Worse, after the initial slice, she had clearly still been alive when another slice had been made up the front of her, spilling her insides onto the floor deliberately.

At fourteen, he'd never seen anything like it in his life. He was still sensitive, an artist, not a killer. Bile had risen, choking him. He heard laughter, and just around the screen, several feet from Chiharu, her two female servants were being hacked to pieces by Eiji and Hachiro. The insanity of the killings made Ricco pause for just a moment, not believing what his eyes were seeing. He'd trained with these boys. They weren't friends, and he knew they were bullies, but he'd never considered they might be murderers.

For the first time, he realized just what he was born for—what was expected of him—and it was brutal and ugly.

He heard Akiko scream and then Nao telling her he'd killed her grandmother and would kill her, and then her brother and sister. He'd wipe out the entire Tanaka family. But first, she would be dishonored. Nao had raped her while Kenta danced around them covered in her father's blood.

The memories were all there in Ricco's head, pouring through the cracks in the walls he'd erected to keep himself from letting them get too close. He'd been carrying the burden of that night alone for so long, protecting his family from the threat hanging over their heads until he was physically, emotionally and mentally used up.

"The Tanaka family only had one child. Akiko," Mariko insisted, her voice shaking. "There were no other children."

Ricco realized she was trembling. He reached out and took her hand, holding it tight, pressed against his chest over his heart. "There were three children, Mariko—two girls and one boy. Akiko was ten years older than her next sibling. Her sister. You, Mariko. You were three at the time of the murders."

She shook her head, blinking back tears. He couldn't imagine what her life had been like once her family was killed. With the way he'd been treated, he knew it couldn't have been good.

"Two servants lay just to the right of Chiharu, cut down by Eiji and Hachiro Saito."

Mariko made a sound of distress. He pulled her closer, sheltering her against his body.

"Osamu hates me with every breath she draws. If what you say is true, I understand so much more," she whispered. She shook her head. "It can't be true. The Tanaka family is a legend. They are spoken of with love and respect."

"What I say is true. I have no reason to lie to you. On the contrary. I don't come off in the best of lights. I came out of the shadows just as Eiji cut down the second servant. The two brothers came at me. I had no choice but to defend myself. I killed them both."

"Are you saying that Eiji and Hachiro murdered the Tanaka family?"

He pulled her into his arms and held her. She was shaken.

Who wouldn't be? The official findings of the Tanaka family deaths were very different. She'd grown up believing exactly what the council members wanted her to believe. Those members were the fathers of the boys involved in the murders.

"They helped. Nao was the leader and he planned the entire thing. Eiji and Hachiro killed the servants and Kenta Ito murdered Daiki Tanaka, your father."

"How could mere boys defeat Daiki Tanaka?" she asked, but he could see she was beginning to believe everything he said.

"Daiki could no longer ride the shadows, and he'd stopped training. He had married an American, a rope model, your mother. When she left him, their shadows were torn apart and he could no longer ride. She couldn't remember she had a family. That's the price we pay as riders. We can't lightly go into a marriage. He wasn't expecting such an attack on his household. He heard Akiko, his beloved daughter, scream and he rushed to save her, just as they knew he would. Kenta lay in wait for him and cut him to pieces with a sword. Nao had already killed Chiharu Tanaka and then he attacked Akiko."

Ricco had heard Akiko's screams, the pain and agony in her voice, while he fought off Eiji and Hachiro. He'd managed to kill Eiji first, sliding in around behind him and breaking his neck. Hachiro had been so shocked that the tip of his sword had tilted toward the ground for that one split second. Ricco had struck hard, slamming the flat of his hand on top of Hachiro's sword hand, going in with three hard chops to the throat.

Hachiro staggered back and lost his footing and then slipped in all the blood on the floor. He went down hard, hitting his head against the ornate woodwork. That, Ricco was certain, was what saved his life. As he went after the other boy, Akiko's screams, more urgent than ever now, hurt his ears, his foot slipped in the blood and left a long trail as he nearly impaled himself on Hachiro's sword. The blade sliced across him, a deep, nasty wound that went across his entire chest.

Hachiro gasped and sliced a second time, this time dragging the tip across Ricco's chest a second and third time before Ricco could catch his wrist, wrench the sword to one side and slam it back with as much of his body weight as possible. Hachiro's eyes went wide and his mouth opened in a silent scream of protest. Of terror. Ricco couldn't look away, and to this day, he woke up staring into those eyes.

The sword had nearly sliced Hachiro in two, the sharp blade cutting through flesh and bone far easier than Ricco had expected. Ricco was swimming in blood. He was certain he'd never get it off his skin. Sometimes, at night, when he woke in a sweat, he'd get in the shower and scrub until he was bleeding. He still felt the thick substance coating his skin.

He cleared his throat and looked down at her. This was the moment when she would understand. When she would condemn him for being late. "Akiko had put her brother and sister into a closet in an effort to save them."

Ricco watched Mariko closely as he told her what her sister had done. Mariko had vaguely remembered being in that closet. With his explanation, she was remembering far more. He saw that the nightmares haunting her were beginning to make sense. She probably remembered bits and pieces of that night, all jumbled together and very horrifying. He hated being the one to tell her what had really happened to her family. Mostly he was ashamed that he hadn't gotten there in time to save them.

"Akiko was very brave. She turned to fight Nao, but he was carrying a sword. Cheating. She'd defeated him in the trials and he wasn't going to take a chance that she could fight him off. He was savage, cutting her up, and then he taunted her, told her he was going to violate her—rape her—and then kill you and your little brother. She screamed for help but I was the only one there to hear her cries, and I was fighting Eiji and Hachiro."

It had taken him so long. Seconds, minutes, he didn't know, only that he had arrived too late.

"What happened, Ricco? Don't stop there."

Her voice was so low he barely caught it. He couldn't make the hearing of the death of her family any easier. There was no redemption for him. There would be that moment of realization that he could have prevented her family's murders and then he would lose his chance at having the one woman he could love so much it terrified him.

He couldn't stop himself. He caught her chin and lifted her face up to his, bending his throbbing head almost blindly to capture her mouth with his. He needed this moment to steady himself. To find the strength to give her the exact truth without trying to make himself anything but what he was: a screwup whose mistake had cost lives—the lives of her family. Nothing was harder to admit, because it meant she would be out of his life, and he'd know, as long as he lived, that he'd lost the one woman he could love through his own mistakes.

He kissed her. Gently. Reverently. Holding back the need and desire so urgent he hadn't known need like that existed. He licked at her lips, tasting her sweetness. The promise of paradise. He savored her taste, grateful she didn't pull away. He took his time, coaxing her lips, apart, teasing with his tongue and teeth, with his lips, until she made up her mind.

When her lips parted for him, he took over, elation and passion rising like a dark tide. His hands cupped her face, fingers sliding along the side of her neck, claiming as much of her as he could. He deepened the kiss, finding tenderness when he'd never had such a thing and never knew it was there inside of him all along, waiting for her.

The pounding in his head receded. The rage in his gut subsided. Peace slipped over him. A new hunger rose, something sharp and terrible in its intensity, tapping into a well of passion so deep he was nearly destroyed by it. He'd had his share of women and had treated sex so casually. Now, suddenly, there was nothing casual about the way he felt toward Mariko. Nothing casual about his kisses, or the way he held her.

He poured what he felt into her, hoping she understood the truth of his feelings—that he even had them was a miracle. It was all Mariko. He'd been alone so long, fighting to keep everyone around him safe, believing he had no chance at anything more than just existence, and then she was there. Out of nowhere. The one he knew would be the center of his world.

But he had to tell her the truth about her past. He had no choice. Reluctantly he lifted his head, his thumb brushing a caress over her lips. Her gaze clung to his, a little shocked, dazed and definitely aroused. He hated to see that leave her, knowing she would never be able to look at him in the same way.

"I have to tell you the rest, Mariko. I don't want to, but you have to know. Your family would never have deserted you. They would have been proud of you. You're a Tanaka, of the legendary Tanaka shadow riders and every bit as good as the best they ever had."

She shook her head, but he knew the denial was more automatic than anything else. She was confused, but not utterly rejecting his account.

"You were that little girl in the closet. Nao pulled your little brother out first, threw him and began stomping on him, over and over. You came flying out just as I rushed in. You hit him hard with a perfect flying kick, right in the groin. When you came down you slipped in Akiko's blood nearly at Nao's feet. Do you remember?"

Tears were running down her face and he used his thumb to brush them away, bending to kiss her temples and then her eyes as if that could make it all better. As if that would somehow ease the terrible tragedy of losing her family to murder.

"You were so brave. Kenta was there and he attacked me. He had a sword. I should have kept Hachiro's sword, but I couldn't take all the blood, and I never wanted to hold a sword again." He had since then. He'd trained year after year, but it had turned his stomach. He touched the long scar on his face. "He did this to me while I was trying to get in a position to keep Nao away from you and still get the sword from Kenta."

Mariko nodded several times, her fingers trembling as she pressed them against her lips. "My nightmares," she whispered softly. "I saw these things in a nightmare."

"Because you lived through them," he assured. "Not nightmares, reality, so imprinted on your brain you can never rid yourself of the sights, sounds and smells." It was like that for him the moment he closed his eyes. He could smell the blood. Hear Akiko's screams. The cries of the little boy, and the sound of his bones breaking as Nao stomped on him over and over.

Ricco couldn't get to Nao and the little boy or girl because he was fighting for his life, trying to get past Kenta, who wielded his sword with the beginnings of expertise. Out of the corner of his eye he saw Nao smirk, deliver another kick to the girl and then go back to the boy.

"Nao bragged that Kenta would kill me, but not before I witnessed what Nao planned to do to your brother and you."

She nodded, her entire body shuddering. "He said they would blame you, a devil from another country. I remember that. I remember him saying that." She looked at him with stricken eyes. "It's true then. I couldn't stop him from hurting Ryuu. He kept stomping on him over and over until he broke so many bones that Ryuu grew up twisted." She put a slender hand to her throat, as if she needed to defend herself and that was all she had.

"You tried, Mariko. At three years old, with only one year of training, you tried. I could hear the bones breaking, and then you went after Nao a second time. Kenta turned his head to laugh. He was covered in blood, and as he stepped, his body turned toward you and Nao. His hand slipped on the hilt of the sword. I took advantage and went inside, hitting the sword aside. He'd gotten me in the face already and there was so much blood I had a difficult time seeing."

The pain had been agony, but he set it aside, hearing the cries of the toddler on the floor, so broken, a maddened teenager attacking the boy so viciously. "It was you, Mariko, who saved the day. If you hadn't found the strength and courage to go after Nao a second time, I wouldn't have managed to kill Kenta."

"I jumped on his back," Mariko whispered. "Kicking and hitting him, pulling his hair. I think I even bit him."

Ricco nodded. "I slammed the edge of my hand into Kenta's throat with every bit of strength and adrenaline I had." All the fear. All the rage. All the knowledge that he was a shadow rider and this was what he was born to do. He might have been late, but Nao would *not* have his last two victims.

"I had a pen I'd picked up off the floor and I jammed it into Kenta's eye. A horrible rattling noise emerged from his throat, as if the sound was being squeezed out." He shook his head. "It was a horrible sound. I picked up his sword and hit Kenta in the head and then turned toward Nao. He had you in his lap."

Mariko touched her throat. "He had a knife."

Ricco had to keep going, to get it all out so she would know the details in her dream were real. "In one move, still spinning, I cut through flesh and bone with Kenta's sword. I wasn't trying to cripple him for life. Only to keep him from killing you and your brother."

Nao screamed, the sound high-pitched, mixing with Ryuu's cries until Ricco couldn't tell them apart. He still remembered those desperate sounds every single night. Sometimes they were so loud he sat in his bed, hands over his ears, trying to drown them out. Behind him, Kenta had crumpled in slow motion, his eyes rolling back in his head so only white showed. In front of him, Nao collapsed, falling into Akiko's blood, his arms thrashing as his legs lay useless. Those images were locked in his brain as well, the artist in him seeing the blood as red ribbons, as crimson rivers, as dark wine pooling below the bodies.

"I ran to Ryuu," she whispered. "His body was so crushed and twisted I just held and rocked him. I remember blood getting onto my clothes and hair."

He nodded. Tears were running down her face, just as they had when she was that little white-haired girl. "Ryuu and Nao were still alive." In shock he called the number to bring the council members to the horrific scene. Then his nightmare had really begun. He supposed hers had as well, and she'd been so much younger. He had his family; she had no one.

"Osamu Saito raised us. Ryuu and me. She hated me with every breath she drew and it got worse every year."

Ricco had felt sick with grief and anger over what the council members had done to him. Forcing him to stay in Tokyo, enduring their threats of telling others he'd murdered an entire family if he didn't cooperate. Afraid they would carry out their threats of killing his family if he told anyone what had happened. He'd felt so alone even in the midst of family who loved him.

Now the rage roiling inside him like dark ominous clouds threatened to spill over, fed by what Mariko had gone through. The men had known how Osamu had treated her, but they'd done nothing in order to protect their reputations. He moved again, closer to her, wanting to hold her, offer her comfort. She moved away from him and he froze, everything inside him going still.

"I need to be alone," she said. "This is a lot to take in."

Her body language screamed not to be touched. To be left alone. What could he say to that? She was asking for space. He knew all about that. He also knew she was separating herself from him. She was rejecting him as surely as he'd expected her to. He nodded and watched her leave his bedroom. She walked away from him without once looking back. Not once. He didn't try to stop her. What was there to say? He'd told her the truth. She knew she was a Tanaka and that her family had been brutally murdered and her brother stomped on until his body was deformed. She knew he had been late. He'd gotten lost.

No way was he ever lost now. He kept a map in his head at all times and he rode the shadows tirelessly every new place he visited until he was familiar with every block. Every rural area. That didn't make up for being late; it would never make up for being late due to him not studying hard enough, but it would ensure it wouldn't happen again. Unless . . . He sighed and lay back down on the bed, his head throbbing again in protest of movement. Unless he was late because he was caught up in something else—*someone* else—like Mariko.

He had to help her. No matter how she felt about him, he had to help find her brother. They needed a place to start. The investigators were already on it, and as soon as Vittorio was out of the woods, he'd ask his brothers and Emme to help. He called Stefano to check on his brother's condition. Stefano would be sitting right there, guarding Vittorio and making certain he didn't slip away.

"Stay home tonight, Ricco, and rest," Stefano said when he offered to take a shift watching over his brother.

"I was late," he confessed. "I was busy with Mariko and I didn't relieve Vittorio."

"You were three minutes late, Ricco. You used the shadows to get to him and that made up the time. We've all been three minutes late."

"I'm never late. He was counting on me."

"He told me he noted the time because Nicoletta had twice come to the window and retreated. He was certain she was vacillating between staying and leaving."

If Vittorio was talking, he was doing a lot better than the last time Ricco had seen him as they loaded him into an ambulance.

"It doesn't make sense that they were outside Nicoletta's home. If they're our enemies, why target her?" Ricco had asked himself that question dozens of times.

"That's the million-dollar question, isn't it?" Stefano asked. "They weren't members of the Demons, nor did they have New York accents. I've reached out to our cousins there, and although the gang is actively looking for Nicoletta and the answer to who killed her step-uncles, there was no flurry of activity as if Valdez knew where she was."

No one but Benito Valdez, head of the Demons out of New York, would be looking for Nicoletta. So why were the assailants outside of her home?

"I think at this point we all have to be very careful and vigilant," Stefano added. "Until we know who our enemy is, we can't take chances."

He hesitated for just a moment and Ricco knew what was coming.

"Are you certain Mariko isn't involved?"

"I hear truth the same as you," he assured. "The connection between us is very strong and when our shadows connect, it's unbelievable. There's no way she could hide anything like that from me." He was silent for a brief time. "She's a good fighter, Stefano. Fast. Efficient. She didn't hesitate. She didn't have to give herself away. She had no way of knowing I was on to her, but she followed me there and then jumped right in. I don't know what would have happened without her."

"You would have killed them all, Ricco, because you wouldn't have had a choice," Stefano assured. "This woman. Are you certain of her?"

"I'm certain she's the one for me. I don't know that she'll stay with me."

"Because of your reputation?"

He sighed. Stefano didn't pull his punches. "I wish it were that. I was late that day, Stefano. I hadn't studied hard enough and I got turned around trying to get to the Tanakas' home. I had to tell her. She had to relive the nightmare of her family dying, knowing I didn't get there in time."

Stefano erupted into a long litany of swear words. Ricco remained silent while he assured him in his usual foul way that he wasn't to blame. He'd been fourteen, and the council was going to have to make amends to the Ferraro family and Ricco especially before this was over. He'd already made inquiries about all the men and their families holding council positions. The New York cousins were investigating, as they were spread thin, but Stefano never wanted Ricco to say it was his fault again.

"Murdering little bastards, their families made them into tragic heroes, pretending they died in a car crash. What a load of shit. Their parents were fucking cowards not to tell the truth and to put it on you to stay quiet. Threatening us?"

Stefano was on a roll and clearly angry. Ricco's head pounded more. "I need to rest for a while if you don't need me at the hospital," he interrupted the colorful tirade. Retribution would take place now that Stefano knew what had happened to his younger brother. Ricco didn't envy the present Tokyo council or the international one.

Stefano instantly cut off the rest of his evaluation of the three families involved and told him to get some sleep. Ricco ended the call and closed his eyes. It was already morning and light was pouring through the long bank of windows, revealing the garden in the courtyard. He had loved the gardens in Japan for their beauty and peace. Right now the light only added to the throbbing pain in his head.

"Drapes." He spoke the word and the thick, dark drapes that covered the window began to descend from where they were rolled up near the ceiling above the glass. He had blood on his clothes and needed a shower, but he couldn't find the energy to get up.

He just lay there on his bed, drifting off, trying not to think about Mariko and the fact that he lost her before he ever had her. At least he'd managed to save her life and he knew she was in the world. Not with him, but alive and a damn good rider. She just wasn't ever going to be his, but that was beside the point. She lived. She deserved to be happy, and he could give her that. He could find her brother for her and make certain they were both safe.

He drifted but he didn't fall asleep. The events of his past were far too close. He had tried to close those doors, but when he lay in his bed, they persistently creaked open. He had thought about the council members so many times over the last years. They probably had been good men at one time, but grief and shame wore them down.

They wanted him to fail. Each time he took the tests, *all* the instructors were present. Ricco had been so determined to be fast and strong that he worked out from morning to night, doing every chore required, but doubling his practice time. He defeated every opponent in the trials, and his times in the shadow tubes were significantly faster than anyone else's, but it didn't matter.

The council members berated him, beat him, used canes and continually jerked him from his bed, throwing him on the floor, kicking and punching and telling him he should have been aware of their presence. None of the other trainees reported they'd been awakened from sleep, but it didn't matter. He trained himself to sleep light, to be prepared for any attack, night or day.

They took his phone from him, had eyes on him at all times. When his family called, they were right there to listen in on every word. The threats against his family were continuous. If he talked, they would kill them all—wipe out the Ferraro family, and no one would ever know who did it.

He needed them. His family. Stefano. He had a poet's soul and the grief-stricken fathers were ripping it to shreds. They had interrogated him for days. Asking the same questions over and over. Wanting the answers to be different. They had talked to little Mariko, and she gave the same answers over and over in spite of their directions to answer differently.

A well of rage inside of him began to form and grow deeper and deeper until it all but consumed him. When he knew he couldn't stay quiet and he was about to erupt into a furious frenzy of anger, playing right into their hands, he went to the training room and spent hours beating on the heavy bag until his hands were bloody. The blows shocking his arms, his body, the pain smashing through his knuckles to his hands steadied him. Grounded him.

That was when Master Kin Akahoshi decided to intervene. He was the martial arts instructor as well as the *hojojutsu* instructor. He had seen the treatment of Ricco, as had all the instructors, but none wanted to go against the powerful council—especially after the "car accident" that had killed their children. Everyone knew they were grieving, but no one knew why they had singled out Ricco for the treatment they gave him.

Master Akahoshi came into the training hall to find Ricco pounding the bag, his knuckles, wrapped as they were supposed to be, bloody right through the wraps. He stood there for a long moment, just observing him, and then he stepped in close and ordered him off the bag. Ricco had whipped around, prepared to fight for his right to use the equipment in off hours, but Akahoshi had held up his hand and simply said, "Come with me."

For some reason he never really understood, he followed the instructor to his home where his private training hall was located. Ricco had known he was the best in the class at *hojojutsu*. He was fascinated with the art and the knots. The tying. The way they looked on his opponent. He began to learn more and more intricate knots and how to lay them perfectly against skin. Immediately he had excelled in his anatomy class, because he needed to learn how to lay the ropes without hurting—or to cause the greatest discomfort possible.

They never talked about the three council members or why they were so hard on him, but his going to Akahoshi's home and being accepted there sent a message to the three men that someone, at least, would hold them accountable. The beatings weren't stopped, but they were fewer. In the meantime, Ricco continued learning the art of Shibari.

Each time he picked up a bundle of ropes, he felt completely grounded. When he tied, he was so utterly absorbed in his art, the anger and fear drained away, leaving him relaxed and at peace. It was the only time he felt that way.

Akahoshi had moved to the United States, specifically Chicago, following three other family members. He had contacted Ricco to see if he wanted to continue with his instructions and of course Ricco had. Now the rope was a part of him and he exceeded his master in training. Still, he returned to compare knots, to talk to the man he credited with saving his life. The council might have driven him to suicide had it not been for Akahoshi.

He'd been conditioned to believe the murders were his fault for being late, for getting turned around. The lives of his family depended on his silence and his skills. He continued to train daily, and at night he haunted the homes of his brothers and sister in order to protect them. He'd developed a thin razor-like strip to attach to the bottom of the door, blocking out all shadows, so no rider could slide through and surprise his family in their sleep. It was easy enough and fast to remove with a single touch, making it possible for them to escape if necessary via the doors.

Sighing, he sat up. When he was like this, restless and unable to sleep, he often visited Akahoshi. His former master always had rope models available to work with and he could lose himself that way. He didn't want to bring trouble to Akahoshi's door, suspecting that because he took Ricco's side and protected him all those years ago, the council members had made it difficult for the instructor to remain in Tokyo.

He could insist that Mariko join him in the studio. He was not 100 percent yet when it came to working out, and his head was still giving him trouble, but although he was paying her, he would never ask her to join him. Not when he was so edgy and moody. His sister Emmanuelle always called this side of him his "dark, scary and very dangerous." No one wanted to be around him when he was like that. If he went to Akahoshi, he usually was brutal in his ties, laying rope in the more traditional punishing knots.

He would never take a chance of accidentally hurting one of the female rope models, let alone Mariko. She needed care. It wasn't that she was fragile, far from it, but she'd obviously never known kindness. She still wasn't opening up to him and he'd practically shoved his entire history down her throat.

He groaned as he sat up, pushing both hands through his hair. The room spun for a moment and then righted itself, letting him know he was a mess. Of course, he'd have to be at his worst when he met Mariko. He prided himself on his abilities, and already she'd had to save the day.

He stripped, tossing his clothes in the vicinity of the hamper. He had bad habits from living alone so long. Emmanuelle told him he was a slob every chance she got—although he knew he wasn't. He just never picked up his dirty clothes until it came time to wash them—something he'd have to get over if he could ever convince Mariko to forgive him and to take a chance on him.

He caught a glimpse of himself in the mirror before he stepped into the double shower. His chest was scarred and he touched one of the long streaks the tip of the sword had left behind in his flesh. His shame was carved into his skin for everyone to see. The number-one question always asked by any woman he was with was how he got those distinctive scars. He made up outrageous stories, turning the moment to laughter when that well of rage always opened up inside of him at the question.

He'd been unarmed and all four boys had extremely sharp swords. The scars should have been badges of courage, but they represented failure to him. He stepped under the pouring hot water and let it ease the pain in his tight muscles. What he wouldn't give for a decent massage. He never could relax enough to get one. He was too busy looking over his shoulder. Even in the shower he felt vulnerable and always faced out toward the room. It was an insane way to live, but he'd been doing it for so many years, he wasn't certain he could live any other way.

He rinsed off the soap and shampooed his hair. It was getting too long. He rarely bothered to have it cut by a professional. He just had Emme chop it off for him. It grew thick and wild, and when it annoyed him, he handed her the scissors. She always shook her head, but she did as he asked and cut it for him.

He pulled on loose-fitting pants, tightened the drawstring, pulled on a tight T-shirt and walked barefoot down the hall into the training room. The moment he set foot inside, he allowed himself to acknowledge his state of mind. This edginess wasn't all about the memories so close, although that was a good part of it. He had lost her—Mariko. And what kind of fate had dictated that the little girl he'd saved would be sent to kill him and he'd fall like a ton of bricks for her.

He pulled on thin leather workout gloves while he contemplated the irony of his fate. He wasn't a man who felt sorry for himself. He got angry, but he didn't wallow in misery. He lived his life in the fast lane to escape the ever-present rage and fear that his family would become a target. He had considered returning to Tokyo and getting rid of the threat, but he knew that would bring disgrace to his family.

Stefano had ways of dealing with threats, and more than once, especially lately, Ricco had contemplated telling him the entire mess. He wasn't all that sorry that Mariko had provided him with the catalyst to do so.

He settled into a rhythm, pounding the bag, moving around it while he jabbed and punched. The sound of his fists hitting the heavy bag along with the jolt of pain as his knuckles slammed over and over into the bag. After a while his thoughts faded from his mind, allowing the craziness to disappear for a short while. He ignored his body's protest. Sometimes the pain in his body was worth the way his mind quieted.

CHAPTER NINE

Mariko cried through her shower and the entire time she was in the soaking tub. The water was cold by the time she could stem the torrent of emotion pouring out of her. She cried for the little three-year-old girl who was told she'd gotten into a car, put it in gear and run over her baby brother. She cried for her brother who went back and forth, along with her, believing and then not believing. She cried for her lost family. She cried to know she wasn't an abandoned orphan no one wanted but a Tanaka, of the legendary riders. Mostly she cried for the fourteen-year-old boy who had killed three boys and permanently paralyzed another to save her, and had been made to suffer a lifetime for his courageous actions.

She understood Osamu's madness just a little better. Her sons had been murderers. They were responsible for several deaths and contributed to the loss of the Tanaka riders. No one would want the stigma and shame of that hanging over them. Osamu and her husband, Dai, were both proud people. The thought that Ricco could at any moment change their lives would eat away at both of them.

Osamu went back and forth between loving Ryuu and hating him. She would, by turns, treat him as the son she had lost and then as the reminder of that loss. She kept him off-balance and always seeking love from her. Mariko she punished for being alive when her sons were not. She would have a hatred for Ricco like no other. He had killed her sons, regardless of the circumstances.

Over the years, Dai and Osamu had grown apart, as her madness had progressed. Dai had retreated, leaving for long periods of time to his apartment in the country, but he always came back. Could Osamu have orchestrated the attempt on Ricco's life? The answer was yes. Certainly. She would have seen justice in using Mariko to kill him. That would explain the note delivered to her room rather than through the mail. But would she involve Ryuu? Risk his life by letting her accomplices kidnap him?

Mariko shivered as she wrapped a towel around her. Ryuu wouldn't conspire against his sister. She was certain of that. He might have swung back and forth between following Osamu's example of ridiculing her and being affectionate, but he would never agree to force her to kill another human being. Ryuu might try to do so himself for Osamu, but he wouldn't use Mariko.

She let her hair down, pulling out the pins so that it tumbled to her shoulders. She should try to sleep, but she wasn't tired. She could hear the echo of a fast-paced rhythm, thuds hitting repeatedly like the beat of a drum. She knew that sound. She knew Ricco must be hitting the heavy bag in the training room. She winced, thinking about the amount of time she'd been noting the noise—certainly the entire time she'd been in the soaking tub. Maybe longer. It was a punishing rhythm, and he hadn't let up for a moment.

She went to the cedar drawers where lingerie had been placed. A red lacy bra and matching panties lay on top. She smoothed her hand over them. She'd always worn plain underwear. Nothing to make her think she was a woman—especially a sexy one. Ricco made her feel beautiful and sensual every time he looked at her. He had a way of focusing on her that made her feel as if she were the only woman he saw. She knew that wasn't true, because she read the tabloids, but still, for the first time in her life, she felt beautiful. More, she felt as if Ricco Ferraro saw only her.

She pulled on the bra and panties, sliding them over her pale skin—skin she'd always hated. Now it felt warm and soft. Sensual. Because she was thinking of him. She hadn't known life could be different. At home, there was always back-breaking, unappreciated work that was never ending. She loved training, but she couldn't train forever. Osamu was always waiting to hand her a list of chores. Even coming off missions, she wouldn't have so much as a night's sleep.

She looked around the room. Comfortable. Beautiful. Spacious. She'd never had anything like that room. Her own bathroom. Drawers and a closet filled with clothes. She pulled a silk kimono from the closet. Blossoming cherry trees ran up the material in soft pinks and browns. It was gorgeous. She wrapped herself up in the long robe and ran her hands down it. The silk felt sensual against her skin, and glancing at herself in the mirror, she was shocked at how she looked.

She studied the makeup in the light-up vanity. She knew enough to make her eyes smolder, but she had never used a red lipstick. Osamu would have been furious and called her all kinds of names. She could barely believe she was so daring as to choose the ruby red. She nearly wiped it off, but then she squared her shoulders.

Ricco Ferraro was a good man. A worthy man. By every account he was considered one of the best shadow riders. If she had a small amount of time left, she wanted it to be spent with him. She wanted to feel like a beautiful woman. She had gone over and over where her brother could possibly be, but she had no clues. No information. Nowhere to start. She could only hope that if Osamu was in on the conspiracy to kill Ricco, after Mariko's death she would have Ryuu released unharmed. In the meantime, Mariko was going to spend as much time as possible with Ricco. She'd continue to try to find her brother, but she knew the odds were stacked against her.

She took one last look in the mirror at the woman she didn't really know and resolutely turned toward the sound of that heavy bag and the pounding rhythm that hadn't once paused. Heart pounding, she continued at the same pace, not fast, not slow, but graceful, silent, moving in the silk of the kimono, feeling it against her bare skin. She had never been more certain, or more nervous, about a decision.

Ricco moved around the bag with the fluid grace of a fighter. She couldn't help but admire him. He was a gorgeous man, a perfect physical specimen if she was going to be clinical. She much preferred to be clinical over the surprising well of emotion he invoked in her.

"You shouldn't be in here right now," he said.

He didn't turn around or even glance her way. She was behind him, their shadows hadn't touched, yet still, he was aware of her. That was good, because she was acutely aware of him.

"You have to stop." He was hurting himself. She knew why. She'd used physical exercise to try to stop the pain and the chaos in her head when Osamu had driven her to want to hurt something or someone—usually herself. Just as he was doing.

"You shouldn't be in here," he repeated. "Give me another hour or so."

"There has to be a better way. Hurting yourself isn't the answer, Ricco." She kept her voice very low, just like his. Her tone was sultry; his was commanding and it vibrated right through her.

He stopped hitting the bag and glanced over his shoulder, his eyes dark and enigmatic. She shivered at the mixture of pain and rage she saw there.

"I have two ways to rid myself of this: working the bag and Shibari. This seemed safer."

She stood her ground, although it took more courage than riding the shadows ever had. "I'm here to be your rope model."

He shook his head. "It isn't safe when I'm like this. I could hurt you."

"No, you couldn't." If there was one thing she was certain of, it was that Ricco Ferraro would never hurt her. She was shocked at how certain she was of that fact. Clearly, when their shadows touched, it revealed far more of him than she understood until that moment. She could spend a lifetime getting to know another man and she wouldn't know him as well as she did Ricco. "You would never harm me. I very much would like to do more rope art with you, that is if you want it, too."

The drumming of her heart was loud in the ensuing silence. She had no idea if she was stepping over some invisible line with him. She didn't know enough about relationships of any kind, let alone the strange one she found herself in now. She only knew that she had to stop him and the only way to do it was to give herself to him.

"I was late, Mariko. You understand if I had gotten there on time, I might have stopped the massacre. I got lost."

"I hesitated coming out of the closet after Nao pulled Ryuu out. I was so terrified, I hesitated."

He swore in Italian. One of the first things all riders had to learn was multiple languages, and she winced at the extremely foul expletives. He finally switched back to English. "You were three fucking years old."

"You were only fourteen," she countered. "You probably would have been killed had you gotten there earlier, and then I would be dead and so would Ryuu. You gave me back my family. Osamu had convinced me I was left on the street. Unwanted. A female devil child bringing bad luck to anyone I encountered. She told me my mother was a whore and that I had gotten into a car, taken it out of gear and run over Ryuu. I know now that isn't the truth. I wasn't the one to hurt him."

He erupted into another long litany of very angry foul language while he jerked the thin leather gloves from his hands. "I will be paying Osamu Saito a visit. The world of riders will know exactly what she did as well as the crimes her sons committed. I can't believe she made up such an ugly story. She had to have done it to separate you and your brother."

She'd never had a champion, someone to take her back. She didn't know how to feel without falling apart. She was offering him her body as a canvas, and that meant his rope, an extension of him, would wrap her up. Instead of feeling frightened, she had felt safe in his ropes. Now she knew why. The shadows connecting her to him had allowed her to see him for what he was—a man to be counted on. For whatever reasons, she'd fallen under his protection, and he took that seriously—every bit as seriously as when he was fourteen years old. Maybe more so.

"What would you like me to wear, Ricco?" she murmured softly, hoping to ease the anger in him.

He went still. "Are you certain? I don't want to frighten you. Having you for a rope model is extremely important to me. My sister says I'm very scary at times."

"Your sister is right," she admitted, "but you don't scare me."

He raised an eyebrow.

She couldn't help but smile. "You *intimidate* me, which isn't the same thing, and only because I'm out of my element."

Immediately she saw tension drain from his face. He still looked—intimidating—but she knew he would always be that to her. Just a little. Just enough to make it interesting. Still, he'd relaxed. She'd managed to tame the demons that drove him, and that made her feel very, very powerful. Once again, *she* had his complete focus. Not the past. Not the problems in the present. Just Mariko.

"You aren't out of your element," he corrected. "I like what you have on. Are you comfortable in what you're wearing?"

She'd chosen the red lace because the color made her feel sexy. The silk kimono with the cherry blossoms across it made her feel at home and exquisitely beautiful. She nodded.

He held out a hand to her. She didn't hesitate to put hers in his. His fingers closed around hers. Hard. Warm. He led her from the training hall toward the studio. Already her breath was coming too fast, but it was from excitement, not fear.

"Will you be uncomfortable if I remove the kimono?"

Could his voice be any gentler? Still, it held that soft, low male note that set her blood on fire. How did he do that?

"I couldn't do this with anyone else." She had to tell him that. Making herself so vulnerable was a gift to him. It took courage. More, she feared she was giving him more than her body as a canvas. Somehow, each time he touched her, spoke to her, or their shadows connected, the threads binding them together became stronger than the ropes he tied her with.

"Mariko. I need to know if you'll be comfortable without the kimono. I can bind you either way, but my preference would be without. The rope will leave marks. Not bruises, just marks, but they'll fade quickly."

"I'm fine with that." Who was going to see them? No one. She had no one. She answered to no one. Here, she had a freedom she'd never had before. She felt safe to explore who she was and who she wanted to be as a woman. For just a short while, she was Ricco Ferraro's woman. She was going to live every single second of that time to the absolute fullest.

He traced the nape of her neck beneath the fall of her hair, just ran his finger down it while they walked together. She felt his touch all the way through her body, as if he had an electric coil that shimmered through her veins and arced bright and hot through her bloodstream. He made her *feel* beautiful, whether she was or not. He obviously thought she was. He stroked her so gently, yet the power of their connection made her feel as if he not only saw through her, but could reach through her skin and touch her soul.

"You don't have to do this. I'm okay now," he murmured as they moved down the hallway.

"I'm doing it for both of us. I'm looking forward to it."

He gave her another one of his smiles. This one lit his eyes for a brief moment and turned her heart over. A reward for her bravery, maybe. Whatever it was, her body responded along with her heart.

He brought her into the studio and walked across the room to the small refrigerator in the corner. Reaching in, he took a bottle of ice-cold water out and returned to her. "The bathroom is over there." He indicated a door with one finger. "This is going to take longer than last time and I want you comfortable. You can get prepared while I ready the room."

He walked away from her and she stared after him, caught in his spell. She didn't understand how he could be so intimidating and so gentle at the same time. So commanding, and yet his voice was velvet soft. He moved with grace, like a large jungle cat, every muscle rippling beneath the thin material of his clothing. He was barefoot and he didn't make a sound as he crossed the room to select music. He was no longer looking at her, but she knew he was as aware of her as she was of him, and that somehow centered her.

She tried the cap on the bottle, found it loosened and drank. It was the little thoughtful things, she decided. He had done that before, loosened the cap so she didn't have to. Opening doors. Walking with her on the inside on the street. Making her feel special and never leering at other women when she was with him.

She contemplated that as she went into the bathroom. When she'd been with him in the restaurant, various women had been trying to make eye contact with him. He had focused on her. He'd been sweet to the waitress, although firm with her. There were a lot of good things about Ricco Ferraro. He might like to live his life in the fast lane, but when he was with someone, he took care of them.

She secured the kimono tighter and stepped back into the studio, found a place to put down the water bottle and caught a glimpse of herself in one of the long mirrors. Her face was flushed. Her hair was a little wild. Her eyes were bright, and the color of her lipstick emphasized the pout of her lips—the pout Osamu had pointed out a million times, sometimes slapping her and calling her a "whore just like your mother." It was the natural shape of her mouth—there was little she could do about it. She hadn't considered that the lipstick would make her mouth even more noticeable. She'd been thinking in terms of what Ricco would like for his rope art.

Or had she? Osamu's voice screeched in her head, a long litany of insults she suddenly couldn't block out. She wrapped her arms around herself, ashamed that she'd come to him dressed in the red lace bra and panties. Osamu was right about her. She hadn't been thinking about rope art. She'd been thinking about Ricco Ferraro.

Movement caught her eye as he turned and looked at her, his eyes meeting hers in the mirror. His handsome features went from relaxed to scary, the lines deepening, his eyes twin black diamonds, hard and cold and very, very piercing as he strode toward her, bundles of black and red ropes in his hands.

"Fuck," he spat out, the sound dark and ugly.

Mariko felt his fury as he strode across the room, the first aggressive move he'd ever made toward her. His rage was tangible, filling the spacious room, an ominous warning of his black mood. She couldn't help but think the ropes were an extension of him, depicting the storms that raged in him in the color and texture of the various coils.

She stood her ground for two reasons. First and foremost, she was a shadow rider—an elite rider—and had confidence that she could defend herself if she needed to. Automatically her mind was already cataloging targets on him. Second, she believed absolutely that he would never hurt her.

Ricco kept coming until he was standing directly in front of her, in her space, so close their bodies were touching. He dropped the coils of rope on the floor and reached for her, his palm curling around the nape of her neck. Possessing her. When he did that, touched her neck, she knew he was connecting them together. Giving her his power. Taking hers. Exchanging. She felt empowered when he did that. Centered. Grounded. More, it made her feel as if she belonged to him and he to her—that there was only the two of them and he saw only her.

"In this room there are two people, Mariko: You. And me. No one else. Ever. Do you understand?" He pulled her hand up to his bare chest, her palm over his heart, her flesh touching slashing scars that told her he had saved her. "You and me. She will never be welcome here. I swear to you, I'll deal with her."

Just like that he made Osamu small and unimportant, because he knew. He saw the real Mariko, everything about her, even her insecurities, and he still wanted her. She could see that in his eyes, feel it in his touch.

She shook her head, dismissing the idea of him having

to confront Osamu. "I stopped letting her hurt me." She wasn't certain he would believe that, because she didn't know if she did.

"Look at me. I want to see your eyes. I want you to see mine because you have to believe that I'm telling you the absolute truth."

She couldn't resist. Who could? There was always that gentle note of command. Steel wrapped in velvet. She lifted her lashes and her heart jerked hard. Her sex clenched. Needy. Hungry. Shocking. His eyes were alive with so much. Rage that Osamu had made her feel less than she was. Hunger. That shocked her. It matched her own, maybe was even more. Something else. Something she'd never seen. It was difficult to recognize exactly what was there, but it made her heart flutter.

"She stole your heritage. At three, and even then, you were magnificent." His eyes blazed with the fire of pure truth. "Absolutely magnificent." He believed that and wanted her to believe it. "You're even more so now. Do you understand me?"

She nodded because she couldn't speak. No one had ever made her feel the way he did. No one had ever believed in her. Or complimented her. Or made her feel of value.

"This room is sacred. She can't come in here and make you think less of yourself. Not here. I have to know you're with me on that."

Mariko nodded again. She didn't want any other person in this room. Ricco created intimacy here—a sensual experience encompassing the two of them. A power exchange to be sure, but one that benefited both. It was mutual. She gave herself to him, trusting he would make the experience good for her. He accepted her gift of trust and made her feel as if she were the only woman in the world for him. Strangely, that feeling carried outside of the room as well.

"Here, you look in the mirror and see what I see. See the incredible, courageous woman I see. You give yourself to me. You stand there quietly, waiting. Believing I'll take care of you. Trusting me. That kind of gift, woman, is beyond any price, but especially when given from a woman born and bred on control and discipline. Don't think for one moment that I'll ever take that for granted. I won't. I know how vulnerable this makes you feel. By surrendering yourself to me, *giving* yourself into my care, you've given me more than any other person could ever give, and I'll treasure that gift for all time."

There was no way for Mariko to continue looking him in the eye. He saw into her soul, into secret places, desires she had pushed down and buried deep. Needs she didn't want to acknowledge. She'd forgotten how to dream. Until she met Ricco Ferraro, she had existed to bring justice to criminals. He had opened an entirely different world for her, and all her secrets were there for him to discover. He was uncovering them one by one.

"Mariko." He said her name in the way that he had. Pouring everything into one word. "You're safe with me. Everything about you is safe. What and who you really are. Outside these walls, you're the shadow rider. Inside, you're all woman. Unbelievably beautiful. Your soul shines through. You can see it in the photographs. I've developed the ones from our last session and they're incredible."

He caught her chin and lifted it, forcing her gaze back up to meet his. "Are you with me on this?"

She was with him on everything. She hadn't even realized she craved human contact. Kindness. Decency. To think that even for one moment she'd contemplated killing him, removing a man like him from the world.

"I came here to kill you," she blurted out. Ashamed. Horrified. Her eyes filled with tears. With remorse. With such guilt she could barely hold her head up.

"No you didn't, *bella*. You came here to save me—and you have."

She blinked. She didn't know what that meant. Save him? He looked at her as if she were special to him. As if she were that one woman. She wanted to be, but she knew better. He was a good man, but a poor bet for a woman to take on. She didn't share. She might not know many things about herself, but she knew that. Still, she could have him for a little while.

She was going to continue to try to find her brother. There was no trail to follow, but she planned to backtrack. She had to have missed something. Sooner or later, her enemy would strike against her, but in the meantime, she would live and enjoy every second Ricco had to spare for her.

A slow smile moved over his mouth, softening the edges but not quite lighting his eyes. He was gorgeous. The scars only made him more so. A beautiful warrior with a poet's soul. She smiled back and nodded that she was ready.

The change was instant, complete confidence in every line of his body. He stepped back but as he did so, one finger slid down the nape of her neck. His claiming. His connection with her. The brush of that finger linked them together, so his confidence became hers. Her vulnerability became his. She ceded power to him and, in doing so, gained his power. She understood that now.

He took her hand and placed it on his chest as he moved first one way and then the other, breathing normally as he did. "We're connected, our breathing, the way we move. I want you to feel me the way I do you. Be aware of me."

She already was. She knew every line of his body, every ripple of his muscles. The way he set his feet on the floor, the way his shoulders moved and his neck turned. She'd never been so acutely aware of another human being. Beneath her palm his skin was hot. His heart beat solidly, a steady rhythm she could count on. She nodded to show him she got it.

He caught up the bundles of rope, his eyes moving over her and then to the ropes. He dropped the red coils, retaining a black bundle, his gaze never leaving her. He circled her, his hands sure as he shook out the rope, sliding it through his fingers, feeling for splinters to keep from hurting her.

She stayed very still, feeling him close, his heat. His power. That absolute confidence. He came back to stand in front of her, one hand reaching down to the knot at her waist where she'd secured the kimono. It took him less than a second to slip the knot and open her robe. Her breath caught in her throat. It was one thing to say she was fine with just her bra and panties, another altogether when he was looking at her under the lights.

He pushed the robe from her shoulders and the silk felt sensual as it slid over her skin. Before the kimono could float to the floor, he caught it, bunched it in his hand, and tossed it toward the table where his camera was already set up. She heard his breath catch and deep inside, her sex clenched and went damp. With just that one small action, he made her feel beautiful, made her realize that the living art form of Shibari was also a sensual expression of sexuality. Hers. His. Theirs together.

"Just so you know what's going on here, before we get started, it's important for you to know I intend to seduce you. That means touching you. If at any time you're uncomfortable with the way I put my hands on you, say so."

Her head jerked up. He spoke matter-of-factly, as if talking about the weather. He always found a way to throw her off-balance. Now she would be waiting. Anticipating. Wondering every moment if he would touch her. Where he would touch her. How it would feel . . .

Her breath caught in her lungs. Her throat closed. His eyes were on her, noting every reaction. He had to see her nipples harden beneath the red lace. He had to know how she responded to his declaration. She inclined her head, wanting him to know she understood and wasn't protesting, but she couldn't speak.

Ricco stood for a moment, sliding the rope through his hand, just drinking her in. Absorbing her. Everything about her appealed to him. She looked sexy as hell in red lace and nothing else. Automatically, he folded the rope in two, finding the center point without looking, keeping it in his hand while he breathed in and out, studying her feminine form. He was pleased that she was courageous enough to acknowledge she wanted him as much as he wanted her. He could read her desire in her body, in her eyes, the rise and fall of her breasts with every ragged breath she drew.

So beautiful. Such a gift she gave him. He focused completely on the soft feminine curves of her body, allowing the world to slip away until there was only the two of them. As he observed her beauty, his vision began to form. Something simple to continue to ease her into the world of his living art, but more than the simple harness he'd used on her before. Adding to that would be good and make her feel secure.

He stepped close to her, inhaling her scent. She was his woman whether she fully accepted it or not. He had a long way to go to convince her, but here, she was all his. No question. He caught her bare shoulders, feeling the cool silk of her skin. She shivered. He slid his hand down her arm to her wrist, moved his fingers over hers several times, to relax her, to ease the tension out of her, to know the temperature of her skin so when she was tied he could tell with a touch if his rope was cutting off circulation.

In the bright light of the room their shadows were connected, and as her apprehension was reduced he could feel other emotions slipping into him. Her feelings. The beginnings of true affection. Hunger. Need. Those deepening passions gave him more power, her power, but it also fed her his as well. She was drifting a little, letting the anticipation take her away from him.

He caught her hands and jerked her close. The movement was swift, hard and unexpected. Her gaze jumped to his. That action certainly got her attention focused wholly back on him quickly. Already he was wrapping her wrists, paying little attention to the actual rope. It was an extension of his body and moved exactly the way his mind instructed.

The moment he took control of her body, erotic dominance consumed him. Became him. Something new. Something to feel that was wild and wonderful. Passion was consuming and he let it take him. He wrapped the ropes around her arms, making certain the lines were perfect on both sides. The rope traveled under her breasts and then above, the coils of black framing the beauty of the red lace just as he knew they would. He was very careful with the underarm hitch. Not wanting to take a chance of pinching her, he slid his finger between her satin-soft skin and the rope while cinching the line.

He couldn't resist using that moment to brush his knuckles along the underside of her breast, a soft, loving stroke. Barely there. Her breath hitched. He didn't smile, but inside, he felt like it. She wasn't fighting being in the ropes; instead she was sinking into the experience.

Ricco laid the lines over her shoulder, paying attention now to his art. To the beauty of the piece he created for her. He could lay in tandem, both hands moving at the same time, so there was no twist in the lines and they lay beautifully against her skin. He laid two pairs of perfectly symmetrical half hitches at her cleavage. Her body was made for this—the beauty of Shibari. The way the rope looked against her skin inspired him.

He was careful not to twist the ropes. The tension was perfect. Each line was in exact symmetry with the other side. He was precise and careful of her comfort. He frowned down at her. She knew he was building the chest harness, and although she watched him, she was allowing her mind to wander. Erotic fantasy or not, she had to learn to stay completely focused on him always.

The rope, like a living snake, slithered through his palms and he let it fall, staying close to her as he did so. Very gently he traced the pad of his finger over the curve of her right breast, down into the valley between and then over the left breast. So very gently. She leaned into his hand, arching her back just a little to give him better access. With his finger circling her nipple, centering her attention there, he reached for the loose rope with the other hand. One swift jerk up and then down.

Mariko's eyes widened, her gaze locking on his as she gasped at the fiery flare of heat radiating out from her breasts to the rest of her body. Coming up onto the balls of her feet, she arched her back even more as he leaned into her, nuzzling her neck.

"Oh. My. God." Desire turned her hazel eyes to a deep amber.

"Breathe, *farfallina mia*. I've got you. I'll always have you." His voice was low, reassuring. She wasn't used to heat and need rushing through her veins like a fireball.

Her head fell onto his shoulders and she breathed deeply, as if drawing him into her lungs. He pressed his body tightly against hers, feeling her softer body melt into him. Very gently he lowered her back onto her feet, steadying her, letting her feel his power.

"I've never . . ." She trailed off.

"I know." He did. He was grateful he had this to give her—something erotic and intimate in exchange for everything she gave him.

Ricco brushed a kiss onto her temple, and then swept more down the line of her jaw to her neck. Moving back in front of her, he tied off the line above her wrists and reached for more rope. The harness looked good on her. He'd chosen to use a diamond pattern and wanted to continue it in the corset he was forming for her.

He measured out the length of rope in his mind to get it perfectly. Already his hands were moving. He quickly wrapped just below her waist where the sweet lace of her panties began, weaving the line into the diamond corset. Using a lark's head knot, he wrapped more rope, careful to keep tension without in any way restricting her breathing. Using a half hitch at her belly button, he tied off the waist lines and pulled to tighten. He ran the doubled line between her legs, front to back, taking extreme care to lay ropes against her sex. He didn't want it tight, nor did he use knots that would have added stimulation. He didn't want it against her clit, that experience would be too much for her second time, although she was extremely responsive in the ropes.

The panties were barely there, a thong only, so he took great care to make certain her skin wasn't burned or pinched as he worked. He wanted to make this a pleasurable experience for her. He wanted every movement in the ropes to heighten her awareness of him all around her, surrounding her with him, to make her feel as if the rope's embrace was truly his hold on her, making her secure. Using another half hitch, he tied off the line at her back.

He slid the rope along her lower lips and then worked it from her back to her front, creating a series of diamonds on her body, all the way around. He used red rope for the diamonds so that the pattern ran through the black, setting the color off and drawing attention to the red lace barely covering her mound and her breasts.

Mariko gasped and writhed in the ropes, her eyes meeting his in shock as the double ropes moved lovingly over her sex. He directed her into position again and she yielded with absolute grace, her body following the guidance of his hands like a dance partner, almost as if she knew where he would place her just by the ripple of his muscle and his steady breathing. Their connection was growing with every diamond he laid against her skin. All the while his fingers brushed against her, judging the temperature of her body, always aware of her state of health. Right now, her desire was heightened, her need for him growing.

With every length of the rope, he was wrapping himself around her. Claiming her. The coils were an extension of him, his desire and lust. His growing love for her and his need to protect her. He gave her diamonds because to him she deserved diamonds. She was a treasure he cherished.

He guided her with his hands, knowing every movement of her body sent that rope sliding over her pulsing sex. He couldn't touch her as he wanted yet. He couldn't use his hands and mouth to bring her pleasure, but he knew other ways and he used them. Ruthless. Wicked. Allowing passion and art to flow together. Talking to her without words. Hoping she understood where his heart was going. His soul. He was laying it out for her as surely as he laid the rope against her skin.

He stood in front of her, looking at his work, the contrast of red and black, the lace and emphasis on her breasts and sex. She looked beautiful, even more so than when he'd started. Her skin was flushed, her eyes bright with desire.

"Are you comfortable? Enough for me to photograph you?" He stayed close to her, absorbing her heat. Her scent.

She touched her tongue to her lips, moistening them. "Yes."

"I'm going to kiss you, because if I don't, I don't know if I'll survive the next few minutes." It wasn't a question. He didn't ask for permission this time. He told her because that was fair.

He pulled her to him, using the ropes to bring her into his body, deliberately allowing the diamonds to rub deliciously over her body as the double ropes sliding between her lips sent darts of fire straight to her sex. His mouth settled over hers, and instantly he was gone. Transported. There was a kind of paradise in the sweetness of her taste. The velvet heat of her mouth.

He heard himself groan. He was so far gone on her. His body hurt from constant arousal, but this was for her. To show her how beautiful she was. How powerful. How much he wanted her. That he was giving himself to her. All of him. Bad and good. He kissed her over and over, deliberately shifting her in his arms to keep her arousal high. He rubbed his chest tight against her nipples, stimulating them as well. When he knew he wouldn't be able to pull back if he didn't stop, he lifted his head and pressed his forehead to hers.

"Thank you, Mariko. Thank you for this." She'd come to him. Initiated their session. Given herself to him to keep him from pounding out his anger on the heavy bag.

She lifted her long lashes and looked into his eyes. He saw her surrender there and his heart stuttered in his chest and he had to let go of her before he lost all control.

"You have to know I want you with every breath I take," he admitted.

She smiled, and it was the most beautiful thing he'd ever seen. Resolutely he turned away to get the camera. He spent the next forty minutes photographing her. Positioning her. Watching her desire rise with every frame he took. Every movement of the ropes. The flush on her skin. The need in her eyes. Her breathing. He captured the moments on film knowing he would never let another living soul see her this way. She was for him. This was private. An intimacy only between the two of them. He also knew he would put some of these pictures on canvas and hang them in his private studio.

Just as he was putting down the camera, judging that she was near her limit and still had to allow him to untie her, his phone vibrated. Not the normal vibration, but the one that was programmed in by Taviano—his genius of a brother who came up with all sorts of gadgets for them. He glanced down at his phone. Emilio. This particular vibration meant one thing: they were under attack.

He caught up the shears he always had on him when working and hurried to her. Wrapping one arm around her, he began to carefully cut away his ropes. "I know you're exhausted, Mariko. You should be lying in my lap, my arms around you, holding you close while you come back slowly, but we don't have time. The enemy has found us here and we're going to be in a fight any minute. I'm going to cut you loose and carry you to the chair. I want you to drink water and then put on my T-shirt."

Mariko nodded, clearly struggling to come out from under the effects of the ropes. "I'm with you, Ricco."

Dio, he loved her. Right then. That fast. She was somewhere deep in subspace, floating in a web of sensual delight, and just like that she was his warrior woman, prepared to fight at his side. Who wouldn't love a woman like that?

The ropes dropped to the ground and he lifted her into his arms and took her to the chair. For one moment he cradled her to his chest and brushed her forehead with his lips. "Drink. Hydrate. The T-shirt. I have no doubt you can fight in your lingerie, but I prefer to be the only man who ever sees you like this."

She nodded, blinking rapidly, reaching for the water bottle, preparing herself, not asking questions, trusting him to get the information they needed to stay alive.

CHAPTER TEN

Teresa Ventura smirked to herself as she pulled on the long gloves, all the while watching herself in the mirror. Her plan was getting closer to fruition. She hadn't thought it would take so long, nor did she think she would like it so much, but Phillip Ferraro was nearly in her net.

For an older man, he wasn't half bad. He certainly had all the moves and put her up in the best of places. Her high-rise apartment had a fantastic view of the city and anyone living there was treated as if they were made of money. The jewelry he bought her was worth a fortune. Now, all she had to do was convince him to get rid of his wife and marry her. She'd have the entire fortune.

"Teresa. What are you doing in there?"

She liked the impatience in his voice. He was always so eager to see her. "I've got a surprise for you, honey," she called back and then winked at herself in the mirror.

She looked good. Better than good. Her thigh-high stockings were sheer black. Her garters, sexy lacy black. She had a great figure. She'd learned in high school the benefits of working out and looking fantastic. Switching on the music, she found the rhythm and danced out of her bedroom.

She was good at dancing. She'd gotten a job in a strip bar and made a ton of money dancing, but it wasn't nearly as lucrative as this venture could be. She began a bump and grind, going to the floor, coming back up again, slowly stripping the glove from her right arm and hand.

Phillip stood in the middle of the room, just where he'd been when she'd danced in. He looked stunned. Good. It was time to step things up. They'd hit a plateau and she needed to up the ante so he'd do his part.

Phillip watched Teresa's striptease from the center of the room. He'd come to tell her it was over. He'd use Eloisa, of course; it always worked when you convinced a mistress that your wife was psycho and capable of anything. He was merely trying to protect his beloved by leaving her. He always left his mistresses happy, weeping but happy with the money he settled on them.

He could appreciate a good striptease, and Teresa had always been excellent. He'd first seen her at a strip bar. She had a good body and a mouth on her that wouldn't quit, but he was bored out of his mind. He was getting too old for this, and Eloisa was getting ready to dump him. He read the signs easily. She'd gone from hurt to angry to indifferent, and now there was a new resolve in her.

Eloisa. Right from the beginning, he'd manipulated her into believing he loved her. Over the years, he found, to his shock, that just might be true. Phillip's phone buzzed annoyingly. He didn't bother to answer it. It was probably the bodyguards. He'd given them the slip to come here, but he'd be back soon. Eloisa was making noises about being on alert, but that was just silly. He was a rider and no one could find him in the shadows.

"Phillip!" Teresa reclaimed his attention. She pouted beautifully. "You aren't watching and I did all this for you."

All what? Put on her working clothes? He was damn tired of lies. His lies. His mistresses' lies. Did Teresa really think she was the only woman he had? Or that he would put her above Eloisa? The phone buzzed again, and sighing, he reached into his pocket.

Something *thunked* hard against the window. It was so loud the sound drowned out the music. He glanced up, and Teresa stopped her dance in mid-grind. The thick glass spider-webbed out from a single source right in the center as if something large had hit it. Maybe a bird. As both stared, a little in shock, two men rappelling from the roof kicked in the window with their heavy boots, shattering the glass and sending shards exploding through the room like missiles. Both had automatic weapons and wielded them with ease, obviously from long practice.

Red and orange spray erupted from the muzzles and Phillip went over backward. He saw Teresa on the floor, her body looking like a broken rag doll, stained bright red. He looked down at his chest. Nothing registered. Not pain. He wasn't certain what had happened. A shadow fell across him and he looked up to see a man with a gun standing over him. The man lifted the gun and aimed it right at his face. A thousand regrets rushed through his mind, the main one Eloisa.

He was a selfish man, a womanizer, and the shadows represented a way for him to carry out his affairs. He'd never once been decent to Eloisa. He knew what she went through, she'd tried to open up to him, tried to make their marriage real, but he had only thought about the fun he could have. Even after they lost their son, Ettore, and Eloisa had needed him, he had turned away from her. He regretted that. He regretted so many things.

I'm dead and I never told her I loved her. He attempted to rise, but he couldn't feel his legs or arms. He could only watch as the man slowly squeezed the trigger and then there was nothing.

The party was in full swing at the Windship Club, one of the most prestigious in Chicago. The event was all about wining and dining the local celebrities so they'd write fat checks for the latest charity Windship was backing. Taviano and Giovanni Ferraro knew it really was about the women, drugs and drink. Vittorio lay in a hospital bed, cut up all to hell, and they were supposed to be snorting coke off a woman's belly, drinking champagne and taking the women into the next room for a quick blow job, or worse, having one crawl under the table and go for it right there in the plush lounge.

Harvey Windship was a sick prick with far too much money. Taviano had never liked the man and Giovanni had a terrible aversion to him. More than once throughout the last hour, Taviano had to be the one to restrain his brother when Giovanni wanted to kick Harvey's ass—and Taviano was known for his bad temper. He couldn't wait to see his brothers and point out just which Ferraro had had to be the peacekeeper.

Laughter erupted all around them and Taviano made certain to put a fake smile on his face. He was good at that. All the Ferraros were. They played out their lives in front of the paparazzi. Very early they learned the art of smiling at parties they didn't enjoy, surrounded by people who weren't their friends.

Harvey flung his cut crystal glass into the fireplace and laughed loudly as it shattered, the remaining alcohol making the flames flare for just a moment. "Gina, get over here," he called.

His wife giggled drunkenly and obeyed, her stiletto heels clicking loudly on the marble floor. She teetered and then fell into her husband's lap when he grabbed her wrist and yanked her down to him. "Having a good time, honey?" he asked, nuzzling her neck.

Harvey was a drunk. He liked his booze, and the more he drank the more amorous he got. He thought of himself as a player, although Taviano knew he genuinely loved his wife. It was his one saving grace. He put on lavish parties and raised millions of dollars for charity, so he wasn't all bad. It was just that his parties were . . . disgusting. Everyone attended of course. The cream of Chicago. Mostly, Taviano was certain, to see what Harvey would do next.

This party was the most garish of all. His wife liked furs so, to thumb his nose at those protecting wildlife, he had decorated the entire club in big-game trophies and real fur rugs and throws. It turned Taviano's stomach just a little, and when Harvey suggested to one of the girls to "do Giovanni" on the leopard skin rug in front of the fireplace, he almost let Gee hit the man. Instead, both laughed, playing their roles for the press. Giovanni declined and they wandered away to give themselves a respite from the man.

Now they were back in the lounge, once again seated in the plush chairs. "Have to go, Harv," Giovanni said. "Vittorio is in the hospital and we're each taking shifts with him." That was a lie and then it wasn't.

Stefano never left the hospital and wouldn't until Vittorio was completely out of danger, but the others came and went. They took care of business while Stefano and Vittorio were out of commission. Still, it was a good excuse and one Harvey would accept. The man was just drunk enough that he might make a scene, and that was the last thing either of the Ferraro brothers wanted.

Both men stood and Harvey tried to get to his feet, too, pushing his wife off his lap. She fell on the floor, landing on her butt. Harvey laughed, subsiding in his chair, his eyes on his wife as she struggled into a full sitting position, her legs sprawled out in front of her. She glared at her husband, who pointed and laughed more.

"Come on, Harvey," Taviano said in resignation. "You don't want to get locked out of your bedroom for a week, do you?" He leaned down to extend his arm to Gina.

Giovanni stepped forward as their two bodyguards turned toward the door where four men had attempted to enter but were stopped by the bouncers. They wore ill-fitting suits and long trench coats over the cheap material.

Two men in the chairs closest to Harvey snickered. "Look at those clowns. Think they can crash the party."

Simultaneously, Giovanni's and Taviano's phones vibrated in the complicated pattern Taviano had devised to alert each of his brothers when an attack on a family member was imminent or happening. Taviano was already leaning down. He dove toward the shadows under the coffee table, slamming Gina back down to the floor with one ruthless arm hooked around her neck.

Tomas and Cosimo Abatangelo, first cousins and bodyguards for the Ferraro family, both shoved Giovanni toward the shadows as they turned, pulling weapons, putting their bodies between the riders and the threat.

Gunfire erupted as the four men pulled automatics from under their coats and sprayed the room with bullets. Screams, cries of agony and the sounds of shattering glass along with the thundering roar of guns filled the room. Tomas leapt for the thick lounge chair as he fired at the man on the outside of the group. Fire raced up his leg and chest as holes blossomed there. He saw his target fall as he hit the floor.

His brother, Cosimo, landed hard just feet from him, his weapon still barking. The assailants separated, came around from all sides, clearly looking for the Ferraros, who were long gone. Tomas stared at the ceiling, waiting for the bullet that would end his life. Cosimo's gun had gone silent, and Tomas could hear him struggling for air, his lungs laboring.

When they couldn't find their targets, the three remaining men turned and hurried out of the club into the parking lot. In the distance was the sound of sirens. Clearly several people had called 911 from their cell phones to report the attack and they'd done it very quickly. The assailants raced toward their van. The driver brought the vehicle beside them, the sliding door open. One by one they dove inside, rolled to make room for the next one and sat up.

"Move this thing, Danny," Brady, the acknowledged leader, yelled, slamming the door shut.

He turned back to see Sean, the youngest of them, lying still on the floor of the van. He kicked at him with his foot. "What the hell. You hit?"

Terry turned his head to observe his younger brother, Sean. He crawled over to him. "Get going, Danny," he added his command to Brady's. "The cops will be here any second." He leaned down to listen for a heartbeat and straightened up quickly. "Shit. He's dead. I didn't even see him take a hit." He scrambled away from his brother until his back hit the wall.

Still the van hadn't moved. Needing an outlet for the adrenaline and grief, Terry screamed at the driver. "Move this fucking van now, Danny, or I'm going to shoot you. Brady, you drive." He lifted his weapon half-heartedly as a threat toward the driver.

Brady sat a few feet away, slumped over, looking peculiar. Something was off about the way he was sitting.

"Brady?" Terry lowered his gun. "Danny, something's wrong with Brady."

Danny turned his head to look. "He's dead. That's what's wrong."

The voice didn't sound right. Staring at the driver, frowning, trying to figure out what was wrong with all of them, Terry scooted toward Brady on his hands and knees. It hit him then. The driver wasn't Danny. It was Taviano Ferraro. Whipping his head around, he tried to think what he'd done with his gun even as he knew it was far too late. Hands were on his head. There was a terrible wrenching. Pain flashed through his body. Excruciating. The wrenching happened a second time and then he was gone.

Taviano leapt from the van just as Giovanni did. They raced back toward the club, one hand sending alert texts to their families. They'd already called 911 and asked for ambulances and cops. Tomas and Cosimo were theirs. They had to know if they had survived and, if so, how badly they were injured.

Eloisa Ferraro hurried outside, nearly forgetting to set the lock on her door. She was tired of Phillip playing around with all his young girlfriends, making her out to be the psycho wife to extract himself when he got bored with the relationship. She'd contemplated divorcing him for some time. A rider didn't do such a thing easily. If she divorced Phillip, she could never ride again. Their shadows had tangled together, and if torn apart, she'd lose her ability to ride, and Phillip would never remember a single thing about the Ferraro family. He'd taken the name and he wouldn't even remember that.

Vinci Sanchez, their lawyer, would help the Greco family plant a lifetime for Phillip. He'd have money and a past, but wouldn't remember a single thing about being associated with the Ferraro family. Not her. Not his children. It was a high price to pay for divorce, but it was time.

His latest mistress was twenty-five years old. Confronting the women for him was becoming harder and harder. She just didn't have the energy or will. So screw him. She was going to divorce him. She'd call Vinci that afternoon, as soon as she got back from visiting Melani Barone, a woman she'd known for years. Massimo and Melani owned Luna's, a favorite restaurant the Ferraro family frequented. The note from Melani sounded very urgent but off a little. Stilted and unlike her. That only served to alarm Eloisa more.

She'd called Henry, the man who had grown up in her family and worked for them for longer than she'd been alive. He took care of their cars. The cars, as a rule, were stored in a climate-controlled garage. Henry kept them in good shape and was extremely loyal to the Ferraros. But he did everything at his own pace and was bossy as hell. Especially to her. The car wasn't waiting in the driveway for her. That annoyed her to no end. Everything seemed to annoy her these days.

Vittorio was in the hospital. Why? No one knew. Probably the teenage girl Stefano and Taviano had insisted risking their lives as well as the family for. Nicoletta something. Who even knew what a girl like that would be like? Slutty no doubt, like that awful Teresa Ventura. Now Lucia and Amo Fausti were at risk as well just because they were sweet enough to foster the girl. By all accounts, the teen had been with so many men already and she wasn't even eighteen, no doubt *exactly* like Teresa Ventura.

Eloisa glanced at her watch, stomped her foot and glared down the driveway. What was holding Henry up? She detested being late to anything. With Vittorio in the hospital, Stefano was in a bad mood, giving her nasty looks just because she wouldn't visit him there. She couldn't, but she wasn't about to try to explain why. Not to any of them. She didn't owe them an explanation anymore, and she didn't care if she was never going to win a mother-of-the-year award.

In the distance, she saw the car coming toward her. Henry was driving very fast. Unusual for him. No, impossible for a man like him. He babied the cars. He would never, not in a hundred years, drive like that. She stiffened, took stock of her surroundings and waited until the car was almost in the driveway. She stepped into the shadows, feeling the familiar pull on her body as she was torn apart to become nothing but molecules. She was whisked from one tube to the next, circling around behind the car as it came to an abrupt halt in her driveway.

Three men leapt out of the still-running car, leaving the doors wide open. A fourth sat behind the wheel, a gun in his hand, tracking the yard. The three men all carried semi-automatics, and they sprayed the shadows along the house and across the wide lawn. She rode the shadows behind the assailant closest to her, sliding out of the tube right behind him, snapping his neck and catching the gun before it—or the body—hit the ground.

She'd been at this far too long to let four idiots take her down. She might be old enough to have grandchildren, but she hadn't lost her skills. And what had they done with Henry? He might annoy the holy hell out of her, but he was family, and if they touched one hair on his head, even after she killed them, she'd come back and chop them into pieces. She found her stomach lurching at the idea of Henry being killed by these men. He was ex-CIA, and before that Special Forces. She had known him since she was a little girl and he was the one constant in her life she could count on.

She shot the two men in front of her in the back of the

neck, using the gun she'd taken from their fallen comrade. Mercenaries. Not very good ones. Whoever sent them probably viewed her as the least of their threats. A society woman. Mother of a bunch of playboys. Old. Damn it all, she wasn't that old. She wasn't twenty-five like Teresa Ventura, but she damn well refused to be old. She shot the driver just as he turned his head toward her, realizing his friends had stopped shooting.

She walked up carefully to each of the fallen men, checking to ensure they were dead. Her car was a mess. Blood all over the windshield and seat. She really liked that particular car. Another vehicle approached, lights flashing, and she knew that was Henry just by the way he drove. She was shocked at the relief she felt that he was alive. Her knees turned to rubber and she almost went down.

He jumped out of the car, a semiautomatic in one hand and a shotgun in the other. "You all right, Eloisa?" He was on her in seconds, kicking one of the bodies out of the way to get to her, running his hands over her to ensure she wasn't hurt.

"I'm fine," she assured.

There was a lump on his temple and another on the back of his head, both bleeding. She touched one of the cuts. It was deep and bleeding profusely. He'd come for her though. As hurt as he was, he'd come for her.

"You don't have your phone on you, Eloisa." It was an accusation. "Ricco sent out a warning that the family was under attack. Everyone tried to reach you, but you didn't cue in the code that you got the message."

She'd left her phone on her nightstand. Purposely. She knew Phillip well enough to know exactly what he'd intended when he left. He was going to try to break it off with his latest mistress and she'd get the call to come and help him. She wasn't doing it. Not again. Not *ever* again. Especially if the woman was twenty-five to her sixty.

"I know, Henry."

"Damn it, Eloisa, you know better. And where the hell are your bodyguards?"

She'd dismissed them. She'd been worried about her children since Vittorio had been put in the hospital and she wanted them to double up on her sons. Tomas Abatangelo was to stay and guard her while his brother Cosimo went with Giovanni and Taviano. She had thought to stay in and decided it was better the two went with her sons instead. They were so shorthanded, all the bodyguards were floating around from rider to rider. She'd pulled rank and they'd complied, because if they hadn't she would have been a real bitch and they knew it. She was good at that.

Stefano would have more leverage than ever against her now. He had decreed the *entire* family have bodyguards, but they were spread thin. Still, he was right. He was always right. She was proud of him, yet at the same time, she resented him, especially the way he was with his siblings. His warmth. Francesca. All of it. He'd been raised in the same cold environment she had, yet he'd turned out so different.

"Who else checked in?" She looked at Henry with stricken eyes.

"There hasn't been time for any of them." When she kept staring at him, her eyes wet, he sighed. "The one thing you did for certain was to teach your children how to survive. How to take care of themselves. You have to trust in that now. We should get this done, Eloisa. We have to phone it in and, before the cops get here, try to get all identifying marks." He indicated one of the bodies and crouched beside another while he pulled out his phone. "I'm calling the police now. We have to do this fast."

"Phillip went to see that woman. He didn't have bodyguards." She had to say it, and the words clogged her throat. Humiliation turned her face red and she couldn't look at Henry. She didn't want to care. She really didn't, but she didn't want Phillip dead.

"Eloisa." Henry's voice went commanding. "Phillip chose his path. We have to get this done. He'll come through this or he won't, but we need to know who is attacking our family."

She liked that. Liked that he thought of the Ferraro family as his own. His familiar bossy tone steadied her and she pushed aside the thought of her children or Phillip being in danger and went down beside one of the bodies.

They examined them for identifying markers. Their clothes, their wallets. Cigarettes. They took pictures of faces, of shoes, the patterns on the boots. They were meticulous gathering information. The family had members in all walks of life and face recognition software was available to them. They took fingerprints for the same reason.

"Enough," she said. "I have to start cleaning you up, Henry, or the cops will wonder why I didn't." In truth, she couldn't stand seeing him bloody and battered. But he'd come for her when she needed him. He always had.

Stefano Ferraro stretched. It had been a long night. Vittorio had lost a lot of blood. Just sitting in the chair beside his bed brought back very unpleasant memories of Ricco's accident. He'd been there at the track. He'd watched his brother's car go into the wall and break apart, metal flying everywhere, flames rising in every direction. He had lost his breath. For one moment the man who could never be anything but strong had lost his ability to move or think.

Ricco had survived, although he was still having headaches and vision problems. He tried to hide them, but Stefano knew him too well. The doctors had assured Stefano that Vittorio, at least, would be as good as new very soon. Behind his chair, Francesca put her hands on his shoulders and began a slow massage, easing the tension from him. She hadn't asked him to go home and rest. She knew he wouldn't. He'd been taking care of his younger siblings since he was a little boy himself and would never be able to rest until he knew they were out of danger and able to take care of themselves.

He'd been uneasy for the last few hours, and it bothered him. Mostly he'd been turning over and over in his mind the things Ricco had told him about his stay in Japan. Was that tied to the attack on Vittorio? Had the target been Nicoletta? It wasn't Stefano's way to sit idly by while someone attacked his family. He'd already sent for members of the International Council, laying out exactly what had happened to Ricco and the truth of the deaths of the Tanaka family as well as what he expected from the council. Still, the nagging in his gut just didn't want to go away.

"I'm going to go for coffee," he said. "Vittorio? Francesca?" The coffee was disgusting and both Vittorio and Francesca looked at him like he was crazy. Francesca stuck her head around his shoulder to give him her "are you nuts?" look.

He laughed, patted her hand and then stood and stretched. "It's better than nothing."

"No, it isn't," Francesca denied. "I think they deliberately make it that bad so no one wants to stick around."

He leaned in to brush a kiss over her temple. Just looking at her made him happy. She could soothe him when he was raging, and had no problem letting him know when his innate bossiness was out of control. She was everything to him. *Everything.* He'd insisted she come with him to the hospital after the attack to keep her from going to work. It was underhanded, but that nagging feeling of unease in his gut had him taking extra precautions with his treasured and very necessary other half.

He walked to the door, stopped and turned back, deliberately going to the opposite side of the bed from his wife. She was already digging through her pack to get out the food for Vittorio she'd brought. She didn't want him eating the hospital food. Vittorio raised an eyebrow but didn't say a word when Stefano leaned down and removed a concealed revolver from his boot and slid it under the covers into his brother's hand.

He caught his brother around his neck and leaned in. "Love you, Torio. You guard her for me. You know what she is to me."

"To us," Vittorio corrected. "Love you, too, man."

They had never had problems stating how they felt to one another. Stefano had initiated that early, when they were just children. He wasn't about to let them enter the shadow tubes without knowing they were loved.

"Is something wrong?" Francesca asked, her eyes on his face.

She was intelligent and quick. She knew him. His every mood. He flashed her a smile because she always made him smile, even when she was as stubborn as hell. "No, baby, just taking precautions. You know me. Security is never good enough. I'm sending Drago into the room while I'm gone. I'll take Demetrio with me." Even as he stated it, he realized he wouldn't. He hadn't meant to lie to her. When he said it, he meant it, but that strange feeling in his gut was getting worse. He'd leave Demetrio at the door, just to be on the safe side.

Francesca nodded, but there was suspicion in her eyes. She went around the bed to intercept him before he made it to the door, planting her body right in front of him. "Stefano, you know, as much as I'm your world, you're mine. Don't take risks. We're going to be fine in here. Take Demetrio with you."

She kept looking up at his face. *Dio*, he loved her.

"Please."

He cupped the side of her face in his palm, his thumb sliding over her smooth skin, feeling love eating him alive. "For you, Francesca, but you do what Drago and Vittorio tell you."

"I will."

He heard his heartbeat, drumming for her. Needing her. Finding her rhythm. He glanced at his brother and then turned abruptly and stalked out of the room. Demetrio and Drago both came to attention as he closed the door. Cousins, they had taken up bodyguarding for the family, following their stint in the service. Both were quick, he'd trained with them several times to get a feel for their abilities. They were younger than Emilio and Enzo, the acknowledged leaders of their protection unit.

"I've got a bad feeling," he told them. "Drago, you stay right here. If trouble comes, get inside the room and shoot anything coming through the door. You get me?"

Drago nodded. Stefano started to tell Demetrio to come with him, but something made him hesitate. He'd told Francesca he'd take Demetrio, but protecting Vittorio and Francesca were far more important to him.

"Gotta go with you, Stefano," Demetrio said, seeing his hesitation. "Whatever your gut is saying, mine is saying the same thing. Get pissed. Don't care. Just doing my job."

His cousin was a pain in the ass and had been trained by Emilio. He was a mini-Emilio, and just to tweak him, Stefano felt like saying so. In a way, he wanted both guards staying in the hospital room because he wanted them protected as well. They were too damned young to die. He sighed. "Suit yourself. I'm just getting coffee."

"Got some in my thermos," Drago said. "Wouldn't drink the poison they serve here for anything."

"Thanks. I need to stretch my legs." And get a feel for the floor they were on. He didn't want any last-minute surprises.

He started down the hall toward the nurses' station where a bank of vending machines rested against a long wall. Demetrio trailed after him. That was another thing that annoyed the holy hell out of him. Demetrio and Drago were family, his cousins. He liked them. The last thing he wanted was for either to die from a bullet intended for him. The least the man could do was walk with him, but if Stefano said anything to him, Demetrio would shrug his shoulders and just do what Emilio ordered him to do.

Since when did Emilio's orders take precedence over his? He sighed. Always. Emilio was damned good at his job and he made certain that the others on the shadow rider detail were just as good.

He was thirty feet from the elevator when it dinged, the

arrow lighting up above it. The doors slid open. Two doctors wearing scrubs and identifications stepped off, talking to each other. One turned his head to look at Stefano. Their eyes met. Stefano felt every cell in his body react. Recognition was there—not of whom but of what. This man was no doctor. He was a hitman—a very experienced one—and he was there for the Ferraros. Simultaneously, Stefano's phone vibrated, the code from Ricco that alerted them to an impending attack.

Recognition that his subterfuge was blown was in the hitman's eyes—Stefano knew what he was doing there. The attacker yanked the other man, a genuine doctor, in front of him as a shield, even as he drew his weapon and fired all in one smooth move.

Stefano took that split second to shove Demetrio away from him. Simultaneously, he somersaulted across the room for the shelter of a crash cart. Not much cover, but as he did so, he fired several bullets, skipping them off the floor to drive the assassin back, hopefully into Demetrio's line of fire.

"Down, down. Get down," he yelled to the nurses and orderlies who had frozen with shock, some in the line of fire.

Horror blossomed on the doctor's face. His eyes were looking beyond Stefano. Stefano rolled, bringing up his Glock just as a second gunman emerged from the stairwell. He had to trust Demetrio to do his job. He turned to face the new threat, firing as he did so, driving him back behind the door.

Demetrio's gun barked several times, and the first attacker answered. Stefano chose a shadow near the stairwell, did another somersault, sending his weapon skidding across the floor toward Demetrio as the pull of the tube took him inside. This was narrow and steep, greased lightning, flinging him toward the small crack beneath the door.

He hit the stairway so fast that he nearly flipped over the bannister. It hit him hard in the belly, doubling him in half.

His head went down toward the floors below, the movement drawing the gunman's attention. The attacker fired several rounds rapidly but the stairwell was lit by bright lights, allowing the stairs themselves to cast shadows.

Stefano flung himself toward one, leaping over the rail, aimed right at it. He hit feetfirst and slid on his knees before swinging around onto his butt. The hitman sprayed bullets through the shadows, up and down and across. Stefano went down to his belly, still moving fast, the sensations horrifying, as if his chest were flying apart and his legs and arms hadn't caught up with him. He'd never been in a tube that moved so fast.

Bullets hit all around him, two kissed his arm and shoulder. He had to do something fast. The shadow curved up the wall behind the gunman. He followed it to the end, leapt out, tackling the man, knocking him down the stairs, kicking the gun from his hand as he did so.

He kicked, first the man's unprotected head and then his throat, following as the body tumbled, not giving him a chance to recover. In a desperate attempt to save himself, the assassin slammed a knife into the stairs to stop his body from rolling farther down them.

He tried to jerk the blade from the metal to attack Stefano with it, but he was already on him, catching him in an arm lock around his head and applying steady pressure. The attacker drummed his heels into the stairs, trying to push himself up. He managed to get the blade free but was already beginning to lose consciousness. The moment he slumped, Stefano transferred his grip and wrenched, breaking the neck.

Dropping the body onto the stairs, he raced back up to the floor where he'd left Demetrio. As he shoved open the door, he saw the body of the gunman sprawled out with the same doctor that the attacker had used as a shield leaning over him. Demetrio flashed past him, running toward Vittorio's room just as two shots rang out. Stefano took off after him.

For a moment Demetrio blocked his way, checking the room first before stepping aside. The body of a woman lay just inside the door to the hospital room, two gunshots to her head. A gun lay inches from her fingers. Stefano glanced down at her, his heart pounding as he stepped over her to peer into the room. Francesca sat next to Vittorio on the bed. Vittorio had his arm around her. His eyes met Stefano's over her head.

"She's good," he assured. "We're both good."

"Who got her?" Stefano asked.

"We both did," Drago said. "Vittorio was fast. Too fast for me to tell him I'd already pulled the trigger. You're bleeding. You okay?"

Francesca was off the bed in a flash, rushing to his side. Stefano put his arm around her and pulled her under his shoulder, sheltering her against his heart. "I'm good, baby. Three dead and none of them ours. Ricco sent a warning. Has anyone heard from him?"

"He's not picking up. Neither is Emilio or Enzo," Vittorio said.

Francesca was fussing with his arm. "You need to get this looked at."

"The cops are here," Demetrio announced.

"I've called Vinci," Stefano said. "Wait for him before you make any statements. The press is going to be all over this. They'll make it out to be a war to take over someone's territory. They portray us as criminals every chance they get. The family should brace for the possibility of being investigated."

He wanted to get to his brothers and Emme, but he couldn't leave without talking to the cops. His siblings weren't answering their phones. He was going to have to get them to have another code to let the family know each was alive and well.

CHAPTER ELEVEN

"Exactly why were you crawling out the window?" Amo asked Nicoletta. His foster daughter hadn't said more than a couple of words since Vittorio had been hospitalized. Through breakfast and now sitting in Lucia's Treasures with his beloved wife and Emmanuelle Ferraro, he gave the teenager his sternest look. "You weren't thinking of taking off, were you?"

Lucia patted his arm. "Maybe we should just drop it, Amo. She's had a terrible night and still hasn't gone to bed." She spoke in her sweetest, most beguiling tone.

Emmanuelle could see why men tumbled at Lucia's feet. She was genuine, too. That sweetness, the caring she had for everyone around her, was the reason the Ferraro family had chosen Lucia and Amo Fausti as Nicoletta's foster parents. The teenager needed unconditional love. She needed to feel it, experience it, and know that it was still in the world and she was worthy of it. Already Nicoletta was under Lucia's spell. How could she not be? Everyone was.

Amo shook his head, a small smile on his face, clearly remembering the times she tried to divert him from chastising their children. "Always the same, my sweet Lucia. Nicoletta, please answer my question."

Nicoletta glanced at Emmanuelle and then ducked her head. "I've been worried since the truck nearly hit me that some very bad people might have found me. They would hurt you and I don't want that to happen."

"Thank you," Amo acknowledged. "That was very brave

of you to tell me the truth. Lucia and I prefer that you stay with us no matter what, whether these people have found you or not. We have the Ferraros to look after us. Your job is to learn as much as you can and be a teenager. Let us worry about whether or not we're in danger."

Nicoletta glanced at Emmanuelle with despair in her eyes. There was no going back from what she'd been through. Yes, this couple had experienced terrible heartache and tragedy with the loss of both children, one to cancer, one murdered, but Nicoletta had been given to three step-uncles living life in one of the bloodiest gangs in New York. She'd been innocent and happy until her mother and stepfather had died in a car accident. That all changed abruptly and her life had been a nightmare until a social worker had appealed to the New York Ferraro family.

Nicoletta nodded her head, again not looking Amo in the eye. Emmanuelle wanted to put her arms around the girl and hold her, but she knew she'd be rejected. Nicoletta didn't allow anyone close to her. Around the Ferraros, she was especially quiet and refused to look at them most of the time. Emmanuelle realized it had everything to do with the girl's past and how she was rescued. They knew. All the Ferraros knew what had happened to her. There was no getting away from it, not when she was guarded around the clock by the only people in town who knew her past. Each time Nicoletta looked at them, she felt humiliated.

She'd been unconscious when Stefano and Taviano had brought her back through the shadow tube. She woke on a private jet heading to Chicago. She'd been terrified after witnessing them kill her uncles. Lucia and Amo had gone a long way toward helping with that, but Nicoletta avoided the Ferraros whenever she could.

Emme's bodyguard, Enrica Gallo, sister to Emilio and Enzo, stirred, just enough to warn Emmanuelle that someone was about to enter the store. Emmanuelle moved slightly to put herself in the shadows. She wore the same pin-striped suit her brothers wore—the signature suit of the Ferraro family. The shadows made it difficult for anyone to spot her immediately.

When she moved, she noticed Nicoletta's gaze flick to her, then to the bodyguard and then toward the door. She was extremely observant. The slightest movement drew her attention. The teen took the three steps necessary to put her body in front of Lucia's. At the same time, she reached down to straighten a wide gold-chain belt. It was heavy and could easily be used as a weapon.

It was too bad the girl hadn't been trained in riding the shadows from the time she was a toddler. She had no idea how special she was or the gifts given to her at birth. She had amazing instincts. Emmanuelle was going to have to ask Stefano about training her. At least in self-defense, but she would make a good rider. It would be a risk to train her, but they'd already risked so much just rescuing her.

The door opened and Signora Agnese Moretti stumbled into the shop, clutching her bag to her chest, looking through the thick glasses she wore, her gaze resting on Nicoletta and then Lucia and Amo. Her mouth pursed and then firmed. She banged the door closed and marched up to Lucia.

"I've heard the most *outrageous* thing and I've come to you so you can tell me this rumor isn't true. I heard"—she glared at Nicoletta—"that your wild daughter has taken a job at Theresa Vitale's flower shop where she will be exposed to that hooligan Bruno. This can't be true. Surely you would never give your permission for such a thing."

Nicoletta turned bright red and her chin went up. Combat mode. Emmanuelle wanted to smile. Signora Moretti, as a rule, ruffled just about everyone's feathers, but she had a heart of gold.

"We thought it would be good for her, *cara*," Lucia said softly, her tone, as always, sweet. This time there was a hint of placating. "All those flowers. Bright and cheerful. Working here part-time and there part-time, she'll come to know the community members so much faster. With you as her tutor, she'll catch up fast. She's so bright, you said so yourself—that she was brilliant."

"Well now," Signora Moretti hedged. "I didn't say *brilliant*."

"You did, Agnese. You know you did. You told Amo and me that she was a genius and would have no problems catching up, that you might be struggling to stay in front of her." Lucia sounded very earnest and innocent. It was all Emmanuelle could do not to laugh.

Nicoletta's eyes widened. She didn't call attention to Emmanuelle by looking at her, but she clearly wanted to. The things Signora Moretti had said about her clearly shocked her.

Signora Moretti made several faces at Lucia in a desperate attempt to quiet her.

"Are you okay, *cara*? Here, sit down." Lucia offered one of the plush chairs, patting the back of it. "Do you have seizures?"

Anyone else would be blasted for asking such a question, but Lucia was just too sweet and innocent for anyone to think she was deliberately teasing them.

Nicoletta turned her face away from the two older women, struggling not to smile. Emmanuelle decided to take pity on Lucia and Agnese. She moved slightly, stepping just out of the shadow. Signora Moretti spun around, her eyes going wide with shock.

"Emmanuelle! Seriously. I've told you and your brothers to stop doing that. You could give an old lady a heart attack." Dramatically she pressed her hand over her heart.

"You aren't that old," Lucia pointed out. "Amo and I have ten years on you at least."

Agnese drew herself up to her full height. "I taught school. All those Ferraro boys. And Emme. That alone added a good ten years to my age." She pretended to shudder. "Just what interest does your family have with this girl?" she demanded of Emmanuelle.

Nicoletta stiffened.

Emmanuelle shrugged. "Stefano knew her stepfather. The service, I think." She lied smoothly. It was the story they'd all agreed on. "You can talk to him." No one, not even Signora Moretti, would want to question Stefano about his personal business.

"She hasn't had schooling." Agnese changed tactics. "Totally neglected, I say."

Emmanuelle flashed her sweetest smile. "Fortunately, as you've pointed out several times, Nicoletta truly is a genius and she'll have no problem catching up. Didn't you tell me, Lucia, that Nicoletta had done one semester's worth of work in a couple of months?"

Amo coughed and turned away. Agnese glared. "I'm *certain* I didn't say such a thing *several* times. I don't believe in making children have enormous fat heads. Nicoletta could easily become vain with her intelligence and looks . . ." She trailed off, scowling. Clearly she hadn't meant to give that compliment, either. "Actually"—she recovered quickly, turning her sharp gaze on Emmanuelle—"I want to know about this woman Ricco showed up with the other morning. He's *never* brought a woman around. He was acting very much the way Stefano acted with Francesca. Although, after seeing all those pictures of him with the Lacey twins in the magazines, I can't imagine a decent woman taking him on."

Emmanuelle took a deep breath to keep from losing her temper with the older woman. Signora Moretti had a kind heart, but sometimes it was difficult to get past her mouth. Emme rarely allowed anyone to get away with putting a family member down.

Enrica cleared her throat, and Emmanuelle spun around to face the window. One of two men she had been keeping an eye on separated himself from his companion and started across the street toward the shop. His friend, trying to look inconspicuous, glanced down the street and then up at the roof of the building next to the one he lounged in front of.

Emmanuelle followed his gaze upward and caught the glint of something shiny. Her heart jerked hard. There were a lot of civilians. "Nicoletta, right now, take Lucia and Signora Moretti into the back of the shop. Enrica is going with you. Don't get near the windows or door until she gives you the go-ahead. I'll be behind you with Amo."

"I have no intention—"

"Agnese." Emmanuelle didn't have time to pull her punches. The man she hadn't taken her eyes from was almost to the sidewalk in front of the shop.

"No need to get snippy, Emme Ferraro," she snapped and pulled a small revolver from her purse. "I understand completely. Let's move." She sounded like a general rallying her troops.

It was all Emmanuelle could do not to roll her eyes. The last thing she needed was for Agnese to shoot someone. "Go," she said to Enrica.

"I protect *you*," Enrica said stubbornly.

Emmanuelle hissed her displeasure, but there was no time to argue. Fortunately, Nicoletta understood the urgency and grabbed Lucia's hand. "Go," she said to Signora Moretti and rushed Lucia and the other woman into the back room, Agnese holding the gun with surprising assurance.

Enrica flattened herself against the wall. Emmanuelle faded into the shadows, leaving Amo busy tidying up the shop. He glanced up as the customer walked in. The man was wearing a suit he didn't look comfortable in. He looked carefully around the store, spotted Enrica partially hidden behind a rack with scarfs hanging from it. She appeared very interested in them.

Amo smiled at the newcomer as he approached him. "May I help you? I'm Amo Fausti, the owner. You are?" He held out his hand.

The man hesitated, looking around him and then taking the extended hand. "Coop," he said gruffly, clearly still looking for the others.

"Looking for something for your wife?" Amo persisted.

Coop shook his head, frowned and then shrugged. "Girlfriend. Shop's a little out of my expertise."

Emmanuelle shifted just enough to allow him to see her. Coop stiffened. He was caught between Emmanuelle and

Enrica very neatly. Amo had stepped well out of his reach, pretending to examine jewelry in a case.

"These pieces are all one of a kind," Amo said, the polite salesman.

Coop didn't bother to pretend anymore. He abruptly swung on his heel, cursing, and hurried from the shop. Emmanuelle, keeping back from the window to prevent a marksman from getting a shot at her, watched as a car with four men inside parked across the street.

"We've got to go now," she said. "Don't bother to lock up, Amo. Enrica, check the alley, make sure it's clear. If not, keep the others inside. I'll clear it for us. Amo, hurry. Right. Now."

Enrica pushed past Amo, disappearing into the back room. Emmanuelle brought up the rear, keeping an eye on the front door. As she did so, her phone vibrated. Ricco's code for the family under attack. It had to be going on simultaneously. She sent up a little prayer that her family members survived as she coded in she understood and was under attack as well.

"We've got at least two covering the alley," Enrica said. "Massive firepower. Might be one on the roof right next to the fire escape above the flower shop. I'll take the rear and keep anyone from coming in from the front. Good hunting."

Emmanuelle nodded and handed Nicoletta a weapon. "Amo? You armed?"

"I am now," he said and pulled a shotgun from behind the watercooler. Lucia gasped but he ignored her. "These thugs after you or our girl?"

"Don't know. Don't care," Emmanuelle said. "They don't get either of us." She had them all move as far back as they could when she opened the door. Mostly it was to keep them from seeing as she chose a shadow, one that led right up the side of the building and stretched to the roof. She would have to take out their marksman first. Two men with rifles. Four in a car. Two more on foot and at least two plugging the back entrance. Whoever the enemy was, they were serious to bring that much manpower.

The pull of the shadow was strong, so much so that it felt as if she were coming apart, her insides flying out of her. She concentrated on seeing everything around her, no matter that she was moving fast. Two men were under cover near the Dumpsters toward the far end of the alley.

Between the attackers and Lucia's Treasures was Giordano's, the butcher shop. A van was parked in the alley unloading. She recognized the Saldi insignia and her heart nearly stopped beating and then began to pound. Could the Saldis be making a move on the Ferraros? The feud dated back centuries. The Saldis were an acknowledged crime family, indicted numerous times, but then the Ferraros were thought to be a crime family and they weren't. She couldn't think about that now. If the first group out on the street decided to attack the shop, they'd catch the Faustis and Signora Moretti in a squeeze. Enrica could only do so much.

Emmanuelle rode the shadow to the roof and spotted the marksman. He had set up shop at the very edge of the railing closest to the fire escape. He had his eye to the scope and kept checking the window. The shadow stopped just short of him. She had to be in the open for one moment before she could step to the next one. She would have to time it perfectly.

She waited until her body felt whole again right at the mouth of the tube, planning her moves so that she proceeded with absolute confidence and no hesitation. The marksman was good. He never took his eye from the scope, watching for her group to come out of the store. She worried for Enrica, who had to keep everyone from being impulsive and trying to leave immediately. Especially Signora Moretti. Who knew the woman carried a gun? She was always leaving her purse in stores. All that time, the high school teacher was carrying a lethal weapon. Emmanuelle would have to have Stefano talk to her. Half the time she forgot her purse all over town.

Emmanuelle took a breath, let it out, stepped decisively out of the shadow, took the three steps to the next one and was in it just as the marksman turned his head, sensing movement. She stayed still, hidden inside the shadow, her heart pounding. She waited for it to settle and for him to put his eye to the scope once again.

She came out directly behind him and caught his head, and using the move she'd been perfecting since she was a child, she wrenched, breaking his neck. She left him there, riding the shadow to the back entrance to Lucia's Treasures. Using a low whistle to signal Enrica she was back and all was clear for them to come out, she studied the van partially blocking the alley about halfway to their destination. There was movement there as someone unloaded large quarters of beef and carried them into the butcher shop.

Emmanuelle knew she faced at least six assailants. They were waiting at the front and back of the alley, boxing them in. The street entrance would be the most dangerous because she had no way to get to the sniper they had on the roof across the street from Lucia's Treasures. That meant taking her group all the way down the alley past the Saldis' van. If the crime family had initiated this attack, that meant the van could hold more shooters.

Signora Moretti pushed close to her. "I'm a very good shot," she whispered. "I might act a doddering fool, but I'm not. No one is going to hurt you or anyone else while I'm around."

Emmanuelle loved her in that moment. She loved her home and every single person in the Ferraro territory because all of them would back her family and one another. They might have their idiosyncrasies but when push came to shove, they stood with one another. She took a deep breath and nodded. "Thanks, Signora Moretti, I think we're going to head down the alley toward the Saldis' van. We need to keep that van between the entrance and us at all times. There are more of the shooters at the entrance. They're working their way down the alley toward us."

She would have to get to the van first and clear it. If the Saldis were part of the attack, she'd confirm with her family and then try to kill anyone waiting to get them. "Enrica, keep everyone together, quiet, and moving toward the van. I'll get ahead and see if I can figure out just where the enemy is."

She didn't wait. They were running out of time. Emmanuelle stepped back into the deeper shadow that ran along the side of the building. At once the pull was there, a strong magnet dragging her into the tube, swallowing her arms and legs and torso. The tube was extremely powerful and she was moving fast. She caught sight of two gunmen making their way along the opposite side of the building, trying to angle around the van to see the back entrance of Lucia's Treasures.

She had to step out of the tube to keep from moving past the van, and that meant exposing herself to the two gunmen just for a moment. She took a breath and dove for the shadow leading under the van. Gunfire erupted. Bullets hit all around, skipping off the pavement, splintering brick and stone. She felt the bite and sting along her left leg and arm. She rolled, desperate to get away from the bullets.

Heavy boots hit asphalt. Valentino Saldi burst from the back door of the butcher shop, his gun roaring as he did so, providing covering fire for Emmanuelle. He reached down and yanked her to her feet, and then thrust her behind him. She cried out as a bullet slammed into her left shoulder, driving her away from Val and back against the wall. She nearly blacked out from the agonizing pain. Her arm was useless. There was no lifting it or fighting with it. No breaking necks. She swore, trying not to shed the tears swimming in her eyes. She'd never felt anything like that pain.

Val kept his body between hers and the gunmen. So much for thinking he was involved. He returned fire, pinning the two men down. She heard running footsteps as the other gunmen broke away from the entrance to the alley, hurrying to join in the firefight.

"Get inside Giordano's," Val ordered.

She shook her head, fighting back nausea. "Give me a gun." She could barely breathe through the pain. The bullet had gone right through her, but it had done a lot of damage along the way. She wasn't certain how much help she was going to be, but she could shoot with either hand.

"Damn it, Emme," Val snapped. "Who the fuck are these jokers?"

He fired off three more rounds and someone yelled. A body dropped. He'd scored two hits, one injured and one most likely dead. Lethal. That's what she needed right now.

Enrica and the others hurried up the alley, forcing Val to turn back to the firefight to cover them. The moment Enrica was close enough, she slapped a compress on Emmanuelle's wound. Fire raced down Emme's arm and to her belly, making it roll. She wasn't about to get sick in front of Val Saldi.

She took the gun Enrica handed her and indicated for the others to get inside the butcher shop. She was certain those inside had already called the police. Amo pushed Lucia and Nicoletta ahead of him and turned back with the shotgun. Signora Moretti stayed as well. The butcher, Berardo Giordano, stepped out carrying a gun as well. Emmanuelle felt a little hysterical. Her little village was the Wild West.

Val glanced over his shoulder, groaning as he saw the others. He didn't ask questions and he didn't order Emmanuelle inside again, but he stayed close to her, so close she could feel the heat of his body—and his anger. He reloaded, rolled to one side and snapped off two quick shots. The moment he did, Enrica fired as well. Emmanuelle took her time, waiting as Val's two shots hit their marks, one in the foot and one through the throat as the man hopped out into the open.

Enrica's shot took out one of the three men running toward them. Amo's shotgun boomed and Signora Moretti's smaller revolver spat. Everything tunneled for Emmanuelle. Shadows connected everywhere, the runners and those hiding unable to keep their shadows from connecting with the tubes. They had no idea she had an exact map to each location.

She glanced at Enrica. Enrica nodded. Emmanuelle stepped out from behind the safety of the van and squeezed the trigger as if she had all the time in the world. One. Two. Three. Four. Five. Bodies dropped. She stumbled back, feeling faint. Val caught her around the waist and dragged her behind cover as return fire sprayed all around her.

The jerking on her body sent another black wave through her. Vision clouded. Bile rose. She was going to go down. Desperate, she caught Val's arm. "Get the others to safety." She choked out the plea. Her knees went weak and she found herself falling.

Val caught her up, cradling her weight in his arms. "Berardo, Enrica, keep them pinned down. Signora Moretti, I'll need you and the kid to stop this bleeding. Call an ambulance. Tell the police to step it up, we're taking heavy fire."

"Shooter on the roof on the main street across from Lucia's Treasures," Emmanuelle managed. She couldn't feel her body. It was one giant pain, but she had no real knowledge of where her fingers and toes were.

"Shut the fuck up, Emme," Val snapped. "I could strangle you right about now. What the hell was that? You trying to commit suicide?"

She would have smiled if she could have. Same old rude Val, even when she'd been shot. Every step he took jarred her body and sent more pain crashing through her. She had to clench her teeth to keep from vomiting all over him. She saw Nicoletta and Lucia as Val hurried past them, their faces white, eyes wide with shock when they saw the blood running down her arm and shoulder, soaking into her suit and covering Val's shirt.

"Here, Val," Claretta Giordano said. She pointed to a couch set up in the back room. She raised her voice. "Angelina Laconi! I need you right now." Angelina's parents owned the kitchen shop and she was a nurse. Her younger brother, Pace, was a senior in high school. Pace and Angelina hurried from the front of the butcher shop to the back as more shots were fired outside.

"You have to get out there, Val," Emmanuelle whispered. "And don't forget the one on the roof across the street."

Val placed Emmanuelle carefully on the couch. "I've got this. Your brothers should be showing up soon. They'll get the one on the roof."

"I think they're under attack as well," she said. "We can't count on them coming."

He frowned. "*All* of them? Someone's going after your family?"

She didn't take her eyes from his and she nodded. Waiting. Hoping. She saw the fierce anger in him covered immediately. He caught up his phone as he pushed the hair that was spilling onto her forehead back, his fingers surprisingly gentle. "I've got this," he repeated. "For once in your life, let someone help you."

She didn't have much choice, but she kept the gun handy. Shockingly, she hadn't dropped it. He turned away from her, texting fast as he rushed outside. She knew he was checking with his father, making certain that Giuseppi hadn't ordered a hit on all of them. For the first time, she wished Val's cousin Dario, the man always acting as his bodyguard, was there. He'd keep Val safe and fight on their side just to do so—and he was fierce with any weapon.

"I can help," Nicoletta said, pushing past Lucia to get to Emmanuelle's side.

Angelina was tearing at Emmanuelle's suit. Claretta handed her scissors. Already the sound of sirens was loud in the distance. She heard running feet—more of the nearby business owners rushing to help. They were all coming. Everyone. Leaving their stores to make certain their neighbors were safe.

Then Giovanni was there, bending over her. "You okay, baby?"

She'd never been so glad to see her brother. "Shooter on the roof across the street," she whispered. It was so good to see him alive. She'd been so scared.

"I'll get him. Taviano's outside with the others."

Angelina all but pushed him away. There was no time to tell him Val had helped, that it couldn't be the Saldis. There was no way Giuseppi Saldi would allow his son to go anywhere without a bodyguard if he was going to war with the Ferraro family. Val might not know that, but she did.

She caught Giovanni's hand as he moved back to allow Angelina to work on the wound. "Anyone else check in?"

Giovanni shook his head. He wasn't about to tell her that Taviano and he had immediately left the scene, riding shadows as fast as possible to get to her. She was their only sister. It was ingrained in them to protect the women. She could produce riders. Nicoletta could produce riders. More than any others, they had to keep them safe. That was the reason they would use, if asked. The truth was, Emmanuelle was their beloved sister and they would protect her at all costs. She was every bit as good as they were at taking care of herself, but that didn't stop them. Emmanuelle would be furious if she knew they'd come for that reason.

He left his sister reluctantly, turning his back on the firefight happening in the alley. He had to get to the sniper on the roof. If Emme said he was there, then he was. He texted Stefano again, and then Ricco with the information that Emmanuelle had been shot and the attack was still going on. He didn't like leaving Nicoletta and Emmanuelle without a seasoned marksman in the room. Taviano and Enrica were outside. Val was as well. It would have been difficult to ask for help from a Saldi, but he would have done it.

He pulled Nicoletta aside, ignoring her wince and her instinctive retreat, trying to pull away from him. "Have you ever shot a gun?" he whispered.

She nodded. "Amo's been showing me sometimes."

The Ferraros should have been the ones to show her. They would have to address her training after they figured out who the hell was after them. He shoved his favorite weapon in her hands. "One's in the chamber. The safety is on. This is how you take it off. Leave it on unless you intend to fire it. You have a full magazine. Don't shoot unless you know what you're shooting at, but you protect yourself and Emme and Lucia. You got that? Don't waste time talking or warning. Just fucking fire if you have to. Understand?"

Nicoletta nodded solemnly and took the weapon from him. She slipped it under her jacket and went to stand up close to Emmanuelle. She didn't realize it, but she was already, to the neighborhood, identifying herself as a member of the Ferraro family. No one would question it.

Giovanni waited until everyone was watching Emmanuelle and the nurse. He slipped into the front of the butcher shop through a dark shadow thrown by the spinning fan light overhead. He made his way silently through the crowd that had gathered there. The shadow took him almost to the front door. He stood just inside the tube, watching out the window, his gaze quartering the rooftops of the buildings across the street. He was careful not to move even as he watched for movement or anything that would give the shooter away.

Across from Masci's, the deli where Francesca worked, up on the roof, he spotted the barrel of a rifle sticking out, just a few inches. The shooter was utterly still, was disciplined. Very disciplined. He kept his aim on the front door of the butcher shop. Not Masci's, but Giordani's. The shooter was in communication with the others. He knew the firefight was taking place in the alley. He also probably knew Nicoletta was inside with Lucia. If he was waiting for them, he would just have to be patient, wait for it all to be over, let everyone think they were safe and kill them as they left the butcher shop.

Giovanni studied the shadows outside. Two made it across the street, both shadows thrown from the position of the sun on the buildings. He would have to change shadows twice before he reached the rooftop. He couldn't get out the door easily without someone leaving or coming in. He waited not so patiently. Inside the mouth of the tube, he couldn't text his brothers or parents to see if they were alive. He mostly worried about Ricco. His brother had sounded the alarm, which meant he hadn't been taken by surprise, but if this was about him, then he was most at risk.

Three men rushed up the sidewalk toward the butcher shop. He recognized Benito Petrov and his son, Tito, along with Tito's nephew, Orlando. Giovanni waited, timing it just right. The moment Benito threw open the door, he stepped out of the tube into the next one. The pull was strong and fast. He ripped past the three Petrov men and out into the street. The switch came up fast and he hopped from one shadow to the next with ease, hoping the shooter was so focused on the butcher shop that he hadn't seen the momentary flash of Giovanni's body moving between shadows.

The shadow tore his body into pieces—or that's what it felt like—as he went across the street and up the side of the building. He ran across the roof, staying low, studying the next building. It had a flat roof. He could chance jumping, or he could go down and back up the other side. Jumping would be faster. If he landed in the shadow, the only one he could spot thrown by a large industrial fan on the roof, the shooter wouldn't see him even if he turned his head. That was a big "if."

Giovanni took the chance. He leapt from the tube and landed just inside the other shadow. Taking a breath, he went still, gathering himself. The shooter looked back over his shoulder, his gaze moving around the roof, noting everything. Nothing was disturbed, not even the dust and dirt on the ground. Satisfied, the sniper turned back, once again putting his eye to the scope, his finger on the trigger, just waiting for the one shot he wanted.

Giovanni took a breath, let it out and emerged from the shadow right behind the sniper. He caught the man's head in his hands, positioning his own body perfectly for the kill.

Saldi men were everywhere. Giuseppi had sent an army to protect his son. Val, Enrica and Taviano had already wiped out those in the alley, although Signora Moretti was insisting she'd killed one of them. Possibly two. When Taviano looked at the thickness of her glasses, he was certain Val and he were very lucky she hadn't killed them.

Taviano had a bad, bad feeling in his gut. He'd learned never to ignore that warning, and the moment it was confirmed that all attackers were down, he turned and ran back down the alley to the entrance of Giordano's. Emmanuelle hadn't looked good. He hoped his radar wasn't going off because of her. He heard footsteps running behind him, glanced over his shoulder as he yanked open the door and recognized Val Saldi. Great. Half the Saldis followed, including Val's bodyguard and cousin, Dario.

Shaking his head, Taviano bent over Emmanuelle. "Got half the enemy right in this room, *bella*. Probably thanks to the prince's fixation with you." He whispered it to her, but he was really inspecting every inch of her. Her shoulder looked bad. Painful. She'd need an orthopedic surgeon, but the wound wasn't life-threatening. He looked around, his uneasiness growing. "Where's Giovanni?"

"Shooter across the street," Emmanuelle whispered back, her voice hoarse. "On the roof."

She hadn't even gotten upset over him calling Val "prince," or him saying their enemy, a family with a long-standing feud against them, had a fixation about her. She was hurting bad and that was more than worrisome.

He glanced to the front of the shop. He just couldn't shake the feeling. "Has Ricco checked in?" He was already moving. He didn't know why, but he couldn't stay in that room with the smell of his sister's blood and the sight of her beautiful face twisted in pain. There were others in the front of the shop, his people, but he couldn't stay there. He had to go. Be somewhere. The feeling was so urgent, he nearly caught a shadow right in front of everyone. At the last minute, he took off running again out the back door.

The moment he was alone, he caught the first shadow leading up over the roof. As he was hurtled along, he searched the buildings across the street he was heading for. He saw his brother coming up behind the sniper. Something else. Something he was missing. Then he saw it and his heart stopped. He jumped from one shadow to the next, desperate to get there before it was too late—already knowing it was. Heart in his throat, he gained the roof where his brother stalked the sniper.

"Shooter, shooter!" he shouted. "Move now!" He hurtled himself across the roof, yelling at Giovanni as he did so.

Giovanni had already applied the pressure necessary, snapping the neck even as he turned toward the sound of his brother's voice and then dove. There was no cover, only the shadow, and it was several feet away. A bullet tore through his left thigh, dropping him to the rooftop just a foot from his destination. It hurt like a mother, and blood geysered up like a fountain.

Taviano reached out and yanked both of his brother's arms, dragging him into the shadow as a second bullet tore through Giovanni's calf. Taviano wrapped his arms around him and slid through the tube, gaining the necessary speed. The sniper above them, shooting from two buildings away, peppered the shadows as if he knew they were using them to escape.

Giovanni bit down hard to keep from screaming. He tried to apply pressure to his leg, but the magnetic effect of the tube was too strong to do anything but let it take him. Blood flew all around them, leaving a trail and coloring Taviano's shirt red. It didn't stop his brother; Taviano took them right to the front door of the butcher shop. He halted, shifted Giovanni to his shoulder, yanked the door open and rushed inside.

Someone screamed. A bullet hit the glass door and John Balboni, owner of the hardware store, fell backward. He'd come to help and his gun was still clutched in his hand.

"Get down!" Taviano yelled, carrying Giovanni on through to the back room. "Angelina, I need you right now. It's bad."

Angelina left Emmanuelle's side and rushed to help him. They eased Giovanni to the floor. Angelina calmly applied pressure to the wound while Giovanni swore over and over. Another bullet tore into the shop and someone screamed for help. It sounded like Claretta, Berardo Giordano's wife. She yelled for someone to help her get John into the back room, that he was bleeding profusely.

"I'm getting that fucking bastard," Taviano snarled. He didn't care if the sniper was shooting into the shadows.

"No. Don't go," Emmanuelle pleaded. "We can't afford to lose anyone else."

He bent to brush a kiss on her forehead. "You know I have to go, *bella*." When he straightened, Val Saldi was there, his bodyguard, Dario, right behind him. They followed him out.

"What do you need, Taviano?" Val asked.

Dario was silent, his eyes on his enemy, probably ready to slit Taviano from groin to chest if he made one move on Val. Taviano wasn't about to turn down a gift horse. "A distraction. Can you move your vehicles around that building? I don't want anyone taking a chance of getting hit, but I want him worried. Packing up." The shooter was probably already doing that.

Val didn't answer him, but looked to his cousin. Dario immediately spoke into a radio and there was a flurry of activity instantly, cars starting up and taking off. Taviano took the opportunity to disappear. He ran around the corner, between the two buildings, back toward the main street, and stepped into a shadow. His body flew toward the buildings across the street.

The Saldi men surrounded the building front and back with their cars, the men leaping out to get under cover of the eaves so the sniper couldn't see them. Taviano rushed past them and up the side of the building. Whoever had sent these men to attack his family had used their own sniper as bait. The men were shooting into the shadows as if someone had told them they needed to watch out for anything in or coming out of the shadows. A shadow rider. Their enemy had to be a shadow rider.

The sniper had finished breaking down his weapon and was putting it into a case. He turned toward the stairwell that would take him down into the attic of the shop below him. Taviano was on him in seconds and he was feeling mean. His brothers called him hotheaded and said he had a volcanic temper. Right now, he was ice-cold.

He stepped out of the shadows right in front of the sniper and caught him by the throat, the other hand in his crotch, twisting while his fingers cut off all air. "You had better believe me when I tell you I'm not playing games with you."

The sniper coughed and struggled, turning gray, but he could barely reach the floor of the roof with the soles of his boots. Taviano was relentless. "Who the hell sent you after my family? I'm going to ease up on your throat and you answer me, or the pain is going to get a *lot* worse." He stared into the sniper's eyes, refusing to look away or allow him to look away.

He took a firmer grip on the groin, twisting that much harder while he eased his hold on the man's throat. The shooter coughed and gasped, tried to shake his head. "Don't know."

Before he managed to get the last word fully out, Taviano's fingers bit deeper into his throat and twisted his groin so hard the man managed to scream in agony despite the hand closing off his airway. Taviano didn't so much as blink. "I can keep this up for hours. You want to hold out, it's all the same to me. I'm going to fucking pull your cock off and shove it down your throat before we're through. You think I can't, you weren't given the full facts about whom you are up against. Let's try again." He eased his hold on the man's throat.

"Don't know." There was desperation in the sniper's eyes. Truth in his voice.

Taviano heard scraping on the fire escape and caught sight of Valentino Saldi as his head came up over the roof. Val leaned on the ladder and regarded Taviano. "And they say my family is crazy. Get it done, Ferraro. Cops are swarming all over this place. They think there's a war going on between the Saldis and Ferraros. Or that we're banding together against another crime family."

Taviano spun the sniper around, caught his head in a vicious grip and wrenched, snapping the neck. He let the body drop. "There's going to be a war, all right," he said, "and the cops don't have a clue what's coming."

"They won't let anyone leave. If you have some place to go, better go now before you're seen here," Val said. "Giovanni and Emme are being transported to the hospital. Gee's in bad shape. Emmanuelle needs an orthopedic surgeon immediately. I'll go as soon as I can and make certain they're protected. In the meantime, I'll send some of my men."

"Stefano's there." Even as he said it, Taviano worried for his brother. The world had gone crazy.

"I'll be at the hospital," Val said decisively.

CHAPTER TWELVE

Ricco caught up his T-shirt and brought it to Mariko. The marks of the ropes were on her body, diamond-shaped patterns marking her pale skin. He dragged the shirt over her head. He liked seeing them there, as if he still surrounded her, held her close—and safe. His fingers skimmed the lines as he pulled the shirt down over her body.

"We're in for a fight. Emilio is watching on the security screens. He'll let us know where the enemy is, but he's saying there's an army coming over the fence from every direction. I'll need him to be our eyes."

He watched her closely. She had to be exhausted. She sent him a faint smile. "I'm good. Stop looking at me like I'm about to break. I'm not porcelain."

No, she wasn't. She was the real deal. A woman. His warrior woman. She'd stand by his side and fight but . . . "I need to know if you trust me, Mariko. Implicitly. With your life."

"Ricco, I let you tie me up." She tilted her head to look up at him.

"It isn't the same thing. I'm going to have you go outside while I'm inside. The house is built to protect the grounds as well as the interior." While he talked, he turned to the wall and laid his palm along the intricate pattern. Panels slid silently aside.

Her breath caught. She stood up carefully, gripping the back of the chair. "You have an arsenal in there."

"I believe in being prepared." He opened a drawer and pulled out two small earpieces. "Wear one of these. It can go through the tube, just like our clothes. You have to get it in the ear. Emilio and Enzo will be our eyes and ears from the control room. I'll be sitting up there." He pointed toward the wing above the Japanese garden.

The house was shaped like a *U* with the garden between the two jutting wings. Surrounding the house was a maze of more gardens with narrow walkways, forcing anyone moving through the extensive outer gardens to do so in single file. Throughout the grounds were many places Ricco had incorporated where a rider could easily slide through the permanent shadows he'd created within the maze.

This was the moment he'd known all along would come. The old council, made up of Dai Saito, Mikio Ito and Isamu Yamamoto, was making its move against his family. Mariko and Nicoletta were caught in the crosshairs. He'd dreaded this moment, had countless nightmares about it, but he was prepared. He just detested that he didn't know what was happening with the others.

He put in the earpiece. "Emilio, Mariko is going out onto the north side. I'm in the north tower. Check on all family members."

"Roger the north side and tower. I checked on all of them, including your parents. No one has texted back. I tried their bodyguards and everyone is silent. We have to assume they're under attack."

Ricco might have gone a little crazy, rage welling fast, guilt all-consuming, but he didn't have the luxury. He had Mariko to protect. He pulled his favorite rifle from the armory and caught up boxes of ammunition. "North garden, Mariko. Stay in the shadows until you hear Emilio or me tell you who and where to hit."

She didn't hesitate, and that humbled him. She was going out into the open in a T-shirt and red lace panties, no weapons, against an army of men heavily armed. Mercenaries by the look of them. Enzo was running facial recognition.

Ricco caught her by the nape of her neck as she turned away from him, jerked her back to him and kissed her. He poured what he felt into her. Passion. Fear. Guilt. Rage. Admiration. Respect. All those things. His need to protect her. He was feeling very protective. She kissed him back and he tasted sweetness. Giving. Passion. Acceptance.

He let her go reluctantly. Their eyes met. She nodded and then slipped into a shadow, riding it down the stairs and out into the north gardens—and absolute danger. She didn't so much as hesitate. He knew he was more than halfway in love with her. She was a warrior woman, totally confident as she walked right into the shadow and disappeared to go face the enemy. She'd made herself vulnerable to him as a woman when she'd come so bravely to him in his studio, providing him with what he needed. No judgment. None. Just a giving of herself. He was falling hard and fast. Irrevocably. No going back.

He sprinted for the northern tower with the bank of windows on three sides. His walls were reinforced and bullets weren't getting in. The closed windows were bulletproof. He had to open a window to protect Mariko and wreak a little havoc of his own.

Outside, the gardens were designed to force anyone on the walkways to go single file and then turn corner after corner, like a maze. The entire outer garden was just that, a maze leading through path after path toward the house. It looked fun and beautiful, but it was deadly to an enemy. With all the shadows cast throughout the garden at any time during the day and with the lights on at night, the advantage was to the shadow rider.

From his vantage point at the window, he could see every open spot where the enemy would turn a corner, and Mariko would be waiting just inside the tube.

"Coming at you in five seconds. Three in a row. Take them at your leisure," Emilio instructed.

Ricco put his eye to the scope and instantly all three men appeared in detail. They had automatic weapons and belts of ammo slung across their bodies. He didn't want to shoot unless he had to. The others coming over the fence would know instantly he knew they were there and they'd probably run a blitz attack. He would prefer to take most of them outside to keep his house from being damaged.

The first intruder rounded the corner and kept going slowly, cautiously, along the narrow path. This was the protected rose garden and the foliage was thorny, making sure the enemy stayed to the ribbon of a pathway. The corners were tight deliberately. The second gunman followed. The first was almost to the next corner when the third rounded the corner. Mariko stepped out of the shadows, smooth and efficient. She reached almost delicately, caught the man's head in the classic kill hold and wrenched, gently lowering the body to the pathway and disappearing in the shadows as the second man rounded the corner.

She slipped behind the second man, killing him, and then the third. She left them where they lay and was once again in the mouth of the tunnel.

"Two pathways over, near the trellis on the outside of the house," Emilio said. "Four more moving slow. They don't like the thorny branches pulling at them." There was a slight snicker in his voice.

Roses had been a good idea, even though Ricco had to make certain they didn't freeze and were protected through the harsh winter months. He watched from the side of the window frame as Mariko slipped back into the shadows. It was strange. He hadn't known her that long, but from the moment their shadows had connected, he felt as if he couldn't be without her.

Over the years, he had honed himself into the best warrior possible. He might be injured, but that didn't matter; when he needed his body to kick into high gear, every muscle was ready. His reflexes were fast and his hand-eye coordination extraordinary. He was a man fully confident in himself and his abilities, everything from killing a man to pleasuring a woman, yet now, with this woman, the one woman, he was hesitant and careful. She felt elusive to him, always ready to slip away.

Mariko emerged, just for one moment, at the mouth of a shadow just behind the four men. That momentary flash of her in the T-shirt that was long enough to be a dress on her, hair falling around her face, tumbling to her shoulders as if they'd just spent hours making love, her skin flawless and her mouth generous, had his body reacting, even in the midst of the danger. Maybe the danger contributed. He thought it was sexy how she could look so delicately beautiful when he knew she was so deadly.

She flowed like the wind, like water moving over rocks, as she came up behind the last man. The intruder didn't get the chance to turn the corner or even step off the path. He was a big man and she looked fragile in comparison. Ricco watched through the scope, his heart pounding in his throat as she leapt into the air and took the enemy down with her legs around his head, her hands already lethal before the man had a chance to know what hit him. She was gone fast, back into the shadows.

"Damn." Emilio's voice was pure admiration. "That woman is *hot*."

Ricco had to agree. He couldn't fault his cousin for noticing but . . . "And she's off-limits. She's the one. I'm going to marry her." He had his eye to the scope, just waiting. She was going to be coming up behind the next man in line. She had to be exhausted, but he couldn't see one hint of that when she was working.

"Does she know that?"

"She does now. She can hear us," Ricco said. That was how crazy he was about her. How far gone. He hadn't even remembered she had an earpiece in. What any of them said, she could hear.

Emilio laughed. "You might clarify, Ricco. You've got guests knocking at your front door. It's rather hilarious. They're actually knocking. Seven of them. Seven more going into the Japanese garden, and you've got seven on the south side approaching the house. Step it up, woman."

There was no answer, or maybe there was. Mariko appeared behind the third man in line as the second one rounded the sharp corner of the maze. She caught his neck and wrenched, her hands slipping off, and then she was back in the tube to move into the next pathway behind the second and then first man in line. She'd taken out all seven attackers without a single incident. He didn't have to fire his weapon to alert the others they knew an attack was under way.

"Thank you, Mariko," Ricco said, steeling himself to let her go. "I want you to go over the wall and get clear. Three blocks down there's a garage with a car in it. Code is seven, six, two, four, five. That opens the door. Keys are hanging just inside the door. There's money stashed in the glove compartment. I want you to get out of here. When it's done, you can come back."

She stepped out of the shadows, looked straight up at him, shook her head, indicated she was going to the south side garden and stepped back into the shadows.

Emilio burst into laughter. "Rebellion. Ferraro men seem to have trouble controlling their women."

"Shut the fuck up. You're a Ferraro," Ricco was compelled to point out.

"But my father's Greco blood saved us."

Ricco strode down the wide hallway to the end, placed his palm on the wall so the panel slid open revealing the armory. He put the rifle in, closed it and took a shadow to the upper story of the southern wing of the house. She was there ahead of him. He cursed as he yanked another rifle from behind a panel that looked just like the rest of the walls. He had them all over the house.

"Slow down, Mariko. I need to get into position to cover you."

She was already in position behind the first of the seven men making their way to the back of his home. They were closer to the house, working their way through the maze, but having trouble with the various twists and turns. No roses on this side. He had planted dozens of flowering shrubs to make the maze thick and impenetrable. His enemies had to follow the paths if they were going to make it to his house.

He took up his position at the bank of windows. "In place." She still had not said a word. He brought her face up on the scope. She looked perfectly serene. She might have been drinking tea in the garden, not chasing killers around the property.

"Emilio, keep trying to find out about the others. I want to know the moment you hear if they're safe." Ricco was anxious about his family, he couldn't help it.

At his soft command, Mariko looked up at him through the window. He saw the compassion there. She understood about loss of family. She'd lost nearly everyone, and now her brother was in jeopardy. That was on him as well. Someone had kidnapped her brother to force her to kill Ricco. His family. Her family. What could he have done differently that horrible night so long ago? What should he have done?

Mariko was on the move, sliding into the shadows and emerging right behind the last man in line. She caught his head in her delicate hands and wrenched. He went down. The second man, having already rounded the corner, suddenly turned back. Emilio hissed a warning and she slipped into the shadows just as the attacker crouched beside his companion and took his pulse while he looked warily into the shrubs. Suddenly she was there, right behind him, wrenching his neck and dropping his body right over that of his friend.

The rest of the men turned back at a shouted command from the third man. He stuck his head around the corner and saw the two bodies lying there. They crowded in along the path, standing shoulder to shoulder, five of them when there was only room for three at the most, and that was pushing it. Three faced one way, two the other, and they sprayed the shrubs and shadows with bullets.

Heart in his throat, Ricco shot the three facing him, one at a time, squeezing the trigger in a controlled movement when he had never felt so out of control. "Tell me where she is, Emilio," he said. "Right now."

The three men fell while the other two turned toward the house, with what looked like a choreographed, slow-motion dance. Their heads went up, eyes found him, automatics spraying up the side of the house in an effort to get to him.

"At your front door, coming around on the run. Seven more, Ricco. Mariko, get into the house, get out of the gardens," Emilio warned.

Mariko slipped along the shadows while the sound of gunfire reverberated in her ears. It seemed as if the intruders had forgotten there might be someone in the gardens with them, instead concentrating all firepower on getting Ricco. Bullets tore up the side of the house, but he'd constructed his home with just such an attack in mind and nothing penetrated.

He calmly shot two more times, not even flinching or hesitating while they adjusted their weapons to hit the window he was framed so perfectly in. Mariko wanted to call out, to tell him to duck, to get out of there, but she remained silent, seeing the other men rushing around from the front of the house to the side garden. She was needed there whether Emilio and Ricco agreed. It was just that Ricco didn't seem to have any regard for self-preservation. The two he'd shot went down as she studied the seven men rushing to help their fallen comrades.

Ricco turned toward those targets. They'd taken care of the seven on the north side and now on the south, but they had more. She was tired, and tired meant mistakes. If she wanted to live, and if she used her brain, she would ride a shadow straight to the car he had stashed in a garage and get clear as he'd insisted. She knew she wouldn't do that.

She lived by a code. That code demanded she back up her fellow riders no matter how dire the situation. She wanted to think she was staying for that reason, but she knew better. She was staying for one man. Ricco Ferraro. She knew she would never leave him in a situation where he was under attack and could possibly be harmed.

He had declared to Emilio that he was going to marry her, but Ricco wasn't the marrying kind. He was a playboy and there were all too many women willing to fall under his spell for as long as he would have them. The only women she could see that had survived more than one night were the Lacey twins, starlets of a popular sitcom. He had to have been joking with Emilio. At least he admired and respected her. That was genuine, she heard it in his voice just as there was truth when he said he was going to marry her—in the heat of the moment.

Movement caught her eye. Another attacker. This one crawled on his hands and knees, sometimes on his belly, using toes and fingers to drag himself along the ground beneath the plants and on the pathway. Weaving in and out slowly. Every now and then he'd look up at the window and then adjust his line of travel.

Ricco's rifle barked twice and two men dropped. He was a damned good marksman. He disappeared from the window and a volley of shots rang out; the attackers that had come from the front were eager to join the battle. She kept her eyes on the man tracking Ricco. He moved quickly right after Ricco shot, and she realized that's how he'd almost gotten into position. He timed the return fire and made his move. Ricco had no idea he was being stalked.

"Emilio, there's a shooter near the small fountain. Can you spot him?" Mariko whispered.

There was silence and then the bodyguard spoke. "I can't. Enzo? Can you pick him up?"

Her heart in her throat, she looked back toward the sniper. He was gone, disappearing into the dark of the maze. Swearing, she slipped out of the shadow and caught the next one with the intention of riding it closer to him. Bullets sprayed all around her, cutting up the leaves and branches.

"What the fuck is going on?" Ricco demanded. "Are they shooting at Mariko?"

"She exposed herself for a second," Emilio said.

Ricco cursed, the mixture of Italian and English blistering her ears. "Stay in the shadows," he hissed. "I mean it, Mariko. And get your ass into this house right now." He stood and squeezed the trigger, dropping two more newcomers, and then he went to the floor as the remaining three returned fire, bullets slamming through the window and hitting the far wall behind him.

Mariko ignored the byplay between Ricco and Emilio. She had to find the sniper moving to set up on him. Ricco could take out the attackers so careless as to use the meager cover of the plants along the pathway. They were lazy and didn't want to get off the path into the maze with its poking branches and thorns. But the sniper . . .

She chose another shadow and stepped into it. That split second of exposure was her undoing. Bullets tore into the shadows and ripped up the carefully planted foliage as she moved fast toward the mouth of the tube. She threw herself onto her belly, hands in front of her, toes ready to act as brakes.

The moment she was exposed, in between the shadows, the attackers saw her and opened fire, giving Ricco the opportunity to shoot two more. Instantly the others fired at him. It was a repeat of what had happened before. Six were down, one left. And the sniper.

She dug her toes into the shadows, sliding with her hands, trying to catch the ground so she didn't tumble out onto the pathway. The sniper couldn't know she was hunting him. Ricco wouldn't stop until he got the last man. There were others approaching the house from the tea garden, but Emilio was watching their every move, and Emilio, Enzo and Ricco didn't appear to fear the enemy entering the house.

Her hands burned from scraping them along the ground, but she managed to stop just inside the mouth of the tube.

She took a breath and looked around her. Time slowed down for her. The sniper was in position in front of her, away from all shadows she could reach, but tucked into the foliage where, from above, Ricco and his bodyguards probably hadn't spotted him.

Heart pounding, she drew herself up, assessing the situation. He was waiting for Ricco to show himself at the window. She knew, before she moved, before she spoke, that it was too late. The shooter outside had ceased firing. Ricco was already in position, and the sniper had him.

"Get down," she warned, uncaring as she moved out of the shadow that the remaining shooter was already searching the shadows for a glimpse of her. She couldn't let Ricco die. She just couldn't. Her eyes were on him. Right there. Framed in the window. He looked invincible. A warrior of old. A samurai determined to stand his ground and defend his castle.

She was almost on the sniper when she heard the whisper of movement behind her. Simultaneously she heard Ricco's voice. "Behind you." Her heart dropped. She desperately wanted Ricco to save himself. He knew the sniper had him in his sights, but instead of dropping low, or flinging himself to the side, he stood there, unbending. Uncaring. Determined to save her. He squeezed the trigger and she *heard* the bullet hit its mark. The sniper fired as well and his bullet drove Ricco back out of the window and into the room where she couldn't see him.

She was on the sniper, knee to his back, pinning him down, staying low so the remaining shooter couldn't get a clear shot. If he sprayed the area he would hit his companion. The sniper tried to struggle, but it was too late; he was impaired by his own rifle as he brought it up thinking he could shoot her. He tried to twist his body, but her hands were already on his head. She wrenched. The crack was audible. She dropped him, and rolled into the shadows, feeling the familiar pull.

The last group of attackers had to have gained entrance

to the house by now. The sense of urgency was great, but she couldn't make a mistake. Ricco might still be alive. She had to stay numb, not think about him or his sacrifice. Standing there, waiting for the sniper to hit him so he could take the shot to save her. What if she'd tried to kill him, just on the off chance it would save her brother? A man like him. With his integrity?

Mariko felt the burn of tears, but she refused to give into emotion. She had a job to do and she was damn well going to do it. Locating the remaining shooter was the first step.

"Emilio." She forced her voice to be calm, although it trembled. "Ricco was hit. Can you get to him?"

Silence answered her while she took a long look around the garden. The maze had done its job, keeping the attackers moving in single file along the paths. All of them had done so except for the sniper. She located the last shooter on the stones just a few feet from her. He was twisting back and forth, trying to see every shadow, while keeping an eye on the window. He stopped watching the window after a few precious minutes, certain Ricco was dead. She refused to even consider that he was dead. She couldn't, or she wouldn't be able to keep going.

The tiny earpiece buzzed. "Ricco doesn't kill so easy," Emilio's voice intoned in her ear. "Get in here."

"I'm on my way." She had one more task and then she'd be inside. Something in her settled at Emilio's calm assurance. She had no idea how Ricco could have survived that shot, but if his bodyguard thought he was alive, she was going to think it, too. Hugging the knowledge to her that he might be alive, she stalked the last shooter, riding the smaller shadows to circle around behind him.

Her prey continually turned in circles, making it difficult to move on him. A shot rang out and the attacker dropped like stone to the ground, blood running from the side of his head. He nearly dropped at her feet. She glanced up to the window, her heart beating wildly. Ricco was there, framed like before, looking scary beautiful in warrior mode.

"Get the fuck into this house right now," he ordered.

She didn't even care that he swore at her. He was alive. *Alive*. She'd talk gently to him later about his language, but not now. Now she wanted to jump up and down with happiness—something completely out of character for her. Instead she acknowledged the order. Calmly. As if Ricco being alive was always a certainty. "On my way."

"They've split into two factions, Ricco," Emilio whispered into their ears. "Enzo is monitoring the gardens, but I think only those in the house are left alive. They're carrying explosives in their backpacks. Two stopped to wire the walls in the great room."

"I can come behind them and sweep up the explosives," Mariko offered. "I have extensive training."

Ricco's voice was a hiss in her ear. "This house is lethal. I want you with me so I know you're safe."

She smiled at the impatience—and concern—in his voice. It was a new experience for her. She liked it—liked that she mattered to someone—especially liked that she mattered to Ricco Ferraro.

She rode the shadows up the side of the house straight to the shattered window, admiring how Ricco had designed his home to maximize shadows from top to bottom, just as he had the incredible gardens. He reached out, hooked her under her arms and dragged her inside, right up against his body. He held her close for several moments.

"You scared the hell out of me, Mariko," he whispered, pulling back enough to look down into her eyes.

Her heart clenched in her chest. It was the way he looked at her—as if she were the only woman in his world. "*You* scared *me*." She knew how he had survived. He was wearing a vest, but still, the sniper could have gone for a head shot. He'd taken a huge chance to save her.

"I'm too mean to die like this," he said. His hand slid down to her elbow. "We have guests. We want to make them feel very welcome." He slid his fingers down her arm even farther to find her fingers with his. It was an intimacy she didn't expect and her heart turned over. He pushed the rifle into the cabinet in the wall, and waved his free hand toward the shelves. "Pick what you're most comfortable with."

There were numerous knives and smaller guns. There was a belt with several holsters and loops. She wrapped it around her waist and slid knives into the loops and the guns she'd chosen into the holsters. She chose extra magazines for the guns and pushed them into the loops.

"Emilio, keep trying Stefano and the others," Ricco said as he chose his weapons.

"I'm on it, Ricco," Emilio assured. "Enemies approaching the target zone," he added. "Three of them."

Ricco pulled down a screen and activated it. At once she could see three men with backpacks moving cautiously along the hallway leading to the kitchen. It was the narrowest of all the hallways in Ricco's spacious home, allowing the attackers to come at them two strong rather than single file, although these men were moving in single file.

Other cameras showed video of groups of men spreading out throughout the lower story. Without warning, a panel at the front of the kitchen, just to the right of the door, slid open. Simultaneously, one behind the attackers did the same. Guns slid out ahead and behind them, trapping the three men in the hall. There was nowhere to go and as the one in front shouted a warning, turning slightly to try to get away, both guns spat bullets. Within moments the three men were lying dead on the floor of the hallway and the guns retracted and slid behind the panels.

"Ricco." She didn't know what else to say. He'd planned for this. He had known sooner or later someone would be coming after him.

"We're good," he assured. He indicated the library. "We're heading there."

There was a long verandah wrapping around the circular part of the room with glass doors leading out to the cool porch so one could sit outside and read when they desired. The library took up both stories, the walls lined with books.

Ladders with safety rails ran along tracks, allowing anyone to move along the long shelves at any level and pick their book. She *loved* his library.

They chose a shadow right beside the window, one that went up to the roof. He kept his hand in hers, as if that contact between them was very important to him. From the roof, they caught another shadow that took them to the verandah on the bottom floor of the library. Ricco leaned into her and brushed his mouth over hers. He indicated she move into the left side where there was a small, darker area on the porch like a little alcove. There was one on the right side as well. He opened the glass doors invitingly. She realized this was also built with defense in mind. She'd been taught, the same as him, that every offense was a good defense, and every defense was a good offense. He'd planned. It occurred to her that no matter what, Ricco Ferraro would protect his family—and he was good at it.

"They're almost to you," Emilio warned. "You have four coming at you, heavily armed with automatic weapons. They have the backpacks so I imagine they also have explosives. They're probably going to try to wire the room to take down the house."

"Wait until I move and pick your targets," Ricco cautioned her.

She nodded, breathing evenly. The relief and elation that he was alive and unharmed was overwhelming. In such a short time, she realized she was already invested in him. It didn't matter if he felt the same back—and she wasn't silly enough to think that he did. He was a playboy. He liked women. Multiple women. That didn't mean she couldn't have him while they were together. The time would be short, and if she lived through finding her brother, she would be the one with the broken heart, but for her, it would be worth it. She'd never expected to ever feel for a man the way she did for Ricco.

"Don't come out of the alcove until you've locked on and can take them both down. Two shots, one after the other."

She sent him a small smile. "I'm good with this, Ricco. I'm a good shot."

He nodded. She liked that he was a little anxious on her behalf, but she was an excellent shot. The doors of the library opened and the four intruders came in, sweeping the room to make certain it was empty. They hurried to the walls to find the supports for the house. Immediately they eased their backpacks from their shoulders and knelt to get to work.

Ricco and Mariko stepped out of the alcoves. She heard the bark of his gun even as she squeezed the trigger twice. Her targets went down and she switched her attention immediately to his. She should have known he wouldn't miss. She started toward the dead bodies and their backpacks.

"Leave it. We should clear the house first. We didn't give them enough time to do anything but set their packs on the floor."

The idea of leaving explosives around disturbed her, but he was right. They weren't going off by themselves. Ricco was already checking all four men, making certain each shot was a kill shot. He pulled down a screen in the corner of the room nearest the verandah. She could see the little squares indicating cameras.

Five attackers were inside the great room, setting up their explosives on the massive columns. One of them coughed. The room looked a little smoky. Metal shields on the windows prevented light from entering, and suddenly all the lights went out, leaving the room in darkness. The one man coughed again. Someone flashed a light on and she could see the smoke was thick now. Much thicker than it had been a few moments earlier.

One of the men tumbled over and lay gasping. His friend went to him and tried to drag him toward the door. He coughed, let go of his fallen companion and tried to make it to the door. He couldn't find the right direction in the murky darkness. A third and fourth man fell. The last one grabbed his throat and tried to cover his mouth at the same time. He gasped and went down, first to his knees and then to the floor.

"Taviano is here," Emilio reported.

For a moment Ricco sagged with relief at the knowledge that his brother was alive. Mariko moved close to him and he locked his arm around her waist, as if she gave him strength. "Tell him to go to the security room. The house is lethal right now. Gas in the great room. Guns activated. Tell him . . . I'm glad he's alive."

"He's reporting Giovanni and Emme both were shot. Emme has a shattered shoulder and Gee has multiple wounds in his leg. He's being prepped for surgery. Stefano checked in with them. He, Francesca and Vittorio are good. Cosimo and Tomas took major hits. They were alive the last time he heard news, taken to the hospital, both in very bad shape. We don't know their status at this time."

"Eloisa? Phillip?"

"He doesn't know."

Ricco indicated they move forward toward the pool room where the last two attackers were busy setting up their explosives. He held her hand as they rode the shadow into the room. Fifteen seconds later, solid steel plates dropped down over the windows. Both men jumped to their feet and stared at the steel.

Ricco took one. Mariko took the other. She was on him immediately, not giving him time to trigger the explosives they already had wired and ready to blow. The moment her hands were on his head, he slammed it backward, trying to dislodge her, his superior weight carrying them six or seven steps back. His elbow crashed into her ribs in another attempt to knock her from him. She leapt onto his back, her legs circling him like a vise.

Her hands never left his head, not even to protect herself when he smashed her back into the wall. She let out her breath and wrenched, snapping his neck, ending his desperate attempt to survive.

Ricco was there instantly, yanking up the T-shirt that

covered her body. "Did he break your ribs? Can you breathe?"

She was very aware she wore only her red bra and lace panties beneath the T-shirt. "I'm fine. He was strong. Is it over?"

He touched the fading marks on her skin from the ropes, lowered the tee and took her hands, turning them over to inspect her palms and the pads of her fingers where she'd taken skin off trying to brake in the gardens.

"All quiet. We've got the cameras sweeping the grounds and house," Emilio said. "Ricco, you took a hit. How bad?"

Ricco kissed the center of her palm and then her fingertips. "Bruising only. My chest feels like someone took a sledgehammer to it. Call Sal in. I want them to do the cleanup here and maybe he and his crew can find some clues to who is doing this."

Her heart stuttered a little at the feel of his lips brushing so gently over her torn skin.

Ricco looked at Mariko. "I'm fairly certain I know, but we need proof."

She knew, too. She'd brought this down on the Ferraro family. "I'm so sorry," she said, meaning it. Very slowly she removed her hands from his. His touch was making it difficult to think. "I had no idea when I came here that this would happen."

"The council threatened me years ago," he pointed out. "This has nothing to do with you and everything to do with me. With what happened."

She lifted her chin. "If you're correct and I'm a Tanaka, then this is my fight. They allowed their sons to get away with killing my family. They made me believe I hurt my brother when one of their sons did it. I'm with you all the way."

CHAPTER THIRTEEN

Riders came from all over the world to attend the funeral of Phillip Ferraro. Each family sent a representative. Every member of the International Council was there. The council was made up of retired riders from around the world. There were five at all times and it was significant that they were all present at Phillip's funeral.

What was more significant was that the Archambault family had come in full force, with the exception of the one always secreted until the family came home. Riders in that family brought justice to any riders and their families if the laws were broken. There were five brothers and one girl, just like in the Ferraro family. Mariko was shocked to see the ruling council as well as the Archambault riders making their presence known to all the rider families. She could see that it made everyone uneasy.

Emmanuelle sat between Vittorio and Taviano. Vittorio was still pale and walked carefully, but he had insisted on coming. Giovanni couldn't be there. Emilio and Enzo guarded him at the hospital. Stefano sat beside his mother, Francesca on his other side. Ricco had insisted Mariko sit with him. He kept his arm around her, his body sheltering hers from prying eyes—and she was well aware that her presence was shocking the world of shadow riders.

A family friend, Henry, sat on the other side of Eloisa, and Lucia and Amo sat with Nicoletta in the family section. Valentino Saldi attended with his father Giuseppi and Val's cousin Dario. There were at least five other men in the Saldi party. Just about everyone who lived or worked in the Ferraro territory was present.

There were seventeen families in the shadow rider community after the loss of the four families in Japan. The murder of the Tanaka family had been a terrible blow, but the loss of the Yamamoto, Ito and Saito families had crippled the riders there. Japan had sent a representative from their remaining family. His name was Kichiro Nakamura, and he had trained with Mariko. He hadn't been mean, but then he hadn't been very friendly, either. He spent a lot of time during the funeral looking from Mariko to Ricco.

She pushed closer to Ricco, sensing his grief. The Ferraro family was shaken, no doubt about it. And angry. Stefano Ferraro was going to have someone's head. She could feel his rage smoldering just beneath the surface—and that rage was nothing compared to Ricco's.

She'd never attended any gathering so grim. Even with the people from the Ferraro territory attending, the family didn't put on their calm, all-is-well faces. They looked angry. They felt angry. By the time they gathered together with the riders in the Ferraro Hotel, their rage wasn't to be contained.

It was a long time to maintain that anger, all through the funeral, then the reception with everyone outside the shadow riding families giving their condolences. Ricco didn't let Mariko slip away from him. Even when she had to use the bathroom, he walked her there and was waiting for her when she came out. Everyone was hypervigilant. There was security everywhere. No one tried to be subtle about it. They were right out in the open, and all of them had guns.

The Ferraro cousins had arrived en masse, bringing investigators, bodyguards and riders. They made it plain that they stood with their cousins and would remain until the threat was gone. Eventually, only the riders were left and they went to the Ferraro Hotel, filing into the large conference room. Catered food and drinks were on the tables, although Mariko noticed not too many people were eating.

Stefano waited for the room to become quiet, holding Francesca's hand the entire time, keeping her close. When the five ruling members of the council indicated they were ready for a meeting, he brought her hand to his mouth. "You will excuse us, Francesca? I'll have Demetrio and Drago escort you up to our home. I want them to stay with you while I'm away from you."

"You keep them here," she protested, leaning into him, anxiety on her face.

"We have our cousins from New York. The riders in this room are skilled."

She looked as if she would protest again, but Stefano shook his head slightly and she subsided, giving him a worried nod. Biting her lip, she turned away from her husband.

Mariko couldn't imagine too many people, man or woman, going against Stefano Ferraro when he had that particular look on his face. Grim. Ice-cold. Eyes gleaming with suppressed fury. It didn't bode well for any member of the council who might think they had reason to oppose him.

"Gentlemen," Stefano said quietly. "Please sit." He indicated the chairs around the table and then waited until a rider from every family had taken a seat as well as the five International Council members. The riders of the Archambault family remained standing, along with the riders from the Ferraro families that had come from New York and Los Angeles. The Ferraro riders looked as grim as their cousins.

"In the history of our existence there has never been a time when riders have turned on one another. There are few of us," Marcellus Archambault said. He was head of the International Council. "This attack on the Ferraro family was aided by someone inside our circle. There is no other possible explanation when those attacking the family members knew to shoot into the shadows."

Beside him, Alfieri Ferraro, another council member, nodded. "This is my family. My cousins. *Our* family. We have to find who did this and bring justice to them."

"Stefano Ferraro contacted us and told us a horrendous tale recording his brother Ricco's time in Japan with our fellow riders there," Marcellus continued. "If this is true, and we've sent investigators to Japan, then our world is about to be shaken. We've provided detailed accounts to all the riders here. Read them and leave the account on the table. Every copy must be returned and then destroyed." He reached for his glass of water to allow the riders time to read the summary in front of them.

Kichiro Nakamura shook his head the entire time he read. He kept looking up to glance at Mariko and Ricco. Mariko moved closer to Ricco. She didn't like the look on Kichiro's face. At. All. From the moment she'd entered the room, he had kept his eye on her, and every time he looked down at Ricco's and Mariko's hands joined, he frowned. It was clear he didn't like them together.

Ricco was very silent, his face an expressionless mask, but she could feel him so close to her. He was a volcano inside. He didn't like any of these men sitting in judgment of him, considering he might be lying or knowing his personal business. He sat straight, shoulders wide and impressive in his pin-striped suit.

"You believe that three of the families conspired to keep this information out of our hands?" Kichiro demanded, tossing the paper onto the table. "You want us to believe that their sons murdered the entire Tanaka family?"

"Everything our investigators have uncovered so far has led us to that conclusion, yes," Marcellus answered. "Isamu Yamamoto committed suicide after his wife died. He prepared a letter that his lawyer sent to the council upon his death. In the letter he admitted that his son, Nao, as well as Kenta Ito and Dai and Osamu's two sons, Eiji and Hachiro, murdered the Tanaka family. Isamu, Dai and Mikio conspired to cover it up. They told everyone their boys were killed in a car accident, when in fact Ricco Ferraro killed them to try to protect the two remaining members of the family, Mariko and Ryuu. Ryuu was stomped repeatedly by Nao, breaking all his bones. Mariko fought to save him as well. She was barely three years old. Ricco fought Nao, causing his existing injuries. In the fight, Ricco was sliced several times with a sword. He has the scars."

The riders around the table stared down at the report and then looked from Ricco to Marcellus as if somehow they could make it all go away.

"This can't be the truth," Kichiro said. "Those houses are respected houses. The Saito family took in Mariko and Ryuu and gave them a home for years."

Ricco stirred then. The first time. Just that small movement brought him everyone's attention. Mariko's heart began to pound. He looked . . . invincible, like he did when he was shooting the attackers coming at him. Calm. Resolute. Scary dangerous. She tightened her fingers around his.

"Mariko was treated as a servant in that home. She was beaten daily by Osamu Saito. She was told she caused those injuries to her brother. Her heritage was taken from her, the legacy of the Tanaka name. She was given a new last name and told her family didn't want her, that they'd abandoned her to the streets. The Saito family didn't take her out of kindness." There was a distinct warning in his voice. One that said if Kichiro persisted, they would do more than exchange words. The fact that, at fourteen, Ricco had managed to kill three promising riders and injure the fourth so severely would give anyone pause before they challenged him.

They shouldn't have worried about him. They should have been watching Stefano. "Are you calling my brother a liar?" He looked relaxed, sprawled out in his chair, a tiger eyeing prey. His voice was very, very soft. So low they had to strain to hear it.

"Stefano," Marcellus cautioned.

"I want to know if he's calling my brother a liar. It's a simple enough question." Stefano didn't take his eyes from Kichiro. Neither did the other members of the Ferraro family, and that included every cousin in the room. The tension stretched out until Mariko wanted to scream.

"Of course I'm not calling him a liar," Kichiro clarified. "Ricco's reputation has always been impeccable. It's just the shock of finding out three of our most legendary families covered up such a brutal event and a Tanaka still remains."

"Why didn't Ricco's family go to the council?" a rider from Russia asked.

"Ricco didn't tell them. He was threatened by the three families. He was told they would kill his entire family if he breathed a single word to anyone."

A collective gasp went up from nearly every rider.

Marcellus continued. "He was also told they would say they investigated and he had committed the murders of the Tanaka family."

The riders looked at one another, frowning. "That wouldn't make sense," the Russian persevered. "All of us would have known if he was responsible; they would have brought him up on charges to the council immediately."

"Isamu Yamamoto was part of the International Council as well at that time." It was Kirchiro who reminded everyone, his voice thoughtful. "He served on both councils."

"The idea that anyone could wipe out the Ferraro family is ludicrous," a rider from England added.

Stefano stirred again, but Eloisa laid her hand gently on her son's arm. She stood up and faced the council members. "I am not the head of my family. That falls to Stefano. But I have something to say. My child was fourteen years old. I sent him off to be trained, believing he would be safe in the hands of those riders meant to guide him. He was not. He was threatened, and he believed those threats as all children do. It changed the entire course of his life and who and what he was. Mariko's life was changed for all time. Compensation must be made to both. Justice must be served. In the world of riders, everyone must know what happened. This I demand as is my right."

Eloisa had thrown down the gauntlet. The council couldn't ignore her demands. She was within her rights. More, Ricco and Mariko, especially, deserved compensation.

"The investigation is ongoing. We have not had enough time—" Marcellus began.

"You have my son's testimony. You have a letter written by Isamu Yamamoto before he died. He waited for his wife to die and then he committed suicide." Her tone suggested she believed Isamu to be a coward. He had been unable to face what his son had done, and he'd taken his life.

"That is true, but of course, Mikio Ito and Dai Saito have denied the charges. We will get to the truth of this matter."

"You know the truth or you wouldn't have given the report to the riders," Eloisa pointed out. "Spare us the bullshit, Marcellus. My son has been through enough. When I found this out, it was everything I could do to keep from seeking justice on my own."

"That is the job of the Archambault riders," Marcellus said, his voice gentle.

"Do you think I care?" Eloisa snapped. "I've lost my husband. I'm not a young woman. Retribution by the Archambault will not deter me as long as I bring these criminals to justice."

Stefano put a hand on his mother's arm. Just laid it there. He said nothing, but she glanced down at it and some of the anger receded from her face to be replaced, just for a moment, by sorrow. That was quickly gone as she struggled to put her mask back in place. She sank back into her chair, looking small and tired.

"I understand how you must be feeling, but we have laws for a reason," Marcellus said. "Those laws are very exacting. When a rider harms another in any way, justice will be served, but not before every single member of this council is convinced we have the absolute truth of what happened. This took place years ago. It is only coming out now."

"You know it isn't coincidence that Mariko showed up here and suddenly every family member is under attack, just as Ricco was threatened all those years ago," Stefano said. "It isn't the first attempt on his life. The crash in his race car was no accident. There were numerous incidents prior to such a costly and coordinated attack."

Kichiro stood. Very carefully he rested his hands on the edge of the table. "A great injustice has been done to Mariko. No rider knew she was from the Tanaka family. I will escort her home and claim her as my bride. She will be given every respect as befitting a Tanaka. My family will welcome her. With the loss of the Yamamoto, Saito and Ito families, it makes sense for us to join together. We need Mariko back in Japan. It is home to her. She will be well taken care of."

Mariko stiffened. The council could very well see this as a solution. Her heart thudded. Kichiro hadn't wanted her when she had no pedigree. When she was an orphan left unwanted on the street and they thought her mother was a whore. His family would have lost it had they known he was ever considering her for a bride.

"That's impossible," Ricco said. He brought her hand to his heart. "I have declared my intentions to marry Mariko. Isn't that true, *farfallina mia*?"

Mariko nodded. This was her worst nightmare—Ricco being forced to stand up for her. To declare intentions he could never keep. She heard the sincerity in his voice, everyone could, but in the long run, he'd never be satisfied with one woman. She couldn't see him cheating, it wasn't his style. He had too much integrity, but he'd never be happy. The alternative wasn't a good one. She wasn't attracted to Kichiro, and his mother was a close friend of Osamu's. Her life would be a nightmare. She was too reserved to be able to stand up for herself in that environment.

There was a shocked silence. Kichiro stared at them in open disbelief. "If Mariko has not given her consent, I would appeal to the council to stop this match. We need Mariko after losing so many families. The Ferraro family is strong. I am an only child. There are no more riders from any of the other families in Japan. Without a wife to provide me with children, we will lose all riders in Japan. We revere Tanaka riders. Mariko would have a good life and can be of service to our world by providing children. The Ferraros already have Francesca to provide them with riders."

Mariko inhaled sharply, feeling a little faint. How had everything turned so suddenly? One moment they were talking about the murders, and now she had to choose a husband and quickly.

Ricco smirked, looking more arrogant than ever. "That only goes to show Mariko she is wanted by me for far more than her ability to provide me with babies."

Kichiro shook his head. "You have the luxury, but I don't."

Mariko started to put her head down. Kichiro was all but saying she wasn't much more to him than a baby machine, but he'd sacrifice. Ricco's fingers on the nape of her neck stopped her. One finger sliding under her hair, just as he did when he was about to start Shibari with her. That one finger alone gave her confidence to face the room full of riders. Face the council with her head held high.

The entire room stared at her. Waiting. Beside her, Ricco looked as arrogant and assured as always, but she felt his tension. Could she possibly humiliate him in front of an entire room of riders? She could always break the engagement when things had blown over, but she would never embarrass him. Not when he'd given her a glimpse of how life could be. Not when he'd given her the confidence to be a woman.

"I'm sorry, Kichiro. Although I've known you since we were children, we never had a relationship like that. I never thought you were even considering one."

"I couldn't before."

"Before?" Ricco raised an eyebrow.

Kichiro nodded. "My family would not have accepted Mariko, but knowing she is a Tanaka has changed everything."

"I don't give a damn whether my family accepts her or not, she's my choice. She'll always be my choice," Ricco stated. "I'm not going to marry her so she can give me babies; I'm going to marry her because she's become my world."

She wanted it to be that way. She knew she was important to him because he'd chosen her to do Shibari. To be his rope model. Suddenly she'd gone from that to his fiancée. He believed what he was saying, that she was his world, she could hear it in his voice. She wanted to believe it, too. Right then, she would allow herself to be his, but she had to remember leopards didn't change their spots.

"Mariko," Marcellus said softly. "Is Ricco your choice?"

"Yes." She stated it truthfully. He was her choice, so much so that she wasn't about to saddle him with her for a lifetime, but she wasn't going to sacrifice herself to be Kichiro's bride, either.

"Then that matter is closed," Marcellus decreed.

"Someone is holding Ryuu hostage at an undisclosed location," Ricco announced.

Again there was silence, as if no one could believe this matter could get any worse, but the more disclosed, the worse it seemed to be.

"I believe whoever took Ryuu is behind the attacks on me personally and my family. They have money. Mercenaries aren't cheap. To find Ryuu before he kills him—and he will—we have to find who is behind all of this."

"Do you believe any other family is in danger?" a rider from England asked.

Stefano shrugged. "No one else has reported any trouble, let alone anyone making a concentrated hit on their family members. We drew the short straw on this one."

"Tell us what you need from us," the rider from Russia said. "We'll help in any way we can. If you need more guards for your family, you have only to ask."

Everyone nodded, including Kichiro. Stefano regarded the riders around the large conference table. They'd come from all over the world out of respect for a rider's fallen husband.

"I appreciate what everyone is offering, and it might be necessary to call on you at some point before this is over, but for now, my cousins are handling it. We know we're under attack and we're taking the necessary precautions."

Marcellus stood up, signaling to the others. "We need to leave this family to their grief. You will all be informed of the outcome of our investigation."

The riders stood and each gave their condolences to the Ferraro family before filing out.

Kichiro hesitated in front of Mariko. "I didn't mean my proposal as it sounded. I was always interested in you, but my family objected when I told them I wanted to court you.

I was elated when Marcellus said you were a Tanaka because, although your mother wasn't one of us, your family is legendary and would be a huge asset. It was *you* I wanted, the woman, not the rider."

The entire time Kichiro spoke, Ricco was coiled and ready to strike. He didn't understand that Kichiro was paying her a compliment. She put her hand very gently on Ricco's knee beneath the table, trying to send him the message to remain silent. She inclined her head to Kichiro, indicating she understood. She gave him a serene smile. "I understand, Kichiro."

He studiously avoided looking at Ricco. "You aren't wearing his ring and I know that is important in his family. If you aren't certain, please consider my offer. It is a sincere one."

Despite the hand on his thigh, Ricco surged to his feet. Since the attack on his family, he had been smoldering for a physical outlet. "You pretentious prick. Get the fuck away from my woman. You insult her and then you insult me. You're lucky I don't throw you out on your fucking ear."

Kichiro drew himself up for the first time, his calm mask slipping. Before he could say anything, Alfieri Ferraro stepped between them. "This is a sad day, gentlemen, and we're all upset. Perhaps it would be a good idea for you to leave now, Kichiro. Thank you for coming. Our family certainly appreciates it."

It was a clear dismissal from one of the members of the International Council. Ricco subsided into his chair, no longer even looking at Kichiro. The Japanese rider nodded his head at Alfieri and then whispered to Mariko, "I hope you will be happy." He turned on his heel and left.

Ricco tightened his arm around her, drawing her beneath his shoulder. "That man doesn't deserve you. I might not, but at least I appreciate you."

Eloisa shot him a glare. "You're a Ferraro," she reminded.

"I'm a Ferraro, a damned good rider, Eloisa," he agreed. "But she's taking a huge leap of faith when it comes to judging what kind of man I am." He brushed a kiss along Mariko's knuckles. "I appreciate it, *farfallina mia*. I swear, you won't regret taking me on."

Mariko had no idea what to do or say. It was all a farce, to save her from Kichiro. Now he had to lie in front of his family—his mother. Worse, he was very, very good at lying. She couldn't hear the lie, and she was very good at it as a rule. Either that, or he believed every word he was saying and his offer was sincere—right at that moment. Moments didn't last.

"I realize this is a terrible situation for you and your family, Ricco," Marcellus said. "But unfortunately, time is of the essence. We would like to interview you and then Mariko."

"His father was just brutally murdered," Eloisa objected.

For the first time, Mariko heard the unrestrained fury in the woman's voice and realized Ricco and his brothers came by their tempers honestly. Eloisa was on the very edge of her control.

"It's all right, Eloisa. We must find out who is behind this. The sooner the council realizes I'm telling the truth, the sooner they'll look at the members conspiring against us." Ricco stood and looked at the council members. "We can use the smaller office right off this room. Mariko was not even three. What she remembers is mostly from nightmares. Her life has been hell, and if you want to talk to her, you'll do it with me in the room."

"Ricco . . ." Marcellus began.

"That's nonnegotiable."

To her shock, Marcellus nodded. "That doesn't seem unreasonable, although you have to know we all would be gentle with her."

"You'll be gentle with her with me present," Ricco declared, not giving an inch.

She couldn't believe he would talk to a council member like that and, more, they'd give in to his demands. She had confidence in herself as a rider, knew she was respected as one, but she wouldn't have had the nerve to speak to a council member so directly, let alone giving them what amounted to an ultimatum.

Ricco nodded toward his brother Stefano. "I'd appreciate you watching out for her while I do this."

"I will be going into the interview with you. As head of the family, that is my right." Stefano was decisive, coming to his feet, his expression grim. "Taviano, Vittorio and Emme will keep her company."

Eloisa glared at him. "I'm still quite capable of defending my family."

Stefano bowed toward his mother. "Of course. Forgive me."

Mariko didn't understand the dynamics of the Ferraro family. Clearly the siblings were close. They all seemed to almost revere Stefano, but their mother, Eloisa, they treated as an outsider—and it wasn't because she was a woman. She watched Ricco and Stefano head toward the small office with the members of the council.

For some reason, her heart beat far too fast as she watched him go. She realized she didn't want him to have to relive the horrors of that day or the subsequent two years that followed in the homes of the families whose children he'd killed. He would have to tell them about how he didn't sleep for years, that instead he guarded the homes of his siblings. He would have to tell them about that terrible night when her family had been massacred by four disturbed boys. She knew the interviewers would question him closely over and over and it would be an ordeal. She realized she wanted to be there with him when he had to go through it all again.

The low murmur of conversation swirled around her and she had no idea of time passing as she tried to puzzle out the enormity of what the three families in Japan had conspired to do. She had grown up there. Japan was beautiful and she loved the country and the culture. The people she'd grown up around were very traditional and held to the old ways, unlike others she'd encountered. Was that part of the problem? Should the riders consider modernizing their training methods? Their society was very small and the ways entrenched. She believed what happened in her country could happen in any of them.

She could understand why their families felt the need to hide the truth from the world. She couldn't understand why they had taken her legacy from her or from her brother, Ryuu. She also couldn't understand how shadow riders could turn so severely on their own kind.

"Mariko." Taviano finally got her attention. "Emilio told us how effective you were in the maze. We appreciate you helping Ricco out when we all know he's still not one hundred percent."

She couldn't imagine how effective Ricco would be when he was at full physical strength. He still had repercussions from the original accident in his race car. She sent Taviano a small smile. "I'm a rider." That said it all. Naturally, she helped Ricco.

"Are you any closer to figuring out who has your brother?"

She shook her head. "Before I went to your brother, I followed Ryuu's trail here to Chicago. He was seen in the airport and he checked into one of the hotels. He never checked out. I went into the room and there was no sign of struggle."

"Where did you go from there?" Emmanuelle asked, moving three seats closer.

She shook her head. "His new job. I went to the company, a software company, small but upcoming, and they had never heard of him. They hadn't sent him the invitation or the ticket to Chicago. I tried tracing the ticket but that was a dead end."

"You believed those you spoke with at the company?" Vittorio asked.

She nodded slowly. "I couldn't detect any lies when I spoke with them."

Eloisa leaned across the table, pinning Mariko with cold Ferraro eyes. "How, *exactly*, did you come to be with my son?"

Without hesitation, Mariko answered. "I was contacted by those holding my brother and told if I killed Ricco Ferraro, they would free my brother."

Eloisa erupted into a long litany of curses in a mixture of Italian and English. "What the *fuck* is wrong with Stefano that he allowed you anywhere near Ricco? Clearly he knew this and didn't tell me. Well, you can just go straight to hell. Don't think for one minute that your little seduction act—and clearly you've seduced him—will get you my son. You may have caught his attention for the moment, because he's intrigued with the idea that you came here to kill him, but trust me, it won't last."

She was shrieking at Mariko, on her feet, her face twisted with a mixture of anger and grief. Her family looked stunned. Mariko would have had great compassion for her, but she could only hear the truth ringing in her ears. A man living under a death threat his entire life would be fascinated by a woman coming into his life to kill him. To have his mother confirm her worst fears—that his interest wouldn't last—was a heavy blow.

She rose and stepped away from the table. That's when the reactions of the Ferraros caught her attention. The compassion lacking for their mother was now on their faces. Emmanuelle immediately went to her mother's side despite the obvious pain she was in with her arm and shoulder in a stiff contraption. Her sons surrounded her, as if they could protect her—and keep anyone from seeing her distress—as the door to the office was flung open and Stefano strode out, Ricco right behind him.

Stefano's face looked like thunder as he emerged—as did Ricco's—but the moment they took in their mother, both expressions changed. Both men went straight to her. "Vittorio and Taviano are going to take you home. They can stay with you . . ."

Eloisa shook her head, pressing a trembling hand to her mouth as if she might be able to take the harsh words that had spilled out back. "Forgive me, Ricco."

"Go home with Taviano and Vittorio," Ricco reiterated. "Everything is fine."

"Henry will stay with me," she said, making an effort to lift her chin. "Vittorio needs rest and so does Emmanuelle."

She looked at Mariko and then back to Ricco.

"Don't." Ricco said one word, but it was a command.

To Mariko's shock, Eloisa nodded and turned toward the door. Despite what she had said, Vittorio and Taviano flanked her as they went out. Ricco immediately went to Mariko and wrapped his arm around her. "Are you all right? Eloisa can be vicious. She's very upset right now and striking out. You were a convenient target."

She couldn't help the small step she took away from him. It was slight. Subtle even. Not subtle enough.

"Mariko." Her name. The way he said it. That voice. The sound slid over her skin to find its way right inside of her where he wound himself around her heart. She was certain she was never going to be free of her obsession with him. Still, Eloisa's words had caused her sense of self-preservation to kick in. It was late coming, but it was there.

She forced a smile. "I'm fine."

His thumb brushed her chin, sending sparks of electricity showering through her bloodstream. "Any man who believes it when a woman uses the word 'fine' is an idiot."

"In this case, I am."

He flashed her a smile that didn't even come close to his eyes. "Come here, *farfallina mia*." She shifted, feigning moving into him. He wasn't letting her get away with it. "Closer to me."

"Come in, Mariko," Marcellus said from the office doorway, saving her.

Ricco remained solidly in front of her. Waiting. She sighed and moved into him. He brought her in close, one hand to the nape of her neck as he bent his head and brushed a kiss across her mouth. "Thank you."

When he did things like that, looking at her as if she rocked his world, it was impossible to believe anything but that she *was* his world. She let him lock her to his side, her hand on his hip, while they walked together to the office. It felt intimate walking beneath his shoulder. He was a solid presence. Protective. She understood in that moment what it would feel like to belong to him.

She found herself nervous, but she refused to allow any emotion to show on her face. If Ricco could face an interrogation, then she could as well.

Marcellus smiled at her as he courteously held the back of a chair for her to sit. She glanced up at Ricco's chiseled features. He was back to his expressionless mask, but that disappeared whenever he glanced down at her. His features softened, his dark eyes gentled, giving her a feeling of being cherished. She had no idea what to do with Marcellus's courtesy let alone Ricco's protective care. She'd never experienced either.

She sank into the chair and took the glass of water from Alfieri Ferraro. "Thank you," she murmured. "I really can't tell you much. I've had nightmares all of my life, but I didn't think it was real."

"Have you already discussed your nightmares with Ricco?" Shaun Holmes, from England, asked. His voice was exceedingly gentle, as if she were a fragile flower.

She nodded. "Yes. Not in great detail, but he told me what happened."

"Your dream," Shaun persisted. "Does it change?"

"Only to add or subtract more detail. Someone wakes me up and takes me to the closet. They put my brother, Ryuu, in with me and tell me to keep him quiet. I hear screaming and threats. There's blood. It's running under the crack in the door."

She was suddenly there, in that tiny, cramped closet, shaking. Terrified. The smell of blood was heavy in the air, making her gag. "Ryuu whimpered and I clapped my hand over his mouth. He sank his tiny little teeth into me." Involuntarily she rubbed the pad of her finger over the little scars there.

Ricco slid his hand down her arm to take her hand, his finger tracing over the scars. Somehow she found it soothing.

"A big boy drags Ryuu out of the closet and throws him. He cries. I'm afraid. There's so much blood everywhere, but the big boy is stomping on Ryuu and he's screaming. I have to do something but I'm so scared. I rush the big boy and kick him as hard as I can the way my father taught me. It makes him very mad."

"Stop." Ricco's voice was very soft. "Stop right now and come back to me."

She blinked rapidly and found herself looking into Ricco's dark eyes. She took a deep breath, gulping at air in an effort to try to recover. She'd been in that closet so many times. It was real and vivid and a place she couldn't seem to ever escape. Ricco's thumb gently brushed at the tears on her face she hadn't known were there.

"We're done with this. She has memories. You can doubt it all you want, but she doesn't need to relive them for you."

"Forgive us, Mariko." Marcellus's voice was gentle. "We're not putting you through hell for our own amusement." He didn't look at Ricco when he said it, but he was making a point.

It didn't seem to matter to Ricco. He'd made his. Marcellus sighed. "Are you willing to take a DNA test?"

Ricco stirred again, and for the first time there was anger spilling into the room. "She doesn't need to do that."

"There is a great deal of money involved. An entire estate, Ricco. As with all families of riders, if there are no survivors, then the estate goes to the league. There will be a demand for proof from every lawyer, including hers."

"I have no problem with that," Mariko stated.

Marcellus nodded approvingly. Ricco pressed her hand to his thigh, his fingers stroking over her skin, making her heart beat fast.

"How were you contacted concerning your brother?"

"A note was on the floor of my room when I returned from a mission. It said they had Ryuu and would kill him if I didn't kill Ricco Ferraro. They gave me three weeks to get the job done."

The council members exchanged long looks. "Why didn't you do it?" Alfieri Ferraro asked.

"A rider doesn't kill another rider, and I certainly wouldn't do so without thoroughly investigating him. I found Ricco to be a good man. I couldn't trade his life for my brother's. In any case, it made little sense to do so. All they had to do was kill Ryuu after it was done and then me."

"Our investigators will help look for your brother. Every

family will send their people," Shaun added. "Do you believe the Saitos or the Itos are involved? And what about Nao Yamamoto?"

"I know that Nao's parents sent him out of the country immediately after. They said it was to give him the best medical care available. He runs one of their companies and he inherited everything when his father died."

"We looked closely at him," Ricco said. "He seems the likeliest candidate, but he's lived here years and has never made a move against us. Still, it's too coincidental that Mariko, the child I saved, would be sent to assassinate me. The note was found in her room. It wasn't mailed to her. Someone went into her home. Whoever is coming after us knows to have their mercenaries shoot into the shadows. We aren't neglecting investigating Nao Yamamoto, but Stefano and I are making a trip to Japan to interview Osamu Saito."

That was the first she'd heard of it and she snapped her head up to look him in the eyes. He pressed her hand tighter against his thigh. She read his silent signal and didn't comment, but she was going to have a lot to say to him when they were alone. *A. Lot.*

The interview went on for some time until finally Marcellus rose, indicating it was over and they were free to go. "Our doctor will be in shortly to take the necessary tests for DNA and then we're finished here."

Mariko nodded. The council, like Ricco, seemed convinced she really was a Tanaka. They hadn't said so, but she was adept at reading people, and every one of them believed her to be from the legendary family. She didn't know what to feel about that.

She was extremely happy the rest of the Ferraros were gone when they emerged from the office. She felt drained and not able to face anyone. Only the bodyguards waited to escort them back to the house.

CHAPTER FOURTEEN

M ariko was quiet on the way back to Ricco's home. He glanced down at the top of her bent head as she sat beside him in the backseat of the car. "I was going to tell you about the decision to go to Tokyo as soon as we got home. Stefano makes up his mind fast. He wants to talk to Osamu." There was no guilt or remorse in his voice, only a quiet explanation. "We both feel there is a high probability she's involved."

She felt there was a high probability as well, although she didn't want to believe it. She looked down at her hands— at the scars from Ryuu's biting her. She hadn't thought about his tiny little teeth in years. She thought she made up the closet incident to explain the scars.

"Why does she hate me so much?" It came out a whisper. She turned her head to stare out the window at the glittering lights of the city as they drove through the streets. The day had passed while they laid his father to rest, had a reception with the townspeople and then the separate meeting with the riders. She hadn't even been aware the sun had set and night had fallen. Now, suddenly, she felt that the sun had set on all of it, her newfound confidence in herself and her secret desire that Ricco Ferraro hadn't been rescuing her when he proclaimed to the world that they were to be married—that somehow he could miraculously become a one-woman man.

"She raised two boys who committed a brutal murder. You were a daily reminder. Why you were placed in her home, I have no idea. My guess, if I had to make one, is that it was all about penance."

She nodded, still staring out the window. What was there to say? Osamu had hated her. Sometimes she hated Ryuu. Most of the time the woman had loved him. She'd set up conflict between Ryuu and Mariko so that he would side with Osamu against her, feel guilty and then be angry at Osamu. Like Mariko, Ryuu was always off-balance. Osamu had been very good at keeping both that way.

Ricco shifted in his seat, reaching for her, drawing her against the protection of his body. She didn't resist. He was warm and felt invincible. She let him hold her because she needed holding. She felt a little guilty over that. They'd buried his father today. Hers had been dead for years, yet he was comforting her.

"You didn't eat much," he said softly, his fingers sliding through her hair. "Are you hungry?"

She should be taking care of him, not the other way around. She felt vaguely ashamed that she could only stare out the window, feeling his hands in her hair, and his body solid against hers. Sometimes she felt completely invisible, as if she not only worked in the shadows but lived there—and she'd wanted to. Like now. Except that Ricco could see her no matter where she was, invisible or not. He could always find her.

"No." She wasn't the least bit hungry. She was sad. Very, very sad. She'd been living in a dream world with him, and it wasn't going to last. She knew the truth somewhere in her head, but her heart had refused to listen and she'd let him in. He was there, inside of her, and she knew she'd never get him out.

Living with Osamu had been a child's nightmare. She'd never understood why the woman would take in two children off the street she despised so much. Osamu had said their mother was a whore and that she had abandoned them. Mariko had been beaten "for her own good," to get the devil out of her. She didn't dare wear clothes or makeup that might be considered attractive to a man. She'd never felt attractive until she met Ricco Ferraro.

"Mariko," he said softly. "Tell me what you're feeling."

It was the last thing she wanted to do. She didn't know what she was feeling—although sorrow was close. He had stolen her heart with his care for her. The way he seemed to cherish her. He made her so much more than she was when she was with him. He gave her a confidence in herself as a woman, as a human. He made her feel beautiful and intelligent. He listened to anything she said. He *wanted* her to speak.

"Mariko."

Her name whispered over her skin. Slid inside her. Wrapped around her heart. How could she leave him? Leave a dream? A fantasy? If she didn't, no matter what happened with her brother, she knew the longer she stayed with Ricco, the more it would tear her apart when she left. She'd have to leave for her own self-respect. She couldn't be in love with a man who would eventually despise her. She'd lived with that all her life and she was done with it.

"I'm okay. Just thinking. The interview must have been difficult for you."

"In a way it was freeing. Just as it was when I told my family. I carried those secrets and the fear that they would all be targeted. They were, but I realized it wasn't through my fault. I did what had to be done. I saved two children. I would do it again even knowing what would happen. Telling the council made me feel vindicated."

He brought her hand to his mouth and scraped at the pads of her fingers with his teeth. She went damp, her sex clenching. He could do that so easily without even trying, his mouth hot against her cooler skin—his teeth moving over her flesh and leaving behind a trail of sparks.

The car pulled through the gates leading to his home, after making its way slowly through a crowd of photographers. Flashes went off continuously while Emilio and Enzo searched through a series of security screens on their phones before taking them all the way up to the house.

The reporters had had a field day speculating that the Ferraro family had gone to war with another crime family, and that the Saldis had sided with the Ferraros. Of course the news media had picked up the story and run with it. Sensation sold, true or not.

All the while, as the car moved through the eager photographers and reporters, Ricco kept his arm over Mariko's head, keeping her face pressed into his chest so none of the cameras could capture her image. Despite her emotional turmoil, the protective gesture made her feel cherished. That was part of his charm, part of the reason so many women—including herself—fell for him.

The moment they were inside the house, she moved away from him. "I think I'll take a hot bath, Ricco," she informed him. She needed the respite from his constant presence. He was overwhelming. Intense. There was disappointment on his face, but he didn't try to argue with her or talk her out of it. Because he left the decision up to her, courage had her lifting her chin. "After, I would very much like to do more Shibari with you."

She was determined to seduce him. He had stated he was going to seduce her, but it was going to be the other way around. When he put the ropes on her, she was always drowning, totally drenched in desire for him. It wasn't the ropes, it was the dark lust she saw in his eyes, the deep passion there when he looked at her. She was totally determined that she would have her time with him before she left. She felt very brave telling him she'd like to have a rope session with him.

His eyes lit up. "When you're ready, Mariko, come into the studio. I'll set up the lights and find some appropriate music."

"Do you have a preference for what you'd like me to wear?" She kept her voice low, looking at him through the long sweep of her lashes, hoping he would cooperate.

"How daring are you feeling?"

Before she lost her courage, she answered, "Very."

It was the right answer. His eyes darkened. He gave her that look she'd come to crave. He was totally focused on her as if she were the only woman in his world. For the time she had with him, she was going to be that woman.

"There's a black lacy robe hanging in the closet. Wear that. Nothing else. Hair up. Red lipstick. Eyes smoky. Sexy."

He was pure Ricco, the one she was so familiar with. His voice was a velvet command that made her shiver with need and want to give him every single thing he asked for—and more. She heard the promise of passion and paradise. She'd never known paradise before—never experienced true joy—but before she left him, before she walked away from her one chance at happiness, she was determined to discover that elusive feeling with him.

She'd lived in a stark, ugly environment her entire life. Ricco accepted her just as she was. He had known why she was there—to kill him—and yet he hadn't judged her. He didn't care if her blood wasn't pure one way or the other. She took a deep breath and nodded her head, to let him know she understood what he wanted before she turned and walked down the wide hall to her suite.

She loved her suite. The large bedroom with its dressing and sitting rooms was so beautiful she couldn't help wandering around each time she entered. She always went to the glass doors leading into the gardens with the views that took her breath and made her feel at peace. Even now, when she should be nervous, she just felt certain. Absolutely certain.

She ran her bath and added the wonderful smelling beads of oil Ricco had left for her there before stepping into the water. So many small touches. She appreciated each of them, but more than anything, she appreciated the confidence he'd given her to be who she was. To make her own decisions. Every step of the way, Ricco had stood back and encouraged her to make choices. He made it clear from the moment she walked into the interview room that she was in control.

Being in his ropes had taught her about the exchange of power. About beauty and the concept of sensuality. Art. Being a woman. Confidence. Above all else, trust. She understood why her mother loved being a rope model. It was freeing. She felt as if she were soaring when she was with Ricco Ferraro and he'd wrapped her up in himself—in his ropes. She also was very aware that she would never allow any other human being to tie her. It was all about her connection to him—and what he needed.

She was careful with her makeup, using a sheer, barely there foundation. She made up her eyes in a smoky, sultry look and added red lipstick to her pouty lips. She stayed naked while she pinned her hair in an elaborate swirl that would come down the moment he pulled out the long, decorative pins.

The robe was sheer stretch lace. Black. Delicate. It flowed down her body as if the material lived and breathed, a sensuous garment that slid over her curves to the floor. There were three pearly buttons at her breasts, but the entire rest of the robe was open so that with every step it opened and closed and slid over her bare skin, making her aware of her femininity and the power she wielded as a woman.

As she made her way to the studio, she knew she wanted this time with Ricco more than anything else in her life. This was her claiming him. Choosing him. She wanted him with every breath she took. Every step toward him. Every step took her closer to what she wanted.

She took a deep breath when she reached the studio doors. There would be no going back from this moment, but she knew she would never be sorry. She was that certain that Ricco Ferraro would always be the man for her—even when she knew she wouldn't be the woman for him forever. But she would be now.

She pushed open the door and stepped through, surprised by the moody music and the dim lighting. Ricco was shirtless, wearing only a pair of soft, drawstring pants. They molded to his butt and hung lovingly on the powerful columns of his thighs. He had his back to her and was looking over the coils of rope. They were all different textures and colors.

He turned to look at her as she came up behind him. She saw his eyes widen, then go dark with sensual hunger and need. She loved that she could put that look in his eyes. He had a rope in his hand, one with several knots already tied on it. She raised an eyebrow and indicated the rope. It was gleaming, midnight black. Made of cotton.

His smile was wicked. "You'll see. You look . . . beautiful. Sexy. Beyond my imagination. Thank you, Mariko, for knowing I needed this even before I did. Already, the ropes are grounding me."

She wasn't certain what the sight of the rope sliding through his hands was doing to her—or the knots . . . She'd felt the vibration of the rope in their earlier sessions and the sensation had been almost more than she could bear. She couldn't imagine what it would feel like with knots . . .

She glanced over to the table where he'd set up the camera. He was going to capture her needs. She knew she would never be able to hide them, especially as he was already preparing to use the rope to stimulate her. She *wanted* him to see, wanted him to know she was aroused. For him.

She knew no other way to seduce him. Each time he'd had her in his ropes, he'd been aroused. He hadn't tried to hide it . . . but neither had she. Her skin had flushed a soft rose, her eyes gone wide with excitement and need. If she was honest with herself, Ricco seemed aroused every time he was with her, which meant he was that way around women. It was Mariko who was made different in the ropes. Because they were his. An extension of him. He wrapped her up with himself. With his power. He gave her a confidence she'd never had before. She knew she was beautiful to him when he created his art with her body as the canvas.

Ricco watched Mariko as she moved around the studio. He loved the way she walked, flowing feminine power she was unaware she had. Her hips swayed, calling attention to her beautiful form. She stretched, completely focusing on warming her muscles, getting her body ready for the vigorous workout of being in the ropes. It gave him the ability to watch her unnoticed. Everything she did, every move she made only served to heighten his hunger for her.

She was very symmetrical, something he found fascinating. He worked with symmetrical patterns because they were so pleasing to the eye. She was already aroused, her body in a heightened state, every nerve ending receptive to the rope—receptive to him.

The rope slid seductively through his fingers, an automatic motion now to ensure there were no kinks. He could tell the burn speed of a rope with that one movement. He felt for splinters, anything that might make her uncomfortable when he laid the rope against her bare skin. For him, her safety and comfort were paramount.

He found the center of the rope easily, his gaze still on Mariko. She moved him in ways he hadn't expected. It wasn't just the way their shadows connected; it was everything about her. He liked her silence. Her flashes of temper. He'd see it in her eyes just before her lashes covered the raw emotion. He loved that. Loved that beneath the serene, peaceful exterior, there was a wealth of passion and emotion. It came out the moment he put the ropes around her.

Watching her, the vision began to take shape, the way it always did. He could see the ropes laid against its beautiful canvas of curves. The halter. The corset. The colors. More, he intended to seduce her. To claim her. To make her believe his marriage proposal was real and he meant every word of it. He knew more secrets with ropes than most and they were all for his woman. He would take her to the very edge of ecstasy, hold her there and then take her to his bed.

He had tied other women, even women he had sex with— the Lacey twins more than once—but it had always been one or the other: sex or art. Never had he wanted to do both at the same time—until now. He'd contemplated it, but he hadn't wanted to taint his art with something he considered casual. His art wasn't casual. By the time he'd considered using Shibari for an erotic time with the twins, he was already so jaded he'd dismissed the idea.

Shibari had been the only thing left to ground him. He'd viewed sex separately. Now, there was no separating anything from Mariko and the way he felt about her. The way he needed her. He had to find ways to tie her to him before she decided to bolt—and she would. Any sane woman of intelligence would take one look at his reputation and run for the hills.

Mariko was intelligent and sane. She was going to come out from under the embrace of the ropes and then she'd want to leave him. He wanted her to look at him and see *him*. The man. Not just the rigger. That was part of him, but it wasn't all of him. He had to find a way to make her see—and love—all of him.

"Mariko."

Deliberately he said her name low, an order, getting her attention. She froze and then turned toward him. He was already close, moving swiftly, using a panther-like fluid motion, deliberately mesmerizing her, forcing her to focus wholly on him. She blinked as he reached for her shoulders, pulled her slightly but very firmly toward him so she was a bit off-balance and had to lean her body into his. Her gaze never left his. She was drowning there. Swallowed whole by him—just the way he wanted.

Her skin was warm to his touch—warm from her bath. She smelled heavenly, a combination of citrus and vanilla. He found that a little ironic because what he was about to do to her was considered anything but vanilla. He inhaled, taking her into his lungs. She was already there, wrapped around his heart. He looked down at her, his heart jerking hard in his chest as she looked back up at him.

Her face was beautiful to him. Classic bone structure, exotic eyes with sweeping, feathery black lashes, and that mouth . . . that fantasy mouth. He couldn't resist bending his head to capture it. Her lips were perfect. Soft. Yielding. One hand went to her throat, his fingers seeking her pulse as he kissed her.

He didn't kiss women while he had them tied. He didn't make love to them or want to make love to them. They were part of his living art, something he needed to balance the rage with the poet in him. Then there was Mariko with her mouth and her smile and the way she moved up behind prey when she made a kill. Sheer poetry.

She tasted like she smelled, like orange blossoms and some exotic spice that blended so well with the vanilla, he was instantly addicted. He couldn't stop kissing her, his arm snaking around her, yanking her into him possessively. He felt possessive. A bit like a caveman. He now understood the urge to carry a woman off and claim her for his own. His need was primitive. Savage.

She kissed him back, and that was his undoing. If she hadn't, he would have found the strength to step back, to change his artwork from seductive to a quick image that would satisfy her, and he'd let her go back to her room alone. But she kissed him back. With her kiss, she took his heart and every bit of good he had in him. He was better with her. He knew he was. More. He was simply more.

He had the rope in his hand, it was always there, an extension of him, and this time, when he grasped her wrists, he was decisive. In charge. He felt her pulse jump and her heart accelerate. Good. He wanted her entire focus on him. He lifted his head just enough to break their kiss, to look into her eyes as he pulled the robe from her body and allowed it to pool at her feet.

He loved the way the black lace looked on the floor around her bare feet. He would photograph her that way, but he knew he wouldn't share that particular picture with anyone else. This was the night he was going to make Mariko irrevocably his. He wanted to read every thought, her body language, the things she said to him without speaking.

When he pulled her arms so decisively behind her back and bound her, he heard—and felt—the air leaving her lungs softly. Her lashes fluttered but not before he caught the flare of desire in her eyes. Her gift to him was precious. Something to cherish. He knew a woman like Mariko would never submit her body this way to a man she didn't trust implicitly. Never.

He was humbled by her generosity. His body was as hard as a rock. He'd never had a problem wanting women. He liked them, and he'd loved sex until a few months before the accident when it seemed everything was the same. He was going through the motions. Jaded. He hated that word, but he knew he'd embodied it.

"You're not getting a bargain, Mariko," he whispered in her ear as he tightened the ropes, declaring his intention to keep her. She might not recognize it yet, but he was talking with the one thing that was always constant in his life. Always grounding. His ropes.

Her lashes fluttered again and then she was looking into his eyes. He didn't know if he was drowning or if she was, but he moved the rope along her back, the sweet curve of her shoulders, fastening the pentacle harness he loved against her skin. This time her breasts were bare and he could worship them as he quickly built the frame of his vision around them, along the tender undersides, laying the ropes carefully on her skin so there was no discomfort.

He worked quickly and decisively, but kept his hands on her bare skin, stroking and caressing, letting the rope subtly help him with licks and bites of flaring heat. He paid attention to the way she sucked in her breath, her eyes widening, the dark of desire creeping into the beautiful hazel, making them pure amber.

He stepped very close again, seeing the haze in her eyes as he kissed her gently. Tenderly. His mouth wandered down her throat over the curve of her left breast. He flicked her nipple with his tongue, teasing, watching her reaction closely. The lift of her breasts as she inhaled sharply. The way she moved into him, not away. Satisfied that she was giving herself to him, he suckled her right breast, bringing every nerve ending to life.

Ricco took his time, a slow dance of seduction, lavishing attention on her breasts even while his hands moved with new rope, the one with the measured knots. One between her breasts, hooking onto the harness there. One just below her ribs and one pressed tight into her clit, almost like before, but this time, right over it where every movement would send a streak of fire racing through her body. He passed the rope under her and back up between her sweet cheeks to attach it to the halter.

When she was drifting in the haze of desire, he caught the harness rope and cinched down, sending streaks of lightning through her breasts as well as rubbing sensuously over her sex. He saw the ripple on her flesh as her body came alive, crying out for release.

Mariko gasped, her eyes flying open, centering on him immediately. Exactly what he wanted—and needed. Her complete focus. He smiled wickedly at her and teased the rope so that it vibrated over her sweet spot, sending more ripples of pleasure through her body. He could give her so much more. *So much.* He wanted her to look at him and feel aroused. He wanted her to see or smell the ropes and feel that same way. Every time she saw a rope, he wanted her to see only him, to want only Ricco.

He'd never used his art for seduction—or for erotic play. He knew his brothers thought he did, but for some odd reason, he had separated the two things in his mind so completely that having a woman in the ropes wasn't a turn-on to him. Women were, not the ropes. He had no interest in bondage other than as an art form. He'd learned because he studied everything about the art. He loved the old prints from Japan and he liked to study the masters' works.

The *art* of bondage was beautiful to him, but he'd never found it particularly seductive. Now he understood why. For him, there was Mariko. Only Mariko. He wanted to give her everything he was. The ropes were a part of him and he had extensive knowledge on how to keep her on the very edge of ecstasy for a long time. He wanted that for her. For them.

He had kept himself separate from the women he fucked. He gave them pleasure, but he didn't give them him. The ropes were part of him. A big part. No matter how sensual other women found Shibari, something in him had always refused to follow through and have sex while they were in the ropes. With Mariko, he wanted sex with or without. Any way he could have her. He wanted ultimate pleasure for her always.

He began to wrap the corset, making certain that each time he moved her body, directing her with his hands, he vibrated the rope. She rewarded him with her gasp of plea-sure. He felt her body melting with each wrap of the rope. Each time he tied her, he had the sensation of wrapping her up in him. His arms. His body. His lust and love.

He laid each line with a firm command, but it was his love he was laying on her body so exposed for anyone to see. He knew she thought she was exposed to him—her secret desires, her needs, even her hunger for him. He saw all that. It was there in her body's response. The peaked nipples, hard as rocks. The damp collecting between her legs—he desperately wanted a taste of that.

She thought it was her exposure, but if she was watching, if she looked with more than her eyes, if she let the shadows tell her, it was Ricco Ferraro laying himself at her feet. She thought she'd given control over to him when she gave him the gift of her body for his canvas. In reality, she had all the control.

He knew with every line, he was exposing his love, his lust, his very need of her. His absolute commitment to her. He'd never felt so raw before or so vulnerable. Every time he'd worked with ropes, he now knew it had been a practice for this moment—with her. The ropes were wrapping her flesh and he knew that each wrap was him sinking into her, deeper and deeper.

He felt his hand tremble, when he was always confident, always the dominant. She did that to him, with the corset of red and black, the deep blue decorative triangle he'd added to the front and the herringbone spine down the back. It was more than decoration. Each pull of the rope sent vibrations teasing her body with the knotted rope wrapped around her, front to back, a part of him seducing her with every touch.

He stepped back to view his creation and it left his heart hammering, his cock hard and pounding with need. He caught the ropes between her breasts and pulled her to him, so that her body melted against his. He took her weight easily.

"Next time, I'm going to tie you on your knees, the ropes in your hair, holding it up off your neck." His teeth teased her vulnerable nape. "I keep seeing the image of you like that. I know exactly how I'm going to tie it." He had to distract himself, but there was no distraction, not even try-ing to think ahead. The moment he thought about tying her on her knees, her head pulled back by the rope in her hair, he couldn't stop the image of her sucking his extremely painful cock into sweet oblivion.

"Would you like that, Mariko? How do you see yourself tied?" He whispered the temptation against her neck, suck-ling gently but persistently until he knew there would be a small strawberry there.

Her breath came in ragged little pants. Her eyes were glazed and she fought coming back from the floating eu-phoria where he'd sent her. He fucking loved that.

"I love any way you tie me," she said. Her voice was soft. Her body squirmed in the ropes. Needed. Was hungry.

"I want to photograph you. For us. No one else. Are you okay with that? Can you stand where I put you?"

She touched her tongue to her lips. He groaned and traced her mouth. "I love your lips. I'm feeling a little desperate to have them under mine—or wrapped around my cock." He said it deliberately, watching her reaction closely. He wanted to seduce her, that was true, and he was willing to use any means at his disposal, but he would never want her to feel so vulnerable in the ropes that she thought he might force her to do anything she didn't want to do.

She licked her lips again, causing his cock to jerk hard. "I've thought about those very same things," she confessed. Her voice was soft, but it was confident. "And yes, I can stand while you photograph me, but my body is burning up."

He flashed another wicked grin. "Good. I love how you look right now. So hungry, *farfallina mia*. I hope all that hunger is for me." He hoped it was for Ricco, the man, not only Ricco, the rigger.

She lifted her chin. "It is." Her eyes met his.

His heart jerked as hard in his chest as his cock did in his pants. He had to move before he did something stupid like take her like a madman right there on the floor. It wasn't what he wanted with her.

He'd been so focused on creating certain images that somehow the person was just a canvas, no matter how sexual the pose. With Mariko, he was so focused on her that every tie was personal, sexual and erotic. He realized, with her, he could easily be into bondage. He fucking loved how she looked in ropes and it was a complete turn-on to use his erotic secrets on her body.

He steadied her, brushed her neck with another kiss, and then checked her hands to make certain they were still warm. "Wiggle your fingers for me. Are you numb anywhere?" As a rider she was in superb physical condition, and he knew that helped.

"No. I'm fine. Just . . ." She shivered. "Needy."

His wicked smile flashed again. He liked her needy. He gave the rope another tug, wanting to keep her right on that edge. He pooled the black lace robe around her bare feet and adjusted the lighting. The camera loved her. He took several pictures with various lenses, from every angle. The longer he looked at her through the lens, the more he wanted her.

Abruptly he put down the camera. He had to know. It was too important to him. His hands automatically went to the ropes. Now they would forever have her scent on them. Her ropes. No one else would ever see or feel them. Slowly he unwrapped her, removing the coils, unknotting each decorative rope, sliding them through his hands to feel her warmth and to make certain there were no splinters.

"Don't slouch, *farfallina mia*. I know you're tired but I don't want any ropes to pull or move on you while I'm untying. I can cut you out if you're too tired."

She shook her head. "I'm not." There was a hint of desperation in her voice.

Standing behind her, his fingers on the knots, removing the coils from around her body, he put his mouth against her ear. "I want you with every breath I take."

"I want you the same way." There was no hesitation.

"Me? Or the rigger? The rope master?"

"It's the same thing."

"No, baby, it isn't." With the corset off, he tugged on the knotted rope so that she cried out softly, her skin flushing a soft rose. "I will agree it's part of me, but I don't want or need ropes to make love to my woman. I need to know if you need the ropes to want to be with me."

Her long, feathery lashes fluttered. Lifted. He found himself falling into those beautiful amber eyes. Flecks of green had intrigued him when he'd first met her, there in the conference room of the Ferraro Hotel. Now her eyes were all amber, exotic, a cat's eyes.

"I came here tonight not to be your rope model," she admitted, looking him straight in the eye. Her voice rang with truth. With absolute certainty. "I wanted to seduce you, and I noticed when you tied me you were aroused. I thought if I came to you the way you asked, dressed in the robe and nothing else, I'd have a chance."

His eyebrow shot up. His hands were moving faster, sliding beneath the rope to ensure she didn't get burned or pinched as it coiled in his hands. "I get aroused because it's you I'm tying. I don't see other women when I tie. Their bodies are canvases I work with or practice on. I don't fuck them after I tie them."

He removed the knotted rope carefully. It was her rope now. He cleaned all his ropes with care, but this one would always be special.

Her eyes didn't leave his. She didn't blink. She looked at him as if he'd grown two heads—or she didn't believe him.

"Mariko, I don't bring women to this house. Ever. I've never had a woman in my bed. I don't sleep with them. Or want to hold them all night. I don't tie them here; I just created this space after my accident in hopes of finding you. When I'm working, it's all about how the creation looks and the right lighting. The poses are sexual, even blatantly erotic bondage, but for me, working with the rope, the art I create centers me. My mind calms and I see only the creation in my mind."

The harness was gone and she stood very still, hands still tied behind her back. She was naked, her body very flushed and aroused, every nerve ending on fire. She was totally aware of him, just as he was of her. His hands went to the last tie to free her. He hesitated. He loved the Japanese artwork depicting beautiful, intricate ties, men and women in bondage, posing in various positions. He never had considered what it would be like to have his woman completely vulnerable to him—so trusting she would give her body completely into his keeping.

"Any numbness in your arms or hands?" He asked the question as his hands moved over her arms, checking her body temperature.

She shook her head. "None."

He stepped back and looked at her from behind. She was gorgeous. His. He made a slow circle around her, taking in her body with his heated gaze. Devouring her. When he was directly in front of her he tipped her face up with two fingers, forcing her to meet his eyes.

"Tell me no if you don't want this, Mariko. Once I have you, there isn't any going back."

He watched her take a deep breath and let it out, her breasts rising and falling, drawing his attention, her thighs rubbing together as if she could alleviate the ache between them.

"You always look so serene," he observed, running the pads of his fingers over her breasts. "Even with your body on fire. It is on fire, isn't it?"

She touched her tongue to her lips and he groaned. She swallowed and nodded slowly. "I need you more than I need to breathe right now. I want you in the ropes or out of them, Ricco. Either way. I'll always welcome you."

He took a breath. Lust and love combined in a fiery need rushing through him like a turbulent storm. He had to stay centered, make certain she was all right before he made his demands. *In or out of the ropes.* He had everything with her.

"Touch me, Ricco."

He smiled. Wicked. Sinful. He felt both. He wanted to be both. He wanted to be her obsession. Her addiction. The love of her life. He took his time, kissing her throat, trailing kisses down to the curves of her breasts. Making her wait while he just blew warm air on her nipples. She swayed toward him, her breath hitching.

"Are you going to untie me?"

He was. He wanted to feel her hands on him. "I'm beginning to understand the appeal of a woman in bondage. When you get out of hand and go all wildcat on me, I'm going to resort to this."

She laughed softly. "You know I'll like it. It excites me to see what you're going to do next."

He obliged and she yelped when his mouth closed over her breast.

She leaned into him. "I don't know about going wildcat."

He did. She had more pent-up passion than he could imagine—and he could imagine a lot. It was in her bold, direct gaze and the smoldering there in the amber of her eyes. She was definitely going to make her own demands, and the thought of that had him wanting to quit teasing her and untie her so he could feel her hands on him.

"You'll go wildcat on me." He said it with absolute conviction and a hint of excitement. "But since you want to touch me so much, I'm going to untie you."

"You're projecting."

He raised his head from where he was nuzzling her breast to look at her, letting her see how wicked he could really be. "You're probably right. The thought of your hands on my cock has been on my mind for a while now. But . . . since you're not ready to be untied . . ."

He dropped down to his knees, taking his time, his hands moving over the curves of her body, his mouth following the same path. Inserting one hand between her thighs, he pressed. "Apart, *farfallina mia*. Spread them apart and give me room."

She made a little sound that vibrated right through his entire body. Playing was fun, but he wanted to get down to the real thing—making her his. Still, he looked up at her, at the desperation on her face. The hunger. The need. There was demand there as well. His woman was no shrinking violet, tied or not, and he fucking loved that.

CHAPTER FIFTEEN

"I'm not sure I can stand up," Mariko said. She was strong, in great physical shape, but Ricco was pushing her right to her limit. Her body had never felt so on fire, soaring, yet the tension building, always building, coiling so hot and deep she thought she might go insane with need.

"Just for a moment. I need to taste you," Ricco said.

She closed her eyes at the sinful, raw truth in his voice. She waited, holding herself still, her heart pounding so hard she was certain he could hear it. One moment. One breath. Ragged. She was barely able to draw air in.

"Mariko."

Her name. Velvet soft. Whispering over her like fingers. She looked down at his upturned face. He looked like sin. Like temptation. Like the embodiment of sensuality. For one moment, their eyes met and she was drowning, *drowning* in him. In her needs. In love for him. She hadn't known love could be so sharp, so terrible. So perfect or brutal.

His hands gripped her thighs, fingers digging into her flesh, and then he leaned into her and put his mouth over her center. She gasped. It was all she could do. His mouth was hot and wild, his tongue as wicked as his look had promised. Stroking. Flicking. She closed her eyes. The flicking was going to *kill* her. No, it was the sudden scrape of his teeth. She wanted to move away. She wanted to stay right there. Pleasure radiated through her like a starburst, yet that tension grew and grew until she wanted to scream.

Her head thrashed back and forth. His hands kept her still, but she had lost all ability to think. She could only feel. Deep inside, that tension wound even tighter. A gathering. A coiling. He had to stop. She didn't want him to ever stop. Secure in his ropes, she was completely at his mercy, and he wasn't feeling very compassionate. His mouth devoured her and his hands were lethal, fingers, by turns, kneading her buttocks and then dancing up her inner thighs to penetrate deep.

She knew she was chanting his name, but she couldn't stop, desperate for release. Her hips bucked against his mouth, grinding, trying to force him to take her where she needed to go.

His finger pushed deep, driving through silken folds. "So tight, *amore,* I have to get you ready."

Ready? She was already losing her mind. She was totally ready. "Please." She managed to get that one word out.

He didn't hesitate; once more his mouth was there, decisive, invasive, so perfect, sending streaks of flames racing through her, so the firestorm exploded, radiating scorching heat through her body. Her mind seemed to break free, taking her somewhere she'd never been, so that for a few moments there was only pleasure surrounding her. She floated in it, that fiery, star-laden place she'd never been but wanted to stay in—with him. Ricco.

She blinked, became aware that his hands were rubbing her bottom gently, smoothing down her thighs, and he was once again on his feet, holding her, surrounding her with his arms. She found herself smiling at him. "That was— extraordinary."

"The beginning," he corrected. "*Dio, amore*, you taste delicious. I could eat you up."

"I want to touch you," she admitted. "I *need* to touch you."

He leaned in to kiss her. She tasted herself on his tongue and it was more erotic than she thought possible.

"I want your hands on me," he said. He reached for a pair of scissors he had on a side table. "Lean into me."

She didn't have any real choice. Her legs were suddenly rubber. She was melting into him. His skin was hot and he was strong and protective. His arms went around her once more and he cut the ropes and began to massage her arms and hands. Mariko tried to stand, alarmed that he was taking her full weight.

"Just lie against me, *farfallina mia*. I've got you."

She wanted him to *always* have her. She felt safer with him, even tied, than she'd ever felt with any other human being. Her bare breasts pressed into his chest. Already she felt a million little sparks leaping from his skin to hers. Now it was even more so. Her nipples brushed over his heavy muscles, and ripples of fire spread straight to her sex.

Her entire body shuddered as his hands gently massaged her arms and hands. There were no pins and needles, nothing to say she'd been tied for a little while. He was that careful where he'd laid the ropes. Still, she groaned when he gently pulled first one arm and then the other from behind her to wrap around him.

"I'm going to pick you up."

Immediately alarm spread through her. She'd been feeling beautiful and sexy until she heard Osamu's voice in her head. *You're big and ugly. You should bind your big feet and breasts so you don't knock into things. You're clumsy and a complete embarrassment. Stay in your room when we have company.*

One arm slid around her back, the other her knees. He lifted her easily, without seeming effort, cradling her almost tenderly against his chest. "Look at me, Mariko."

She curled into him, both for strength and to hide her body just a little from his dark, piercing gaze. He could see through shadows. Into them. Beyond them. He could see into her mind. She lifted her gaze to his and instantly desire poured into her again. It was there in his eyes. So much she was drowning in it.

"Stay with me, Mariko. Don't go there. Not ever again. She has no place here. Not in this room and not in this house. I want you to throw her out of your head and hear and see only me. Look at yourself the way I see you, not her. Do you need me to show you the images in the camera? When you see them, you'll see only beauty."

She allowed her gaze to drift over his face. Her fingertips went to the scar, tracing it from his eye, following the curve to the corner of his mouth. He'd gotten that scar saving her life. The ones on his chest had been put there for the same reason. She slid her hands around his neck and locked them there. For whatever reason, Ricco Ferraro wanted her, and she was going to have him. Again, she knew it was her choice. Having him for one night, or a few nights, and walking away brokenhearted was better than never having him at all. *He* was her choice.

Using her hands, she brought his head down to her uplifted one and took his mouth. The man could kiss. The moment her lips touched his, featherlight, teasing, tracing his lips with her tongue, his hand slid up her back to bunch her hair in his fingers. How he could hold her so close, so steady, without so much as a tremble she didn't know—or care—because she had her mouth on his and it was . . . perfection.

He took over the kiss, deepening it. She followed his lead, tasting his hot, masculine flavor, savoring it, wanting to devour him. He kissed her over and over and she found herself drowning, every nerve ending on fire for him, so aware of him, of the muscles rippling against her bare skin as she floated through the air like some princess in a fairy tale.

He carried her through the house straight to the master bedroom. His territory, where he'd said no woman had ever been. She literally felt as if she were floating, his mouth on hers, kissing her senseless, as he took her through the spacious halls straight to his bed.

He stripped the comforter off while holding her with one arm, still cradled in tight against his chest. That ability was enough to take her breath away. Then she was on the cool, silk sheets, sprawled out on his bed, eyes on his, because there was no looking away from him. Even if she did, it wouldn't have mattered. He was all she could see. Everything she could want.

Ricco stood at the bottom of the bed, his hands on his drawstring pants, but his gaze on her. "You're so beautiful."

She smiled at him. She couldn't help it. He made her *feel* beautiful. "You did suffer a major blow to the head. Sooner or later you're going to come to your senses." That much was true, but in the meantime, she was going to enjoy every single second with him. "You have too many clothes on."

He did. He *so* did. She had dreamt of his naked body entwined with hers, and that had been long before she met him—when she was doing research on him. She'd seen photographs taken of him in a hot tub with the Lacey twins, his bare chest showing. She'd been a little disappointed that he wasn't standing. To her, he was physically gorgeous. She was grateful to realize that everything she'd learned about his character matched his body. He was a good man, a really good man.

"I don't want to scare you off," he teased, his thumbs in the waistband of his trousers. They sat low on his hips and he looked delicious standing there with that confident smile that bordered on arrogant.

She smiled and shook her head slightly. "That's not possible." This night was for her. She hoped she'd be memorable enough that he'd always cherish their night together. She knew she would. The movement of turning her head reminded her she had her hair up and she'd used long pins to secure it. She reached to take them out.

"Don't take the pins out of your hair, let me." He pushed the material down his hips, his gaze holding hers.

She couldn't help but look. She knew her eyes went wide and she remained staring. "You aren't going to fit." There was disappointment in her voice.

He laughed softly. "I'll fit, *farfallina*. You were made for me."

She tried not to look skeptical, but when his laughter reached his eyes, she knew she hadn't succeeded. He knelt on the foot of the bed looking so intimidating she had the unexpected urge to fling herself off the bed into the nearest shadow. God, he was beautiful, such a predator, a man born to ride shadows and dispense justice. His hips were narrow, his chest defined with heavy muscles that rippled along with his abs that she was a little jealous of. She couldn't help but look lower, her breath catching in her lungs. "You really are a beautiful man."

His smile tugged at her heartstrings. She hadn't noticed him smiling with others. She felt like he'd given her a gift when he gave her that slow, sexy smile that lit the dark of his eyes. He caught her ankles and tugged her legs apart, all the while keeping his gaze on hers. That was what allowed her to obey his unspoken command and spread her legs for him.

She felt a little wanton and very sexy. The silk sheets under her bare skin slid over her back and bottom like a caress. He crawled up her, looking every inch the predator he was. His cock dragged along her thigh, heavy and full. She found him shockingly sensual. Everything in her responded to him.

"Thank you." His voice smoothed over her skin the way the sheets did. He reached for her right hand, his gaze moving over her forearm and hand while he massaged. "You're certain no numbness? You were in the ropes a long while and you aren't used to it yet."

The way he cared for her, as if she were extremely important to him, made tears burn behind her eyes. She'd never had that caring. Not, at least, that she could remember. "I'm in good physical condition."

His grin was nearly a smirk. "I'm counting on that."

For some reason that made her blush. He placed her arm carefully on the sheets beside her and massaged the other one. He held himself over her, as if it were an easy feat with one hand. She loved that he was so strong. She'd grown up feeling large and clumsy in the very small house with its narrow hallways, and Osamu beating her back with a broom because her body had brushed the table or chairs as she'd walked through a room.

She knew she would never regret this night. Not one single minute of it. Ricco Ferraro would always be her choice. *Always.*

Mariko was looking at him with stars in her eyes. A man could get addicted to that look, pay any price, do anything to keep that look right there for all time. Ricco placed her arm gently on the sheets and reached behind her head to pull the pins from her lush hair. He loved her hair, all that silk, thick and wavy, framing her face, brushing across her vulnerable neck, spilling on his pillow just the way he knew it would when he set it free. Her hair always seemed as if it had a life of its own. He loved that she looked so feminine, so delicate, and yet each pin he took from all those silky blond waves was lethal.

She was magic to him. All those years of heartbreak, of anger, of no sleep, watching over his family and feeling terror for them, came down to this woman. She was worth every single second of those years. Every moment he felt alone and apart from the others. He had saved her. He didn't need a DNA test to know that Mariko was a Tanaka, and yet it wouldn't have mattered if she hadn't been.

If she were forever Mariko Majo, he would want her. He knew now how important what he'd done all those years ago was.

She was sexy to him. Everything about her. How sweetly feminine she could look and then she'd turn tiger and step into a shadow, snap a neck and return as serene as ever. The moment he saw her, his body reacted. Sometimes, like now, it was a slow burn, but other times, like in the studio when he'd tied her, it was a brutal inferno, but he always reacted to her.

He kissed her because kissing her was as necessary as breathing. When he kissed her, her arms went around him, her hands were on him, moving over his body, claiming him almost without her knowledge. Her fingers moved over his skin and his heart reacted, hammering loudly. Thunder roared in his ears and his cock pounded with hunger.

He couldn't explain joy because he'd never felt it until Mariko. How could joy be wrapped up in the savage, primitive way she made him feel? He wanted to pound into her, be surrounded by her, taken deep. He wanted them to go at it so hard they rolled off the bed onto the floor and didn't even realize it. At the same time, he wanted gentle for her. Tender. He wanted her to feel the love overwhelming him, the joy sweeping through him. He wanted her to know she made him . . . *more*. Whole. Better. So much more and better of a man. Every cliché he'd heard and thought was total bullshit. He felt all those things for her.

"God, I love kissing you," he whispered against her throat. "I could kiss you forever." He wanted to watch her undress slowly, or come to him just as she had in the studio. He couldn't get enough of her, clothed or otherwise. She was . . . spectacular.

The rain started, drumming outside, hitting the roof and the sides of the house as the wind kicked up and drove it into the windows. Tears, he thought. Tears neither of them had shed when they should have. He kissed his way down her throat, feeling her pulse jump under his lips. Tears of sorrow. Tears of sheer joy.

He'd never felt skin like hers, softer than silk. He'd noticed that the first time she'd modeled for him, and he'd found every excuse possible to touch her skin. That was a first for him, too. Always before, with other models, his entire focus had been on his art. With Mariko, he was totally focused on her. Just as he was now. He lost himself in her.

He'd been right about her. She was a little wildcat in bed. There was no shyness, no holding back. Her hands were everywhere, stroking, caressing, urging him to move faster. He didn't, of course, because she needed to be ready for him and he wanted every experience they enjoyed together to be more than just good for her.

Mariko couldn't get enough of touching his skin. She *loved* the way he felt against her bare body. All the hard muscles covered by a satiny texture that she couldn't resist. His mouth was at her breast, pulling strongly. Hot. Hard. His tongue rasping against her nipple, then the sharp scrape of his teeth sending fire streaking through her. It was so beautiful she wanted to live in that moment.

She scraped her nails down his chest, savoring the feel of his muscles rippling beneath the hot satin of his skin. Her gaze was on his face, watching him shudder, watching his eyes go dark, drenched with a desire so dark and intense it stole her breath. He breathed her name, a whisper of sound that moved in her soul.

She kissed his throat, feeling his pulse hammering beneath her lips. The heart of him. Every beat. For her. She would remember this moment for the rest of her life. Each separate beat under her lips, on her tongue, beneath her palm. She inhaled, drawing him into her lungs. Deep. Holding him there. He smelled fresh, clean, with that faint outdoor scent that was so elusive.

Outside, the rain poured on the roof and beat a rhythm against the window, drenching it so the water ran like a waterfall off the glass. The sound was beautiful to her, like a symphony, violins weeping in the background, her heart and his drumming a beat that she knew she would always remember.

He was never still, his hands and mouth as busy as hers. She loved that, too, that need in him, the driving hunger, as if he had to know every inch of her body. She felt that way, almost desperate to touch every single inch of his skin. Her fingertips followed the path of his scars, the long ridges that took her to the rows of muscles along his abdomen. Her mouth followed, kissing those scars, the signs of his courage and integrity. The marks he wore proclaiming he'd saved her.

He made a sound, deep in his throat, a dark, sexy groan that made her sex clench and her body shudder with desperate need. He'd given her release with his mouth in the studio, but that tension was back and this time it was a thousand times worse. Every nerve ending was on fire for him. She couldn't get enough of touching him, of having every part of his body touching every part of hers. She felt almost frantic for the sensations he gave her with his hands . . .

Her head went up and she looked at his face, realizing it wasn't the sensations so much as the need to be as close as possible. To give him pleasure. She wanted him to feel the way he'd made her feel. More, she wanted to worship his body the way he always seemed to worship hers. His hands moved over her, his mouth trailing kisses on her shoulder and down her arm, while his palms took in as much of her flesh as possible.

It was Ricco's face that caught and held her attention—made her breath catch in her lungs and a million butterflies take wing in her stomach. For the first time, she looked beyond the dark sensuality carved so deep in the lines of his face, beyond the desire, the passion, and saw something else there she realized she'd seen before when he was with her. There was a vulnerability that was never there with anyone else.

She'd seen it on the street when he'd been thrown off the hood of the truck and was injured. She saw it when they were in his studio and he was creating his art. It was there now on his tough, handsome features. He was beautiful, and in that moment, he was all hers. She wished she could fully interpret that look, because she knew it was hers alone, but all she could do was memorize it and hold it close to her heart.

She breathed him in with every breath she took, wanting to gorge on him, absorbing every sensation, so that every detail was imprinted on her soul. She wanted to keep this memory, have this part of him, for all time.

Her heart clenched. Hurt so much. She rested her forehead against his belly as the realization swept over her. Not a moment. Not a memory. She desperately wanted him for her lifetime—beyond if she could. She had thought the ropes intimate, their connected shadows intimate, but this, the way he touched her body, so reverently yet at the same time with such dark passion—this was true intimacy. Not the ropes. Not the shadows. Not even the sex. Tears burned her eyes. She wasn't going to ever get over him.

At once he lifted his body slightly up, propped himself up on one hand and looked down at her, studying her expression. There was no getting away from those dark, piercing eyes. He saw everything. Saw right into her.

"*Amore*, tell me."

His palm curled around her throat and then moved down her chest to cover her right breast. She was acutely aware of his heat. Her nipple pushed right into the center of his palm, just as her heart had beat into it. She couldn't tell him she knew he was going to have a night with her and, as with all the rest of his women, that would be enough for him. It would never be enough for her.

"Mariko." His voice was gentle. Tender even. "You have to talk to me. You promised you would."

She had, but in the ropes. Not lying under his gorgeous body without a clue what she was doing, but wanting it desperately. Wanting him desperately. She had to think of something fast if she was going to keep one shred of dignity.

"I've never done this," she blurted. "I've never kissed anyone else or touched anyone else. I don't have a clue what I'm doing." That was the strict truth. She was terrified she'd do something wrong and he wouldn't want to be with her. She hadn't wanted him to know ahead of time. She'd read extensively, but no man would court her, not with their mothers being friends with Osamu. No one wanted to incur her wrath and her never-ending revenge.

She held her breath. Anxious. Waiting.

His smile was slow in coming, but when it did, it was the most beautiful thing she'd ever seen. He stroked his finger from the base of her throat down to her belly button. "I know what I'm doing, *farfallina mia*. Have no worries in that department. I swear I'll be gentle with you."

Ricco had never felt possessive of a woman in his life. He'd never wanted to belong to a woman or have one belong to him. He didn't remember being innocent or vulnerable. He'd worked too hard to shed both after the experience in Japan. He needed to be tough and scary. He went through women, not because he needed variety but because he'd never found the one that he needed. He hadn't found Mariko. She was everything he wasn't. Vulnerable. Delicate. Innocent. She had the heart of a warrior and could dispense justice as easily as he could, but her heart had not been hardened by the harsh experiences of her life.

He cupped her face in his hand—that beloved face. He wanted to wake up every morning to her face, to the gentleness in her eyes. That soft, sweet voice. Her body. All his. He bent his head to take her mouth. Her lips trembled under his. He loved the shape and feel of them. He teased her lower lip with his teeth, nipping and easing the sting with his tongue. He traced the seam, waiting for her to part her lips so he could be inside.

Kissing Mariko was like transporting himself into an erotic world of feeling, of heat and fire. Once he'd kissed her, he knew he could never rid himself of the obsession— and he didn't want to. He'd surrendered himself before he'd known he was in any kind of danger. He kissed her over and over until he felt her body relax beneath his.

He breathed her name, his own personal magic, and kissed his way down her throat. One knee slipped between her legs, nudging them apart. He felt her tense, and he murmured to her softly against her bare skin. "Relax for me, *amore*. Trust me to keep you safe."

"I feel like I'm flying again," she whispered, her voice shocked. "How can you do that when you're just kissing my skin?"

"You do that for me." He gave her the truth when he never would have told another soul.

"I do?"

Her hands were on his shoulders, fingernails digging into his skin, flares of heat shooting down his spine at the streaks of fire the action produced. *Dio*, he loved her hands on him. He loved the evidence of her wildcat, the one that emerged when she wasn't thinking too hard.

"You do," he assured, taking the opportunity to slide his other knee between her legs, wedging them open so he could sweep his hand from her belly button to her mound. He went up on his knees so that he was kneeling.

She gasped. Her gaze jumped from his face to his hand. "What does that feel like?"

Her eyes went back to his face, her gaze searching his. He waited patiently, his hand gently moving, fingers finding her damp and ready. He didn't take his gaze from hers. He watched her take a breath, her breasts moving with the air in her lungs.

"Fire. A trail of fire."

"What does this make you feel?"

He pushed his finger into her, stretching her slowly, forcing his way through the tight folds. His cock throbbed and jerked, so in need. So ready to feel her sheath surrounding him. He felt like he'd waited his entire life for this moment, this woman.

Her gaze dropped to his cock as he circled it with his free hand. Her eyes widened. She looked a little frightened, but her slick cream coated his finger, allowing him to slip a little deeper.

"Needy. Desperate."

He loved that she was honest with him. He loved the way her hair was wild, spilling over the pillow, the way her exotic eyes had gone to amber, and her skin felt like silk. He wanted to see her like this every night. Wake up every morning to her.

He reached over to the nightstand, thankful he'd remembered to put condoms close. He was going to make certain to protect her. He wanted her to know that he wasn't marrying her for the rider community. To have children. He wanted her to always know she was first in his heart. His choice. No, even more than that. He rolled on the condom, loving the way she watched, as if it was an important detail she would need to learn. Twice her tongue came out to moisten her lips, and when he caught her legs and pulled them around him, she made a sexy little sound that sent a vibration right through his cock. Once more his hand tested her.

"You're ready for me, *amore*."

"I *feel* ready," she admitted. "*So* ready. I want to just scream at you to get on with it, but I'm scared, too."

He loved that she trusted him enough to admit both to

him. She wasn't coy or shy; she was willing to make her own demands even if she was a little afraid.

He pressed the head of his cock to her damp entrance. Heat flared through him and he caught his breath. His body trembled with need. That had never happened to him before.

"Ricco." Demand was in her voice.

He flashed his wicked grin, but he didn't let her impatience hurry him. He wanted this to be good for her, and no matter the cost to him, he was going to give that to her. He sank into her hot, wet, tight sheath. The sensitive head of his cock felt on fire. Gripped hard. Squeezed. Stroked. He clenched his teeth and forced his body to stay still when his hips wanted to thrust forward hard, to bury his cock deep. Instead, he made slow circles with his fingers on her hips, trying to ease her tension.

"I can't breathe."

She was panting, her breath coming in ragged little gasps. He felt like doing a little panting of his own. Fire could be exquisite, and the tight sheath surrounding him was just that. He inched forward and her eyes went wide and shocked. He had to breathe deeply as her muscles clamped down like a vise. A sweet, hot vise.

"You're too big. It burns." Her hands went to his, although she didn't push him away.

"You're very tight, Mariko," he said, using his rope master voice, the one that always steadied her. "Give your body a minute to adjust. It will. Trust me, *amore*, you were born for me."

Her gaze clung to his and he waited, her hands on his until the tension drained out of her and left her face. She nodded. "Much better."

He wanted it great for her, not just "much better," but she was new at it and he wasn't the smallest man ever born. Patience. He chanted it over and over in his mind. He slipped in another inch and then he was bumping her thin barrier, all the while watching her face.

She was squirming now, making it difficult for him to go slow. Every shift of her body sent ripples through her tight muscles so they danced and massaged and milked his cock. He threw back his head, beads of sweat dotting his forehead. He deserved fucking sainthood for this. *Dio*, he'd never felt anything like it.

"Ricco, I need—"

She broke off as he surged forward, past her barrier, pushing through the tight folds so they opened for him, just enough to let him in. He wanted to howl it was so good, the fire streaking up his cock, spreading through his groin and up his spine. He buried himself deep and stilled again, giving her body time to adjust.

"You good?" She had to be. He wasn't certain he was going to survive.

She nodded her head, a slow smile curving her mouth. She was good. That meant so was he. He bent over her, his cock stroking inside her. She gasped and her muscles clamped down on him, the friction incredible as he slowly withdrew. Planting a hand on either side of her head, he began to move in her. Slowly at first, to make certain she could take it, and then, when her body responded with more damp fire, he set a fast, hard rhythm.

Fire surrounded his shaft, an exquisite burn as she clamped down like a silken fist. He threw back his head, breathing deeply, his gaze locked on her face to absorb the perfection of the sensation and the beauty of the passion there. Her breath came in little pants. Her skin was flushed, her eyes dazed, gaze clinging to his for reassurance.

Her body writhed on the sheets and her fingernails streaked more fire down his back. *Dio*, he loved that. Loved every second with her. He plunged deep and hard, burying his body again and again in her, the scorching friction creating flames burning through his body like a raging firestorm.

Mariko couldn't look away from his face and the dark passion stamped there. He looked utterly sensual, completely focused, an ancient samurai warrior claiming her for his own. He moved in her faster and harder. Every hard thrust sent jolts of pleasure rippling through her body like waves taking her higher and higher until fear began to creep in. She couldn't let go. She didn't know how.

She wasn't certain if she was going to live through her first time. Her breasts brushed his chest, so sensitive she felt as if pinpoints of fire brushed over her nipples each time. Lightning seemed to rip through her body, sizzling through her bloodstream with a rush of white-hot heat connecting her breasts to her sheath.

Fire roared through her, threatening to destroy her. She couldn't quite catch her breath, and there was no stopping the sensations swamping her. She looked up at him. Ricco. She felt him in her then. With her. Connected. His hands were steady and certain. His shaft swelled, the friction growing even hotter. She found his dark gaze with her frightened one. She could see tenderness. Something more she was afraid to name.

"Let go, *farfallina mia*. Let yourself fly with me."

She was used to that dark velvet voice. She knew his strength and power. She knew he would catch her. Breathing deeply, she let go. The ripples gathered in force until the sensations were giant swells. Thunder pounded in her ears. Her blood rushed hot and wild through her veins. Flames kissed her skin. Her body clamped down on his shaft, squeezing and milking, taking him with her. His arms tightened around her as she felt herself flung out into the stars, whirling around and floating, soaring, flying high with him. With Ricco. A shocked cry escaped and she heard Ricco's hoarse chant as he emptied himself into her. Then he collapsed over top of her and she took his full weight.

She stayed very still, afraid if she moved she would lose that feeling of euphoria. She stroked her fingers through his dark, thick hair, breathing shallowly, determined that she really didn't need air to breathe, she only needed to hold on to him. He groaned and pushed up slightly.

"That was beautiful. Wild." He brushed her eyelids with kisses. "Are you okay?"

She nodded, not wanting to speak at all, not wanting the moment to end. Her heart had begun to settle, the roaring in her ears subsiding. Her body still felt as if it were floating, but now she no longer felt connected to him. She honestly didn't know if she was withdrawing, or if it was Ricco, but she forced a smile. He frowned and withdrew, his heavy cock sliding over the sensitive bundle of nerves, triggering another orgasm.

She gasped and rolled, turning on her side, so she could draw up her knees.

"I'll be right back, Mariko." He knotted the condom and moved off to the bathroom.

She lay there, still a little dazed, but panic had set in. Heart pounding, she sat up, looking wildly around. He'd made it clear he didn't hold women all night or have them in his bed. What was she supposed to do? She should have asked before she'd gone to his room. It would have been so much smarter to go to *her* room and then he'd have to leave, not her. She had no clothes. Her robe was in the studio.

There was only one thing to do. A shadow. She had to get into a shadow and find a way out of his room before he came back from the bathroom. Her first inclination was to grab the sheet and cover up, but the sheet wouldn't go into the tube with her, as the specially made clothes for the riders did. She flung it aside and leapt to her feet.

She felt him on her skin. Inside her. *Everywhere.* He was branded deep in her body, but more—and she'd known it would happen—he was there forever in her heart. She wrapped her arms around herself and stepped into the nearest shadow that was thrown toward the door. It led right under it, except she was forced out of the tube right at the door itself. Nothing got under there. She'd run into that before when she'd first gotten there and wanted to explore his room.

What did people do? She reached for the doorknob, feeling foolish. He hadn't locked her in. He didn't keep women, he discarded them immediately. She wasn't about to be the awkward situation in his home he couldn't get rid of.

"Whoa. Stop, Mariko. Where are you going?" He reached around her, his hand above her head, preventing the door from opening. "What's wrong, *farfallina*?"

She went very still, wishing she knew how to disappear. It used to work when she was a child, but Ricco saw her no matter what—and he was so close. His body pressed right up against hers. She could feel every inch of him, all man, all muscle, against her back and bottom. His cock, the moment he came into contact with her, skin to skin, went from semihard to just plain hard.

His finger slid down the nape of her neck. His breath was warm, stirring the thick mane of hair falling around her shoulders. "*Amore*. Where are you going?"

"Back to my room." She said it to the door. That thick, heavy door with something stopping shadows from sliding underneath.

"Why?" His hand moved her hair so that he could trail kisses down the nape of her neck, following the path his finger had taken. His hands slid up and down her arms, warming her when she shivered.

She was shivering, not because she was cold, but because she couldn't resist his touch and she wanted—*needed*—to be strong.

"I know you don't like women in your bed, Ricco. I'm not going to make this difficult. You saved me from having to have an arranged marriage with Kichiro and I appreciate it. I really do." She stayed still, facing the door, feeling him breathe. Feeling as if they still wore the same skin. His hands never stopped moving, caressing her arms, up and down, his breath on the nape of her neck, lips so close she felt them pressed into her neck.

He remained silent, giving her time to pull her scattered thoughts around her like a cloak. "A good shadow rider never goes after someone until he or she is totally convinced beyond any doubt that the person deserves justice. I had to research you. Thoroughly. You aren't a man ever to be satisfied with one woman. That doesn't make you a bad person, but you're not husband material. I won't be that woman in your bed that you wake up resenting."

She was so proud of her voice. She kept it even. Low.

Nonjudgmental. Most of all, the bone-deep sorrow she felt wasn't there. Not even a hint of it.

Ricco groaned and pressed his face between her shoulder blades, his arms circling her under her breasts, holding her tightly so she was more a prisoner than she had been in the ropes. There was a moment of sheer panic, and then she felt his distress. His breathing had changed subtly, but it had. His heartbeat had accelerated.

"I'm honestly not trying to hurt you. I want you to know you're off the hook. I'm not expecting marriage and fidelity just because we had sex. I knew what I was doing and made the decision myself. I wanted to be with you. I wanted you to be the one *I* chose, not the council. Not the riders. You were my choice, and I'm all grown up, Ricco. You have no responsibility toward me at all. As soon as we can, we'll announce that the engagement didn't work out."

There. She'd absolved him. Every man would like that, right? He had to let go of her before he noticed her trembling. Her reaction to him. The sorrow eating away at her at the loss of her silly dream. She knew better than to dream. Or to hope. Or to want or wish for something. Especially something as big and real as Ricco Ferraro. A good man. The man who had managed to penetrate her heart. He was there for good. But she wasn't a silly schoolgirl. She knew the difference between husband material and a man who would be miserable with one woman. His mother had it right.

"Are you finished?" he asked softly.

Fingers of desire danced down her spine. His lips were against her skin, speaking there so she felt every word formed. His hold on her hadn't loosened at all.

"Yes." She could barely get the word out.

"Then come back to bed."

She couldn't. If she went back there with him and he seduced her all over again, she'd be so lost she would agree to anything, and she knew she'd regret it. Self-respect was the only thing she had left to her. She shook her head because she couldn't speak. She couldn't actually tell him no.

She wanted to go back to bed with him, but pride wouldn't allow it. Pride and self-preservation.

Ricco shocked her by letting her go, turning her around and catching her under her legs to lift her. She had no choice but to grab on to his neck to hold herself upright. He looked down at her upturned face.

"Do you know how amazing you are?"

She shook her head but stared at the door, afraid to move or breathe.

"I have family. I've always had them. No matter what happens in my life, they're here for me. You only have your brother, yet of the two of us, I'm the far more broken one. That alone speaks to your incredible strength, Mariko. Beautiful, strong and so ready to sacrifice for me. No, you're right, I wasn't the marrying kind. I never wanted to have a woman spend the night with me because I knew she wasn't the right woman. You are that woman. When a man looks his entire existence, waiting to find her, and she shows up, believe me, *amore*, he recognizes her."

She was afraid to move or speak. If she misunderstood him, or dared to believe him, she might shatter. She could only stare up at him, wondering how he could say such things to her, afraid to believe him.

"I'm willing to give you just about anything in this world you want, Mariko. I have the means to do it. You don't want to be a rider, you don't have to be. You don't want children with me, you don't have to have them. I don't give a damn what the council says. I'll stand in front of you, beside you or watch your back. But you're not leaving this room until we have an understanding. I've had everything I don't want. Believe me when I tell you, I recognize what I do want and I'll do anything to keep it."

CHAPTER SIXTEEN

His past had finally caught up with him. Ricco stared down into Mariko's beloved face. He detested that he had hurt her in any way. She'd been hurt enough by the people who had taken her into their home—the ones who should have shown her love. He brushed her forehead with his mouth and placed her back in the middle of his bed, following her so that she had no chance to escape if she was so inclined.

"I think, before we go into explanations of why I'm so fucked up, and how I need you to save me, I think you need to be aware my marriage proposal was very sincere."

She shook her head. "Don't, Ricco. I was there. You were saving me from Kichiro, which was very gallant of you and I really appreciate it, but I'm certainly not going to hold you to it." She scooted up to the headboard, sat with her back to it, drawing up her knees and pulling the sheet up to her chin.

He wanted to tell her if she thought she was safe—she wasn't. He had ropes in the room and could easily tie her to the bedpost if that was the only way he could get her to stay and listen. He almost laughed out loud at his crazy thoughts. He was in full-blown panic mode, another new first for him as an adult. He'd prepared for every situation but finding the woman he could love and losing her through his own stupidity.

"You're giving me far too much credit, Mariko," he said,

raking his fingers through his hair in agitation. "I'm not the kind of man who goes around saving women."

"You're *exactly* that kind of man."

"I told Emilio I was going to marry you," he pointed out.

"In the heat of the moment. Joking."

"Woman." Exasperated, he glared at her.

"Would you mind putting on some clothes? A robe? Anything? I can't think straight."

She sounded a little desperate and that took some of the tension away. She couldn't be so bent on leaving him if she couldn't look at him naked with a clear mind. He sank down onto the bed, facing her.

"Does that help?"

She nodded. "Thank you, I appreciate it."

He almost smiled at her prim voice, but caught himself just in time. He reached for her hand, threaded their fingers together and dropped them to his thigh. Up high. Close to his stirring groin.

"Do you think I've ever proposed to a woman before?"

She bit her lip, her eyes wide. *Dio*, he loved her eyes. He could spend eternity looking into her eyes. "The answer is no. I haven't. Not even in the heat of the moment. Not when I won races or came out of the tube needing sex more than I needed to breathe. Only with you. Do you think I ever brought another woman to this home? The answer is no. Only you. I haven't had one in this bed. Just you. I haven't touched another woman sexually when she was in the ropes. Just you. By taking you to Ferraro territory I declared my intentions for everyone to see, and that was before the heat of the moment."

She pressed her lips together, her gaze never leaving his. Her lashes fluttered, drawing his attention. Long and dark, they curled, feathery soft and so feminine around her eyes. He brought her hand up to his mouth, kissed her knuckles and brought it back to his thigh. His cock jerked hard at the close proximity. He wanted to point out that even his cock recognized her but kept that to himself.

"I have your engagement and wedding rings in my night-stand. I wanted to ask you properly."

Her head went up. "That's impossible. Any ring on a rider must be specially made, just like our clothes. There's only one jeweler . . . *Damian*." Her voice dropped almost to reverence when she named the store. Damian Ferraro used his first name for his famous designs.

"One of my cousins."

"Even so, it takes forever to get anything from him. He also makes regular jewelry and his designs are exclusive and sought-after. He couldn't possibly have designed a ring and gotten it to you in that short amount of time."

Her voice was a challenge, and it made him smile. Keeping her hand on his thigh, he leaned over and opened the nightstand drawer to take out a box. "You can't wear gems in the tube. Only this alloy." He took out the small jewelry box and flipped it open with his thumb.

Mariko drew back when he pushed it across the short distance. For a moment, she continued to look at his face, and then her gaze dropped to the ring. His cousin was a renowned jeweler, his designs so sought-after, celebrities, multimillionaires and kings and queens from other countries went to him for a personal piece of jewelry.

His cousin Damian had a gift. He could design the perfect piece of jewelry that suited an individual. His wedding rings were so sought-after that you had to go to him years in advance to get an individual piece. Each one of the Ferraros had gone to him when they turned twenty-five, knowing they would have to marry whether or not they found the love of their lives. It was a tradition in their family.

In truth, he'd been upset when he saw the rings Damian had designed for him. He watched as Mariko slowly picked up the box and stared down at the rings. Both were bands. The engagement ring was wider than the wedding band. The wide band had two Japanese swords carved into the metal. They were exquisitely detailed, the hilts ornate. Twisted into the hilts of both swords was the Ferraro family crest. Inside had been carved *Sempre la vostra spada e scudo.* Always your sword and shield.

He'd thought his cousin was insane and he'd locked the rings away, never showing them to his family. Now he understood why everyone thought Damian was such a genius. His gift was to know exactly what his client needed long before the client did. Ricco knew he would always be both a sword and a shield for Mariko. He would always be her samurai warrior. Always.

"Do you understand?" He'd had to apologize to Damian when he'd sent the ring to be sized. "I've made mistakes, Mariko, far too many. I'm no saint and I never will be. I like sex, lots of it. I'm not going to pretend I don't, but my entire focus is on you."

Deliberately he moved her hand to his cock, wrapping her fingers around the thick, very hard shaft. She didn't try to pull her hand away, rather she gripped him tightly. His hand around hers kept her there. It was heaven and hell all rolled into one. Her palm burned like a brand. He wanted her with every breath he took, but he forced himself to be still. It was Mariko who started the slow glide. She moved her thumb over the broad head of his cock, smearing the leaking drops so that the glide was smooth as she pumped up and down almost lazily. It was enough to kill any man.

"What if you get tired of me, Ricco? You know that's a possibility. One woman isn't going to satisfy you for the rest of your life, and I'm not a woman to cheat on. Nor would I want you miserable."

"I can understand your fears, Mariko." *Dio*, how could he think when her fingers were dancing up and down his shaft, and then her fist squeezed him so tightly it robbed him of breath. "But truly, really listen to the answer. You hear truth. I can't lie to you, nor would I have a reason to do so. I want only you. I fell in love with you almost from the moment you walked into the interview. Every moment spent in your company has deepened what I felt until I know with absolute certainty that I love you and you are the only woman I want in my life."

Her hand stopped moving, although her fist remained tight. Her eyes stared directly into his. "You never told me you loved me."

"I did. In a thousand ways. With my ropes."

Her eyes widened and her hand tightened. He held his breath. He needed her to move that hand. Every cell in his body was tuned to that one body part. He could count his heartbeats there. He knew she could, too.

"You never told me in words."

"I laid myself bare to you, Mariko." He said it quietly. She couldn't deny it. He had.

"The Lacey twins? Two women at one time?"

He said nothing because he was guilty as hell and he couldn't take it back. He could try to explain the need to run all the time, to get rid of the rage in him. How he needed the adrenaline rush every moment of his existence to just live. He'd lived and played hard. He'd done so in the spotlight. There was nothing he could do about it now.

"I don't share well with others," she whispered.

"Neither do I. I can't change my past, Mariko, but I can promise you my future. My word is good."

She began that slow pump again, moving her tight fist up and down, sending waves of heat rushing through his body to his veins, spreading it like a slow drug through his entire system.

"Are you going to marry me?" His fingers bunched in the sheet. *Dio*, he was already as hard as a rock.

"Probably." She was no longer looking at him, but at his cock.

His shaft jerked hard at her long contemplation, leaking more drops for her to smear around. She'd increased the tempo.

"That's not an answer. Fucking say yes before I lose my mind."

"Don't swear at me." A ghost of a smile curved her mouth and he found it as sexy as hell.

"I didn't swear at you." How in hell was he going to convince her when he no longer had a brain? He dragged the sheet slowly from her body, using his fingers to bunch it and then push it down so he had access to her. He circled her ankle with his fingers and then stroked up her leg to her thigh, applying pressure, a silent command to part her legs.

Mariko sat up straight, her back to the headboard, her eyes on his, hand still working him. Very slowly she parted her thighs and then let her knees fall open, watching him with that sexy little smile on her face. She was deliberately taunting him. Playing with fire. He closed his eyes briefly, savoring his victory. She was already wet and slick, wanting him the way he wanted her. The evidence of his earlier possession was there to remind him to be careful of her. He loved how she looked, there on the bed, her breasts jutting toward him, her hair a wild mess of tousled waves, her legs spread open, her sex glistening. All for him.

"Say yes, *farfallina mia*." Just to be certain, he pushed his finger into her hot entrance, stroking and caressing, spreading small circles around her clit.

"Are you going to be a crazy man? Race cars? Play cards? Get into trouble?"

He couldn't help smiling. "Yes. But you'll be there with me." He could do wicked, sinful things with his fingers—and he did. He wasn't above seducing her into saying yes, although he'd already read her consent when she'd opened her thighs to him.

"I suppose someone has to take you on," she said. "I'm strong, I guess it should be me." She moved her hips in rhythm with the two fingers he was moving in and out of her. Her fist kept that same beat, so tight around his throbbing cock.

"You could be a little more enthusiastic," he pointed out, adding his thumb to the stroking rhythm. He used it against her clit, watching the color flush her skin and her breasts heave with the effort to get air.

"Oh. I'm sorry." She gave him a wide-eyed, innocent stare. "Am I doing it wrong?"

She gripped him harder, pumping his cock at an increased pace. He lost his own breath and knew he wasn't going to last. It was a combination of the way she looked, knowing she was his, and her hand that continually moved, fingers busy, fist so fucking tight he was losing all control.

He caught her ankles, yanked her toward him, and flipped her over all in one decisive move. She gave a little laughing yelp, fisting the sheets as he caught her hips and jerked them back and up, forcing her onto her knees. One hand on her back kept her head to the pillow. He almost came just looking at her bottom, up in the air, waiting for him. Once again, he knelt behind her, spreading her thighs ruthlessly, knowing she was in superb physical shape and could stretch a good distance.

"Amore." He groaned the endearment. "Can you reach over and get one of the condoms out of the drawer?" He should have been prepared.

"I'm on birth control. It's a mild one to regulate me, but it's still birth control. If you're clean . . ."

Dio. His heart clenched hard in his chest. She was so trusting. He knew he was clean, but she just gave herself to him. Trusted him with her body.

"Are you certain, Mariko?" More than anything he wanted to be inside her with nothing at all between them.

"I'm certain."

His hand slid to cover her sex. She was hot. Damp. So ready for him. He didn't wait, and this time he entered with one hard thrust. Her inner muscles protested, tried to keep him from invading, reluctantly giving way when he drove deep. At once he was surrounded with heat and fire. "You're so fucking tight, *amore.*" He clenched his teeth against the streaks of fire racing up and down his body, radiating from his groin.

Mariko's breath hissed out of her as Ricco all but slammed her to the bed. He was stronger than she'd ever imagined a man could be, his hands always sure when he touched her. He liked touching her nearly as much as she liked him doing it. When he jerked her hips up and back toward him, her body had gone liquid with need. Her skin felt hot and her breasts ached, nipples on fire against the cool of the sheets.

His hands stroked her back, down her spine, and rubbed her bottom. All the while his cock pistoned into her, every stroke hard and dominant. She'd loved how gentle he'd been the first time, his touch reverent, almost as if he worshiped her with every caress. This was different, a wild, almost abandoned taking of her.

He reached places he hadn't before, his cock sliding heavily over the bundle of sensitive nerves, sending streaks of fire racing through her body. The tension inside her wound higher and higher, tighter and tighter. Her breath came in little sobs. Her breasts ached, nipples brushing back and forth on the sheets with every forceful thrust. It was glorious. Beautiful. So perfect.

He leaned over her back, repositioning. A little cry escaped her throat. So good. She'd never known anything could be so good. He drove out the voices in her head, the ones that argued reasonably that leopards didn't change their spots. The voices that told her she would never be enough woman for a man like Ricco.

Ricco *showed* her, in so many ways, that he wanted *her*— Mariko Majo, the female devil. How could he touch her with such beauty? Even in his wild, his touch was all about love. She felt that, and there weren't any shadows connecting them together. She felt his love with every stroke of his cock. The way he put her pleasure before his own. Every time he changed position it took her higher. When she gasped because the pressure inside her grew until she feared she would lose all control, he leaned into her and whispered into her ear.

"Let go for me, *farfallina mia*. Fly. Fly with me."

He reached down and found her clit. The relentless stroking of his cock, pushing his way through her tight folds, the feel of it, strong and male, the connection, making it so they shared the same skin, all came together with the realization that Ricco Ferraro had showed her things he'd never showed another woman. He'd told her things he'd never told another woman. He allowed himself to be as vulnerable as she was. He'd given her power over him. He'd told her he loved her, and she hadn't said it back.

The feelings were overwhelming, turbulent love and lust mixed together until she couldn't separate the two. She pushed back against him with a little half sob of pure happiness, her muscles locking around him, squeezing down like a vise as his cock pistoned into her, spreading flames everywhere. She felt him swell, pushing against her sensitive muscles even as the fiery friction sent her hurtling over the edge.

She screamed. In her entire life, she'd never screamed over anything. It wasn't done. Certainly not with such abandon, but the sound was wrenched from her as the fire consumed her. She felt the hot splashes of his release deep inside her and then he collapsed over top of her. His arms held her tight, his body crushing hers.

Still on her knees, head down, she turned her head to look at him over her shoulder. His eyes were on her. Dark desire was stamped into his hard features and every sensual line of his face, but there in his eyes, she could see love. She'd never seen it before. Not ever. She hadn't recognized it for what it was, but now it was so plain to her. She smiled at him.

"I can't move." She couldn't. She was exhausted, her body feeling like a wet noodle. "If they come for us tonight, you'll have to do all the fighting. I'll watch and cheer you on."

His smile was slow, genuine and beautiful. So beautiful, what little breath she had in her lungs rushed out.

"That might be difficult, *amore*. I can't move, and we're attached."

She laughed. She couldn't help it, and the sound startled her. He'd given her so many beautiful moments. So many things she'd never expected to have. Lying on his bed, surrounded by his body, his arms tight around her, the feel of his hair sliding over the bare skin of her back, it was all surreal. Perfection.

"You have to find your rings. They were somewhere on the bed." Ricco turned his head to survey the sheets.

"In my hand," she said and lifted her fist from the sheets to show him the little box had been guarded carefully.

He pressed kisses down her spine, making her shiver. He gripped her hips suddenly, as he was withdrawing. "Mariko. I don't want this to be over." Once more he laid his head on her back, just holding her. "I don't suppose you could go to sleep like this."

Laughter bubbled up and she shook her head. He eased out of her, the movement triggering another ripple of pleasure mixed with muscles burning a bit in protest. She gasped and rolled over as he sank back to his heels.

Ricco caught her ankle as she drew up her knees. "What's wrong?"

"Nothing."

"There it is. The other thing women say that is total bullshit. If it was 'nothing' you wouldn't have gotten that particular look on your face."

She found herself smiling. Feeling happy. Shocked at the realization that despite the circumstances with why and how they met, she was happy when she was with him. She loved that he paid attention. "When you moved, I had another mini-orgasm that was really, really nice and at the same time realized I was a little sore." There. She'd told him the truth and managed not to turn beet red. She was a bit of a rose color, but not lobster red.

He rolled off the bed in one smooth motion, coming to his feet. "Stay right there. If you don't, I'm going to find other uses for my ropes than decorative art."

She let him get to the door of the master bathroom before

she answered. "You've already found other uses for them and we both like it." That was daring of her, but she liked teasing him.

He paused at the door, looking back at her. His cock jerked and he fisted it. "Woman, you're going to kill me." He gave her a wicked grin and then disappeared into the bathroom. "You need to soak in the tub. I don't want you so sore we can't continue."

A bath sounded nice, but really, she was just too tired. She closed her eyes and let herself drift.

Ricco tested the water, making certain it wasn't going to be too hot, but he needed it hot enough to soothe her body. When he returned to the room, she was sound asleep, curled up on her side by the edge of the bed. His rings were on the nightstand, still in the jewelry box. He took the engagement ring out and slipped it on her finger.

She stirred, her lashes fluttering, and then she was looking at him. As it always did when their eyes met, his stomach performed a strange flip. She was magic. He knew he was the only one responsible for his happiness, but finding Mariko certainly went a long way toward helping.

"Come on, *cara*, bath time."

"You take a bath," she murmured sleepily. "I'm going to sleep."

She looked sexy lying on the silk sheets, her hair spilling everywhere, her naked body curled up like a sleepy kitten. He reached down and picked her up easily, cradling her against his chest. Had she been more awake he would have slung her over his shoulder and carried her off like a pirate hoisting treasure just to hear her laugh again. He loved the sound of her laughter.

"Bath, then sleep," he said decisively.

"Oh no." She gripped his shoulder looking alarmed. "I'm full of you. Of us. And it's leaking everywhere."

"I like you full of me and us." He stepped into the bath and lowered his body until he was sitting, legs stretched out, Mariko on his lap.

She wrapped her arms around his neck and turned her face into his shoulder. "This is nice. I don't mind this at all. But I'm going to sleep."

"Are we good, Mariko? Is my past going to haunt us?" He knew uncertainty was in his voice. He certainly needed her far more than the other way around, which put him at a disadvantage. He didn't care if she knew. He wanted her to be happy. "Is there anything else we need to put to rest?"

She tipped her head back to meet his gaze. "I choose to believe you, Ricco. That you love me and that you're certain I am the one for you. I choose to believe you will always feel that way. Love doesn't seem to work out for so many people, and I'm scared. I'm not going to pretend I'm not, but I don't know what's good or bad in a relationship. I'm going on faith and you're the person I choose to have faith in."

Her sincerity humbled him. Every moment in her company only made him love her more. "I can only promise you that I'll try every single day to be a man you can be proud of."

She reached up and traced his lips with her fingertip. "I love being with you, Ricco."

"Why?" He couldn't imagine why a woman like Mariko would choose him, with his past and his failures.

"Aside from the fact that you're very, very good at what you do"—she swept her hand down to encompass her body—"you're the best man I know."

"You can't have known very many," he protested.

"Not in the biblical sense," she agreed, teasing him. "But I'm a rider. I've seen things."

He liked the teasing note in her voice. "What countries did you travel to when you were training?" He'd been curious about that from the beginning, as had Stefano. The investigators found few riders able to give any information on Mariko outside of Japan, which was unusual.

"I wasn't allowed to travel to other countries. The council followed Osamu's advice. She believed I'd dishonor the riders of our country and they took her word that I was . . . difficult."

"Difficult?" he prompted, trying to hold at bay the building rage on her behalf.

She squirmed. "I don't like talking about Osamu's opinion of me."

"It is only her opinion," he pointed out. "The council should have done an investigation if they were worried. That's their responsibility." Every muscle in his body wanted to tighten up, but he forced himself to stay relaxed.

"Dai was the adviser, along with Isamu. Isamu is Osamu's brother. They both backed up her opinion and the council dropped it. They refused to send me for training outside the country due to the fact that I might bring disgrace and dishonor down on our riders."

There was no bitterness in her voice, but he could taste it in his own mouth. "I should have followed up, Mariko. I believed them when they told me a family had taken the two of you in because, of course, there was truth in their voices. Still, I should have asked who the family was and insisted on seeing you."

She shook her head, the silky strands of her hair tickling his skin and sending shock waves through him. He'd always had a strong sex drive, but now it seemed doubly so. More, he was utterly aware of her at all times. The way the water lapped at her breasts. How they floated, the pink areolas framing her nipples, drawing his attention. The thatch of curls at the apex of her legs, the curve of her body, so feminine. All of her. Every inch of her.

"How silly, Ricco. You always try to take on too much. What fourteen-year-old boy would ask beyond if we were safe? Especially when he was being threatened. You saved us. What happened after that is not on you. It wasn't all bad. I had a roof over my head and food to eat. I was allowed to train as a rider and I excelled at it—enough that Osamu couldn't stop me or interfere. I had a space that was mine and I could read of faraway places. And I had Ryuu."

Her brother. He kept his worries to himself. "Kiss me."

Her head came up. "What?"

"Kiss me. I need you to kiss me." He ached for her taste.

"If I kiss you, that might lead to other things, and I'm so tired I'd fall asleep and miss it all," she teased.

His eyebrow shot up. "Fall asleep? When I'm making love to you?"

"It could happen."

"It could *never* happen." He growled and bit her neck.

Laughing, she caught his head between her hands and brought it up. Leaning into him, she brushed kisses over his eyes. "I haven't told you yet . . ." She kissed his nose and along his rough jaw. "Thank you for my beautiful ring." She kissed the corners of his mouth and then brushed her lips back and forth over his.

It was tantalizing. Sexy. His overactive cock stirred to life. Just at her touch. Her teeth nipped at his lower lips and she shifted position, still in his arms, straddling him, pressing her breasts against his chest as her teeth bit down and drew his lip out and then let go so she could use her tongue over the small sting.

Groaning, he reached between them to grasp his cock in his fist, right at the base, with one hand. With the other, he guided her hips so that he could lodge the broad head in her. With both hands, he gripped her hips and pushed her down while he surged up. There it was . . . home. He drove through those tight muscles, slick with the two of them, hot as hell, an inferno he welcomed, more, he needed.

Once she was fully seated on him, her sheath pulsing around him, so tight he could count her heartbeats through his shaft, he bunched her hair in his fist and pulled her head back. "You're teasing me."

"I am," she admitted.

He took her mouth. Hard. Dominant. Sweeping her into another level of his world. Sex could be many things and he wanted to show them all to her. Tender, wild, rough, it didn't matter, not as long as she trusted him and she tasted love on his tongue and felt it in everything his body did to hers.

He shouldn't have been surprised when his woman

matched him, fire for fire. There was no holding back from her; she kissed him, using her tongue, following his lead, sending flames flickering down his spine and heat rushing through his veins. Of her own accord, without his urging, she began to move, riding him as if she'd been doing it for a hundred years. She was grace and fluidity, undulating her body so that he could feel every ripple, every vibration.

She reached behind her and planted both hands on his thighs so her breasts jutted temptingly, giving him a show as she rode him. Slow at first, and then when he thought he might have to take over, she picked up the pace. Water lapped at his skin, giving him the sensation of tongues on him. He cupped the soft weight of her breasts in his palms, thumbs brushing, watching her skin flush. He tugged at her nipples, gently, watching her reaction.

Those tight inner muscles squeezed him like a vise as scorching heat saturated him. He tugged again, this time harder, a little rough. Her body clamped down on him and she moved faster, obviously close.

She threw back her head. "Again," she demanded.

He did as she requested, tugging and rolling, alternating gentle and rough.

She rode him hard, her body so tight around his cock, the friction was nearly unbearable. Watching her get herself off on him was one of the sexiest things he'd ever seen.

She moaned, her breath hitching then coming in ragged pants. "More. Harder."

"Use your hand at your clit," he instructed and waited to oblige her until she had obliged him.

He watched her hand slide between her legs, felt her fingers seeking her target and then heard her breath hiss as she stroked and pulled. He tugged and rolled her nipples and then began to match her rhythm, surging into her as she came down over him. The beauty of her stretched out on a rack of pleasure, desperate for release, would be forever branded in his memory.

Her mouth opened. Her eyes went hazy. Her skin was

flushed. Her sheath clamped down on his in a vicious grip, forcing his cock to swell. *Dio.* He clenched his teeth. His breath rushed out of his lungs in a long symphony of guttural sound.

His warrior woman was utterly abandoned, grinding down, taking him with her, forcing his cock to give her what she wanted—wringing every drop of his seed. Hot and vicious, it rocketed out of him in strong spurts as if she milked him ruthlessly. She cried out his name as she came, half sobbing, half shocked moans.

Mariko collapsed against him, her arms around his neck, her head on his shoulder, breasts pressed into his chest. He held her to him, so overwhelmed with love for her that he couldn't speak. He had it all in her. A partner. A woman willing to be his friend and have his back, as she had when he'd been injured in the streets of Ferraro territory. A rider to help defend the helpless. An extraordinary lover, one willing to match his passion and his adventurous ideas outside the norm of sexual boundaries. As ferocious as she was, she was still willing to accommodate him and even enjoy the sessions in his studio when he needed to practice Shibari to ground him. She was willing to take that further and incorporate it into their lovemaking.

"I love you, Mariko Majo Tanaka."

"Love you, too." She sounded very sleepy, already drifting.

He nuzzled the top of her head, liking the way the dark bristle on his jaw tangled with the blond silk of her hair.

"Marry me soon."

"Hmm?"

His hand slid down her back, following her spine to the curve above her buttocks. He stroked caresses there and felt her relax more. "Marry me soon."

"Okay." Her lips brushed his collarbone.

Just that small, intimate gesture shocked him. He was sated for the time being. Still deep inside her, still sharing her skin. Connected to another human being as he'd never been—not just physically but emotionally.

"Give me your word of honor."

Her lips curved. He felt her smile imprinted in his skin. He loved that. Wanted more.

"You don't want much, do you?"

The drowsy note in her voice sent heat shimmering like sheet lightning through his veins. He was done. She'd taken everything he had—for the moment—and yet he was still thinking about sex. That made him smile. He leaned his head against the back of the tub and closed his eyes.

"Promise me, *farfallina mia*." He murmured it softly, tightening his hold on her.

"Yes."

It was so soft that he almost didn't hear. "When I say."

He felt her laughter like a melody of soft notes against his skin. The rain poured on the roof, ran down the windows. Steam rose around them, enclosing them. Enfolding them. He waited. She wasn't quite asleep, but she gave him most things he wanted. He *really* wanted her promise. Mariko wouldn't break her word to him, and he had a bad feeling that things might not go well with her brother.

The feeling had been growing for some time. He knew Stefano had that same gut intuition he had. He didn't want to chance losing her, not if things went horribly wrong. Too much time had gone by and Ryuu had been gone far too long for the outcome to be very good.

"You always want your way."

He loved that voice, drowsy, sexy, drifting in a sex-induced exhaustion.

"I do." He reached down to release the plug and let out the water. As much as he didn't want to move, the water was growing cold, and he needed sleep, too.

"Okay."

"Say you promise." He stood, using the strength in his legs to stand them both up. Reluctantly, he had to allow his body to slip out of hers. "Grip the edge of the tub for me. It won't take a minute and I'll get you in bed."

She didn't protest or even open her eyes. She leaned over and grabbed the edge of the bathtub. Very gently he washed her, enjoying the task of taking care of her, grateful that she allowed it, extremely grateful that she wasn't shy with him. He wrapped a towel around her and carried her to the bed, drying her off quickly before putting her in the middle of the sheets again.

"Mariko. Don't go to sleep without promising me."

"You're a badger. You're badgering."

She turned on her side, curling her body, looking delicious. He knew he would always look forward to the times they went to bed. He hoped he'd never fall asleep first, just so he could have these moments when she was drifting off, goofy as hell, adorable and all his.

He laughed softly. "I can keep it up for hours. Better to give in now."

"Fine."

He knew she deliberately used that word because she lifted her head and gave him a quelling look. Laughing, he slid into bed, curled his body around hers and drew up the sheet. "I'll take that 'fine' as your promise, *amore*." He wrapped his arm around her, cupping one breast in his palm. "Go to sleep. We're getting on a plane in a few hours."

She pushed back into him, her only answer, and then she was perfectly relaxed, already asleep.

CHAPTER SEVENTEEN

Mariko stood in the doorway of the amazing jet they'd used to travel to her country. The aircraft was more of a luxury hotel than a plane, complete with bedrooms. She'd spent more time awake than asleep, but she didn't regret one moment of her time with Ricco. He was a demanding lover—but then, so was she.

The lights of the city lit up the sky in every color of the rainbow. She loved everything about Tokyo at night. When she was a teenager, so upset with Osamu's treatment, or hurt that Ryuu had said something mean to her to get into Osamu's good graces, she'd ridden shadows all over the city. Sneaking out had been easy enough. Sneaking back to bed when Osamu was waiting for her hadn't been.

"You don't have to go with us," Ricco said, coming to stand behind her. His hand went to the nape of her neck. One finger slid over her skin in that caress she knew so well. The one that always seemed to give her confidence.

"I do." She glanced back at him over her shoulder and met his dark gaze. She wanted him to know she *had* to face Osamu—to see for herself once and for all. She'd be able to read Osamu even if the woman was adept at lying.

He didn't argue with her. He didn't want her to go. He'd made that clear enough. She knew he wanted to protect her from whatever they might find, and she loved him even more for that. Sometimes she didn't know how to take his protective streak, but she was always grateful for it.

She leaned back against him to show she understood it was difficult for him to have her go with them to confront Osamu Saito. The woman had been so harsh with her and yet she was the only mother Mariko had ever known. If Osamu was behind Ryuu's kidnapping, Mariko honestly didn't know what she would do.

"Let's get it done then. We have to be in and out of here fast," Stefano decreed. "You follow our lead, Mariko, and if things go to hell, hit the first shadow and ride it back to the plane."

She nodded because she knew the Ferraro brothers now. How stubborn they were. They'd stand there until hell froze over before they moved if she didn't agree to Stefano's orders. There wouldn't be an argument. They didn't argue. In any case, although she had complete confidence in herself and her abilities as a rider, she knew this would be an emotional journey and it was going to take its toll on her.

She looked down at the ring on her finger. It wasn't just any ring. It was a rider's ring—specially crafted by the famous Ferraro jeweler in New York. She touched the band, rubbed at it, feeling the solid presence surrounding her finger the way Ricco's ropes surrounded her, the way his arms did.

The ring was a part of her and it would break down just as she did in the shadow tubes. She could carry it with her everywhere she went, which meant having Ricco with her. His strength. His power. His belief in her.

Stefano reached out and clapped Franco Mancini, another cousin and the Ferraro pilot, on the shoulder. "We'll be back in a couple of hours. If not, you know what to do."

Franco didn't smile, and Mariko could see, despite his expressionless mask, that he was worried. She wanted to reassure them that Osamu would be gracious to them. It was only to Mariko—and sometimes Ryuu—that she showed her mean streak. Franco's gaze shifted, just for a moment, to her and then moved away, out toward the large asphalted area where he had taxied the plane, brought it in nose first, and parked. Was he worried about her? She glanced at Ricco's face again.

"I'm going to be fine," she assured him, although she was really reassuring *all* of them. She'd gone from just having Ryuu—and that was often part-time—to having what seemed an enormous family. Siblings and cousins treated her as if she were already a part of them.

"I wish you'd stay with Franco here where I know you're safe," Ricco said. "I've got a bad feeling, *il mio amore*." He wrapped his arms around her and nuzzled her neck. "I wouldn't make it very long without you. I'd much rather know you're safe than take chances."

"Seriously, Osamu is no threat to us. Her husband was a rider. As far as I know, she stopped riding shadows when she had children, but she always respects a rider."

"Except for you," Franco murmured.

Stefano's head jerked up. "Osamu was trained in riding shadows?"

Mariko frowned and nodded. "She told me once that she was. She was upset because I'd beat everyone's times in the trials. We had to go from one end of Tokyo to the other. There were checkpoints to ensure we didn't cheat, as if any shadow rider would. She detested that I was given any recognition and she told me she could have easily beat my times when she was training."

Stefano's eyes met Ricco's over her head. "That information is not common knowledge, Mariko. All trained riders are known within the community. Osamu was never registered as a rider."

"I asked Dai about it. He said she didn't like being in the tubes, but that she was trained and, despite feeling sick when she was inside, was very good when she was young." She looked from Stefano to Ricco. "What difference does it make? She's married to a shadow rider. She produced children and they were riders. She respects the riders even though she didn't want to go out on missions or continue into her adult years. There are many riders who try but don't make it for various reasons."

"Everything makes a difference, Mariko. The more knowledge we have the better," Ricco said, his voice gentle. "We investigate everyone we target thoroughly."

"We aren't targeting Osamu," Mariko pointed out. She looked from one brother to the other. "Are we? Isn't it possible she was just given the note and put it in my room?"

As terrible as her childhood had been, Osamu was still the only mother she had. Grief had lived in that house every single day. Osamu had been a good woman, a rider, a mother of two little boys she adored. A wife. Dai loved her despite how sorrow had weighed her down and changed her. He'd always come back, and more than once, Mariko had seen him holding Osamu as she cried. She didn't want the Ferraros to think Osamu was all bad. People had layers to them. She had never experienced the compassionate, good side of Osamu, but she'd seen it in her interactions with Ryuu and Dai. She'd heard her laugh with her friends.

"We're just investigating," Stefano said. "And we need all the facts."

"I'm sorry, I guess I didn't think to tell you that she had trained. She was never an official rider nor did she go out on missions. Something about being in the tubes made her violently ill."

"Mariko," Stefano said. "There's a reason we don't investigate close to home. You're missing important facts because you don't want to see the truth."

"You admitted to me that you believed Osamu slipped the note under your door," Ricco pointed out gently, giving his brother a quelling look. He wrapped his arm around her waist and drew her back against him, holding her close.

She didn't want to be the cause of an argument between the brothers, but . . . "It's occurred to me that any shadow rider could have put that note in my room. It would have been easy enough to do."

"True," Stefano said. "And just as easy for Osamu. You let us do the talking."

There was no looking away from those dark, compelling eyes. Even with Ricco surrounding her with the force of his personality, with his strength and protection, his older brother was just plain scary. She nodded, not because she was intimidated, but because, as a rider, she knew he was right.

She was too involved emotionally. Her brother's life was in jeopardy—if he was still alive. There had been no word from the kidnappers. None. That wasn't a good sign. She couldn't let herself think about that. She had to believe he was alive and that somehow the Ferraros or the International Council, in their investigations, would find Ryuu's trail.

"Get ready," Ricco cautioned.

Stefano nodded to Franco and his cousin stepped in front of them, a small device in his hands. Lights flickered, went out and then shone brightly across the entire area where the plane had been parked. Shadows raced in every direction, rushing up the steps, drawn by the strange magnetic compositions of their bodies.

Ricco took the lead, stepping into a tube without hesitation, choosing one that connected with so many others. Mariko went in after him, her body feeling as if it were flying apart. It was easy to see why some potential riders didn't make it. Having one's body torn apart time after time was hard. One had to stay in top physical shape at all times to endure using the tubes to get from one place to another. The aftermath could often be feeling extremely ill as Osamu had. Even within a family of riders, it wasn't unusual for some members to be unable to work as riders.

Mariko hesitated coming out of the tube, even knowing she was blocking Stefano from emerging right at Dai and Osamu's doorstep. Just looking at the house made her feel different. Her newfound confidence wavered at the sight of the home she'd grown up in. She felt like that unwanted girl, daughter of a street whore, despised by Osamu and her friends.

The circle of women was very powerful. They could do good or they could be very ugly in their judgments. Their voices could sway their husbands' opinions and shape the opinions of their children. Osamu's voice had been loud and her friends' had been louder. Their disdain had colored her life, spilling over to the other riders.

She had known the riders training would have been her friends had their host families not told them to stay away from her. Kichiro had admitted that his mother wouldn't have wanted her as a daughter-in-law.

A hand on her shoulder made her jump. Stefano leaned into her, half in, half out of the tube. "You don't have to do this, *la mia sorellina*. If you're doing this out of pride, just know that you're one of us and we have no problem doing this without you. We protect our own. I would expect you to lend me a hand if I needed it. Family is everything."

Calling her little sister. Including her as family. She'd never had that before. She took a deep breath just as Ricco stepped close to her, worry in his eyes. He pulled her under his shoulder.

"Tell me what you need, Mariko."

She was *so* in love with him. One hand had gone to the nape of her neck, his fingers massaging the tension out of her there. One finger slid down her nape. That one small gesture he always used just before they began Shibari together. He always grounded her. Centered her. Made her feel powerful with that tiny, intimate gesture.

"You just gave it to me," she assured. "Both of you. I'm ready and I'll follow your lead."

"Stay in the background as much as possible," Stefano advised.

She was good at that. Good at being almost invisible. She'd practiced not drawing attention to herself since she was a child. "I will," she said, because they needed to hear that she was strong enough, that she had her confidence back.

The three went up the front steps. The stairs were wooden

and led up to the home. It was considered luxurious, in a good part of Tokyo, where residents had small yards with trees and foliage in abundance. It was small, and although it had four bedrooms, it only had one bath. The entire house could fit into her suite at Ricco's estate.

Osamu answered the knock and her eyes widened as she stepped back to allow Stefano, Ricco and Mariko to enter. She didn't greet Mariko, but she inclined her head out of respect for the riders. Dai came forward immediately, alarm on his face.

"Stefano. Ricco. It is good to see you." He didn't sound as though it was good to see them.

Mariko knew the International Council had already questioned him and he had been adamant that his sons had been killed in a car accident—that the Tanaka family had been as well.

He waved the riders toward chairs. Mariko didn't say a word but slipped into the corner where she'd spent most of her childhood.

"We've come to speak with Osamu about a very pressing matter," Stefano said. "It is extremely important."

Dai looked shocked that they weren't confronting him about his testimony to the International Council. Relief settled over his features and he almost relaxed. "Osamu." He raised his voice to summon his wife, who had gone into the kitchen to make tea.

She came immediately, so fast Mariko was certain she hadn't been in the kitchen.

"These gentlemen need to speak with you."

Osamu smiled and inclined her head. "Mariko. We need tea." She didn't even look at the corner where Mariko had settled as she gave the order.

"Mariko no longer resides in your home," Ricco said. "Nor is she your servant."

Osamu looked confused. "She may no longer reside here, but she is still my daughter. Has she forgotten I took her in and raised her when no other would have her?"

Mariko went very still inside. Osamu had used the "mother" mask often when they had company, pointing out Mariko's failings as a daughter. Dai seemed to buy into it every single time. Stefano and Ricco both acted as if they had adopted Nicoletta into their family. They might believe that Osamu thought of her as a daughter. That subtle reminder of "I took her in and raised her when no other would have her" was all about letting others know she'd come from the streets.

"Mariko hasn't forgotten a single thing," Ricco said. "Now she is here as my fiancée, not your daughter, and what we need to discuss with you concerns her. She needs to be here."

He made it clear, and there was no subtlety about it, that Mariko was under his protection. Osamu didn't fail to understand. She shot Mariko a look of pure poisonous hatred. She settled into the chair beside her husband and glared at Ricco.

"Fiancée?" Disgust twisted her voice. "You are a shadow rider with a great name. You allow the daughter of a whore to seduce you into giving her a ring?"

Ricco shocked Mariko by settling back in his chair, steepling his fingers and regarding Dai over the top of them. "Since when is rudeness to shadow riders and their families tolerated? This family has fallen a long way since I was a boy. There was a time the name Saito was highly respected. Now your woman insults both my fiancée and me in your home right in front of you. It is sad that your wife disrespects you so much that she would insult a fellow rider in your own home. You have my sympathy."

Stefano stirred, nodding his head. "Mine as well, Dai."

It took every ounce of discipline Mariko possessed to remain still and quiet in her little corner. Osamu looked as if she might have a stroke. Her face was mottled a beet red and she sputtered, trying to get out a protest. Dai shot her a look of resignation and disappointment.

"Enough, Osamu. You are to answer questions, not give

your opinion." His voice was low and defeated. He hung his head and reached for worry beads he always kept on him.

Mariko knew Osamu detested those beads.

"We're looking for Mariko's brother," Stefano said. "Do you know where he is?"

Osamu cackled, sounding exactly, to Ricco's ears, like the witches from horror movies. The strange laughter had Dai leaping to his feet and beginning to pace. He glared at his wife. She kept up the screeches, rocking herself back and forth, looking for all the world like an old crow.

At one time, Mariko had considered Osamu beautiful— the most beautiful of all the women in their circle. There was none of that beauty now. She looked old and evil. She could barely look at her, barely see the woman Mariko had hoped would one day come to see she'd tried her best to be a good daughter.

"Osamu!" Dai pressed his hands to his ears. "Stop that this instant."

Osamu sobered immediately, as if her husband had slapped her across the face.

"Answer Stefano's question." Dai paced across the room, turning his back on her as if disgusted.

Osamu bared her teeth at Stefano. "Of course I know where he is, but you'll never find him. *Never*."

"Osamu," Mariko whispered. "How could you be a part of harming him?"

Ricco shook his head, the gesture barely perceptible, but Mariko nodded, ashamed she'd broken her silence when both men had specifically asked her not to.

"You didn't do your job, Mariko, and it was so simple. Just like the jobs I gave you in the house. The cooking and cleaning. Very simple tasks, but you always messed them up."

Osamu's attention was wholly on her now. Mariko realized why the brothers had asked her not to speak. Her very presence was inciting her.

Osamu leaned toward her. "You were a horrible child,

always looking to get out of work. I had to beat you to keep your attention on your tasks. You needed attention all the time. Every second of the day. You ran over your own brother so he wouldn't be able to be trained. You wanted all the accolades for yourself."

"She didn't run over Ryuu," Ricco objected. "Have you forgotten that I was there that night? I saw them all. I witnessed what they did. Nao Yamamoto stomped on Ryuu. I saw Mariko save him. She kicked Nao and drew his attention away from her brother."

"You lie!" Osamu shrieked, her face once more twisted. "Why do you lie, Ricco? We always treated you like a son. Why would you lie about such a girl?" Her features turned sly. "You're *fucking* her, aren't you? I knew you would. Her mother was a whore on the street and her daughter is just like her."

"*Enough*, Osamu," Dai snapped, his back to her. Both hands were behind his back, his fingers clenching and unclenching in two tight fists. "Answer them immediately. Where is the boy?"

At the lash of Dai's command, Osamu sank back into her chair, looking small and defeated. She began to rock herself, her arms around her middle. "Where is he? Where is he?" Her voice rose in a singsong. "Where is he?" She chanted it over and over.

Dai turned from where he was staring out the window to look at his wife. To Mariko's horror, there were tears in his eyes. "Osamu, please. Tell them where Ryuu is, so they can go. You're becoming agitated again."

It was very difficult to watch Osamu's madness—there was no question that Mariko was looking at a woman totally insane. By turns she would look crafty and then, when she looked at her husband, she crumbled completely. It was all she could do not to go to the woman and try to comfort her. She must have made a move toward Osamu because Ricco's hand suddenly shot out and caught her wrist in a viselike grip.

The action drew Osamu's gaze and instantly her expression changed again. Hatred was stamped in every line of her face. "You're such a vile creature. Tempting men just like your mother. She ruined Daiki. *Ruined* him. He was a rider of unimaginable talent, but he was so weak, letting himself be seduced by that bitch."

Dai shook his head and left the room, his face lined with age and fatigue, with a terrible sorrow that was beyond all words. His shoulders slumped and he looked to Mariko as if he'd aged right in front of her.

"Osamu." Stefano's voice was very low, almost too low to hear, but the woman's attention immediately swung to him. "You were going to tell us where Ryuu is."

She shook her head and began to cackle again. "You'll never find him."

"Does Nao Yamamoto have him?"

Osamu tapped her knee hard with her fist. "He doesn't have long to live. Time is running out for him." She swung her head toward Mariko again. "You should have killed Ricco Ferraro, not fucked him." She threw back her head and began laughing hysterically as if she'd told a great joke. "Not that it would have done you any good, but the other riders would know how you broke the code and killed another rider."

"Osamu." Stefano brought her attention back to him. "We need to know where Ryuu is."

"You need? The oh-so-perfect Ferraros need something from Osamu?" She glared at Ricco. "I want my sons back. *He* took them from me. Give me back my sons and I'll tell you what you want to know."

"You know that's impossible, Osamu." Stefano continued to use her name in an attempt to keep her attention focused on him.

She leaned toward Ricco. "You're going to die, but before you do, you're going to suffer. Everyone you love will die, including that bitch in heat."

Ricco remained passive, refusing to rise to her bait, nor

did he change expression. He merely looked at the woman. Mariko had the unfamiliar urge to shake her, to bring Osamu out of the craziness that seemed to take her over.

"What did Ryuu ever do to you?" The question burst out of her. "He loved you, Osamu. Like a mother. He thought of you as his mother. How could you help Nao hurt him? You never liked me, I accept that, but Ryuu was loving to you."

The fingers shackling her wrist tightened to the point of hurting her. She knew neither of the men wanted her speaking, but Ryuu was her brother, Osamu the only mother either of them remembered. Surely she had to have *some* feeling for Ryuu. He'd only been a baby when they were given to Osamu.

She tried to yank her hand out of Ricco's restraining fingers, uncertain whether or not she was going to fling herself at Osamu and force the woman to tell them where her brother was being held. He refused to let go of her.

"You tell me where my brother is right this minute," Mariko demanded.

Osamu surged out of her chair, flying at Mariko, hatred twisting the once beautiful face. In her hand she clutched a dagger she'd drawn from inside her cardigan. Ricco shoved Mariko aside as Osamu leapt the short distance between them. His chair went over with a crash as he stood, trying to judge when she would slash in the hopes of disarming her before she cut him.

Time slowed down. Tunneled. Mariko landed on the floor but her entire being centered on the dagger in Osamu's hand. In that moment, she knew there was no living without Ricco. He was her choice. He would always be her choice, and she'd risked him by not listening to the two men. They were so right. A rider couldn't be emotionally involved, and now she was close to losing the man she loved.

She tried to scramble off the floor, to distract Osamu enough that Ricco could take control of the dagger. Osamu looked right into Ricco's eyes, fury, determination and hatred on her face as she slid under his arm to reach her goal.

A shot rang out. The sound was so loud in the confined

space that Mariko's ears hurt. A red hole blossomed in Osamu's chest, right over her heart. Osamu's stricken gaze shifted from Ricco's face to over his shoulder. Mariko followed her gaze. To her horror, Dai stood there with a gun in his hand, looking at his wife, his expression so sorrowful Mariko felt the burn of tears.

Very slowly, Osamu's body crumpled, in increments, her knees giving out, and then she bent forward and toppled to the floor. Ricco and Stefano didn't take their eyes from Dai and the weapon in his hand. Ricco extended his hand to Mariko but didn't look at her.

Mariko took his hand and he pulled her up but thrust her behind him. "Stay there." It was a command, nothing less, and the tone carried a hint of a promise of retaliation if she didn't listen.

"Dai," Stefano said, speaking in that soft voice he always seemed to use. "Give me the gun."

Dai stepped back out of reach, shaking his head. "None of this was her fault."

"You need to give me the gun."

"This wasn't her fault. None of it," Dai reiterated, tears streaming down his face. He moved carefully around Stefano and Ricco until he was standing beside his wife. "It was that boy. The Yamamoto boy. He was sick. Insane. His parents knew it. We all did, but no one wanted to go against Isamu."

"Dai, give me the gun and let's call the council," Stefano said.

Dai slowly lowered himself to the floor, his grip on the gun never wavering. He pulled Osamu's body into his lap and began to rock back and forth as if he could comfort her. "Isamu was my brother-in-law, Osamu's brother. She worshiped him, and no matter what I said about allowing the boys to be with Nao, she wanted to please her brother. I knew better, but I couldn't bear to see Osamu unhappy."

"Dai." Stefano moved closer. "Give me the gun."

Dai shook his head. "Leave us, Stefano. Take Mariko and go." His watery eyes lifted to Mariko's face. "You are a Tanaka. A rider of the first quality. I gave you and Ryuu to Osamu hoping it would give her something to love. Instead she was cruel to you. Even then I couldn't step in and take you from her because she didn't have any other outlet. In the end, I failed everyone, but most of all, myself."

"Dai, give Stefano the gun," Mariko pleaded, without much hope.

"Go, my dear. Leave us now."

"Do you know where Ryuu is?"

Dai shook his head. "Regrettably, I hid out in the country when Osamu would get too bad. I do know that whatever conspiracy she came up with, she wasn't alone. I don't know who was helping her, but when I was here, she spoke often in whispers to someone on the phone. Now please go and leave us in peace."

Ricco reached for her hand, threaded his fingers through hers and tugged until she was under his shoulder. He turned her away from the only father she'd ever known. She stumbled once but kept walking with him, Stefano behind her. The gun sounded overly loud in the house, like a boom of thunder, hurting her ears. Even expecting it, she cried out, wincing. Ricco kept walking, his arm tight around her.

She didn't understand. Osamu was totally insane, and yet Dai had loved her all those years. Clearly there had been something between Osamu and Daiki Tanaka at some point, and Osamu resented Mariko's mother because she'd somehow stolen Daiki from her. Why wasn't Osamu happy with the man she was with, the one showing her so much love and understanding over the years they were together?

"We have to get into the shadows as we leave," Ricco whispered, his lips brushing against her ear. "No one can see us. We can't hide the plane, but Stefano has business in Tokyo and it will just look as if he came here for that."

Mariko nodded, still too numb to think clearly. Dai had shot his wife and then taken his own life. Osamu had refused to tell them where Ryuu was. She acted as if it were hysterically funny that they were looking for Ryuu and she had hidden him so well with his kidnappers that no one would ever get to him before it was too late. Mariko pressed a hand hard over her pounding heart. She had to slow her breathing before she stepped into the shadow. She was a rider. She had to pull it together.

"Mariko." Ricco stopped just inside the door, turning to her, lifting her chin with gentle fingers, his body blocking Stefano from seeing the tears burning her eyes.

It was his gentleness that undid her, the tender look on his face. She didn't know what to do with love. She'd never had it, had never known that the feeling could be so overwhelming.

"We'll find him," Ricco assured. "The investigators are looking for him as well. We'll get it out of Nao."

She nodded because she knew he meant it. She was losing hope, but she had to cling to her belief in him. He had a way about him that shouted confidence. He didn't seem to think Ryuu was dead. His palm curled around the nape of her neck the way his ropes curled around her body when he tied her—the way his arms felt when he held her. Solid. Safe. Connecting them.

His forehead touched hers. His breath was warm against her lips. He kissed his way up to her left eye, his tongue taking the few tears that had managed to trickle down her cheek. He left a trail of kisses from her right eye down to her mouth, sipping away the tears.

"We have to go, Ricco." Stefano's voice held an urgent note as well as a compassionate one.

"I'm going to get you through this," Ricco promised, not turning or acknowledging his brother's warning.

Still, she knew he heard. He just wasn't going to rush her before she was ready. "They were the only parents I ever knew. Dai was kind at times and indifferent at others. She sometimes accused me of flirting with him. That started when I was around ten, so we were careful to never be alone. He became mostly indifferent after that."

She took a deep breath. His palm curling around the nape

of her neck, his thumb sliding along her cheek in a small caress, his breath, warm and as steady as the beat of his heart, gave her a sense of calm. She squared her shoulders. "I'm ready."

"You're my woman, Mariko. I know I was born to be with you. To love you. When things are bad, you have me." Ricco lifted her left hand to his mouth, kissing the ring on her finger. "You have my family. You aren't alone, *amore*."

She nodded, although she didn't know why. She had no understanding of anything anymore. She was terrified for her brother, and even at the last, when Osamu had the chance to be a mother to both Ryuu and her, the woman had chosen not to. She would rather sacrifice Ryuu's life than do one decent thing for Mariko.

Ricco jerked his chin toward the door. Stefano had been watching the shadows as the lights around the houses threw patterns on stairs, landscape and into the streets. He opened the door and was instantly swallowed by a shadow. Ricco stepped back to allow Mariko to precede him. She did without hesitation. At once the shadow pulled her apart, hurtling her after Stefano.

For the first time, the tube felt comforting despite the terrible pressure on her body. It was familiar to her. The strange feeling of being pulled apart. The weird spinning sensation as if the tube were a giant wave that rolled over her and was about to collapse on her head. She had ridden the shadows from the time she was two years old. It felt like more of a home to her than the house she'd grown up in.

In the privacy of the tube, she could admit that she was devastated, that Osamu's betrayal of Ryuu was so unexpected and heartbreaking she could barely comprehend it. She had always believed that Osamu cared about Ryuu. Maybe she didn't love him as a normal mother loved her children, but she'd raised him from the time he was a toddler. He had continued to live with Osamu until just a couple of years earlier.

She followed Stefano's lead, switching from shadow to

shadow until they were back at the airport. Franco was waiting, the door of the plane open, the lights providing the necessary shadows to slide up the stairs right into the privacy of the interior. As soon as Ricco was safely inside, Franco spoke into his cell and a car made its way to the plane.

Stefano immediately turned to Mariko, touching her cheek gently. "I've got to get to this meeting. You stay out of sight. I'll be back as soon as I can."

She knew his meeting was their cover, the reason the Ferraro jet was in Tokyo. She nodded.

"I'm sorry, Mariko. There was nothing we could do to prevent that. Osamu clearly was out of her mind."

"Dai couldn't take it anymore," she murmured.

"You know it was more than that," Stefano said gently. "The International Council was investigating their crimes. Dai knew they'd be found guilty, and he didn't want to face the lies they'd told their friends and family. He was a proud man, but a weak one. He allowed the Tanaka name to be taken from you and your brother. He allowed you to be treated badly in his home. Don't mourn Dai or Osamu Saito. Neither deserve your tears or sorrow. Justice was coming for them, and Dai took the easy way out." He swept her into his arms for a brief hug and then stepped out into the open, as if leaving the plane for the first time.

Ricco wrapped his arms around her and walked her deeper into the luxurious interior. "He's trying to say you have a family, Mariko. We love you and we'll help you find Ryuu."

"Do you think he's alive?" She couldn't help but ask, even though she wasn't certain she wanted to hear the answer.

"He's alive," he assured.

Her gaze jumped to his face. It was, as usual, impossible to read. Something in his tone sent goose bumps swarming over her flesh and she rubbed her arms. Ricco could be very intimidating when he chose.

CHAPTER EIGHTEEN

"I wondered how the hell they were able to know where we all were," Taviano said. "Which shop Emme was in. Where Nicoletta was. Even Phillip's mistress. How did our enemies keep tabs on us without our knowledge?"

Stefano's apartment was once again the gathering place for all of Ricco's siblings. The penthouse smelled delicious. Francesca and Taviano had whipped up a dinner after a brutal training session in Stefano's very large training hall. It was the first time Mariko had ever trained with them, yet they didn't go light on her. She was happy they respected her enough after watching her work out to treat her as a real opponent. She didn't do that badly against them, either.

Only Stefano, Ricco and Taviano could spar with her, and Stefano watched over Ricco like a hawk. Emmanuelle was still wearing the immobilizer and sling to keep from moving her shoulder. Vittorio was out of the hospital. He watched the sparring matches but was still forbidden to fight one of his brothers or sister. He worked out a little on the mat, but mostly it was stretching. Giovanni's femur had been broken and needed extensive surgery. He had rods and pins in his leg. It was kept immobile by a long brace. Recovery was a minimum of four months, but more likely six. It was imperative that all metal be removed if he was going to ride again. He was there, pale and hurting, but he didn't complain.

"Did you figure it out?" Stefano asked as he reached for

the basket of warm sourdough bread smothered in butter and garlic salt. "And what's with their fixation on Nicoletta? Have you figured that out?"

Giovanni reached for the pasta, couldn't quite make it, so Mariko added the pasta to his plate. She added two pieces of the garlic bread and a very large helping of salad before serving herself.

"Thanks, *mia sorellina*. I appreciate you feeding me." He glared at his brothers.

Vittorio shrugged. "I'm kind of liking you not being able to reach the table properly, Gee. More food for me and I don't even have to work at it. He's not going to starve without a few meals, Mariko."

"Vittorio," Francesca protested. "That's so mean."

"He's kicking me while I'm down," Giovanni pointed out, clearly looking for sympathy and an ally from Francesca.

"Vittorio." Francesca sent him a stern look. The Ferraros burst out laughing. Mariko had to smile as well. Francesca didn't look nearly as stern as she tried. She looked sweet, much like Lucia. She could see why the family regarded her as their center with Stefano and were protective over her. She felt a little protective toward her as well.

Stefano passed his plate to his wife and she put a healthy helping of pasta on it. "Taviano. What did you find?"

"Cameras. All over the village. At Eloisa's house. In the hotel lobby and positioned across the street recording all entrances. Once I realized we virtually had our own reality show, I checked everyone's homes. Cameras were positioned across the streets, and sometimes in the garages." He took a bite of the pasta, chewed, swallowed and continued. "The cameras were installed some time ago. Long enough that there's signs of rust on the mounting bolts. Whoever he is, he's damn good with surveillance. Knows what he's doing." He took another bite of pasta and chewed, then waved his fork at them. "I'd guess whoever put those cameras up also fucked up Ricco's car."

Mariko stole a quick glance at Ricco. He was sitting close to her, close enough that their thighs were touching. He did that a lot the last couple of days. They'd returned from Japan and he'd stayed close to her, very protective. She had nightmares and he was always there, holding her close, telling her everything was going to be all right and she wasn't alone.

She was terrified she was going to lose Ryuu. He was all the family she had left. It had hurt to discover just how much Osamu hated her. Dai knew, he knew exactly how Osamu had treated her, and he hadn't stepped in. Mariko had been a child. She'd been three years old when her family had been massacred. Now . . . She fought back panic. She *couldn't* lose Ryuu.

Ricco shifted in his chair, his palm curling around the nape of her neck. She blinked, looked around and discovered the entire family was watching her. All of them. Compassion on their faces.

"We're with you, Mariko," Emmanuelle said. "All the way. We're with you. You're Ricco's, but you're ours as well."

She flashed a smile, but it hurt even to curve her mouth when she wanted desperately to cry. They had one another. They always had. No matter how bad it got for them, they had a circle of absolute love and loyalty. She'd never even known it. It was a struggle to believe it was real, and they were extending that love of family to her. She wasn't certain she could make herself believe she was worthy of it when she'd been told so often she wasn't.

Ricco's finger slid down her nape, steadying her. Connecting her. She didn't know why it worked, but it did. The moment she felt that small caress, she felt strong again. Complete. Not because she was with him but because he had somehow managed, through his rope art, to empower her as a woman and a human being. He was offering her his life. More than once he'd made himself vulnerable to her. She had to hold that to her. Remind herself every time she felt uncertain that Ricco felt she was worthy. His family felt that way. *She* had to come to that realization, and Shibari had started her along that path.

"I try not to think about Ryuu and what he must be going through. Osamu had him so conflicted, he probably thinks I'm not looking for him."

"Everyone is looking," Stefano said gently. "The International Council and every rider we have. We're all trying to pick up the trail."

Yet no one had. That was what was so disturbing. She forked pasta and put it in her mouth, although it tasted like cardboard to her. The shock of seeing Dai shoot his wife and then knowing he killed himself . . .

"We didn't actually see Dai's body," she said, turning her head to look at Ricco. "What if he didn't kill himself and just wanted us to think he had. He's smart. He could be behind this."

Ricco's fingers tightened around her neck. He shook his head. "The police came and found them. The bodies were taken to the morgue and members of the Japanese council as well as the International Council viewed them. They died when we were present."

Emmanuelle frowned. "What does that mean? They suspected you of killing them?"

Stefano held up his hand when his siblings protested loudly. Mariko's heart thudded wildly. She could very well get the entire Ferraro family in trouble with the council.

"*Farfallina mia.*" Ricco leaned into her, his lips brushing her ear. "They were always after me. You were sucked into *my* mess. Just the fact that Taviano could tell the cameras had been up for a long while means they were planning this for a good amount of time."

"Either I'm losing my poker face, or you can read my mind," she objected.

"You never actually had a poker face," Ricco said, "but that blow to my head gave me psychic ability. I *can* read your mind."

"What *exactly* is it saying right this minute?" she asked,

trying not to laugh. He could always make her laugh, even in the worst of circumstances.

"Even I can read that message," Giovanni said. "He'd better eat the pasta if he wants to keep what's left of his head."

"That would be correct," she agreed.

The siblings erupted in another round of laughter. This time, she joined them, feeling a part of them. They had a way of wrapping one another up, just like Ricco's ropes, snug, laying the line perfectly to keep one safe.

"Cameras can be traced," Vittorio pointed out when they all sobered. "Pass the garlic bread, please, Giovanni. Stop eating it all. You're going to get fat sitting on your ass and eating Francesca's fine cooking."

"Vittorio." Francesca tried another severe look.

"I'm *helping* him. Good advice, you know. He can't work out for a while, which means watching the calories. Garlic bread"—he nabbed three pieces—"is high in calories."

"You're not exactly working out right now." Giovanni managed to snag one of the pieces of bread off his brother's plate. "If you call that stretching crap work, I'm going to call you a girl."

Emmanuelle's head shot up. She scowled at her brother. "What does that mean? I'm a girl. Are you saying I'm not badass because I'm female?"

Vittorio grinned at his brother. Giovanni flipped him off and then smiled lovingly at his sister. "No one would dare say you're not a badass, *bella*."

"Hmm," Taviano mused. "I do believe the prince, Val Saldi, might have something to say about that. He was sure hovering over her, acting like she didn't know how to shoot a gun and he'd have to teach her."

Emmanuelle's face flushed and she opened her mouth to retaliate, glaring at her brothers as they all burst out laughing.

"Taviano." Francesca used a warning voice before Emmanuelle could say a word. "If you want to keep eating, you are going to get off that subject right this minute and leave

Emme alone. She has enough to contend with without you constantly teasing her about Val Saldi. She can't help who crushes on her."

"It isn't like that," Emmanuelle muttered. "He can't say a nice word."

"Maybe not," Stefano said, "but, obnoxious or not, son of our enemy, he saved your ass when it was needed and for that, I'll tolerate him."

"We're all here," Ricco said, looking around. "Who's on Nicoletta? I swear that girl is going to take off if you don't talk to her, Stefano. She's worried about Lucia and Amo, and with three attacks with both present, I'd say she has reason to worry."

"Enrica pulled guard duty tonight," Vittorio said. "What's the word on Tomas and Cosimo? I called yesterday and Cosimo was back home and already doing his PT. Tomas wasn't given the go-ahead yet."

Stefano sighed. "Like Giovanni, they're both acting like they can jump right back to work. I told Emilio absolutely not until the doctors clear them and they've had several months of training. I told them to go to counselors as well." He flashed a grin at his brothers. "That was Francesca's suggestion, and a good one."

Immediately, all smiles were gone and the brothers nodded their heads, looking solemn. Francesca looked around the table and then to Mariko. "What? They almost died. They want to be bodyguards again and they should at least have someone to talk to about it. Don't you think that's a good idea?" Before Mariko could answer she turned to Stefano.

Instantly he reached for her hand. "We're teasing you, baby. Tomas and Cosimo are throwbacks to the caveman days. Asking them to go to counseling is worse than anything you can imagine, but you're absolutely right, and I told them they had to go. Tomas is rebelling. Cosimo agreed to make an appointment with the counselor I suggested. She's going to be renting the small studio over Biagi's and using the office next to it. She's French. Young. Her name is Oceane Brisbois, moving in next month. Our one and only counselor is retiring. That should give Cosimo and Tomas time to come to terms with the idea. She was thoroughly investigated before we allowed her in."

"Let's get back to Nicoletta," Ricco said. "She's fierce in a fight. I know we can't teach her to ride shadows, but she should be taught to defend herself. We could have her train with both hand to hand and weapons. I think she'd be more inclined to stick around if she was training. She'd feel more in control and able to defend Lucia and Amo."

"I totally agree," Vittorio said. "She's a little hellcat and needs something to channel all that aggression. Maybe eating more pasta." He scooped more onto his plate.

"You're going to turn into pasta if you keep eating like that," Giovanni pointed out. "I agree as well. Train that girl, but then we'll have to read about her doing in every high school boy making a pass at her."

A collective groan went around the table. Mariko hid her smile. There was genuine caring in their voices. Nicoletta might not know it, but the Ferraro family had her back.

"I think it's a brilliant idea," Emmanuelle said. "And you can only hope she's doing in the high school boys who make a pass at her rather than partying every night like certain ones sitting at this table did."

"Don't be ratting us out," Vittorio said. He tried to look innocent but failed.

Everyone laughed, including Mariko. She loved sitting there listening to all of them. She knew she would always love it. Beside her, Ricco was solid and warm, his hand on her nape or holding hers against his thigh. He touched her often, gently, barely there, but enough to let her know he was close and aware of her.

"You deserve to be ratted out as many times as you stopped me going out the window," Emmanuelle said, pretending to glare at her brother.

"Because you were meeting the prince," Taviano said.

"That was strictly forbidden, but you did it anyway. You were in high school, and he was not only too old for you, but he is the enemy."

Emmanuelle rolled her eyes and took another bite of garlic bread. "Taviano, what do you think about training Nicoletta?"

"I think it's a good idea. I agree that it might make her less likely to run and we can all get some sleep. We do need bodyguards assigned to her on an everyday basis."

"She's not going to like that," Emmanuelle said with a little sniff of disdain. "Especially if Emilio trained them and they're under his jurisdiction."

Stefano set his wineglass back on the table. "Nicoletta is family whether she likes it or not. We took her in when we made the decision to get her out of that situation. She'll have bodyguards whether she likes it or not, and because she's family, that means they'll be trained by and work under Emilio." It was a decree, nothing less.

Mariko found it fascinating to watch the interplay within the family. They all got a vote, but Stefano had the last word and everyone accepted it as such. No one ever appeared to really argue with him. Maybe Francesca, but it seemed she didn't have to argue much. Stefano clearly gave her anything she wanted.

Mariko glanced up at Ricco and found herself blushing. He was looking down at her with a look on his face that took her breath and made her heart flutter. No one looked at her like that. It was the same look Stefano got on his face when he looked at Francesca. Adoring. Loving. She felt the burn of tears. She didn't have a clue what to do when Ricco looked at her that way. Everything he was offering to her was new. Sometimes she felt like she was in the garden maze, trying to find her way.

He leaned down and pressed his lips against her ear. "I think it's a Shibari night. A special one. You. Me. The ropes. A very erotic pose. I've been sitting here looking at you and I can already see the exact image I want."

She shivered. Her sex clenched. She was aware of her body beneath the modest clothes she wore. The lacy demi bra and sexy little panties that left her buttocks bare, but had a small bow right at the base of her spine with three strands of cord wrapping around to the front. Ricco liked lingerie. Once, in the ropes, he'd whispered that he liked knowing she wore it just for him. That no one else could see what she gave him.

"We have Nicoletta covered," Stefano continued. "She's got Enrica right now, but when this is over, I'll put the two new men on her. They're good. Emilio has them well trained and both were Special Forces before they came home. I like them."

"Too fucking young," Taviano objected simultaneously with Vittorio.

Mariko had to hide her smile again. It was funny how the brothers all talked alike. Thought alike. Had similar expressions. Voted alike. She smiled up at Ricco, blushing, the color moving up her body like the touch of his hands. She wanted the ropes around her. She wanted to see desire building in Ricco's eyes. The lines of lust carved deep into his face. Mostly she wanted that feeling of belonging. Of being so seductive he couldn't resist her.

"Taviano, I know damn well you didn't just stop at the cameras," Stefano said, sitting back in his chair, reaching for his wineglass. "What else did you learn?"

"The software he's using is very advanced. *Very*. I traced that directly to Forward Technologies."

Mariko gasped and sat up straight. "That's the same company that supposedly sent my brother the ticket to come to the United States. They booked the hotel room for him using a company card, but the card was later reported as stolen."

"To find out the owner of the software company took a bit of doing. Vinci got involved as well as Rigina and Rosina. After we peeled off all kinds of layers, it seems the Yamamotos own the software company, along with the company that produced the faulty casing on the race car. The Yamamotos also own a leading security company complete with the exact same cameras used to keep track of all of us." Taviano picked up his glass of wine, smiled at his siblings and took a drink.

"Nao Yamamoto," Stefano said. "Why wait so long?"

"He didn't make his move until after his father died. He wouldn't have wanted to shame them further," Mariko said. "I suspected Nao and actually watched him for several days before I came here. There was nothing out of the ordinary happening with him. He has a caretaker who is with him at all times, but he went to work and then went home. I checked his home and his offices. Ryuu isn't being held there."

"If he had these companies hidden, he probably has more," Stefano said. "Our family certainly does. I'll get Vinci and the others on it. We're all looking, Mariko. Everyone is."

She inclined her head, because around the Ferraros it was difficult to keep her composure. She either wanted to laugh or cry, or join in their ridiculous arguments. She loved the family. She loved the way they gathered at Stefano and Francesca's home, even if they lived in a penthouse in a hotel. Francesca had made the space into a beautiful, warm, welcoming home.

"Next time we come," Ricco said, "Mariko and I will be doing the cooking." He stood up and leaned over to kiss Francesca on the top of her head. "Are we paying Nao a visit later tonight?"

Stefano nodded. "Let's go around two. His caretaker will have settled down by then and we can have a private chat with him."

"You two taking off already?" Giovanni asked, nudging Taviano. The two men grinned at each other. Vittorio smirked and winked at her.

Mariko blushed all over again, but she didn't mind the teasing. She knew it was meant to be affectionate. It made her feel part of their family. More, Ricco moved closer and wrapped his arm around her.

"See you at two, Stefano," he said, shooting his brothers a quelling glance. He kissed his sister on the cheek and urged Mariko toward the door with his palm in the small of her back. He was silent in the elevator, withdrawing a little, although he held her close to him. She had noticed he did that before he practiced his art.

Just the thought of having him alone with her in the studio was exciting to her. She loved the way he moved, his confidence, how he handled the ropes as if they were a part of him. She couldn't wait to see just what he had in mind. The sexual tension stretched between them until every nerve ending in her body was so aware of him, she was certain she could orgasm without him touching her. He just had to speak.

Emilio drove them to the house and let them off at the side entrance. She realized, after the attack on the house, that even from above, the entrance was protected from every eye. Not even a marksman would be able to get either of them as they slid from the car and made their way into the house, the thick walls of the entry on either side of them.

"Are you up for this tonight? Physically? It may take time to tie you the way I want."

She nodded. "I'm ready."

"You know how to prepare yourself. Wear the red lace one-piece for me. The red stiletto heels. Nothing else."

His voice stroked her skin with velvet over steel. Dominant. Confident. So completely Ricco. She nodded, already so aroused she could barely speak. She loved that he could do that to her. That it was only Ricco who could see her this way. Needy. Hungry for him. Vulnerable. Somewhere between lust and love.

He reached out to cup her cheek, his thumb sliding over her high cheekbone, his dark eyes so intense she shivered again.

"I love you, Mariko. Never, never doubt that. I love you with everything in me."

The pad of his thumb, sliding back and forth over her

skin, was mesmerizing. His eyes were hypnotic. She was so far under his spell she knew she would never get out, and she didn't want to. She wanted to spend her life with this man.

"I love you, too."

"If at any time I do anything you don't like, you tell me and we stop. If a tie hurts, you say so. Don't stay too long because you want to please me. It wouldn't. Shibari, to me, is decorative tying. I want to edge us into something more erotic. If you are uncomfortable or don't like it, you speak up. Do you understand me? The most important thing we have is communication."

She was already damp, and getting more so with every word. She wanted him. She wanted his art on her body. His ropes. His hands. His mouth. All of him. She had hoped he would take their art that one step further. "I will," she promised.

"This time, come to my room, not the studio."

She blinked up at him. They always worked in the studio. Just the thought of going to his room sent a rush of heat through her body. "I will," she said, not asking questions. She knew he wouldn't answer anyway, but he had something planned and she was certain she would be the beneficiary of that plan.

He brushed a kiss across her temple and then abruptly turned and walked away. She watched him go. He moved like a cat, all fluid muscle and rippling power. She knew, no matter how old she got, or how long she was with him, she would always feel that secret thrill when she watched him walk toward her or away from her.

She took her time with her routine, bathing in scented water, hydrating, doing her hair and makeup. She loved the way she felt in front of the vanity—so very feminine. That was a feeling she wasn't certain she would get used to. The red catsuit was stretch lace and it framed her curves with a delicate pattern, lying against her skin so lightly she almost couldn't feel it. The neck was low, but not plunging.

The suit would have been modest if it hadn't been made of the fragile lace, leaving skin exposed everywhere.

With every step toward him, her excitement grew. Her heart hammered out a rhythm. There was an accompanying throbbing deep in her sex. Her clit felt swollen, her pulse pounding right through it. She hesitated at the door, unsure whether to knock or just go in. She'd been sleeping in his bed the last few nights so it seemed silly to knock. Still, he'd been fairly formal after leaving Stefano's apartment.

She took a deep breath and pushed open the door. Ricco looked up immediately. He had rope in one hand and bamboo pole in the other. He didn't smile, but his gaze drifted over her possessively. His eyes darkened and the lines in his face were carved with sensual lust. He looked sinful in his low-cut, button-up jeans. Only two of the four buttons were done up so she could see his muscle, the dark ripple of hair and the vee that was so intriguing, disappearing into his jeans.

She turned around for him and then, turning back so she could watch him, she did slow stretching. She needed to warm up her muscles before he began tying, especially if it was going to be a long, complicated tie. His camera sat on the nightstand. He intended to take pictures.

He walked toward her, his stride confident, nothing lazy about it. He was all business, his features serious, a look she loved on him when he was practicing his art on her. Her heart jerked hard in her chest as she caught the scent of the rope. Sweet grass. He was using hemp. The texture of the rope was different than what he'd been using on her. Ricco was mesmerizing as he slid the rope through his hand, checking, she knew now, for splinters and burn speed to ensure her comfort.

He caught her hands decisively, tied them and pulled them up and over her head. The movement was very controlled, setting her heart pounding. She didn't know why she had such a reaction to Ricco when he was so dominant, but she loved how he took control, even when she knew one word from her and everything stopped.

His breath touched her neck as he lifted the heavy fall of hair and began braiding it. The tug felt like a massage on her scalp, and it wasn't until he pulled her arms down behind her that she realized her hair was braided into the rope and her head was tilted at an angle so that she couldn't move. For one moment panic set in. It was silly really; she'd been tied so completely she couldn't move, and yet it was immobilizing her head that caused her to become anxious.

His lips slid down the nape of her neck. "I've got you, *farfallina mia*. I'll always have you." His arms came around her and he pulled her back against his body. He was rock hard, his body strong, his heart beating against her back, his cock pressed tightly, intimately against her bottom. "Do you want to stop?"

She didn't. She wanted this with him. Just as it grounded him, it did the same for her. The connection between them was so intense when he tied her, she craved that closeness. She felt like she could see into his soul—and he into hers.

"Your breathing changed." His hand moved up her body to circle her throat. With her head slightly tipped back, her throat was exposed and his palm wrapped around it easily, so that it seemed as if her heart beat right into his hand. "When I'm with you, Mariko, my focus is wholly on you. Always you. I see everything you do. The way your body responds to me, to my art."

His fingers trailed down her chest to the upper curves of her breast. One finger continued, sliding over her right nipple. The lace was open and allowed him to touch bare skin. Her nipples were already peaked, tight little buds. The brush of his fingers sent fiery darts shimmering through her body straight to her sex. She wasn't certain she would survive.

"The feel of your skin is so warm and soft, better than silk. The lace, so fine and fragile, and the rough of the hemp in contrast. With your arms up over your head, your breasts are lifted in invitation. Such a beautiful temptation."

The words, murmured in such a low, compelling voice, sent goose bumps over her skin, flutters in her belly and had her sex clenching, spilling more welcoming drops of cream for him.

His hand moved under her breasts and settled on her hip for a moment before he stepped back, the rope in his hand. "This is a tortoiseshell body harness, but I see it on you a bit different than I might tie it normally. Your skin . . ." He trailed off and continued working, bringing a double line around under her breasts, laying the ropes along her rib cage to ensure they didn't interfere with her breathing. "The lace, so fragile, and the harsher texture of the rope will look beautiful with this tie." His arms went around her, the rope snaking around, and then his breath was once again against her ear. "Every time I look at you, you take my breath away."

His fingers moved down her back, following her spine to the base, where he laid his palm briefly. The contrast between his skin on hers and the rougher brush of the rope he held sent waves of heat crashing through her. She wasn't certain how much time passed after that as he built the tortoiseshell body suit. He worked fast and then slow. He touched her often. Her hair, running his lips down her exposed throat, his tongue touching the nipple peeking out through the lace, a brush of his hand over her buttocks.

She was acutely aware of him at all times. Her body waited for his touch, craving it. A string of knots went down her front from under her breasts and down her back as well in perfect symmetry, and she found herself squirming a little, wanting those knots in other places. He didn't give her that, but he worked close, his head down sometimes, brushing across her nipples until they felt on fire.

"Stop squirming," he murmured absently, and his teeth nipped at her buttocks. She couldn't stop the little cry of need from escaping as his hand slid down her leg, following another long knotted rope. He was on his knees now, in front of her, his breath adding to the heat building in her sheath until she thought she would fragment into a million pieces. The tension coiled tighter and tighter with no relief.

She tried to concentrate on the music, to take her mind off the need that had grown out of control. She'd never felt so sensual, writhing in the ropes at times, trying to rub her thighs together in an effort to alleviate the terrible ache that grew every moment. She found herself living second to second, waiting for his touch. Waiting for his breath. The brush of his hair. The rope was tight, wrapped around her like his arms.

Her mind began to chant, *please, please, please.* She couldn't think, she could barely breathe with needing him. The rope slithered down her left leg and he began tying with that decisive precision, his concentration seemingly on his work while all her concentration was centered on him.

Her skin felt raw with fiery nerves. The sensitive bundle of nerves inside her feminine sheath pulsed and burned. His tongue was suddenly on her inner thigh, licking at the wetness there. She cried out, writhing again, unable to be still when her body was no longer her own but entirely his. His hands gripped her thighs, fingers digging into the flesh beneath rope and lace, holding her still while he indulged himself. His tongue was wicked, sinful, sliding up her inner thigh, dancing along the crease of her lips, flicking at her clit hard, so that her entire body shuddered, and then it was gone, back to her other thigh.

"Ricco." She hissed his name. A demand. A plea.

He lifted his head to smile up at her. "You taste delicious."

She wanted to scream when he went back to his tying, leaving her on fire. There was no way to rub her thighs together, he was wedged between them as he worked. His hair brushed her inner thighs, the sensations keeping that tension inside of her winding tight until she thought she would go insane with desire. Then he was moving her, pushing her down to the floor, spreading her legs even farther apart.

He drew up her left leg and deftly wove rope from her shin to her upper thigh. He did the same with the right, forcing her knees up with her legs wide apart. He wound the rope around one of the bedposts and slipped it into the loop of the tie on her right and then did the same with the left. His eyes on hers, a small, very wicked smile on his face, he cinched the rope, and she gasped as it drew her left leg wider apart. He cinched the other rope and her right leg was pulled wider.

He stepped back to survey his work, his gaze burning on her wet, needy sex. All she could focus on was the bulge at the front of his trousers. She licked her lips. He stepped closer, right between her legs. Her head was tilted up, and if he had been naked she would be at a perfect angle to get what she wanted, and suddenly it was all that she wanted.

"What is it, *farfallina mia*?"

She hadn't realized she was making frantic little mews. "You." He just stood there, looking down at her, stretching her need out until she wanted to scream. "Your cock. In my mouth. *Right. Now.*" The last was a demand, nothing less, because if he didn't give her what she wanted, she was going to lose her mind.

He reached for the last two buttons of his jeans, undid them and began to slide the material off his hips. He seemed to move in slow motion. Every cell in her body focused on him. His hands. His skin. The slow revelation of his beautiful cock. Full. Hard. Long and thick. All hers. All for her. He stepped away from her and she cried out, straining in the ropes toward him.

He shimmied out of the jeans, turned and placed them over the back of a chair and reached for the camera.

"Ricco." Now it was a plea. Her body needed. Craved. Was obsessed with having him. She *had* to be touched. Her skin burned for his touch. Her sex wept with need and there was no way to hide it from him with her legs drawn apart. She supposed she should have been ashamed, humiliated,

that he could see her need of him, but instead, she wanted him to see his effect on her.

"You look so beautiful. Your throat." He trailed his hand down her throat. "Your breasts." The position of her arms had her breasts jutting out toward him, nipples, twin tight peaks, desperate for his attention. He massaged first one and then the other. In one motion, he suddenly shredded the delicate lace, leaving both breasts bare, framed by red lace and hemp.

He stepped back and took several pictures from several angles while she panted, her breath so ragged, her sheath on fire. Everything he did inflamed her body more.

He came closer again and leaned down, once again, his hand on her throat, feeling her heart beat into his hand while his wicked fingers and thumb tugged at her nipples. Then his mouth was there, hot and demanding. She was helpless, unable to move or touch him. She realized just why some women and men found the ropes so erotic. The sexual tension built beyond anything she could ever have conceived. His mouth on her breasts had her shuddering with desire. Her sex clenched and throbbed, burning in need.

He took several pictures of her. She couldn't see her breasts but she knew his marks were there. He knelt, his hand going low, sliding between her legs, finger moving the lace aside to brush over her clit, making her entire body ripple with pleasure. The pleasure was so intense it bordered on pain. His finger probed deep and her needy body clamped down instantly, trying to draw him deeper. Her muscles were tight and they held him inside her, where he could feel the fiery heat. His finger moved and she cried out, moving her hips, desperate for release.

He removed his finger, licked, then sucked, his eyes on hers. Another small cry escaped and he smiled and reached down, once again ripping lace. The action nearly sent her over the edge, her orgasm so close she reached for it with everything in her. He moved back, just out of her reach and she moaned with the loss.

"Beautiful," he murmured, and snapped several pictures.

"Ricco. Please." She couldn't manage anything else. She hadn't known a woman could be so aroused.

He set the camera carefully down and once again moved between her legs. His hand circled his cock, his thumb sliding over the head to smear the pearly drops all over. Her gaze was riveted there. Her tongue went out to moisten her lips. She couldn't move her head forward the scant inch to reach him. She could only watch as his fist did a slow slide up and down.

"Is this what you want?"

She tried to say yes, but it came out sounding like a sob. He smiled and stepped that inch closer, the head of his cock sliding over her lips. She opened her mouth but he just traced her lips, just enough that she had the hot masculine taste of him setting up the addiction. His hand slid into her hair, fisted there. When he pulled her head farther back, every rope on her body vibrated, sending shock waves through her.

She cried out as her body reacted, the nerves going wild. His cock slid into her mouth and she closed her lips around him, drawing him in, grateful she had something to concentrate on instead of the need raging through her like a firestorm. She'd read books, learned technique by practicing on a banana or cucumber. It had been a silly idea, but she was so glad she had. She used everything she'd learned, flicking her tongue. Dancing it. Fluttering it against the spot right beneath the crown that sent shudders through his body.

His hips began to move, a slow, gentle rhythm. She didn't understand how he could be so gentle when she felt wild and out of control. She suckled strongly while he did the work. She couldn't move her head so he set the speed. She should have been afraid, but when he slipped deeper, she welcomed him, trying for more.

She wanted to swallow him down. Take him deep into her. Surround him with the damp heat of her mouth the way the ropes surrounded her. Her eyes never left his face. She needed to see the desire there, the way his breath hitched. The shudders running through his body as she worked him.

She was powerless in the ropes and yet at her most powerful. This man trembled before her.

"Farfallina mia." He began to withdraw slowly.

She clamped her lips tighter with a small cry of dissent. She could feel him swelling even more, growing thicker and hotter. Drops of his essence leaked into her mouth and she eagerly swallowed them down, taking his length deeper still.

"I'm not going to be able to stop and you'll have to swallow," he warned.

She suckled harder. Her tongue teased and danced, fluttered up and down his shaft as she worked him. His hips thrust deeper. The fist in her hair tightened on her scalp, setting the ropes in motion so they flicked her skin with tiny bites and flares of heat. She kept her eyes on his. The lust there. The love. The need in him matching the hunger in her.

Then he was erupting. Swearing. His head thrown back. His throat as vulnerable as hers. She could barely keep up with the rocketing stream jetting down her throat. It was perfection. But her sex clenched and wept and needed until she wanted to cry. Even taking him into her body, swallowing him down, bringing him practically to his knees, didn't ease the burning. If anything, it only made it worse.

He withdrew slowly from her mouth and she licked her lips, her gaze clinging to his, silently begging for more. For anything. For his touch. His kiss. His everything. He bent his head and brushed his lips across hers, his hand going to the back of her head, to the ropes. One handed, he released her hair so she could straighten her head. The action sent more vibrations singing against her sensitive skin.

She cried out and he caught at the rope around the post, releasing first one and then the other. He caught her up, her legs still spread wide, still in the crab position, her knees up and tied to her shins. That left her sex completely exposed and open to him. He set her on the bed, one hand went to her belly and he pushed her back. Her hands were under her shoulders, but she didn't care. All that mattered was his mouth on her.

He didn't wait. There was no pause. No warning. His tongue stabbed into her, fingers spreading her wide, and then he was devouring her. She fell over the edge, screaming, her body throwing her mind into chaos, into somewhere she'd never been. He didn't stop as her orgasm rushed over her like a freight train. His tongue was wild, licking, slashing, fluttering against her clit, following his fingers as he plunged two into her, pushing through tight folds to find her most sensitive spot. She exploded again, fragmenting, thrown deeper into a world of pure feeling, so deep she feared she might never return.

She was helpless under his onslaught, that wicked tongue and sinful fingers extracting more and more cream. The moment one orgasm stopped, the next began to build. Each one seemed stronger than the last. Then he was once again over top of her, his cock slamming deep without preamble. She was hot and slick and screaming as he drove into her because nothing had ever felt that good.

He took her hard and fast, driving into her, leveraging with his arms on the bed while his hips surged into her over and over. Streaks of fire raced through her body from toes to breasts and radiated to her arms and legs. Every hard thrust sent her body skittering on the mattress, pushing her deeper so that the ropes vibrated and sang, flicking at her skin, taking tiny, heated bites, so it felt like Ricco was touching, kissing and nipping at her everywhere.

The need coiled tighter and tighter. Built higher and higher. Her head thrashed from side to side. He had to stop— he could *never* stop. It was terrifying. Beautiful. Brutal. Perfect. His cock swelled, pushing at the tender tissue, triggering the gathering explosion. She came apart. Completely and utterly apart. So many pieces. So good. So bad. So everything. She heard her keening wail, the only sound that could possibly emerge when she'd fractured into a million pieces and all were floating somewhere in subspace.

She felt the hot jet of his release filling her, triggering another orgasm so her body rippled and the ropes vibrated and sang while he lay over her, fighting for air. He brushed kisses into her belly button and over the underside of her breasts. He lifted his head to look at her, his eyes still dark with the intensity of their wild joining. "I should have been a little more gentle."

Mariko's head was still spinning. Euphoria was difficult to come down from. "I didn't want gentle. I wanted perfection and I got it."

He kissed her and then stood up, looking very male and very satisfied. Instead of beginning to untie her, he caught up the camera again. She touched her tongue to her lip. "What are you doing?"

"If I can get my hands to stop shaking, I'm going to take a picture of you. *Dio*, you're beautiful. I'm getting hard just looking at you." He snapped several more pictures from various angles and then put the camera aside.

She didn't have to ask—he was already releasing ropes and he was fast at it. The moment he had her untied, he began massaging her arms to ensure her circulation was in no way impaired. He shredded the red lace, tossing it aside so he could massage the rope marks on her skin. "You'll wear these for a few days," he said.

"I hope they last a long time." She was truthful.

She couldn't keep her hands off him. She wanted to touch him everywhere and she did, stroking, caressing, kissing, biting, licking at him. Her fingernails moved over his back and down to his buttocks.

"What are you doing?" he asked.

"We have until two o'clock and I'm making every single second count."

"I'm human, Mariko. Coming twice is . . ."

She pushed him to his back. "Then I get to play."

He laughed softly as she kissed his throat and down his chest to his nipples where her tongue flicked at him. "Play all you want." His hands covered her bare buttocks, fingers digging deep in a massage.

She kissed her way down to his cock, already semihard. Yeah. She was going to get her way.

CHAPTER NINETEEN

Ricco detested that his woman had insisted she go along. He was proud of Mariko for her decision and knew she would never do less, but he was determined to find out where the kidnappers were holding Ryuu. His methods might not meet with her approval.

She was exhausted as well. Coming out of the ropes was usually a slow process, but they'd had wild sex several times. More than he'd ever thought possible, before both had fallen asleep. She had been draped over his body when he woke, her breasts against his ribs, her arm around his waist. He'd fallen asleep on his back and stayed that way, something very unusual for him, but he loved his woman lying over top of him. He'd slept soundly, again something very unusual.

Nao's condo was on the top floor. There were security cameras everywhere. Shadow riders were required to hear lies, disrupt electricity and be able to be pulled apart and put back together. Most could compel the truth as well. That was a specialty of Ricco's and he'd damn well get the truth out of Nao.

Stefano held up his hand at the entrance to the tube and indicated a camera pointed right at them. It wouldn't be able to capture their images, hidden inside the tube as they were, but the moment they stepped out, it would record them. He raised his hand, a gesture that wasn't strictly necessary, but one all of them made. It was a human gesture. The disruption really began in their brains and had nothing to do with hands. Stefano concentrated, and the dim lights flickered. The camera smoked and then abruptly went dead. He looked cautiously around, seeking any other devices that might be a problem before he stepped out into the hallway and beckoned to Ricco, Taviano and Mariko.

Taviano moved ahead of Stefano. He was extremely powerful at disrupting electrical equipment. He would ensure no cameras worked as they made their way through the condo to Nao's private quarters. The walls were decorated with expensive paintings, most depicting ancient tortures of men in various stages of undress with ropes done in intricate knots. Ricco recognized the ancient art of *hojojutsu*. He paused to look at the prints. Nao liked ancient weapons and ancient tortures.

A few very ancient prints and extremely rare books were kept under glass. Above them along the wall were weapons of every kind throughout the history of Japan. The collection was museum-worthy. Hundreds of weapons from every era. Ricco would have loved to have the time to study all of them, because there were three he was absolutely certain were ones he'd bid on and lost to an anonymous bidder. The first had been ten years earlier. The second, seven, and the last, five years ago. If he was correct about the items, then Nao had been keeping tabs on him for a long, long time.

He kept walking, following Stefano, but that strange nagging feeling in his gut only intensified. He noticed four empty spaces, as if the wall had been prepared for four more weapons, but Nao hadn't found them yet.

As they passed the door to the caretaker's room, Ricco hesitated. His gut was still talking to him, telling him something wasn't quite right. He stopped and motioned to the others that he wanted to check the room. He waited for Stefano's acknowledgment and then stepped into the larger shadow that slipped beneath the door.

The suite of rooms was spacious and very clean. The caretaker was a neat freak. Every single thing was put precisely in place, from the books on the shelves in alphabetical order to the coffee mugs with their handles turned the exact same way. Glasses were lined up in cupboards, plates slipped into slots so that they stuck out precisely a quarter of an inch. Everywhere he looked, the rooms were perfect.

He slipped into the bedroom. The bed wasn't made, the blankets flipped back, but no one was in it. One pillow was military straight, the other cocked at an angle. He glanced toward the bathroom. There was no light spilling out from under the door indicating the caretaker was in that room.

Ricco looked around, checking the kitchen area, what passed for a living room and the bedroom before he decided to look in the bathroom. There was no sound coming from the dark room. He turned the doorknob cautiously. It wasn't locked. He took his time opening it, slowly, inch by inch. Waited for sound, for anything indicating the room was occupied. If anyone was in there, they were holding their breath, and doing it for a very long time.

He moved into the room with confidence, treading silently as he examined the main area where there was a wide sink and a large Jacuzzi tub. The toilet was in a separate section, wide, with a large towering cupboard behind it, rising all the way to the ceiling.

Puzzled, he looked around. Even if the caretaker had been given time off, research the investigators had discovered indicated that another caretaker always took his place. The man's name was Darin Salsberry and he'd worked for Nao five years, much longer than most of his caretakers had lasted. The substitutes came and went, most fired after two or three days with Nao. He apparently liked the way Darin took care of him, or Darin was just able to put up with the constant abuse Nao heaped on the heads of those working for him.

It didn't surprise Ricco in the least that Nao was a bully. He had been a bully when he was seventeen. His father had not only lied for him, but he'd shielded him from the consequences after murdering a family, crippling a child and causing the deaths of three other boys. More, Yamamoto had placed his son in a position of authority from early on in their overseas companies, removing him from possible retaliation from the Saito and Ito families.

The investigators said male prostitutes regularly visited the condo. Often, several returned, no doubt because Nao had millions to burn. He definitely had enough money to fund an elaborate attack on the Ferraro family. He could afford mercenaries, and most of the mercenaries, Eloisa and Henry had discovered, came from South Africa, and they weren't cheap.

So where was Darin? He wasn't in his condo. Had Nao called him? Was he with his client? That was the only explanation, yet for some reason, Ricco felt uneasy. He made his way twice around the apartment, but couldn't find what was setting off the reaction in his gut. He stood in the middle of the bedroom, breathing deeply, listening, certain something was wrong but he couldn't quite put his finger on what it was. There were several closets, and he ignored those.

Curious, he opened the two remaining doors, one built into the bedroom and one the main living quarters. Both opened to narrow corridors. When he opened the door, LED lights lit up along the ceiling, illuminating the hallway. Ricco followed each hallway. One led to the kitchen, the other to Nao's master bedroom. When Nao had guests, clearly he didn't want Darin to be seen.

Finally, knowing he was taking up far too much time, Ricco slipped into another shadow that allowed him to reach the others faster than he could have walking. Taviano had cleared the cameras so they could move quickly to the master bedroom.

Nao's bedroom was enormous. The bed was king-sized with a mirror on the ceiling. One wall held a long floor-to-ceiling mirror. The walk-in closet was designed for someone in a wheelchair, the clothes set lower to be easily accessible. Both doors were wide open, revealing the huge room, one that was nearly as big as some apartments. Nao obviously liked clothes and shoes. Every kind of shoe and boot was lined up in neat rows. Hundreds of pairs.

The door to the passageway Darin used was in the corner to the front of the room and left of the main entryway. Two panels on either side of the bed, from floor to ceiling, were lights that would instantly illuminate the room if Nao turned them on. It also made the man feel safe.

Stefano and Ricco exchanged a long look. Nao was vain. The wheelchair hadn't affected his narcissistic personality in the least. From all reports, he was a master manipulator and closed deals faster than his father—who had been renowned for being a closer—had ever done. It was rumored—but not proven—that threats were often used and companies caved immediately after speaking with Nao. Ricco, having witnessed the extent of his sociopathic behavior, believed all the rumors about the man.

The shadow took him to the left side of the bed. Stefano went right. Taviano searched the other rooms thoroughly and shook his head to indicate Darin wasn't anywhere to be found. More, with Nao soundly sleeping, there was no evidence that the caretaker had been there in the last few hours. He slipped back into the shadows in order to protect them. Ricco waved to Mariko to position herself at the head of the bed, so the first thing Nao would see when he opened his eyes was her. The men looked at her and she nodded.

"Nao," she called softly. "Akiko wanted me to give you her regards."

Nao shifted uneasily in his sleep, a frown chasing across his face.

"Did you think she wouldn't keep an eye on you? She doesn't like that you would attempt to harm the rest of her family."

Nao scowled and batted at the air. "Go away." His hand fluttered in midair and then dropped to his chest. "Stop coming here."

There was some satisfaction in knowing that Akiko was still on Nao's mind. Ricco pressed his knee into the mattress to help wake him. The movement caused the man to thump his fist into the pillow and scrunch his eyes closed tighter.

"Go away, Akiko. You're dead."

"Yes," Mariko said. "I'm dead. You killed me. That means I can come visit you anytime I want to. You've been sending men after my sister to kill her. I don't like that. Wake up and look at me." She put command into her voice.

Nao's eyelids fluttered and then he forced himself to peek at her. His sudden inhale was audible and his eyes widened with shock. He reached behind him for the crosspiece running along the four posts, gripped with both fists and pulled himself into a sitting position, the entire time staring at her. He fumbled for a moment and then hit a button. The large panels on either side of the headboard lit up, throwing a dim light across the room.

"Who are you?"

"Mariko. Akiko's sister. Where is my brother, Ryuu?"

Ricco was proud of the low demand in her voice. She didn't overplay it or act theatrical, she just stated the truth softly.

"How the fuck should I know where your twisted wreck of a brother is? That double-crossing bastard stole my companies' research right out from under me. Hacked into our computers and then got his company the patents without doing any of the work. Osamu put him up to it. Feeding him lies about me, blaming me for Eiji's and Hachiro's deaths. She never wanted to believe they threatened my family if I didn't go with them."

"Where is he?" Mariko persisted.

"Get out of my bedroom before I call the cops." As Nao gave the order, he reached for the phone beside his bed. Ricco's hand was there first, so Nao's fingers tried gripping his. Nao's head swung around and he gasped in alarm. "Ricco Ferraro."

"Not dead, Nao. Wet work didn't suit your team of assassins."

"I heard your father died."

Ricco nodded. "He did. No one else."

"That's too bad."

Nao grinned, looking both sly and evil. Ricco didn't like

that his attention kept straying to Mariko. He wanted Nao's entire focus on him at all times. There was just something nagging at him, something he couldn't put his finger on, but he was worried. He didn't want Mariko anywhere near Nao or danger, and he sensed they were all in danger.

"Where's Ryuu?" He kept his voice low but commanding.

"I told you, I have no idea." Nao gripped the bar behind him tightly and dragged himself into a very upright sitting position. He glanced at the bell on his nightstand, the one that presumably called his caretaker, but made no move toward it. Instead, he clasped his arms behind his head and leaned back, his eyes on Mariko.

"Osamu told me you'd fuck Ricco. You really are a little slut just like your mother. Osamu and the other women did their best to tell your father, but he wouldn't listen. He was weak. We didn't need weak riders. We can't tolerate weak riders. It was our job to weed them out."

"Whose job?" Stefano spoke for the first time, and Nao's head swiveled to face the new threat.

Ricco watched him closely. Nao had that same superior look he remembered so vividly in his nightmares from his teenage years.

Nao leaned toward Stefano. "All of us. All riders. We can't allow the gene pool to grow weak. It should be pure."

"Pure?" Stefano echoed, one eyebrow shooting up. "Pure what?"

"Not tainted by weak men or women."

"Akiko defeated you," Ricco reminded. "I was there. I saw what she did. You couldn't take that a woman was stronger than you."

"She wasn't stronger." Nao spat the words at him, glaring now, his famous temper rising. "She was slutty, just like her mother. I heard the talk about Tanaka. What a worm he was. Throwing away greatness. His name. His honor. All for what?" He sneered the last as he looked at Mariko. "A whore."

"She wasn't a whore," Ricco said softly, his voice so low Nao swung his head back toward that thread of a sound. "We investigated her, just as your father's family would have done before he married her." He didn't look at Mariko, he couldn't. He knew he was revealing far too much. She would know his family had investigated her. "Marie Hammond was a good woman, not a whore. Osamu and the other women were jealous that Daiki Tanaka married her instead of one of them, and they were vicious, turning everyone against her. The lies Osamu told Chiharu caused her to turn on Marie."

"The International Council investigated *your* family," Stefano said, drawing Nao's attention to him. "Their findings were interesting. Four of your family members were quietly killed by other family members. Do you know why? They went mad. The Archambaults destroyed two others. Osamu has been hospitalized twice in a psych ward and your father once."

"For depression!" Nao screamed, his face turning bright red with anger. Both fists clenched. "For *depression*. My father lost everything thanks to that twisted troll and her . . ." He spat toward Mariko.

"Actually, Nao," Ricco said calmly, "your father was out of his mind. He tried to kill several nurses after he'd physically assaulted them."

"You liar. You're a fucking liar. You fuck a whore, you don't let them lead you around by your dick. She's *infected* you with her weakness. With depravity." Nao leaned forward, his hands sliding along his mattress as he did so. Instantly the lights on either side of him went out, plunging the room into darkness.

Instincts kicking in, Ricco dove for Mariko. He was too far away to get to her fast enough. Stefano made the same dive from the other side of the bed. It was Taviano who took her to the floor, landing on top of her, his body covering hers. Ricco and Stefano hit the floor on either side of her, wrapping arms around their brother so no part of Mariko's body was exposed.

A faint hum shimmered in the air for one moment. A *thunk*. Ricco turned his head away from the bed, peering into the darkness behind them. The door to Darin's passageway was open and a shadowy figure, holding a crossbow, suddenly turned to run. As the intruder turned, three figures emerged from the shadows, and Ricco recognized three of the Archambault riders.

"Cover me," he hissed in Stefano's ear. He patted Taviano on the back and rolled toward the partially open door.

Stefano and Taviano stood, both between the French riders and the door to the passageway. Taviano gallantly helped Mariko to her feet.

All three stared at Nao. An arrow protruded from his chest. His mouth was open grotesquely, as if he'd seen death coming and had tried to stop it with a shout.

"Maxence," Stefano greeted, looking to the oldest brother. "What are you doing here?" He knew it looked bad, but they were all empty-handed. Still, the French riders would know Ricco had been there as well.

"The investigations are complete. We were here to bring justice to Nao Yamamoto. Where is Ryuu?"

There was something in Maxence's voice that had Mariko turning pale and Stefano feeling like an old man, tired of always being right. "We don't know," he said. "Why?"

"Osamu Saito trained Ryuu as a shadow rider and used him as an instrument of revenge against the Yamamoto family. He began taking their companies apart by hacking in and stealing research and selling it to the highest bidder. He proved to be extremely good at industrial espionage. He also managed to transfer most of Nao's personal fortune into an account he'd set up for himself offshore."

Mariko stepped back, away from Taviano and Stefano, shaking her head. Taviano made a move to slip his arm around her, but she stiffened and stepped back farther. "That's impossible," she whispered. "My brother's bones were broken and twisted. He couldn't ride the shadows, as much as he wanted to."

"You're certain Osamu trained him?" Stefano asked, already knowing the answer. The International Council would never have sent the French riders if they weren't 100 percent convinced that they had all the facts.

Maxence nodded. "I'm afraid so, Stefano. Ryuu and Osamu are behind the attack on your family. They used the money Ryuu stole from the Yamamotos to fund the mercenaries. We traced the money back to the account Ryuu set up. They also targeted the Yamamotos. Sango Yamamoto was pushed onto the tracks. Witnesses said another woman was with her. We believe that woman, from the description, was Osamu."

Stefano shook his head. "Osamu had to have been totally insane."

Maxence agreed. "She had been courted by Daiki Tanaka when they were young, but at the last minute he backed out. There is a small trail that leads us to believe she began plotting revenge on him. Certainly she was known to say things against Daiki to her friends and her sons. We believe she tracked Marie down and killed her. She was in the same small town at the same time as Marie's death, and that's just too big of a coincidence for us to swallow."

Taviano moved closer to Mariko. She was pale, her eyes looking like two bruised flowers pressed into her head. At his movement, Stefano glanced back at Taviano. Somewhere, in the house, Ricco was hunting right at that moment. Ricco and Stefano had been worried that Ryuu was involved somehow. To what extent they didn't know, but nothing about the kidnapping made sense.

Stefano wanted Taviano to get his hands on Mariko. She was a very intelligent woman and she was going to realize that along with the Ferraro family, her brother and Osamu had targeted her. The moment Ricco realized who was in the passageway, his expression had turned murderous. He would want to protect Mariko before anything else, not realizing that if he killed her brother, she might not ever forgive him.

"We do our own investigations and our findings differed from the police's when it came to Isamu's suicide. We kept those findings secret, but we knew he wasn't alone when he killed himself. More than likely Ryuu put a gun to Osamu's head and forced Isamu to kill himself to save his sister. He just hadn't realized that his sister was bent on revenge."

"Do you think Dai knew his wife was behind those deaths?" The last thing Stefano wanted was for one of the French riders to come across Ricco killing Ryuu. He tried to stall them.

Maxence shrugged. "Everyone knew he loved her, and yet he killed her. He wouldn't have killed her unless he knew there was no other way out. He had to know the moment the International Council launched an investigation into the deaths of the Tanaka family that we would uncover Osamu's conspiracy to take down all the families involved."

Stefano sighed. "If Dai knew all along and did nothing, he was as guilty as she was."

Maxence nodded. "Agreed. We found evidence that the Ito family was next in line for the pair to take down. All along Ryuu had been pretending to help Nao. Nao was obsessed with Ricco. From the evidence we gathered, he admired Ricco. He began pitting himself against Ricco by trying to outbid him for various items they both collected. Ricco's collection came first, but Nao was determined to rival it. During that time, he trusted Ryuu and gave him access to his computers without realizing it. That enabled Ryuu to begin his destruction of the Yamamoto empire."

Stefano's investigators had known someone was stealing from Nao Yamamoto and that his personal assets as well as companies were slowly being drained in a variety of ways. "Ryuu changed the compound for the making of casings for the race cars, didn't he? That was Yamamoto's company."

Maxence nodded again. "We believe he made certain that your brother's car received the bad casing. He's been watching your brother for a long time."

"Ricco worried for years that someone was entering his house. He made certain no one, not even a rider, could."

Maxence's eyebrow shot up, but he didn't comment on that bit of information. "Ryuu killed Darin Salsberry. His body is in one of the hall closets. We're certain that Ryuu is somewhere in this house. He could use the passageway without fear that Darin would stumble onto him. My brothers are hunting him as we speak."

A small sound of distress escaped before Mariko could stop it. Not her brother. He wouldn't do this. He would never conspire to kill an entire family, just wipe them out because Osamu told him to. Would he? She pressed trembling fingers to her lips and took another small, gliding step back away from the men and toward the passage where Ricco had followed Nao's killer.

She could not believe that Ryuu would do this, but a part of her was already recognizing the red flags she'd chosen not to see. The many times Ryuu had laughed when Osamu had shamed her. He'd come to her room later and tell her he was sorry, it was just that Osamu looked so funny with the broom, bashing at her as if she could sweep her under a rug. Although his laughter had hurt at the time, she'd allowed him to coax her into smiles after.

There were so many incidents growing up that she'd overlooked because she'd needed to believe Ryuu loved her. Someone had to love her. Now he was somewhere in the house with Ricco after him. Ricco. Her heart stuttered. Ryuu could kill him. Ricco had a gentle heart. He might hesitate because Ryuu was her brother. How would she feel if he killed Ryuu? She didn't know. Her normally calm mind became utter chaos.

She turned and dashed for the passageway. She didn't care if the French riders were angry at what she was doing. She had to find her brother. She needed answers. She needed to know that he hadn't done these things and Osamu hadn't turned him completely against her. Fighting back emotions that threatened to overwhelm her, she raced down the passage, looking for shadows that would tell her which way they went.

Ricco sprinted down the narrow passage after the shadowy figure he knew was Ryuu. He had begun, almost from the very beginning, to worry that Mariko's brother was involved. When she had lost the trail and then the investigators had said there was no trail, he had looked at the surveillance footage of the hotel cameras himself. He and Stefano. Neither had said one word of their suspicions to Mariko. Ricco had wanted to be wrong. He'd even sent up a prayer or two, and he wasn't a praying man.

There was plenty of footage of Ryuu walking to his hotel room, but none of him coming out of it. Stefano and Ricco had watched every inch of the recordings, identifying the guests and following up to make certain each person entering the hotel had legitimate business there. No one had come to kidnap Ryuu, and seemingly, he'd never left his room. That left only two ways possible. Someone could have tampered with the cameras, but there was no evidence of that. Or, Ryuu was a shadow rider and he had left that room on his own. If that were the truth, then he had to be a big part of the conspiracy against the Ferraro family.

It explained a lot of other things as well. Nao's collection mimicking Ricco's so closely. Ryuu could have been entering Ricco's home and photographing the weapons for Nao. Ricco had always suspected someone was coming into his house. As a shadow rider, Ryuu would know about the Ferraros using shadows to travel and he could have warned the mercenaries to attack the shadows.

Ricco opened the door leading to the caretaker's rooms cautiously, mindful of the attack on Vittorio outside the Fausti home. He somersaulted into the room, scanning as he rolled across toward the door. It appeared empty but the lights were on, throwing shadows across the room. He kept rolling until he was just at the mouth of one of them, the largest that led under the door to the next room, and then he leapt up and into it.

Ryuu tried to take his head off with a vicious kick right to the exact place he'd taken such a beating in the accident on the track. Expecting the attack, he dropped low and swept Ryuu's leg out from under him. Ryuu went down, but as he did, he dove forward, deeper into the shadow, letting it swallow him.

Ricco raced after him. The shadow tore him apart, reminding him he wasn't 100 percent physically. He consoled himself with the knowledge that Ryuu's body wasn't perfect, either, and the brutal pull of the shadow on him had to be just as painful. There was some satisfaction in that.

As he neared the end of the tube, he slowed, hating to lose precious seconds, but he couldn't take chances. Ryuu was nowhere in sight, but again, shadows raced up the walls and under the doors. Ricco stepped into the nearest one and followed it under the door of the caretaker's suite, to the outside, private entrance provided for Darin.

Ryuu was waiting, standing draped against the ornate column just outside the door. Ricco couldn't see any resemblance to Mariko. Ryuu was almost the spitting image of his father, Daiki Tanaka. He grinned at Ricco.

"Ferraro."

"Tanaka."

"So you know."

Ricco nodded. He took the time to allow his body to catch up with itself. His heart needed to find a calm, steady rhythm while he assessed his opponent. Ryuu couldn't stand straight. His back appeared to be twisted just enough to throw one shoulder higher and his frame on the right side forward. Still, he was a handsome man by most standards.

"I see Nao stomping you into the ground when you were a baby didn't stop you from learning to use the shadows," Ricco said. Ryuu was an intelligent man. He would need to show Ricco how smart he'd been. The more they talked, the better the chances that Ricco could find every weakness.

"Nao had nothing to do with my bones. That was my dear sister—the woman who claims she's my sister. She was playing in a car and took it out of gear. It rolled over me."

Ricco shook his head. "I suppose Osamu told you that lie. She was very good at manipulation. Mariko told me you were intelligent, but that can't be true if you didn't recognize Osamu's madness and hear the lies in her voice."

"Riders can hear lies," Ryuu informed him. "I'm a rider and I never once heard a lie in my mother's voice."

"Your mother was Marie Tanaka."

"My mother was Osamu Saito," Ryuu explained patiently. "Daiki Tanaka was my father. Look at me if you don't believe me."

"I am looking at you, and I see a fool."

Ryuu smirked. "I spent so much time in your house I know the entire layout by heart. I photographed it foot by foot for Nao. He was obsessed with you. Totally obsessed. He thought you were a god. The perfect rider." He snorted his derision. "I was right under his nose and he didn't even know it. All those years, sucking his company dry and he never suspected until I let him know it was me." He laughed softly. "Nao, sitting on this throne, believing he was better than me because he had the pure blood of a rider."

"It must have been difficult listening to his bragging. I knew him when he was seventeen. He was a braggart and bully then, too."

Ryuu shrugged. He moved position just slightly, easing his weight from his right leg. "I found him tedious. I was stealing him blind, right under his nose, and all he could do was wonder what you were doing, what you were up to, how many women you'd screwed, what paintings you were acquiring."

"Why?" He didn't take his eyes off Ryuu, breathing evenly, his body relaxed now and waiting. Coiling to strike. To defend. Every defense was an offense.

"He wanted to be you." Ryuu smirked again. "I used to talk about you with him, show him all the magazines. He went to every race you were driving in. I switched out the casing for your car and made certain he was at the race to watch you go right into the wall. I had a difficult time deciding who to watch—you crashing or him watching you crash. I chose him. The expression on his face was well worth it."

"Why would you hate him so much if you don't believe he was the one who twisted your bones? He's Osamu's nephew."

"He took Eiji and Hachiro from us—my true brothers. Both were great riders and he was jealous of them. He tried to dishonor them. He was driving the car that killed them and he'd been drinking."

Ricco shook his head. "Eiji, Hachiro, Kenta Ito and Nao murdered the Tanaka family. Nao pulled you out of a closet and stomped on you. Mariko saved you by kicking him in the groin. She was just a baby, too."

"That's bullshit. Everyone knows the story, apart from Nao's guilt. His father refused to allow anyone to tell the truth of it. My brothers were lost to us and the entire rider community. No one did anything about it."

"Ryuu, does that really make sense to you? She raised you on hatred and revenge. Every moment of your existence, she forged a weapon against those she perceived as her enemies."

"They were her enemies. They were enemies to the entire riding community."

"Mariko was an innocent child, just as you were. Why would Osamu target her? Why would she have you turn on your own sister?"

"She's *not* my sister," Ryuu spat the venomous statement out, his face twisted with hatred.

Behind Ricco, Mariko gasped. He silently swore. He didn't want her to hear any of this, to see the evidence of just how far gone her brother was. He'd been raised by a madwoman and he believed every word she'd said.

"She's a Tanaka. Even if Marie wasn't your mother, Ryuu, by your own admission, Daiki is your father. That makes Mariko your half sister."

"A *whore*? Osamu said she would sleep with you, and she has." Ryuu raised his gaze to his sister's face. "Haven't you?"

It was the small distraction Ricco waited for. He slid across the entryway, slamming the ball of his foot into Ryuu's right thigh, his full body weight behind the kick. Ryuu went down hard and Ricco was on him. He couldn't just kill Ryuu, not with Mariko watching, and that gave Ryuu a huge advantage. He hit him hard in the pit of his stomach and Ryuu jackknifed his body, drawing up his knees and slamming his feet into Ricco's chest, knocking him back.

Ryuu leapt to his feet, limping now but coming at Ricco, pressing him hard. Ricco feigned falling back a step or two and then went to the right, kicking the leg again, this time a solid round kick, targeting the exact same spot. Ryuu's face paled a little, but he kept moving, switching to a left-handed stance to better protect his leg.

"Stop. Ryuu, stop," Mariko pleaded. "You don't know what you're doing."

"Shut the fuck up," Ryuu snapped, never taking his eyes from Ricco. "You don't talk to me. You're dead to me. You always have been. You're nothing but a little whore like your mother."

"Ryuu, you don't mean that."

Ricco winced at the pleading in her voice. He hated this for her. He knew there was no taking back all those years of Osamu whispering to Ryuu, turning him into her instrument of revenge. He had wanted to be loved, and Osamu loved him as long as he did exactly what she said.

"I *despise* you." Ryuu spat on the floor. "She took you in and even allowed you to become a rider, but you were never grateful. You were just like your mother, always flirting with Dai until she had to send him away. When he pleaded to come home, she relented, but there you were, trying to lure him to your bed."

"I didn't," Mariko denied.

Ricco heard the tears now. His woman was crying. Her heart breaking. He feinted a punch, forcing Ryuu to turn his body just enough. He landed another solid kick.

Ryuu's gaze went desperately around the entryway, seeking a shadow. His right leg had to be numb, a dead leg. Ricco had many of those during early training years before he'd learned to protect his legs. Ryuu had been taught to ride the shadows and he definitely had trained in hand-to-hand combat, martial arts and street fighting, but he didn't have the years of training and experience that Ricco did.

Ricco circled him, keeping him away from the shadows, forcing him to drag his right leg around to keep Ricco in sight at all times.

"She lied to you," Mariko said. "She lied, Ryuu, about everything."

"I told you not to talk to me," Ryuu said, his voice low and vicious. He kept his attention seemingly centered on Ricco, moving awkwardly forward with a series of punches. At the last moment, he flung himself to the side, right at Mariko.

There was a large shadow directly behind her. Mariko stood her ground, and Ryuu slammed into her hard. He punched her twice in the mouth.

"Keep your filthy mouth shut," he spat at her as he rolled, coming up on his feet triumphantly right at the front of the tube.

She staggered back under the assault, but didn't lose her footing. She reached out a hand to her brother. "Ryuu." Just his name whispered.

He looked back at her.

Mariko cried out. *"Don't."*

The last was said to Sacha Archambault. He emerged from the shadow directly behind Ryuu and caught his head in both hands.

"Justice is served," Sacha said as he wrenched hard.

There was an audible crack. Mariko screamed and went to her knees. Sacha dropped the body and looked at Ricco.

"I'm sorry she was here," he said softly.

Ricco nodded and went to her, wrapping his arms around her, forcing her to her feet. They had to get out of there and leave the cleanup to the people in charge. They were riders. They dispensed justice.

"It's over, *farfallina mia*. Let's go home." What else was there to say? Now he had to find a way to keep her with him.

CHAPTER TWENTY

"It's been a month," Mariko said softly. She'd filled her days with making Ricco's house her home. He'd told her to change anything she wanted and she took him at his word. The International Council had decreed that the families pay restitution to her and Ricco. Hers was an enormous sum, one she could barely deal with. She'd turned the headache of all that money to Ricco's financial people.

She made her way through the house to the Japanese garden. It had become her favorite place since her brother's death. There was no reason to go back to Japan, although she would always love her country. She couldn't bear going there when there was no one to go to. She crossed the bridge over the koi pond, pausing to watch the fish swimming lazily. She found peace in watching them, naming them, studying the variety of koi and trying to identify them.

Ricco had been more than good to her—always patient—never asking anything of her. They shared the same bed and he hadn't touched her until she'd turned to him. He was gentle with her, loving, never going wild, and she often sensed the restraint in him but hadn't had the energy to tell him she wanted his wild. Or his Shibari. She'd heard him several times in the workout room, hitting the heavy bag, and she hadn't gone to him. She should have.

"Mariko?"

Emmanuelle's voice made her smile. She looked up and both Emmanuelle and Francesca were walking toward her.

She stopped at the entrance to the elaborate tea house that Ricco had built in his garden. It was traditional style and very beautiful. She loved it and spent quite a bit of time there meditating. Emmanuelle and Francesca came every day to see her and knew to find her in the tea house.

She flashed a genuine smile, the first she'd felt in a month. "I'm glad you've come," she greeted. "I'll make us tea. There are things that need to be said."

Emmanuelle and Francesca exchanged a worried frown. "Things that need to be said?" Francesca echoed. "Do you need us to get Ricco? Are you all right?"

"Finally. I'm finally all right." Mariko stepped into the tea house and looked around it. There was peace and serenity in this building. "Ricco told me he'd built this place of meditation hoping someday to find a woman who would enjoy it with him. I know I'm that woman. I was born to be that woman." She said it with absolute confidence.

Francesca and Emmanuelle looked relieved. They followed her into the building and sank down onto the comfortable low chairs across from her. The sound of the waterfall traveling downhill over the rocks to fall into the pool soothed her. She looked at their faces. She had come to love them in the last month. They'd been as patient as Ricco with her. Neither pushed, but they let her know they were there.

"I have to let Ryuu go. The brother I loved so much died that day when I lost the rest of my family. He never had the chance to have a normal life. I was clinging to the man I wanted him to be, the one I made up in my head in order to survive. That man wasn't my brother." She looked down at her hands. "I've grieved long enough for someone who didn't exist."

She looked up at the two women who had been her constant support. "I have a family now, and I'm not going to risk losing it to cling to someone who never actually existed. I'm sorry it's taken me so long to come to that realization."

"You have the right to take all the time you need,"

Emmanuelle assured. "We are your family and we'll always be here for you."

The dark shadow in Mariko, the one that had been weighing her down for so many weeks, lifted even further. "I've never been a part of a family that I can remember, so I'm going to make mistakes. I hope you both will find it in you to be tolerant."

Francesca laughed softly. "We're Ferraros. We *have* to be tolerant of one another. You might want to remember that today."

"*Today?* What's different about today?"

Francesca and Emmanuelle exchanged another look and then both turned their full attention on her, eyes sparkling with mischief, reminding her of Ricco when he was up to something—which was often.

"Oh dear. What are you up to now? If you make me a part of it, how upset is Ricco going to be?"

"Ricco isn't as patient as he might be, not when it comes to you," Francesca said.

Mariko shook her head. "No, he's been amazing. Far better than I deserve. I lost sight of what I had right in front of me. I'm lucky he is so patient. Another man might have walked away."

"If he walked away, Mariko," Emmanuelle said, "he didn't really love you in the first place and you'd be better off without him."

There was something in her voice that had both women looking sharply at her. She flashed them a smile that didn't quite reach her eyes. She shook her head and forced a smile. "We've come to help you get ready."

"Ready for what? There's nothing on the calendar. Did I miss an important event?" Her stomach tightened. They really were up to something, and her gut told her it was big.

"Just the fact that you're getting married today."

Mariko's breath stilled in her lungs. Ricco had been watching her closely, but he hadn't brought up marriage other than to have her fill out the necessary papers to apply for residency since she wasn't from the United States. "That's impossible."

"Ricco is a Ferraro. Nothing is impossible. We brought everything for you to get ready. Stefano is giving you away and we're standing up for you." Emmanuelle looked immensely pleased at the idea.

"But I've been so difficult lately," Mariko said. "No." She shook her head. "I need to talk to him first." She had to tell him she was sorry for spending so much time mourning a brother, mother and father who were never real in her life.

Francesca flashed another smile. "At least you aren't protesting getting married. If you did, he said we were to remind you of your promise."

Mariko rolled her eyes. Of course he would throw that silly promise at her—that she'd marry him at the time he chose. So, he was choosing now. She was thankful that she'd come to the realization that the family she had right in front of her, the people willing to love her, were worth far more than the ones who had rejected her.

If he was insisting on marrying her without any preparation, at least the wedding would have to be small, not the huge event the paparazzi would attend and splash across the cover of every magazine. She didn't want a billionaire's wedding. Or even a celebrity's wedding. She wanted the ceremony to be about them, not about the hundred-thousand-dollar dress and fifty-thousand-dollar cake.

"We need to get started," Emmanuelle said. "Ricco might have decreed you get married today, but he doesn't know what we've got planned."

"Rose petals for your bed. Tons of them," Francesca said.

"I've got a few plans as well," Mariko said. "Let's get started. At least I've just bathed." She'd been late getting up and Ricco had already been gone. She was upset with herself over that. He liked early morning sex and yet he hadn't disturbed her. That might have been the catalyst for her finally realizing she was throwing away something good over something unreal.

The next two hours went by very quickly. The two women styled her hair simply, pulling it back to let it hang in loose curls down her neck. They did her makeup flawlessly, smoky eyes and an accent of dark lipstick that made her look terribly sexy.

Her gown was her dream gown, one from a designer, Yumi Katsuri. She'd loved her work and often looked at the gowns online, never thinking she'd actually get married in one of her creations. She had mentioned the designer one time to Ricco, in passing, and he must have remembered. Of course he had. He remembered everything she said to him. If he thought it important enough, he took the time to get whatever it was, or do it for her immediately. He had discussed having the designer make her a one-of-a-kind gown, but she didn't want to spend that kind of money.

Even though she now could buy anything she wanted, she had been very frugal growing up and living on the tiny amount she was given. Everything she bought had been carefully chosen. She'd seen so much poverty and so many others in need that she'd been very grateful for what she had. She wanted to stay that way, and she wanted her children to value what they had and be aware of what others didn't. In her mind, it was a splurge to have a wedding gown so beautiful, and as it was, she knew the gown chosen was expensive, just not by Ferraro standards.

It had a modified ivory halter top, fitted to her perfectly. The dress dropped into swirls of white tulle, layer after layer, so it appeared light and airy.

Mariko touched the dress reverently and then brushed her hand along the Swarovski crystals adorning the top. "I love the crystals." It was becoming real now that she had the dress on. Her heart began to pound. She was marrying Ricco Ferraro. She would be his wife, beloved by him, cherished by him. It seemed a fairy tale, something she might have read about in one of the thousands of books she'd read. She never believed she would find a man who would really love her, let alone make her the center of his universe.

"Um, honey," Francesca said. "Those aren't crystals."

Mariko frowned, her eyes meeting Francesca's in the mirror. "They are. Believe me, I've read the description of this dress a million times. I've always loved it."

"This dress was specially made for you. Those are diamonds."

Mariko's breath caught in her throat. "He didn't."

"I'm afraid he did," Emmanuelle said. "It was fitted just for you and the neckline made with diamonds. He said something about how he loved the way diamonds looked on your bare skin and he wanted to see that when you came up the aisle toward him. He also sent these earrings and a necklace."

She produced chandelier earrings dripping with diamonds and a matching necklace. They felt cool against her skin, and when she looked in the mirror she was shocked at how beautiful she appeared. She had to blink back tears. Ricco had given that to her as well. She never would have considered herself beautiful if he hadn't made her see herself that way.

She might have protested the diamonds, but she knew he was referring to his Shibari—no—*their* Shibari. He was talking to her the way he had with his ropes. Telling her he loved her, and she heard every word. She refused to dwell one moment longer in her past. She hoped he heard her when she told him back.

She didn't ask questions, but let Francesca and Emmanuelle get her ready. They spent time getting ready and then the limousine was there to pick them up. Enzo was driving and he whistled softly as she was escorted out. Stefano was already inside and he smiled at her as Emilio handed her in.

"You look beautiful, Mariko," he greeted.

"Thank you. You look quite handsome in that tuxedo." He did. Ferraro men were made for suits.

"Are you ready for this? He's railroading you."

"You're helping."

He laughed. "Of course I'm helping him. You don't think I'm going to chance the best thing he's ever had in his life getting away from him, do you?"

"Your family is the best thing that ever happened to him, Stefano. Maybe within that family, it's you. You're the one who gave your siblings that closeness."

Francesca and Emmanuelle had both slipped into the limousine as well. "You got that right," Emmanuelle agreed, flashing a loving smile at her brother. "Of course, he's terribly bossy."

Stefano's eyebrows shot up. "Bossy isn't the same thing as boss."

"You're both," Francesca and Emmanuelle said in unison.

Even Emilio smirked a little at that. Mariko looked down at her hands. She felt the love in the vehicle, emanating from the others. Even Stefano's cousins. She was part of that circle because they'd made room for her. The brothers treated her just as they did Francesca and Emmanuelle, as if she were the most precious treasure in all the world. It was a little disconcerting after she'd been ignored, beaten or shamed for her entire life. Some days she wasn't certain how to respond so she stayed very quiet.

After realizing that her depression and grief over losing her brother were keeping her from enjoying what she had, she was determined to grab life with both hands. Every single day with Ricco would be a miracle to her. She knew she loved him and she believed he loved her. She knew there would be doubts, she was conditioned to doubt herself, but she would use the ropes to stop the voices, just as Ricco did.

She should have asked where they were going. She didn't because it hadn't mattered—until she got there. She thought a small ceremony, just the family. It was a church, and not only the family but half or more than half the people living and working in the Ferraro territory were seated, waiting for the bride. She knew because she peeked out the door where she waited with Stefano, Emmanuelle and Francesca. She should have known. They were so loyal to the Ferraros, going so far as to try to defend them when they were under attack. It stood to reason that the family would invite them. She recognized Nicoletta, Lucia and Amo near the front, right behind the family pew. Signora Moretti was there as well. That was all she recognized in the sea of faces because she began to feel a little faint.

She was a woman of the shadows, not just when she was working but when she was home. She tried to disappear into corners, not be in the spotlight. She didn't know if she could follow through and walk out there, even under Stefano's protection. She shut the door and leaned against it, fighting for air.

"He invited everyone."

Emmanuelle nodded, going to her side to urge her to sit. Francesca brought her a glass of water. "Our cousins from New York are here, that's why the church seems so full. We have a lot of family. We wanted all the cousins to know you."

She knew why. They were all close and they protected one another, unlike the family she grew up in. "I need him."

"He can't see you before the wedding," Francesca protested.

"I need him right now," Mariko said, desperate. If he didn't get there, she didn't know what she would do. Run? She'd never humiliate him that way, but she might faint, or worse, throw up on her way down the aisle to him. "Please go get him."

Stefano slipped out the door, and Mariko counted her heartbeats until Ricco came in. He looked a little wary, as if she might be about to tell him she was going to run, but he went straight to her. She stood and he gasped, his eyes moving over her. Something in her settled at the look on his face. She had no idea how he had come to love her so much, but she not only saw the intensity in the naked emotion on his face, she felt it as well.

"*Dio, farfallina mia*, you are the most beautiful woman I've ever seen."

He believed that, too. She let her breath out, not realizing she'd been holding it, waiting for him. "I needed to see you. I know it's supposed to be bad luck before the wedding, but . . ." She trailed off. She didn't know exactly what she needed from him or why, only that it was imperative or she couldn't walk out of the safety of the room.

He smiled, and his smile was gorgeous. He took the step separating them and pulled her into his arms. He smelled like Ricco. Wonderful. Familiar. Hers.

"*Don't* kiss her, you goof," Emmanuelle ordered. "You'll mess up her makeup."

His finger slid down the nape of her neck, a gesture that always steadied her. That's what she needed. To know she was his. That she belonged. That he thought her strong and confident as a woman, just as she was as a rider.

"Emme, don't you have more lipstick? You're killing me here. Look at her. Don't you want to kiss her?"

"Well, of course, just not quite in the same way," Emmanuelle replied, her voice droll.

Mariko burst out laughing. "I'm fine now. Go wait for me."

"That's it? You're okay now?" His eyes searched her face.

She nodded. "I just needed to see you. To know."

He understood. "You should always know. Now that I've seen you in that dress, you know every second of the reception is going to be hell."

The reception was hell. Every touch, every look. The dances. The slow music while he held her in his arms, her body moving in perfect rhythm with his. She loved dancing with him. Loved it. Being in his arms and floating across the floor together was an experience she never thought she'd have. She didn't know too much about dancing, but he was extremely good at guiding her every move.

"I'm sorry it took me so long to realize that grieving for Ryuu when he didn't love me, when he conspired to help Osamu kill all of us, me, you, your entire family, even Nao, was ridiculous." Even saying it still hurt. Her brother. Her one family member wanted her dead, refused to even acknowledge a connection between them.

"Don't apologize, Mariko. You loved him. There's nothing wrong with your feelings for him. You loved him all these years, just as you should have. He's the one who was poisoned." He brushed her mouth gently with his.

The touch of his lips against hers sent butterflies winging through her stomach. She knew she'd always feel that way just looking at him.

"I'm just sorry it took so long to come to the realization of what I had in my life."

He whirled her out of danger when another couple came too close. "The truth is, *amore*, I would wait a lifetime for you."

There was honesty in his voice and it set her heart beating double time. She had a family. A man who loved her. It was everything she'd ever wanted. They danced the evening away, Mariko feeling like a fairy princess. The limousine took them home. She loved the sight of their house, the high fence and iron gates surrounding the extensive gardens.

"I can't wait to get you inside," Ricco said.

The sensual lines carved deep in his face took her breath. She felt as if she'd been waiting a lifetime, her body so sensitive and ready for his. She was grateful she wasn't alone in the way she was feeling.

He held her hand into the house as if he thought she might run from him. He led her straight to the elevator to the second floor instead of taking the stairs. In the elevator, he began slipping the long row of pearl buttons down her back from their loops. She loved that he was so focused on getting her out of her dress that he stopped in the hallway to finish, encouraging her to step out of the lace concoction. Mariko did so, standing in the hall in her ivory lace, barely there, thong and garters, high heels and stockings. He unsnapped her matching bra at the door of the master bedroom, leaving her breasts bare.

"We're flying out of here for our honeymoon in the morning," he promised. "We own an island and we can have it all to ourselves. I won't mind imposing a no-clothes rule."

"I'll just bet you won't." She held her breath, waiting.

He turned his head and looked at their bed, dripping with

rose petals and covered in bundles of rope of all colors and textures. She was talking to him. Telling him she loved him and she needed his Shibari to ground her as much as he needed it.

Ricco reached for her, pulling her close to him. "You're certain?"

"Absolutely. I realized we both need it. You've been capturing our journey together on film, and this is our wedding night. We should have at least one picture, even if it's simple." She hoped he knew what she was saying to him. He'd spent the last month pounding the heavy bag when he needed relief from his demons. She'd gone to the tea house out in the Japanese garden. Shibari joined them together in their struggles.

"It makes me stronger, Ricco. I realized I need it as much as you do."

He draped her dress across the bed, the rose petals all around it. He placed three coils of rope near the ivory lace and then her bra over one of the coils of rope.

"You already know what you want to do."

"Get ready."

His voice was *that* voice, the one she had become so familiar with. She nodded and headed for the bathroom, excitement coursing through her. She couldn't wait to see how he tied her. Already her sex was hot, clenching and so damp. She knew her wedding night was going to be spectacular, and then she had the honeymoon to look forward to . . .

Bellisia Adams stared at herself in the mirror. Beside her was JinJing, a sweet woman, unaware that the man she worked for was an infamous criminal or that the woman beside her was no more Chinese than the man on the moon. Bellisia's hair was long and straight, a waterfall of silk reaching to her waist. She was short, delicate-looking, with small feet and hands. She spoke flawlessly in the dialect JinJing spoke, laughing and gossiping companionably in the restroom during their short break.

She kept her heart rate absolutely steady, the beat never rising in spite of the fact that she knew just by the heightened security and the tenseness of the guards that what she'd been looking for this past week was finally here. It was a good thing too. Time was running out fast. Like most of the technicians in the laboratory, she didn't wear a watch, but she was very aware of the days and hours ticking by.

JinJing waved to her and hurried out as the chime sounded, the call back to work. Anyone caught walking the halls was instantly let go. Or at least they disappeared. Rumor had it that wherever they were taken was not pleasant. The Cheng Company paid well. Bernard Lee Cheng had many businesses and employed a good number of people, but he was a very exacting boss.

Bellisia couldn't wait any longer. She couldn't be caught in the restroom either. Very carefully she removed the long wig and lifelike skin of her mask and rolled them into her white lab coat. She slipped off the laboratory uniform, revealing the skintight one-piece bodysuit she wore under it—one that reflected the background around her. Her shoes were crepe-soled and easy to move fast in. She removed them and shoved them in one of the pockets. Her pale blond hair was braided in a tight weave. She was as ready as she'd ever be. She slipped out, back into the narrow hallway the moment she knew it was empty. Acute hearing ensured she knew exactly where most of the technicians were on the floor. She knew the precise location of every camera and just how to avoid them.

Once in the hall, she climbed up the wall to the ceiling, blending in with the dingy, off-white color that looked like it had seen better days. As she moved from the hallway of the laboratory to the offices, the wall color changed to a muted blue, fresh and crisp. She changed color until she was perfectly blending in and slowed her pace. Movement drew the eye, and there were far more people in the offices. Most of them were in small, open cubicles, but as she continued through to the next large bank of offices, the walls changed to a muted green in the one large office that mattered to her.

She could see the woman seated, facing away from her, looking at the man behind the desk. Bernard Lee Cheng. She was very tempted to kill him, take the opportunity of being so close and just get the job done. It would rid the world of a very evil man, but it wasn't her mission, no matter how much she wished it were. The woman, Senator Violet Smythe-Freeman—now just Smythe—was her mission, specifically to see if the senator was selling out her country and fellow GhostWalkers, the teams of soldiers few even knew existed.

There was no way into the office, but that didn't matter. She moved slowly across the ceiling, hiding in plain sight. Even if one of the men or women on the floor happened to look up, they would have a difficult time spotting her as long as she was careful to move like a sloth, inching her way to her destination. She positioned herself outside the office over the door. Muting the sounds around her, she concentrated on the voices coming from inside the office.

Cheng faced her. Even if she couldn't hear his every word because he'd soundproofed his office, she could read lips. He wanted the GhostWalker program. Files. Everything— including soldiers to take apart. Her stomach clenched. Violet's voice was pitched low. She had the ability to persuade people to do what she wanted with her voice, but Cheng seemed immune.

She wanted money for her campaign. Maurice Stuart had named her his running mate for the presidential election. If elected, she planned to have Stuart assassinated so that she would become president. Cheng would have an ally in the White House. It was a simple enough business deal. The origins of dark money never had to be exposed. No one would know.

Violet was beautiful and intelligent. She was poisonous. A sociopath. She was also enhanced, one of the original girls Dr. Whitney had found in orphanages and experimented on so that he could enhance his soldiers without harming them. She used her looks and her voice to get the things she wanted. More than anything, she wanted power.

Cheng nodded his head and leaned forward, his eyes sharp, his face a mask. He repeated the price. Files. Ghost-Walkers.

Bellisia remained still as Violet sold out her country and fellow soldiers. She told him where to find a team and how to get to them. She also told him there were copies of the files he wanted in several places, but most were too difficult to get to. The one place he had the best chance was in Louisiana, at the Stennis Center.

Cheng responded adamantly, insisting she get the files for him. She was just as adamant that she couldn't. He asked her why she was so against the GhostWalker program.

Bellisia tried to get closer, as if that would help her hear better. She wanted to know as well. Violet was one of them. One of the original orphans Peter Whitney had used for his own purposes—a "sister," not by blood but certainly in every other way. She'd undergone the same experiments with enhancing psychic abilities. With genetics, changing DNA. There was no doubt that Whitney was a genius, but he was also certifiably insane.

Violet's murmured response horrified Bellisia. The woman was a GhostWalker snob. Superior soldiers were fine. DNA of animals was fine. Enhancement met with her approval, but not when it came to the latest experiments coming to light—the use of vipers and spiders. That was going too far and cheapened the rest of them. She wanted anyone with that kind of DNA wiped out.

There was a moment of silence, as if Cheng was turning her sudden burst of venomous hatred over and over in his mind, just as Bellisia was. Bellisia could have warned Violet that she was skating close to danger. Violet was a GhostWalker. Few had that information, but with that one outburst, she'd made a shrewd, extremely intelligent man wonder about her. He had a GhostWalker right there in his laboratory.

Violet, seemingly unaware of the danger, or because of it, swiftly moved on, laying out her demands once again. The two went back to haggling. In the end, Violet began to rise, and Cheng lifted a hand to stop her. She sank down gracefully, and the deal was made. Bellisia listened to another twenty minutes of conversation while the two hashed out what each would do for the other.

Bellisia calculated the odds of escaping if she killed the senator as the traitor emerged from Cheng's office. They weren't good. Even so, she still entertained the idea. The level of the woman's treachery was beyond imagination. She despised Violet.

A stir in the office drew her attention. Guards marched in and directed those in the smaller offices out. She glanced into the hallway and saw that the entire floor was being cleared. Her heart accelerated before she could stop it. She took a slow breath and steadied her pulse just as the siren went off, calling everyone, from the labs to the offices, into the large dorm areas.

Lockdown. She couldn't get to the restroom to retrieve her uniform, lab coat and wig before the soldiers searched, nor did she have enough time remaining before the virus injected into her began to kill her. She also couldn't remain in one of Cheng's endless lockdowns. He was paranoid enough that he had kept workers on the premises for over a week more than once. She'd be dead without the antidote by that time. Cheng would be even tighter with his security once the clothes and wig were discovered.

She began the slow process necessary to make her way across the ceiling to the hall. She couldn't go down to the main floor. Soldiers were pouring in and every floor would be flooded by now. She had to go up to the only sanctuary she might be able to get to. There were tanks of water housed on the roof that fed the sprinkler systems. That was her only way to stay safe from the searches Cheng would conduct once her clothes were found. That meant she had to take the elevator.

Cursing mentally in every language she was fluent in— and that was quite a few—she hovered just above the elevator doors. The soldiers would go into the elevator and that meant she had to be very close to them. The men were already on alert and gathering in front of the elevator. The slightest mistake would cost her. Although she could blend into her environment, it took a few seconds for her skin and hair to change. Her clothing would mirror her surroundings, so she would have the look of the elevator over her body but her head and hands and feet would be exposed for that couple of seconds.

Heart pounding, she slowly edged over to the very top of the elevator. Should she try to start blending into that color now, or wait until she was inside with a dozen guards and guns? She had choices, but the wrong one would end her life. Changing colors to mirror her background was more like the octopus than the chameleon, but it still took a few precious moments. She began changing, concentrating on her hands and feet first until she appeared part of the doors.

A ping signaled that she only had seconds to get inside and up the wall to the ceiling of the elevator. She waited until soldiers stepped into the elevator and slipped inside with them, clinging to the wall over their heads. The door nearly closed on her foot before she could pull it in. The men crowded in, and there was little space. She felt as if she couldn't breathe. The car didn't have high ceilings, so they were mashed together and the taller ones nearly brushed against her body. Twice, the hair of the man closest to her— and it was just her bad luck that he was tall—actually did brush against her face, tickling her skin.

She rode floor to floor as men got off to sweep each, making certain that all personnel did as the siren demanded and went immediately to the dormitory where they would be searched.

The last of the soldiers went to the roof. She knew this would be her biggest danger point. She had to exit the elevator right behind the last soldier. It was imperative that all of them were looking outward and not back toward the closing doors. She was a mimic, a chameleon, and no one would be able to see her, but once again it would take precious seconds to complete the change in a new environment.

She crawled down to the floor and eased out behind the last man, her gaze sweeping the roof to find the water tanks. There were six banks of them, each feeding the sprinklers on several floors. She stayed very still, right up against the wall until her skin and hair adjusted fully to the new background. Only then did she begin her slow crawl across the roof, making for the nearest tank while the soldiers spread out and swept the large space.

Up so high the wind was a menace, blowing hard and continuously at the men. They stumbled as it hit them in gusts. She stayed low to the ground, almost on her belly. She stopped once when one of the soldiers cursed in a mixture of Mandarin and Shanghainese. He cursed the weather, not Cheng. No one would dare curse Cheng, afraid it would get back to him.

Cheng considered himself a businessman. He'd inherited his empire and his intellect from his Chinese father and his good looks and charm from his American movie star mother. Both parents had opened doors for him, in China as well as the United States. He had expanded those doors to nearly every country in the world. He'd doubled his father's empire, making him one of the wealthiest men on the planet, but he'd done so by providing to terrorists, rebels and governments classified information, weapons and anything else they needed. He sold secrets to the highest bidder, and no one ever touched him.

Bellisia didn't understand what it was that drove people to do the terrible things they did. Greed. Power. She knew she didn't live the way others did, but she didn't see that the outside world was any better than her world. Maybe worse. Hers was one of discipline and service. It wasn't always comfortable and she couldn't trust very many people, but then outside her world, the majority didn't seem to have it much better.

The cursing soldier stopped just before he tripped over her. She actually felt the brush of the leather of his boot. Bellisia eased her body away from him. Holding her breath. Keeping her movements infinitely slow. She inched her way across the roof, the movements so controlled her muscles cramped in protest. It hurt to move that slowly. All the while her heart pounded and she had to work to keep her breathing steady and calm.

She was right under their noses. All they had to do was look down and see her, if they could penetrate her disguise. She watched them carefully, looking out of the corners of her eyes, listening for them as well, but all the while measuring the distance to the water tanks. It seemed to take forever until she reached the base of the nearest one. For*ever*.

She reached a hand up and slid her fingers forward using the setae on the tips of her fingers to stick. Setae—single microscopic hairs split into hundreds of tiny bristles—were so tiny they were impossible to see, so tiny Dr. Whitney hadn't realized she actually had them, in spite of his enhancements. Pushing the setae onto the surface and dragging them forward allowed her to stick to the surface easily. Each seta could hold enormous amounts of weight, so having them on the pads of her fingers and toes allowed her to climb or hang upside down on a ceiling easily. The larger the creature, the smaller the setae, and no seta had ever been recorded that was small enough to hold a human being—until Dr. Whitney had managed unwittingly to create one.

Her plan was to climb into the water tank and wait until things settled down and then climb down the side of the building and get far away from Cheng. She was very aware of time ticking away, and the virus beginning to take hold in her body. Already her temperature was rising. The cold water in the tank would help. She cursed Whitney and his schemes for keeping the women in line.

The girls had been taken from orphanages. No one knew or cared about them. That allowed Whitney to conduct his experiments on the female children without fearing repercussions. He named them after flowers or seasons, and trained them as soldiers, assassins and spies. To keep them returning to him, he would inject a substance he called Zenith, a lethal drug that needed an antidote, or a virus that spread and eventually killed. Sometimes he used their friendships with one another, so they'd learned to be extremely careful not to show feelings for one another.

She started up the tank, allowing her body to change once again to blend in with the dirty background. The wind tore at her, trying to rip her from the tank. She was cold, although she could feel her internal temperature rising from the virus, her body beginning to go numb in the vicious wind. Still, she forced herself to go slow, all the while watching the guards moving around the roof, thoroughly inspecting every single place that someone could hide. That told her they would be looking in the water tanks as well.

A siren went off abruptly, a loud jarring blare that set nerves on edge. It wasn't the same sound as the first siren indicating to the workers to go immediately to the dorms. This was one of jangling outrage. A scream of fury. They had found her wig, mask and lab clothes. They would be combing the building for her. Every duct, every vent. Anywhere a human being could possibly hide.

She had researched Cheng meticulously before she'd ever entered his world. It was narrow, rigid, autocratic, with constant inspections and living under the surveillance of cameras and guards. Cheng didn't trust anyone, not his closest allies. Not his workers. Not even his guards. He had watchers observing the watchers.

Bellisia was used to such an environment. She'd grown up in one and was familiar with it. She also knew all the ways to get around surveillance and cameras. She was a perfect mimic, blending into her environment, picking up nuances of her surroundings, the language, the idioms, the culture. Whitney thought that was her gift. He had no idea of her other abilities, the ones far more important to the missions he sent her off on. All the girls learned to hide abilities from him. It was so much safer.

The guards reacted to the blaring siren with a rush of bodies and the sound of boots hitting the rooftop as they renewed their frenzied searching. She kept climbing, using that same slow, inch-by-inch movement. It took discipline to continue slowly instead of moving quickly, as every self-preservation cell in her body urged her to do.

She relied heavily on her ability to change color and skin texture to blend into her surroundings, but that didn't guarantee that a sharp-eyed soldier wouldn't spot her. The pigment cells in her skin allowed her to change color in seconds. She'd hated that at first, until she realized it gave her an advantage. Whitney needed her to be a spy. He sent her out on missions when so many of the other women had been locked up again.

She gained the top of the tank just as one of the soldiers

put his boot on the ladder. Slipping into the water soundlessly, she swam to the very bottom of the tank and anchored herself to the wall, making herself as flat as possible. Once again she changed color so that she blended with tank and water.

She *loved* water. She could live in the cool liquid. The water felt soothing against her burning skin. In the open air, she felt as if her skin dried out and she was cracking into a million pieces. She often looked down at her hands and arms to make certain it wasn't true, but in spite of the smoothness of her skin, she still felt that way. The one environment she found extremely hostile to her was the desert. Whitney had sent her there several times to record its effects on her, and she hadn't done well. A flaw, he called it.

The soldier was at the top of the tank now, peering down into the water. She knew each tank had soldiers looking into it. If they sent someone down into the water, she might really be in trouble, but it appeared as if the soldier was just going to sit at the edge to ensure no one had gone in and was underwater. Once it was dark, the soldiers should have completed their search and she should be able to slip up to the surface and get air.

Right now she was basking in the fact that the water was helping to control the temperature rising in her from the virus. Whitney had injected her every time she left the compound where she was held, to ensure she would return. She'd always managed to complete her mission in the time frame given to her, so she had no idea how fast-acting the virus was. The water definitely made her feel better, but she didn't feel good at all. Her muscles ached. Cramped. Never a good thing when trying to be still at the bottom of a water tank with soldiers on the lookout above her.

Night fell rapidly. She knew the guards were still there on the roof and that worried her. She had to be able to climb down the side of the building, and she couldn't even get out of the tank as long as the guard was above her. She also needed air. She'd risked blowing a few bubbles but that wasn't going to sustain her much longer. She needed to get to the surface and leave before weakness began to hit. She had been certain the soldier would leave the tank after the first hour, but he seemed determined to hold his position. She was nearly at her max for staying submerged.

Bellisia refused to panic. That way lay disaster. She had to get air and then find a way to slip past the guard so she could climb down the building, get to the van waiting for her and get the antidote. She detached from the wall and began to drift up toward the surface, careful not to disturb the water. Again, she used patience in spite of the urgent demands her lungs were making on her.

After what seemed an eternity, she reached the surface. Tilting her head so only her lips broke the surface, she drew in air. Relief coursed through her. Air had never tasted so good. She hung there, still and part of the water so that even though the guard was looking right at her, he saw nothing but water shimmering.

A flurry of activity drew the guard's attention and she attached herself to the side of the tank and began to climb up toward the very top. She was only half out of the water when the shouted orders penetrated. They wanted hooks dragged through the containers to make certain no one was hiding in them with air tanks. So many soldiers tromped up onto the roof that she felt the vibrations right through the container. Spotlights went on, illuminating the entire roof and all six containers. Worse, soldiers surrounded each one, and more climbed up to the top to stand on the platforms.

Bellisia sank slowly back into the water, clinging to the wall as she did so, her heart pounding unnaturally. She'd never experienced her heart beating so hard. It felt as if it would come right out of her chest, and she wasn't really that fearful—yet. Her temperature was climbing at an alarming rate. She was hot and even the cool water couldn't alleviate the terrible heat rising inside of her. Her skin hurt. Every muscle in her body ached, not just ached but felt twisted into tight knots. She began to shiver, so much so she couldn't control it. That wasn't conducive to hiding in a spotlight surrounded by the enemy.

She stayed up near the very top of the tank, just beneath the water line, attached to the wall, and made herself as small and as flat as possible. There was always the possibility that she could die on a mission. That was part of the . . . adrenaline rush. It was always about pitting her skills against an enemy. If she wasn't good enough, if she made a mistake, that was on her. But this . . . Peter Whitney had deliberately injected her with a killer virus in order to ensure she always returned to him. He was willing to risk her dying a painful death to prove his point.

He *owned* them. All of them. Each and every girl he took out of an orphanage and experimented on. Some died. That didn't matter to him. *None* of them mattered to him. Only the science. Only the soldiers he developed piggybacking on the research he'd conducted on the girls. Children with no childhood. No loving parents. She hadn't understood what that meant until she'd been out in the world and realized the majority of people didn't live as she did.

All of the girls had discussed trying to break free before Whitney added them to his disgusting program to give him more babies to experiment on. The thought of leaving the only life they'd ever known was terrifying. But this—leaving her to die in a foreign country because she was late through no fault of her own. She had the information Whitney needed, but because he'd insisted on injecting her with a killer virus before she went on her mission, she might never get that information to him. He liked playing God. He was willing to lose one of them in order to scare the others into compliance.

Something hit the water hard, startling her. She nearly jerked off the wall, blinking in protest against the bright lights shining into the tank. Her sanctuary was no longer that. The environment had gone from cool, dark water—a place of safety—to one of overwhelmingly intense brilliant light illuminating the water nearly to the bottom of the tank.

A giant hook dragged viciously along the floor, and she shuddered in reaction.

A second hook entered the water with an ominous splash as the first was pulled back up. The next few minutes were a nightmare as the tank was thoroughly searched with hooks along the bottom. Had a diver with scuba gear been hiding there, he would have been torn to pieces.

She let her breath out as they pulled the hooks back up to the top. They would leave soon and she could make the climb out of the tank and across the roof. Already she could tell she was weaker, but she knew she could still climb down the side of the building and get to the van where Whitney's supersoldiers waited to administer the antidote to the poisonous virus, reducing it to a mere illness instead of something lethal.

The hook plunged back into the water, startling her. She nearly detached from the wall as the iron dragged up the side of the tank while a second hook entered the water. This was . . . *bad*. She had nowhere to go. If she moved fast to avoid the hook, she would be spotted. If she didn't, the hook could tear her apart. Either way, she was dead.

The sound, magnified underwater, was horrendous on her ears. She wanted to cover them against the terrible scraping and grinding as the point of the hook dug into the side of the tank. She watched it come closer and closer as it crawled up from the bottom. The other hook came up almost beside it, covering more territory as they ripped long gouges in the wall.

She tried to time letting go of the wall so neither hook would brush against her body and signal to the men on the other end that there was something other than wall. She pushed off gently and slid between the two chains, trying to swim slowly so that movement wouldn't catch eyes. She stroked her arms with powerful pulls to take her down, still hugging the wall as best she could below the hooks. If she could just attach herself on the path already taken, she'd have a good chance of riding this latest threat out.

The advantage of going deeper was that the light didn't penetrate all the way to the bottom. She just had to avoid the hooks as they plunged into the water and sank. Once she was deep enough, the soldiers above her wouldn't be able to see even if she did make a jerky movement to prevent the hook from impaling her.

She made it about halfway down when the hooks began their upward scraping along the wall. Once again she stayed very still, the sound grating on her nerves, her heart pounding as the huge hooks got closer and closer. This time she did a slow somersault to avoid getting scraped up by either hook. The dive took her lower into the tank. She didn't see how they could possibly think anyone could stay under water that long, and by now they certainly would have discovered a scuba tank.

The soldiers were thorough, plunging the hooks deep and dragging them up the walls without missing so much as a few inches of space. Bellisia realized they had to have perfected this method of searching the tanks by doing it often. That made sense. The tanks were large and Cheng was paranoid. No doubt the many floors and laboratories were being searched just as thoroughly.

There, in the water, listening to the sound of the chains scraping up the walls, she contemplated the difference between Cheng and Whitney. Both had far too much money. Whitney seemed to need to take his research further and further out of the realm of humanity and deeper into the realm of insanity. No government would ever sanction what he was doing, yet he was getting away with it. At least his motive, although twisted, was to produce better soldiers for his country.

Cheng wasn't affiliated with his government as far as she could tell. He worked closely with them, but he wasn't a patriot. He was out for himself. He seemed to want more money and power than he already had. She'd researched him carefully, and few on the planet had more than he did.

Still, it wasn't enough for him. Yet he had no family. No one to share his life with. He didn't work for the sake of knowledge. He existed only to make money.

Bellisia was aware of her heart laboring harder and the pressure on her lungs becoming more severe. That was unusual. She'd taken a large gulp of air and she should have had quite a bit of time left before she had to rise, but it felt as if she'd been underwater a little too long, even for her. Of course Whitney would find something that would negatively impact her ability in the water. He didn't want her to use that means as an escape route.

She had no choice but to begin her ascent. She tried to stay to the side of the tank they'd already dredged. It was terrifying to be in the water as the large, heavy hooks slammed close to her again and again. It was inevitable, given the many strikes the soldiers made at the water, and it happened as she was just pushing off the wall to allow her body to rise slowly, naturally. A hook hit the bottom of the tank and was jerked upward and to the left, right across her back and arm. She folded herself in half to minimize the damage, but it hit hard enough to jar her, even with the way the water slowed the big hook down.

She felt the burn as the point ripped her skin open. It was a shallow wound, but it stung like hell and instantly there was blood in the water. She had to concentrate to close those cells to keep from leaking enough blood that the soldiers would notice. Under her skin she had a network of finely controlled muscles that aided her in changing the look and feel of her body's surface skin. Now, she used them to squeeze the cells closed and prevent blood from pouring into the water, at least until the spotlights were turned off.

It seemed to take forever as she continued to rise, her lungs burning and her muscles cramping. All the while the horrible splash and scraping of the hooks continued. Twice she had extremely close calls, and once more the tip barely skimmed along her body, hitting her thigh, ripping her open.

It was much harder to control the bleeding this time as she was weaker and needed to break the surface before her muscles went into full cramps.

She was relieved when the hooks were pulled from the water and the soldiers began to climb down the ladders back to the roof. Instantly she kicked the remaining four feet to the surface and took in great gulps of air. She clung to the side for several long minutes, resting her head against the wall while she tried to breathe away the inferno inside her. She couldn't keep doing this for Whitney. She wouldn't survive. He made them all feel as if they were nothing. She knew she wasn't alone in wanting to escape because they all talked about it, late at night when one or two could disrupt the cameras and recording equipment and they were alone in the dorms.

She had tried planning an escape with her best friend, Zara, but before they could attempt to carry out their plans, Zara was sent on an undercover mission and Bellisia was sent to ascertain whether or not Violet was betraying Whitney. Whitney had set Violet up as senator, taking over when her husband had been killed. Whitney didn't trust Violet, but Bellisia suspected that he had paired them together. If that were the case, then that physical attraction evidently didn't stop Violet from conspiring against the man who had experimented on her.

Bellisia began her slow climb out of the water tank. She would have to dry off before she could make the trek across the roof to the side of the building. If she didn't, one of the soldiers might discover the wet trail leading to the edge. The platform around the tank was warm from the high-powered lights, and she lay down, allowing her body to change to the color of the dingy planks.

She didn't dare sleep, not when soldiers still guarded the roof, but they seemed content with pacing the length of it in patterns, checking every place that could possibly hide a body over and over. She realized the soldiers were as afraid of Cheng as she and the other women in her unit were afraid of Whitney. Life was cheap to both men, at least other people's lives.

She began her slow crawl down the side of the tank once she felt she wouldn't leave behind a trail. Her body was hot now, so hot she felt as if her skin would crack open. Her muscles cramped, and she couldn't stop shaking. That didn't bode well for crossing the roof, but at least it was very dark now that the spotlights had been turned off. If she shook when a guard was close, hopefully the darkness would conceal her.

It took her just under forty minutes in the dark to climb down the side of the building. The virus he'd given her was vicious, her fever high, her insides searing from the inside out. For someone like her, someone needing more water than most people, it was sheer agony. It was as if he'd developed the strain specifically for her—and he probably had. That only strengthened her resolve to escape.

She rested for a moment to get her bearings and plan out her next step. She needed the antidote immediately, and that meant putting herself back in Whitney's hands. She had no other choice. Bellisia made her way across the lawn to the street where the van was waiting for her. It was parked one block down to be inconspicuous, one block away, which put it right next to the river.

She was staggering by the time she reached the vehicle, and Gerald, one of the supersoldiers sent to watch over her, leapt out to catch her up and jump back into the van. He placed her on a gurney and immediately spoke into his cell to tell Whitney she was back. She closed her eyes and turned her face away, as if losing consciousness.

"I need the information she has," Peter Whitney said. "Get it from her before you administer the antidote. Take her to the plane immediately. Your destination will be Italy."

Her heart nearly jumped out of her chest. She knew several of the women had been taken there to ensure they became pregnant. The GhostWalkers had destroyed his breeding program in the United States. No way was she going to Italy.

"Whitney needs a report," Gerald said.

She kept her breathing shallow. Labored. Eyes closed, body limp.

"Bellisia, honey, come on, give me the report. You need the antidote. He won't let me give it to you until you give him what he wants."

She stayed very still. Gerald and his partner, Adam, were her handlers on nearly every mission. The three had developed a friendship of sorts, if one could be friends with their guards. She knew how to control her breathing and heartbeat, and she did both to make him think she was crashing.

"We're losing her, Doc," Gerald said while Adam caught at her arm, shoving up the material of her bodysuit.

"Be certain. She could be faking," Whitney warned.

"No, she's out of it. She got back way past the time she was supposed to. We might be too late to save her. They locked the building down and she was still inside." Gerald's voice held urgency.

"Did you see Violet or any of her people going in or coming out?" Whitney demanded.

"I never saw Senator Smythe. I have no idea if she was there or not," Gerald said. Bellisia wasn't altogether certain he spoke the truth. He may very well have seen the senator, but Gerald and Adam didn't always like the way Whitney treated the women.

"Be sure Bellisia is really out."

Gerald prodded her. Hard. She made no response.

"She's burning up. And she's bleeding on her back and thigh."

"Inject her. She'll need water."

"Adam, give her the antidote fast. We'll need water for her."

She felt the needle and then the sting of the antidote as it went in. She stayed silent, uncertain how fast it was supposed to work. She hated needles; the sensation of them entering her skin often made her nauseous. The double row of muscles caused the needle to spread a terrible fire through every cell.

"Doc says get her water."

Adam held up a bottle. "She's not responsive enough to drink." That showed her how upset on her behalf Adam was—he knew she would need to be submerged in water. He wasn't thinking clearly.

"Not drink. Pour it over her."

The cool water went over her arm and then her chest. She nearly lost her ability to keep her heart and lungs under control, the relief was so tremendous.

"That's not enough. Get the bucket and fill it up at the river."

Adam threw open the double doors to the van and hopped out. Her acute hearing picked up Whitney hissing in disapproval. He didn't like that they'd parked by a river. That was her signal to move.

She leapt from the gurney, onto the ground right beside a startled Adam.

"Grab her," Gerald yelled.

She raced across the street with Adam rushing after her. The tips of his fingers brushed her back just as she dove right off the edge into the river. Water closed over her head, the cool wetness welcoming her.

Do you love fiction with a supernatural twist?

Want the chance to hear news about your favourite
authors (and the chance to win free books)?

Keri Arthur
Kristen Callihan
P.C. Cast
Christine Feehan
Jacquelyn Frank
Larissa Ione
Darynda Jones
Sherrilyn Kenyon
Jayne Ann Krentz and Jayne Castle
Lucy March
Martin Millar
Tim O'Rourke
Lindsey Piper
Christopher Rice
J.R. Ward
Laura Wright

Then visit the Piatkus website and blog
www.piatkus.co.uk | www.piatkusbooks.net

And follow us on Facebook and Twitter
www.facebook.com/piatkusfiction | www.twitter.com/piatkusbooks

piatkus